DEFILED

DEFILED
A NOVEL

MIKE NEMETH

New York

DEFILED
A NOVEL

Published in New York, New York, by Morgan James Publishing. Morgan James and The Entrepreneurial Publisher are trademarks of Morgan James, LLC.
www.MorganJamesPublishing.com

The Morgan James Speakers Group can bring authors to your live event. For more information or to book an event visit The Morgan James Speakers Group at www.TheMorganJamesSpeakersGroup.com.

Shelfie

A **free** eBook edition is available
with the purchase of this print book.

CLEARLY PRINT YOUR NAME ABOVE IN UPPER CASE

Instructions to claim your free eBook edition:
1. Download the Shelfie app for Android or iOS
2. Write your name in **UPPER CASE** above
3. Use the Shelfie app to submit a photo
4. Download your eBook to any device

ISBN 978-1-68350-001-8 paperback
ISBN 978-1-68350-002-5 eBook
ISBN 978-1-63047-868-1 hardcover
Library of Congress Control Number:
2016904323

Cover Design by:
Chris Treccani
www.3dogdesign.net

Interior Design by:
Bonnie Bushman
The Whole Caboodle Graphic Design

In an effort to support local communities and raise awareness and funds, Morgan James Publishing donates a percentage of all book sales for the life of each book to Habitat for Humanity Peninsula and Greater Williamsburg.

Get involved today, visit
www.MorganJamesBuilds.com

Habitat for Humanity®
Peninsula and
Greater Williamsburg
Building Partner

Note to Readers: Dolphin Beach and Cortes County cannot be found on any map of the state of Florida, and yet, readers familiar with the geography will recognize them as representative of Florida Gulf Coast environs. Predictive analytics is an emerging branch of science being applied to everything from online shopping patterns to baseball pitching tendencies. At the same time, advances in computer technology now make it possible to decode and store DNA strands in large volumes. I imagined that the two branches of science could be combined to create a commercial entity known as Atlanta Medical Analytics. Whether a similar company exists somewhere in the world or is on the drawing boards in Silicon Valley is not known to me; but, if there isn't such a company today, there likely will be in the near future. I have attempted to represent scientific facts and legal processes accurately, but readers may discover that I took small liberties, sometimes intentionally and other times mistakenly, in order to enhance the story's dramatic impact.

For Ginger and Wanda
R.I.P.

First there is a mountain,   First we know,
Then there is no mountain,   Then we do not know,
Then there is.   Then we know.
Popular Zen verse   Mike Nemeth
                                    Atlanta, Georgia
                                    January 2016

ACKNOWLEDGMENTS

This story became a novel because of the tough love of Aviva Layton, who read the first draft and set me on the right path.

This book would not have been possible without the patience and empathy of my wife, Angie Nemeth, who is an inexhaustible source of encouragement and feedback.

My deepest gratitude goes to the team at Morgan James Publishing—Fiction Publisher Angie Kiesling, Managing Editor Keri Wilson, and freelance editor Cheryl Ross—who tolerated all the quirks of a novice and cheerfully provided gentle guidance.

CHAPTER ONE

A soft knock on my office door broke my concentration. I knew it wasn't my wife, Carrie—she often burst into my office hoping to catch me at something shameful—and no one else would interrupt my work for anything less than a fire. That certainty caused the hairs on my arms to dance and my stomach to fall into my lap. For three months, a tenuous ceasefire had been in effect as my wife and I had moved into separate bedrooms and isolated areas of our large house. Except for the kitchen, our demilitarized zone, every room was off-limits to one of us. As I verified a complex algorithm that predicted debilitating diseases for people with certain DNA signatures, I didn't want to lose my train of thought, so I scribbled a note to mark my place in the long list of calculations before saying, "Yes?"

The door cracked open only far enough for me to see panic in the eyes of our maid, Rosa.

2 | MIKE NEMETH

"Mr. Randle, a gentleman is here to see you." Without waiting for a response, she withdrew and pulled the door shut.

Loud enough to be heard through the door, I said, "Who is it, Rosa?"

She didn't answer, so I had no choice but to trot after her. From my third-floor perch, I scurried down the back staircase to the second-floor gallery and down the ceremonial staircase to the ground floor. Carrie stood beside the staircase, in front of the formal dining room, flanked by Rosa and our yardman, Larry. They were lined up like "See no evil, hear no evil, and speak no evil" until Carrie inched back and behind her two protectors, like a quarterback retreating into the pocket formed by burly linemen.

I looked at them with a question on my face, and they stared back. As always, my wife appeared to be a store mannequin in the department where they sell male attractions—buffed and polished, garnished with jewels, adorned in linen and silk. At five-foot-two, Carrie reached only to my shoulders, and in contrast to my lean, long-limbed torso, she was an eye-catching confluence of tanned, sweeping curves. Trying not to leer at her oversized bosom was like trying not to gawk at a car crash. Short blonde hair in the spiky style favored by sexually liberated women, sapphire-blue eyes beaming like expressionless gems on a ragdoll's face, acrylic fingernails done in the trendy French style, and toenails painted a purplish color completed the picture of a forty-four-year-old woman who actively sought the attention of men of all ages.

Today a yellow stone the size of a man's thumb hung from a platinum chain and rested on two inches of her exposed cleavage. Dangling earrings matched the necklace. A diamond-studded anklet encircled one sharply contoured ankle, and rings decorated one thumb and one index finger, but no wedding rings were in evidence.

I paused and shot the three another quizzical look. In return, I got nervous stares, so I headed to the front double doors that stood wide open. A slight black man I didn't recognize fidgeted on my porch. He hadn't been invited in, and he looked too nervous to have accepted. My heart rate changed from a lope to a sprint; everyone was nervous that something bad was about to happen. When I reached the porch, I saw that the visitor had parked his car facing the street on the circular drive, blocking Carrie's red Jaguar convertible on the carriage porch. Carrie reserved that spot for her car because it afforded weather-protected access to the private spaces of the house. Guests used the front double doors that led through the foyer to the formal dining and living rooms. Rosa and I used the garage entrance. This guest had left his engine running and the driver's door open, ready for a getaway, like a bank robber.

I said, "Can I help you?"

"Are you John R. Marks?"

That confused me for a moment. Then I realized he was referring to me. "Yes, I am."

As soon as I identified myself, the nervous young man thrust a thick envelope at me and I reflexively accepted it.

"You've been served, Mr. Marks."

The process server whirled around, trotted down the steps, and jumped into his car. Without a wave goodbye, he stepped on the gas and accelerated down the driveway.

It was not likely that my neighbors had served me some benign summons. It was not likely that I had been served with a business-related lawsuit at my home. There was only one possibility, and it had me swinging between anger and shock.

The three of them were behind me, waiting for a reaction, so I tore the envelope open with my back to them and read the top page of the document.

IN THE CIRCUIT COURT OF CORTES COUNTY, FLORIDA
Carrie T. Marks, Plaintiff v. John R. Marks, Defendant
SUMMONS

An italicized paragraph of pretentious eighteenth-century legalese demanded that I file a response to this complaint with the clerk of court within thirty days or face a summary judgment in the case. Below the legalese a number of notarized signatures—Carrie's, the circuit court clerk's, and that of Carrie's attorney, a woman named Roberta de Castro with an address in Largo—made the document official. I wasn't accustomed to seeing my name written as "John R. Marks." As a youngster, people had called me "Jack" and my mother had called me "Jackie." Still did on the rare occasions we saw one another. When I enrolled at Georgia Tech, I became J. Randle Marks, person of importance, and I asked people to call me "Randle," my mother's maiden name.

I flipped to the second page and found an oversized bold-type banner:

PETITION FOR DISSOLUTION OF MARRIAGE

Twenty pages of text followed the banner, but I didn't bother to read them. I spun on my heel and charged toward Carrie and her bodyguards. When I was within ten feet of her, I tossed the document at her like I was throwing a Frisbee to a dog. She sidestepped the missile and it came apart, a big chunk flying under the formal dining table, two pages separating and twirling to the floor like elm tree seedpods falling in the springtime.

"You've quit on us! You should be ashamed of yourself," I said as I turned toward the staircase.

Carrie cowered behind Larry and said, "Randle, you have to read this. You can't stay here."

"Don't worry about that. I don't want to be here."

Seeing an opportunity to earn his keep, Larry said, "We don't want any trouble."

I leaned over the bannister and said, "Who's 'we,' punk? You're not involved in this. In fact, you're trespassing, so get out of my house."

Carrie said, "I have possession of the house, Randle. You're the one who has to pack up and leave."

"Keep him on the ground floor where he belongs," I shot back. "If he puts one foot on the stairs, I'll call the cops."

"When are you leaving?"

"I'm going to make some calls. I'll leave when I'm ready."

I continued up the stairs to the second floor and heard Carrie say, "I'll call my lawyer!"

As I walked across the gallery past guestrooms, I shouted, "Call the TV news for all I care."

At the end of the hallway, I climbed the narrow set of stairs to the third-floor attic, my private portion of the residence. In one half of the attic I had stored my life before Carrie—all the paintings Carrie wouldn't hang on her walls, all the framed pictures she wouldn't display, all the trophies and masculine trappings for which there wasn't appropriate space in "her" house. The other half was an enclosed home office, my refuge.

The office measured twenty feet by thirty feet, with blood-red walls and an indestructible Berber carpet. Bookshelves lined two walls, and two dormer windows overlooked the pool and wooded backyard. A nine-foot-long spindle table served as my desk, and an overstuffed couch often served as my bed. After a particularly vicious fight, I had moved out of the first-floor master bedroom and stored my clothes in a second-floor guestroom. I preferred sleeping in my office, however, because the door locked, the stairs squeaked, and I could keep my pistol within reach. I locked the door now and took a seat behind my desk.

My first call went to the cell phone of Tony Zambrano, my best friend and nominally my lawyer. He didn't answer, so I hung up and sent him a text message: *SOS answer the damn phone.* About five minutes later my cell phone rang.

Tony said, "I was putting. Where's the fire?"

"I've been served."

"I assume you're not referring to breakfast."

"Cut the crap, Tony. Carrie filed for divorce, and I've been served."

"Okay, okay, stay calm. What does the summons say?"

"We have to answer within thirty days."

"Sure, that's routine, but what does the filing say about terms of separation?"

"I guess it says I have to leave the country house. That's what Carrie said."

"You don't know? Take a look and tell me are there any exhibits or notices attached to the summons."

"Ah, I don't have it in front of me, Tony. I threw it at Carrie, and it's scattered around the dining room floor at the moment."

"Dammit, Randle, you're going to screw this up before we can fight it. Pack your bags and move to the beach house. Now!"

"Sure, just didn't want her to think I was scared of her."

"You should be scared. Your life as you knew it is now over. Don't do anything stupid. Don't even talk to her. Drop the summons at my office on your way to the beach house, and come see me tomorrow."

"How is this going to work, Tony?"

"Tomorrow, Randle. Right now I have to hit my tee shot. These guys are drooling over the money they're going to win from me. Drop in the bucket compared to what you have at stake."

My second call went to my daughter's cell phone. She didn't answer either, most likely on duty for the Tampa Police Department. I left her a message that I would be at the beach house for the foreseeable future, in the remote chance she needed to reach me.

I was spurred to action by the realization that I was an isolated combatant in enemy territory, like a soldier separated from his platoon in the jungles of Vietnam. I packed two briefcases with my laptop computer, product designs, papers, pens, and business cards. Then I grabbed two large traveling suitcases from the storage room and carried it all down to my temporary bedroom on the second floor. There I packed business clothes as I had plenty of casual clothes at the beach house. I made two trips down the stairs to get it all into the garage before I stuck my tail between my legs and crawled around the dining room floor, gathering the pages of the court summons. Larry watched from the safety of the foyer, Rosa peeked around the corner of the kitchen, and Carrie stood in the hallway leading to the master bedroom. They guarded what Carrie considered valuable as though I were a thief in my own home.

With that embarrassment out of the way, I got into my aging Ford Bronco parked next to Rosa's generic sedan on the garage apron. Before I could put the car into reverse, Carrie ran up to the window and said, "Give me the house keys and the garage door opener."

"We both know you'll change the locks before I get out of Cortes County, so what's the point? And I'll want your keys and garage door opener for the beach house in exchange. You got those handy?"

"I can get them."

"You do that."

When Carrie turned to go back into the house, I put the Bronco in gear and backed around Rosa's car. As I sped down the driveway, Carrie waved in my rearview mirror. Probably the keys; probably not bon voyage.

⸻⸺❀⸺⸻

In less than an hour I reached Tony's office in a high rise at the intersection of Fourth Street and Fourth Avenue North in downtown St. Petersburg, dropped off the summons, and made an appointment for the following morning. Then I drove on Central Avenue to Dolphin Beach on the Gulf side of the peninsula.

Our "beach" house, which I had purchased before meeting Carrie, was not on the beach. It was a traditional Florida bungalow—a single-story cinderblock rectangle built on a concrete slab with a Mexican tile roof and electric hurricane shutters. The house had no curb appeal, and the interior added no charm—just a series of small square rooms adding up to less than two thousand square feet of living space. Located on an inlet off the Intracoastal Waterway, three blocks from Gulf Boulevard and the beaches, the house was off the beaten path of spring breakers and the locals who came out in the heat of the summer. At the back of the property, a wooden dock and boatlift sat unused because the inlet provided insufficient depth at low tide for anything but rowboats. As a result, I kept my elderly Carver aft cabin cruiser at the municipal marina in St. Petersburg.

I loved the bungalow because the floors were terrazzo and the carpets were Berber, a screened porch was fitted on the back, and the backyard was dominated by an in-ground pool and a hot tub on a slab. When I wanted to, I could climb out of the water and walk into the house dripping wet to get a beer without harming anything. Trees, hibiscus, and sea grape separated the bungalow from the neighbors, so I could skinny-dip day or night although I could never convince Carrie to do it with me. In fact, Carrie hated the bungalow and insisted that I put it up for sale. She loved the beach, but she was haunted by the reminders that I'd had a life before I met her. She said she wanted something different, something truly "ours." The Realtor's sign was in the front yard, but the Realtor was under strict orders from me not to show it and not to encourage buyers. No way would I ever sell my favorite place on earth.

I pulled the Bronco into the circular drive and unloaded the luggage. When I opened the front door, the alarm system didn't beep its warning to enter the security code. While I was in Atlanta on business a couple of weeks ago, Carrie and her girlfriends had stayed at the bungalow, and apparently she had forgotten to set the alarm when they left.

I dragged the luggage indoors and found the interior stifling hot and humid. I flipped a light switch so I could see the air conditioning controls on the wall, but nothing happened. The switch controlled table lamps in the living room, but one of the girls must have turned off the lamps. The first lamp I tried didn't work. Neither did the second. Like a fool I went from lamp to lamp and wall switch to wall switch, hoping for light long after I knew there was no electricity.

As I walked through the house, intending to go out the back door to get some daylight to use my cell phone, I discovered that the dining room furniture had vanished. Peeking around the corner into the family room, I found it empty too. Outside, the wicker porch furniture was gone. Where the chaise lounge chairs should have posed beside the pool there were only leaves and twigs from overhanging trees. Without electricity the pool pumps weren't running so the pool was full of trash and the still water had stagnated. I raised the lid on the hot tub and the smell of foul water ringed by green scum assaulted me. Two abandoned wineglasses sat side by side in a corner of the tub.

Sitting with my legs crossed on the Cool-Crete surface surrounding the pool, I dialed the power company and navigated the maze of menus until I reached a customer service representative, who informed me that the electricity had been disconnected because the bill hadn't been paid in three months. As a result, I would have to pay past due charges, plus late fees, and make a new deposit to reopen the account. A succession of calls to the gas company, the cable company, and the municipal utilities produced the same results. Carrie paid the routine bills, so I had no idea the utilities had been turned off.

Just to be doing something other than wallowing in pity, I grabbed the pool skimmer and removed the leaves and seedpods from the pool.

Then I drained the hot tub and carried the wineglasses into the kitchen. Lipstick smeared the rim of one glass but not the other. A quick tour of the interior revealed that Carrie had taken the guest bedroom furniture as well. Her closets and dresser drawers were empty. The glass-doored wardrobe in the living room had been emptied of keepsakes and statuettes. The only rooms that were still furnished were the small living room and the cramped master bedroom. Behind my back, Carrie had taken everything she wanted from the beach house.

As I moved from room to room, my footsteps echoed in the empty spaces, drowning the echoes of an ex-girlfriend's laughter. Several murals painted by the girlfriend, Susanne, dominated rooms now devoid of furniture and turned them into small museums. An underwater scene of a coral reef and colorful fish decorated one wall in the family room; dolphins played between windows in the guest bedroom; and yellow seahorses hid behind the shower curtain in the guest bath. For me, the murals added a touch of class to an otherwise classless bungalow. To Carrie, the murals were my way of holding onto a former girlfriend and a former lifestyle. She was probably right; I had allowed the conflict to cause friction between us like a pebble in a shoe.

I dialed my wife's cell phone and reached a recorded message informing me that the number had been disconnected. Smart girl.

The refrigerator contained moldy food and spoiled milk, so I drove to the local Publix and bought a cooler, a bag of ice, and a case of beer. In the garage, I found a ratty old folding chair, placed it in the shade of the screened porch, and took stock of the situation. While pretending to work on our failing relationship, it was apparent that my wife had prepared for today's events over a long time. Carrie had shared the hot tub with someone who hadn't worn lipstick. Instead of sharing the financial windfall that was on the immediate horizon, Carrie had opted to run off with as much as she could grab and pull the center pole from the rickety tent of our marriage.

All my dreams dissolved like cotton candy on my tongue, except there was no sweet aftertaste. Yes, they had been dreams—a crowning success after a career studded with entrepreneurial failures, enough money to cut my commercial business ties, enough money to devote my time to writing and lecturing—and finally they had been within reach. Until there came one soft knock on my office door.

CHAPTER TWO

Tony Zambrano looked up from the file on his desk with something like alarm in his sleepy brown eyes. "You look like something that crawled out of a sewer," he said.

I flopped into the client's chair and said, "There's no electricity or water at the beach house. Carrie hasn't paid the bills in months so last night I slept on a lawn chair in the backyard because it was cooler outside than inside. She probably had a good laugh about the housewarming gift she left for me."

Tony leaned back in his leather chair and fingered his tie knot. One of his many affectations was dressing like a Cambridge professor: striped tie on a striped shirt under a chalk-striped suit.

He shook his finger at me. "We're not going to retaliate, Randle. We face stiff competition, and the judge's sympathy will be with the plaintiff until you tell your side of the story. Assuming you have a story to tell."

The large window behind Tony's desk overlooked The Vinoy hotel on the left, the city marina dead ahead, the city pier to the right, and Tampa Bay in the near distance. At the municipal marina, my cabin cruiser rocked in its slip on gentle swells off the Bay. The morning sunlight caused me to squint, and Tony came in and out of focus as he leaned forward or back.

I said, "Do you know this lawyer, Roberta de Castro, that Carrie has hired?"

"Oh yeah, a ballbuster. She has a reputation for winning outlandish awards for her female clients. Around the courthouse, opposing attorneys call her 'Bobbie the Castrator.' She likes the nickname; it's good for business."

"Is she just intimidating, or is she good?"

"Both. She's very expensive, but she's very effective, so someone gave your wife good advice about who to hire. Your wife's legal fees will cost you an arm and a leg."

"I'll have to pay her to divorce me?"

"It's customary."

"Terrific. What does the summons say?"

Tony flipped through the file on his desk. "Nothing unusual. The only legal grounds for divorce in the State of Florida are that the marriage is 'irretrievably broken.' They'll want to prove that you broke it. So what do they have on you, Randle?"

"Like what? I'm clean as a whistle."

"No one is 'clean as a whistle,' Randle. I never met Carrie; never saw her with you at the club. Describe her for me."

I shrugged. "We don't have any mutual friends. If you had met her, you'd remember her—she's sexy, eye-catching, in her prime. She'll be forty-five in November."

A big smile played across Tony's face. "And you're older than dirt."

"I'm only fifty-eight, Tony. The gap isn't important at our age."

Tony just smirked at me. "What I meant was describe who she is as a person. If you had to use one word to describe her, what would it be?"

It took only a moment to think of an appropriate word. "Amoral. If it's good for Carrie, it's right; if it's bad for Carrie, it's wrong. She has very high standards for the rest of us but not for herself."

Tony wore a lascivious grin. "So she was young and sexy and you fell for a honeytrap. How'd you let that happen?"

I flushed with heat. "I was in love, my friend. You should try it sometime." Tony's wife had left him a year ago.

Tony held up two hands, palms facing me to ward off an attack. "Sorry."

I got out of the chair and walked to the window behind his desk. Of course, I had asked myself that question many times. My first wife, the mother of my daughter, was a free spirit, the owner of a New Age store, an experimenter with religions, into Zen and yoga and vegan diets. Nothing wrong with that for many men, but I couldn't relate to it. Our relationship was pure Teflon—no arguments, no ups and no downs. Carrie was the opposite: uneducated but street-smart, provocative, pigheaded, alluring, uncontrollable—a tantalizing challenge. We disagreed about almost everything, but sorting through the issues drew us closer and connected us like two pieces of Velcro. I had always wanted a Ferrari, and one day I woke up with one in my driveway, so to speak. And like a Ferrari owner, I soon found I couldn't drive it anywhere to exploit its speed and handling, couldn't afford the gas and maintenance. But I still wanted the car.

Tony looked over his shoulder at me. "Okay, we'll assume they're trying to scare us into accepting an outrageous settlement. De Castro only takes cases where the husband has a boatload of money. Are you hiding a fortune I don't know about?"

The company I had helped found—Atlanta Medical Analytics (AMA for short)—had pioneered the mathematical modeling of relationships between DNA, disease, and therapies, and our imminent IPO had Wall Street buzzing with anticipation.

"I'm cash poor and carrying more debt than is healthy, but I hold stock options that will be worth a couple million when my company goes public. I'll get royalties once my patent applications are approved."

"There you go," Tony said, as though he had confirmed the Big Bang Theory. He positioned a yellow legal pad in front of him and grabbed a Mont Blanc pen from his drawer. "Okay, tell me about your income, the stock options, the royalties, and all of that."

I quoted him all the numbers: two hundred thousand dollars per-year base salary; one hundred thousand dollar annual-incentive bonus; and two hundred thousand stock options. Thirty thousand options had vested when we formed the company, before I met Carrie. During the marriage another ninety thousand had vested on company anniversaries, and thirty thousand would vest in six months, on the fourth company public and would vest on the IPO date.

Head down, writing, Tony asked, "What are the options worth?"

"We'll go public at twelve to fifteen dollars a share, so the options could be worth as much as three million dollars before taxes. The royalties on the patents could pay me another million over ten years. Depends upon how successful we are at licensing other companies to use our technology."

Tony wrote that all down, then scratched his head with the pen. "The base salary isn't enough for de Castro to chase. Even base plus bonus wouldn't get her panties wet, so it's the options and royalties they're after. We'll argue that the stock has no value until your company goes public and that you have to be present to win, like at a church raffle. The thirty thousand shares that vested before you married are certainly a premarital asset. We'll say that the royalties are post-divorce ordinary income."

Tony sucked on his pen, deep in thought. I waited. As though to himself, he said, "When does your company go public?"

"In sixty days. Can we get this done before then?"

Tony rubbed his chin and raised his eyes to the ceiling. "Afraid not, my friend. The average Florida divorce takes six and a half months."

"So, she wants the IPO to happen before the divorce goes final."

"Sure. If the IPO happens before the divorce is final, the remaining shares will become community property. Maybe the royalties too."

"Whoa! Wait a minute. How are the royalties a part of this? I haven't earned that money yet."

Tony tapped the pen on his legal pad and gave me a sad look. "They'll argue that you earned the royalties while you were married, you just haven't collected the money yet. Anyway, the court will include them in the calculation of future income when establishing alimony."

That stunned me. I had worked for peanuts for twenty years, refining my theories of medical predestination, before joining a high-tech startup that could commercialize the science and provide me with the vehicle to disseminate the science broadly and not just to people who could afford to be healthy. Simplistically, I had assumed that our wedding day and our divorce date would be definitive brackets around my financial obligations to Carrie Marks. Now I had the sensation that I was tiptoeing through a legal minefield and I could lose a figurative arm and a leg.

"You can't let that happen, Tony. This is my future we're talking about."

"Of course we'll fight it," he said. He leaned on the desk, moved closer to me. "Once the money is in the bank the split is straightforward, but the division of future earnings is tricky. So why did Carrie file now, Randle?"

I leaned back in my chair, not wanting to be more intimate with Tony Zambrano.

"We argue about money," I said. "The credit cards are maxed out, so I took them away from her and cut them up. I moved our savings, fifty thousand dollars, out of a joint account and into a CD in my name so she couldn't spend it." What I hid from him were the arguments about how to support her parents. They were old, retired, and destitute, a condition I hoped wouldn't befall me. Since Carrie spent all our free cash, there was nothing to give her parents until the stock options could be cashed. Another pebble in the shoe.

"No more of that," Tony said as he pointed a crooked finger at my face. "One of the exhibits to the filing is an injunction against financial changes. It's mutual. Your assets are frozen, and neither of you can buy anything more expensive than groceries." He paused and then added, "You can pay your legal fees of course. Ha ha."

"Of course." I didn't laugh.

"Her complaint asks for temporary maintenance as well as permanent alimony, so the filing gets her financial relief."

"Does 'permanent' mean forever?"

"That's how Webster's defines it."

"Dammit!" I slammed my fist on the desk.

Tony gave me a disgusted look. "You sound like those billionaires who get taken to the cleaners. You flash your money around to attract sleazy younger women, and you expect them to love you just because you're you. Then you make the mistake of marrying them and you never give a thought to what the divorce will do to you, but you expect your lawyer to work a miracle and make it all go away."

"Okay, I deserve that, but I'm drowning and you're my life preserver."

Tony puffed his cheeks and blew stale air into the room. "Any other reasons she might want to file in a hurry?"

Lots of them. The straw that broke the camel's back may have been an incident in late June or early July. I was watching a golf tournament in the family room—my designated space—when Carrie waltzed in and said, "I want you out of this house."

I had feigned a dumbfounded look and replied, "I must have missed the memo, the one that said you're in charge here."

"Go live in the beach house. You're happier there anyway."

"No," I said, "I'll hang around here and keep an eye on things." Meaning an eye on her.

She flushed crimson. "I have friends who can throw you out of here."

I shrugged. "Good luck with that. I lock my door and keep my pistol cocked and loaded on the bedstand at night. You should do the same thing."

She growled and kicked an end table, toppling and shattering a three-hundred-dollar lamp. I never cleaned it up and neither did she.

To Tony I said, "I refused to move out of the country house. Southern women believe they can kick their husbands out of the house whenever they get angry and make them crawl back asking for forgiveness. It's a game they play."

"It's not a game anymore. Another exhibit to the filing gives her possession of the Cortes County house and a restraining order against you. You can't come within one thousand feet of the house. Means you can't even drive by on the road."

"Gee, Tony, this is all going so well. Any other legal gems I should know about?"

"Nope, that's pretty much it: standard grounds; temporary and permanent alimony; you pay her legal fees; she gets possession of the country house; restraining order; your assets are frozen. Now it's our turn at bat."

"Finally. What's the plan?"

"I'll file an answer ASAP, ask for expedited mediation. The answer will be simple; we're not contesting the divorce, are we?"

"No, not this time."

Tony was surprised—his eyebrows danced and his eyes twinkled like a midsummer Santa Claus. "You were separated before?"

"Yes, during our first year of marriage. I convinced her to get help and give the marriage another chance."

"Psychological help or marriage counselor?"

"Mental health counseling for her erratic behavior, mood swings, violent reactions."

Tony frowned. "Tell me about the violence."

"She throws things at me when she's angry. She dumped a serving bowl of salad on me once, and another time she threw a heavy crystal ashtray at my head."

Tony smirked.

"It knocked a hole in the wall."

Tony stifled a laugh.

"One time I returned from a business trip and found that she had emptied every drawer in the house, gone through all my clothing, dumped the clothes on the floor of the closet, and tipped my filing cabinet over. I said, 'What the hell?' and she said, 'A wife can look anywhere she wants.'"

Tony flipped his hand. "Legally, she was right."

"Tony, the slightest hint of criticism provokes an explosive reaction. There's a name for it in psychology: avoidant personality disorder."

Nodding, Tony said, "You need a psychiatrist's professional opinion for any mental diagnoses."

"She takes meds prescribed by a psychiatrist. She filled out an application for employee benefits through my company, and she listed the medications she was taking. I looked them up and found they were antidepressants and pills to prevent anxiety attacks."

Tony leaned his head to the side, interested. "Did she take her meds?"

"Not always. She said they made her gain weight."

"Hmm." The lawyer cocked his head again. "So she's mentally unstable and it was impossible to maintain a marital relationship."

"That's right. She's looney tunes."

"We'd need a third-party opinion, not yours."

"Then let's get one! Let's fight back."

Staring off into space, he recited lines he may have read as a second-year law student. "There's a law called the Baker Act that regulates all mental health facilities, practitioners, treatment regimens, and processes in the State of Florida. Under the Baker Act, as a close relative, you can petition a judge to have your wife examined involuntarily. You would have to show proof that she is a threat to herself or to others. It's like a probable cause hearing in a criminal case."

"I have plenty of evidence."

Tony leaned back, gazed at the ceiling, calculating. "If she were adjudged insane, she'd lose credibility. You'd get a better deal on alimony and fringe benefits too."

"Let's do it. File a petition."

He cleared his throat. "Okay, write everything down for me, all the incidents that might indicate mental instability, and include the names of any witnesses we could call. I'll run it past my partners, see if they think it's a good idea."

"Thanks, Tony, but be careful what you wish for. I could write *War and Peace* and not cover it all."

Tony jotted another note on his yellow legal pad. He said, "Were you planning a divorce too? Did she beat you to the punch?"

"No, I didn't want a divorce, but I think she's been cheating on me. I wanted proof or a confession or an apology. Something."

He looked at me in disbelief. "You'd stay with her just to get an admission she cheated?"

I turned back to the window. It was hard to think with him staring at me. To the world beyond the window, I said, "I'd hoped she'd morph back into the woman I dated."

Tony laughed as though he had heard a joke. "Single women and married women are two different species, and they only evolve in one direction."

Turning around, I said, "I want to countersue for divorce, take away her advantage as a plaintiff, and I want a restraining order too. You can serve her at the country house. The process server knows the way out there."

Tony swiveled to face me. "You're turning this into something it doesn't have to be."

"Trust me on this one, Tony. We're not doing Vietnam—incremental escalation—we're doing Desert Storm—shock and awe." I looked down at my lawyer, sitting in his big executive chair. "We have to let her lawyer know you're not a pushover. If she's going to intimidate you, she'll want you to know up front she's going to turn you to mush."

Tony drew a deep breath. "This is a good time to let you off the hook if you want to go a different way on counsel. We're buddies, and this lawyer/client thing is a little uncomfortable for me. You know there are guys out there, sharks like de Castro, that you could hire."

"No, Tony. I want to go through this with someone I know and trust."

Tony looked pleased and maybe scared too. "Okay, but if this starts going south, you can change at any time. No offense taken."

I patted my buddy on the shoulder. "We'll make you famous—the guy who beat Bobbie the Castrator." At that moment, I actually believed it.

CHAPTER THREE

At six-thirty a.m., Tony's phone call woke me from a dream in which I was lost in a large convention center and couldn't find my colleagues. Down passageways, into the basement, through spaces reserved for hotel employees, I had searched in vain. What would Freud say about that? How about, *Randle seeks allies for his battle with Carrie?*

"What are you doing, Tony? There are still stars in the sky."

"Sorry, mate, but I've got a, ah, meeting in a few minutes, and I thought you'd want to know that we filed your counterclaim yesterday . . . in case you hear from your wife."

Tony playing golf again. Fitting me in between his tee times. "You send the process server out there? Embarrass her the way she did me?"

"No, the countersuit is your answer to her complaint, so we filed it with the Clerk of the Circuit Court. The service, if you want to call it that, was a copy delivered to de Castro by messenger. That's how it's done once both parties have representation."

I rolled out of bed and stretched. As I headed to the kitchen, I said, "Okay, step one in our defense. Thanks."

"Don't thank me. It's like firing on Fort Sumter. It's gonna start a war."

The way I remembered it, Carrie had fired the first shot, but I didn't quibble with the analogy. For divorce lawyers, the plaintiff's complaint was merely a demand for a settlement. The reaction to the demand initiated the battle. I popped a Gevalia coffee pod into my Keurig.

"A war is what we want, Tony, not a surrender."

I took my coffee outside to the screened porch and settled onto a chaise lounge chair.

Tony covered his mouthpiece and said something to someone at the golf course. When he came back on the line, he said, "I've got to run, Randle. Do you have anything else for me on this fine morning?"

It annoyed me that Tony had forgotten he had initiated the conversation. "Yes, I want the rest of my stuff from the country house. I'll need movers to help me."

"Can't you just leave the stuff out there till mediation?"

"No, Tony, there won't be anything left. It needs to happen ASAP."

He sighed. "Okay, I'll draft a motion."

"Thanks. Go break a hundred."

"Yeah, a hundred-dollar bill." He hung up.

A second cup of coffee had me fully awake when Jamie, my daughter, called. I said, "I was getting worried."

"Sorry, Dad. I'm on the night shift, and I sleep during the day. Just leaving work now."

"Guess you got my message? Carrie served me with divorce papers on Monday."

"Good riddance. Should have happened a long time ago."

"Don't sugarcoat it. Let your feelings out."

"I'm not trying to be mean, Dad. Your life will be a thousand percent better without her. Let her have the money. She's like those lottery winners who are broke in a year. You can always make more money."

"I'm running out of time to do that, but I'm glad you have confidence in me."

"Does this mean I can see you without seeing *her*?"

I hadn't seen my daughter in more than six months and only a handful of times in the last two years. She wasn't fond of Carrie, and she wasn't all that fond of me. "Sure," I said. "Tell me when."

"How about Sunday? I have to work tonight and sleep tomorrow, but I'm off tomorrow night." She paused for just a millisecond. "I'd have to bring Mom. She's spending the day with me."

Jamie was referring to my ex-wife, Glenda. I said, "Okay. Why not?"

"One thing you have to promise, Dad: Don't charm her socks off. She still talks about getting back together with you, and now there's an opening."

"But she's happily married, right?"

"Yes, and he's a good husband for her. So don't mess it up."

It took several hours to write *The Mental Health History of Carrie Marks*—ten thousand words recounting every odd and scary event during our marriage. The more I wrote the more I remembered and the more I had to write. The act of writing it down on paper was cathartic. *I'm not crazy; she's crazy.* I attached the Word document to an email and sent it to Tony.

CHAPTER FOUR

After three days alone in the beach house, I imagined myself to be a balloon on a string. Some little kid had lost his grip, and now I was floating higher and higher and farther away. It felt like unrestrained freedom, and it felt like a loss of control. My desire for control was stronger than my desire for freedom. I was scared.

I didn't realize it was a Saturday until Carrie's sister, Connie Tomkins, called and told me it was. She said I should get out of the house and join her for lunch at the International Plaza in Tampa. Connie frequently asked me to lunch to share work gossip that was of little interest to the rest of Carrie's family. Usually I found a way to graciously decline. Today I didn't feel magnanimous or sociable. I was still recovering from the idea that Carrie had planned the divorce for months; however, I wanted to hear what Connie knew about Carrie's plans, so I agreed to meet her.

After I hung up, I shaved, showered, and dressed in my best business-executive-on-a-day-off duds and drove across the causeway to the Westshore Drive exit. Around the back of the International Mall, past Nordstrom and Nieman Marcus, stood a row of restaurants I frequented—sometimes with business associates, occasionally with my daughter.

I left the Bronco with the valet and walked to the open-air tables in the courtyard. After a bit of searching, I found Connie sitting under an umbrella at a Cheesecake Factory table. As I wound my way through the tangle of tables, Connie stood to greet me. She wore a silk blouse the color of dried blood over linen slacks and flats. I walked into her embrace and got kissed flush on the mouth. Diners at nearby tables might have assumed we were lovers. Connie always kissed me as though she were my girlfriend, even in front of Carrie.

We sat at a round wooden table, both of us on the same side of the umbrella post growing out of the middle. The umbrella was open and tilted to shade us from the early afternoon sun. Hiding our nerves, we exchanged small talk while the pink elephant waited nearby. When the waitress appeared, Connie ordered a salad and sweet tea and I ordered guacamole dip, hot and spicy, and a Blue Moon.

Connie was the "business manager"—the accountant—for a community hospital in Manatee County. She also played multiple roles within the Tomkins clan—fixer, tour guide, family bank, and more mother than aunt to Travis, my stepson. As Connie jabbered about work, I surveyed my sister-in-law. She was a few minutes older than her twin, an inch taller, and ten pounds lighter, but otherwise a carbon copy of Carrie without the paint, the glitter, and the breast augmentation. She had short hair the color of West Texas tumbleweed—the color Carrie's would have been without help from the salon—and the high cheekbones and prominent brow that were the products of Cherokee blood mixed into the Tomkins gene pool a hundred years ago. Today she had left several blouse buttons unfastened. There wasn't much to see—a hard white sternum and a bit of black lace bra—but it was far more than I had glimpsed in the four years I had known her.

Connie had married her college sweetheart after graduation, and the mistake had lasted only ninety days. She hadn't dated anyone in the four years I'd known her. Nonetheless, if she tried a bit harder, she could attract men. But, unlike her sister, whose primary endeavor and only talent was attracting men, Connie made no overt effort to attract the opposite sex.

The food arrived but Connie continued to regale me with minutiae. Her mother, Annabelle, had grown feeble, her health failing. "I don't have time to take care of her, and Daddy doesn't know how, so Carrie has been an angel, over there all the time."

Yeah, right. I scooped guacamole with tortilla chips, smiled at the right times, made eye contact, and waited for Connie to get around to the real reason for doing lunch. At one point, I thought a skanky young man with limp, long hair, sitting at a table across the aisle and behind Connie, had used his smartphone to take a picture of us. For a while, I watched the young man surreptitiously, but he never looked our way again.

Connie noticed that I was distracted and looked back over her shoulder. The young man looked in our direction, and Connie must have made eye contact with him, but she made no comment. Instead she said, "You're not listening to me, Randle. The whole family is devastated by the divorce."

"You didn't know this was going to happen?"

"We knew there was trouble in paradise, but we hoped you guys could work through it. Everyone likes you, Randle, so it will be a shame to lose you."

"I didn't file for the divorce. Carrie did."

Connie took her time to consider that as the waitress appeared and asked if we wanted to see a dessert menu. I ordered another Blue Moon.

When the waitress departed, Connie resumed the conversation. "Carrie says you forced her into it. You were controlling her, spying on her, accusing her of things she didn't do."

I scoffed at Connie and said, "A divorce has been Carrie's plan for at least six months. She prepared for this like a general prepares for an invasion."

Connie made a hurt sound as she sucked air. "You're wrong. Carrie loved you, and she's brokenhearted that she had to file for the divorce."

The young man with the smartphone got up and left without looking our way.

"Divorce wasn't her only option. I convinced her to see a marriage counselor, but Carrie didn't think it was fair that I brought up the issues I had with her. She thought marriage counseling should be about her problems with me, so she refused to go a second time."

"I heard about it. You refused to compromise."

"Compromise is a lose-lose proposition; neither person gets what they really want."

"All you wanted was sex."

The hostess seated a couple with three small kids at the table next to us. I waited for the commotion to settle and then leaned closer to Connie so the neighboring table couldn't overhear me.

"Is that what Carrie says? What we discussed was Carrie's inability to care about anyone but herself. We all know what a lack of empathy implies."

Connie glared at me. "Carrie says that was a smokescreen, and you wanted to embarrass her in front of the counselor. You know she has issues with sex because men come on to her all the time, and she doesn't know how to deal with it—let them do whatever they want or fight them off."

"Predators and victims identify each other instinctively. Carrie invites men to come on to her with the way she dresses and the way she behaves because it boosts her self-esteem when men want to get her into bed."

Connie reacted to my words as though she had been slapped. Although we couldn't be heard over the racket at the next table, she leaned in close and whispered, "Carrie discusses her problems with a professional."

"Her clinical psychologist? Those sessions are like sugar pills for Carrie. I went along once to see what it was like. Carrie cried on the woman's shoulder and blamed the rest of us for everything that's wrong in her life."

Connie slowly leaned back in her chair, her eyes wide, her mouth forming an "O." After she gathered herself, she said, "When we were kids she blamed me for the things she did. She'd wet the bed and blame me, but Momma knew who did it. Another time she killed the cat and hung it from the clothesline. It was just a stray so Momma didn't do anything about it."

Carrie had always depicted her childhood as a fairy tale so I was shocked by these revelations. And I knew what animal cruelty implied.

"See, Connie, she's been sick since she was a child."

"Carrie takes her mental health seriously now, takes her medications, sees her counselor regularly."

I spun my beer bottle around and picked at the label. Carrie wasn't diligent about her mental health, but it wasn't worth an argument with Connie. "Sorry, Connie, I'm not going to give in to her because of her mental condition." *In fact, I'm planning to exploit it.*

Connie became irate and huffed and puffed like a cartoon dragon. "Let me give you a piece of advice, Randle: From a sister-in-law who loves you, stay away from Carrie until this is over. Don't violate your restraining order. Don't go out to her house or confront her about anything. Do you know she has a gun?"

With all the bombast I could muster, I said, "Yep, and I've got a bigger one. I have a protective order too. If she shows up on my doorstep, I'll blow her away. There are laws in Florida that make it legal."

"My God, you're both scary."

"Well, forgive me for being indignant. Little pipsqueak threatening me with her peashooter. If you care about her, take that gun away before she gets hurt."

"Stop antagonizing her. You didn't have to file a countersuit."

So that's why we're having lunch. "The divorce wasn't my idea."

"Now we're going in circles." Connie sat back and waited for me to finish my beer. When I was paying attention, she said, "She seemed so happy when she found you. What happened?"

I had considered that question hundreds of times. "Neither of us got the person we thought we wanted. Carrie thought she wanted a business executive—a guy with no dirt under his nails, a classy guy with some money who could improve her social status and make her life easy. In reality she likes roughnecks with a pickup and a gun rack, guys who listen to sad country music."

"She tried that twice. Both ex-husbands are good ol' boys."

I leaned back in my chair and thought about that. "Phil Simmons seems like the right kind of guy for her." Simmons had been Carrie's second husband.

"He cheated on her."

"And she cheated on him for revenge."

Connie looked like she had just been told that Santa isn't real. "She told me she's never cheated on any of her husbands."

"That's a lie. She told me how she punished Phil. She felt bad about seducing a married man, but she had to screw somebody and he was handy."

Now Connie looked like a deer in the headlights. Absentmindedly, she stroked her neck, tugged at her blouse. "Look, Carrie's not easy,

I know that. On the other hand, the divorce can be easy. She doesn't want a big fight in court, Randle." Connie waited for a reaction, but I didn't give her one. "Is that what you want? A big show to embarrass the family?"

The waitress arrived with the check, wanting to turn the table over and line up her next tip. Connie said this one was on her, and I surprised her by letting her pay it.

Knowing Connie would pass it along to Carrie, I said, "She can have a divorce, but she's got to be held accountable for her behavior. We've charged her with inappropriate marital conduct." It felt strange coming out of my mouth, like a line from a movie.

Connie straightened her collar. "She didn't do anything wrong, Randle."

"Then she has nothing to fear." I stood. Lunch was over for me.

Connie remained seated, holding me in place. "Why waste your money on lawyers and countersuits? Drop your suit and save the money for yourselves."

I leaned on the table for effect and said, "I filed the countersuit because Carrie won't negotiate in good faith unless she feels threatened. I take it from our chat today she feels a bit threatened."

"You should feel threatened too."

I continued as though she hadn't spoken. "The lawyers are scheduling a mediation session. If we can reach a reasonable agreement, this will all be over."

Connie got out of her chair and grabbed her purse. "Okay, that's all we can ask."

We filed between the tables and moved onto the sidewalk.

"Where did you park?" Connie said.

"I used valet parking."

She motioned toward the far end of self-parking and said, "I'm way over there," but she walked alongside me to the valet stand. I handed an attendant my ticket. We stood in silence for a few moments before I blurted out a confession. "I lie in bed at night wondering how I got myself into this mess."

Serious, she said, "You chose the wrong Tomkins sister."

Had my mouth been full of beer, I'd have spit it all over her in shock.

"Don't look so surprised. You're not the first man to make that mistake." She kissed me on the lips and turned to walk away.

I wasn't surprised that Connie felt she was a better match for me than Carrie. What surprised me was that she thought I had made a choice. Connie didn't have the slightest reason to think I was attracted to her.

I said, "What!?"

Connie looked over her shoulder. "A story for another day, Randle. Call me sometime."

I watched her walk down the way and then across the street to the parking lot. As she crossed, she saw me watching her. She waved.

I imagined the scene as a movie, a chick flick. The male lead would come to his senses and chase after the good sister. He would wrap her in his arms. He would beg forgiveness for his mistake. He would kiss her passionately. He would pledge undying devotion. Fade to black. The problem with that scene was that the premise was all wrong; there was no good Tomkins sister.

CHAPTER FIVE

A t lunchtime on Sunday, Jamie called and suggested an early dinner. We agreed to meet at four-thirty at Maggiano's at the International Mall in Tampa. Lunch with "my family" would be a welcome distraction from the divorce process. I couldn't help but mentally rewrite history: If I hadn't divorced Glenda I would not have met Carrie, would not have suffered through four years of a bad marriage, would not be in the middle of an ugly divorce, would not feel guilt for abandoning Glenda and Jamie. All because I was bored and wanted a new adventure. *What an idiot.*

The restaurant lobby was packed and overflowed onto the sidewalk. As I elbowed my way to the hostess station, Glenda appeared out of nowhere on my right and Jamie slid beside me on my left. Both women wrapped an arm around me and kissed me on opposite cheeks.

"Hello stranger," Glenda said, and fitted herself into my embrace.

Arm in arm, we shuffled to the front of the line—three tall, distinctive people whom others watched with interest. Glenda was five-foot-five with a mass of artistically messed copper-colored hair and freckles everywhere. Everywhere. In heels, her height was a good match for my long frame. For her part, Jamie was a mixture of her parents. A couple of inches taller than her mother, with auburn hair worn short to accommodate her uniform headgear, she resembled Glenda facially but had my brown eyes and athletic grace. Today, I admired their contrasting outfits—Jamie wore jeans and sneakers, while Glenda wore sandals and a long print skirt below a mint-green blouse that matched her eyes.

As the hostess led us to a table on the mezzanine overlooking the main floor, I trailed behind and watched Glenda's hips sway rhythmically, like the women in Africa who balance urns of water on their heads. Seated at the table, we perused our menus and commented on the entrées we might order. After deciding on my choices, I looked up and glanced toward the lobby. What I thought I saw was the long-haired kid who had sat near Connie and me at the Cheesecake Factory yesterday—the guy I suspected had taken our picture with his smartphone. But maybe it wasn't the same guy. People milled around and changed positions, and I lost sight of him. If he had been there at all.

Jamie, ever the cop, noticed my distraction. "What's the matter, Dad?"

"Nothing." I picked up my menu again but peeked over the top. There he was, for just a moment, and then gone again. I was pretty sure.

The waiter brought drinks and took our order while I surveyed the lobby crowd for another glimpse of the stalker. Glenda chattered away, something about her husband, and I struggled to catch up and appear attentive.

She finished by saying, "So he doesn't make me go with him to see his mother anymore."

"Wesley went to see his mother?" I said. "Doesn't she live in Lauderdale or somewhere down there?"

"Yeah, she's in a high-rise condo, and she does nothing but complain about not having a boyfriend. At eighty-four years old! There aren't enough men to go around, so the women compete by cooking for the men, doing their laundry, cleaning their apartments. She says there might be three or four casserole dishes sitting outside a guy's door every night. I'll bet the women do more than clean and cook for the men." She winked at me.

"That's what I want to be when I grow up," I said, "one of the survivors that women fight over."

"Women have always fought over you, Randle. Including me. Of course I always lose to some bimbo."

"Mom!" Jamie said.

"It's true. I never understood how you could marry Carrie. She doesn't play golf."

Even Jamie laughed at that, but I was annoyed again that everyone wanted to criticize my choice of mates. Glenda read my face.

"Just having fun with you, Randle," Glenda said. "My mother says *we're* destined to get back together someday. You know how clairvoyant she is."

"Yep," I said, "just like those TV commercials at three a.m. Ought to have an 800 number."

"Don't make fun of my mother, Randle. She's always right."

Our food arrived, but Glenda picked up the conversation thread without missing a beat. "Now that you're single again, will we see each other?" As an aside to Jamie, she said, "While your father was married to Carrie, he wouldn't spend time with me, but when he was single he couldn't get enough of me, even though *I* was married."

"Mom," Jamie said, "let's not go down that path."

"Why not? It was fun. I would pick your father up in the Publix parking lot, and he'd duck down in his seat until we were in the garage so the neighbors wouldn't see him. It was one of the best times of my life." She smiled at me, hoping for confirmation.

Instead, Jamie said, "It's disrespectful to Wesley. He's been very good to you, and I hope you won't do that to him again."

"Why not?" Glenda said. "It's not cheating if you slept with the man for eighteen years."

"Stop her, Dad."

What I never quite understood is that Glenda and I enjoyed dating one another, but we bored the snot out of each other when we were married. If it wasn't wrong and risky, it wasn't fun for us. In some twisted homage to morality, I had never cheated on my spouse, but I had not hesitated to exploit Glenda's affection for me, no matter her marital status. Now that the shoe was on the other foot, I vowed I would never do that again to a brother husband.

I cleared my throat. "That brings up a point I wanted to discuss." Both women waited with interest for me to continue. "My divorce may end up in court, in front of a judge." I turned to Glenda. "They could ask you about the time when I was separated and staying at your husband's condo. Carrie thinks we were cheating on her."

Glenda said, "Ha!" Then to Jamie she stage-whispered, "I was ready to hop in the sack, but your father wouldn't do it. Some misplaced sense of loyalty."

"T.M.I., Mom," Jamie said.

Glenda just kept talking. "You poor thing," she said to me. "Our divorce was so easy—we shared a lawyer, no custody battle, no child support, got it done in thirty days."

We had waited until Jamie was eighteen so there was no question of custody, although I funded Jamie's education and supported her until she graduated from the police academy. Our divorce had been amicable—two people who had drifted apart and wanted to start life over. I had abandoned her, looking for excitement with other people. After many failed relationships, Glenda had found Wesley and my guilt subsided somewhat.

"Those were the good ol' days," I said.

While the waiter cleared the dishes and refilled sweet tea glasses, I looked again to see if the long-haired kid was watching us. The kid was not in sight. Maybe he had all the pictures he needed. Or maybe he hadn't been there at all.

"Let's change the subject," Jamie said. "How is Wesley doing? Is he okay?"

I didn't think this was a great conversational direction either, but Glenda responded in a breezy tone. "You mean is he clean? You can just say it, I don't mind. Yes, he's sober. What he's learned is to stay away from AA meetings. They tell alcoholics to change their playmates, then they throw them in a room full of people who want to get high. Do you know that all of those people are addicts?" She snickered.

Jamie said, "Wesley is good for you, and he seems committed to his sobriety."

"Good ol' Wesley," Glenda said. Then to me she said, "Will you come outside with me? I need a cigarette, and I don't want to stand out there alone."

I glanced at Jamie. "Go ahead," she said. "This is my treat. I'll meet you outside."

Glenda and I thanked her and headed outside. We walked away from the doors, around the corner to a shaded spot. Glenda fished a cigarette out of her purse, and I took the lighter and played the gentleman.

Exhaling, she said, "I'm trying to quit again. I've cut back to when I'm nervous and after sex. Since I don't have a sex life, I hardly smoke at all."

I chuckled.

She eyed me. "What are your plans? Will you leave us again and go back to Atlanta?"

"No, why would I do that? My house and boat are here. You and Jamie are here."

"Your company is in Atlanta, and that means more to you than anything."

"I can work from here."

"I hope so, Randle, because Jamie would follow you and then I'd be alone again."

"I don't plan to leave, and you do have a husband, Glenda."

"Wesley is alright." She gave me a rueful smile. "He adores me, but he's not you. There's no emotional connection for me."

"There are worse things than a husband who adores you."

Glenda stepped over to a trashbin with an ashtray on top and stubbed out her cigarette. When she returned, she said, "If you've got nothing better to do, why don't you follow me home? We could bake cookies or something."

I didn't answer. I stared at the parking lot, and Glenda followed my gaze. "What is it?" she said.

I saw him: The long-haired kid was between cars and taking pictures of us with his phone.

I shouted, "Hey, what are you doing?"

The kid raced down the line of cars, and impulsively I chased after him. He was young, and I was too far behind to close the gap. Before I could catch up, he jumped into a white panel van and squealed tires as he took off.

I walked back to the restaurant, where Jamie now waited with her mother.

"What was that, Dad?"

"Carrie has a private investigator following me. He's not Magnum P.I., but he got pictures of your mom and me. We'll see those again at trial."

"Unbelievable!" Jamie said.

Glenda frowned. "Uh-oh."

I said, "Yeah, no cookies today."

Glenda and I laughed while Jamie looked at us like we had lost our minds. Then it was hugs all around. Glenda held her hug for a long time before she walked off to her car, but Jamie hesitated.

"As you can see, Mom is still carrying a torch for you, but if you get involved with her I'll never speak to you again. Get it?"

I held up my hands in a defensive posture. "I will not get involved with your mother. I promise." I meant it.

She shook her head. "Please don't. I'd like to have a normal relationship with both of you. Maybe we could get together sometime, just the two of us."

"Sure," I said, "I'll call you." I meant that too.

CHAPTER SIX

As soon as Tony's law office opened on Monday, I called his paralegal, Melissa, and asked for an appointment with him. She said his calendar was full but I could meet him at the club for lunch.

I took Gulf Boulevard all the way to Belleair Beach. Along this route I passed the massive beach at Treasure Island, the Madeira Beach Marina, where Carrie's father kept his Boston Whaler, the condos in the Reddingtons, and the upper-class homes in Indian Shores, before I reached the beachfront mansions rumored to be owned by Christian Scientist celebrities. It took a lot longer than Route 19, but I liked the views of the Gulf to my left and the Intracoastal to my right, at times less than a hundred yards from the roadway. Like all Florida beach communities, the peninsula between St. Pete Beach and Clearwater Beach had a somewhat decadent, decrepit ambience that made me feel at home.

It wasn't until Gulf Boulevard became a two-lane road between North Reddington and Indian Shores that I realized the white van had followed me. I used the Belleair Causeway to cross the Intracoastal Waterway to Belleair Bluffs, turned onto Indian Rocks Road, and entered a middle-class neighborhood of mature trees and homes built in the '70s and '80s. Fearing he might lose me in the neighborhood, the kid in the white van clung to my bumper like a NASCAR driver drafting and preparing for a pass. Without warning, I yanked my Bronco into the parking lot of the Belleview Biltmore Country Club and stood on the brakes, blocking the entryway. The kid swerved to miss me, hit the far curb with his left front tire, and skidded to a sideways stop. Dazed, he stared through his windshield at me and the white-with-blue-trim, sprawling wooden structure of the Belleview Biltmore clubhouse.

I flipped him off and parked my Bronco. As I walked toward the entrance, the kid eased away down the leafy street. In the main dining room only half the tables were occupied on this weekday, populated by retiree foursomes that had played golf early to avoid the stifling heat of the afternoon. Tony sat alone at a table away from the prying eyes and ears of old guys with nothing better to do than eavesdrop on a private conversation. Later the old guys would go home to their old wives and recount all the juicy details of other people's lives. That would be their afternoon entertainment.

Tony was dressed for golf and drinking a Scotch.

"You'd play better if you drank after the round," I said.

"Not true. I've tried it sober, and I'm worse. I'm playing with a prospective client and my boss, so I need to be loose."

Tony motioned to the chair across from him, and I took a seat. Almost immediately, a waitress appeared with a menu and asked for my drink order. I had never seen her before, but she was the same as all waitresses in Florida beach towns: older than her years, as tan and leathery as a horse saddle, used up by a nomadic life. Before I came back to the club, she'd be gone, off to find new drug connections or better luck or just a man who wouldn't beat her.

I ordered a sparkling water then told Tony, "I'm being followed by some amateur private eye. He's taking pictures of the people I meet."

Tony looked terrified. "Anyone you shouldn't be seeing?"

Even my lawyer distrusts me. "Once with my sister-in-law, who invited me to lunch, and once with my daughter."

He leaned back and pursed his meaty lips. "I told you they'd counterattack after we filed the countersuit."

"Can we do something about it?"

"You can behave yourself. Let me know if he harasses you."

"He followed me all the way up here. He's invading my privacy." The old geezers stopped eating and started listening. Ours could be the exciting conversation they'd later relate to their wives.

"You have no privacy in public places, Randle. Ask the Hollywood stars if you don't believe me."

"Terrific. Guess lunch is over."

Tony ignored the sarcasm. "Not yet. Ms. de Castro called this morning to introduce herself, and she gave me an earful."

"Wants to turn you to mush?"

"No, she wants to turn you to mush." Tony pointed a fat stubby finger at me.

"Same thing."

"Not really."

The waitress—her nametag identified her as "Sally"—served my sparkling water. Tony ordered a shrimp Caesar salad while I glanced at the offerings. I wasn't hungry but I ordered a tuna melt, and before she retreated Sally told me it was her favorite.

"So what did de Castro say that has you so concerned?"

"De Castro says you're a horrible husband, just to get that out of the way. Who's Susanne?"

The abrupt change in direction took me by surprise. "My ex-girlfriend. Why?"

"Do you know where she is?"

"Orlando, last I knew."

"You've taken business trips to Orlando, haven't you?"

"Sure, we've attended industry events and conventions in Orlando."

"They say those trips were excuses to hook up with Susanne."

I felt my face flush. "I dumped Susanne to date Carrie. I had to pay her moving expenses to get her out of the beach house before Carrie discovered she was there."

Sally arrived with the food, and Tony ordered another Scotch. While he dug into his salad, I stared out the window at the practice putting green and allowed my tuna melt to grow cold.

After swallowing a mouthful of Gulf shrimp, Tony said, "They say you had extramarital relations with your ex-wife, Glenda."

"Glenda is a friend, and we share a daughter. Carrie can't handle that. When Glenda and I separated, I had nowhere to live. The country house was under construction, and we were living in the beach house. So I graciously let Carrie stay in the beach house, and Glenda let me stay at one of her husband's vacant rental properties."

"And?"

"And nothing."

"They could call Glenda to testify."

"Tony, they're trying to intimidate you. Doing a good job of it too."

Sally arrived with Tony's Scotch refill and put her hand on my shoulder. She asked if my tuna melt, untouched, was okay, and I told her it was fine.

Tony wiped his mouth with his napkin and sipped his Scotch. He pulled a piece of notepaper out of his pocket and referred to it as he said, "Ms. de Castro had plenty of other things to say. You abused your wife physically, mentally, verbally, and sexually." He waited for rebuttal.

"Got her list from a Hollywood divorce manual?" I said sarcastically.

"You restrained her during arguments, grabbed her shoulders, and shook her. You called her names, yelled at her."

It was true that I had defended myself against Carrie's physical assaults, and I had called her the c-word in response to being called the a-word. So what?

Tony prattled on. "You forced her to have unwanted sex." The lawyer glanced at me with a boys-in-the-locker-room sneer, then continued, "Pressuring your wife into unwanted sex is rape, even within a marriage." I reacted with a dismissive huff, so Tony referred to his notes again. Not looking at me, he sheepishly said, "Your wife claims you coerced her into committing shameful sex acts. She says you're a sex addict and should go to rehab."

Shameful? I suppose, but they were Carrie's idea. "She complained to her counselor about our sex life and the counselor told her there's no such thing as sex addiction." My lawyer looked doubtful, so I said, "The American Psychiatric Association refused to include it in the *Diagnostic and Statistical Manual of Mental Disorders* in both 2010 and 2012."

"Odd that you should know that. De Castro also gave me a list of demands, says your wife will want the country house and the furniture, alimony of course, plus her car and legal fees and life and health insurance."

I was flabbergasted. "I'd have to make her car payments?"

"You signed for it. According to de Castro, all the debts are in your name."

"Well of course they're in my name. She couldn't get credit at a fruit stand."

With a big smile, Tony said, "I did win one point with de Castro: no temporary alimony. Just use the money as you did before the divorce was filed. Because you're sharing the money, the judge will see you as a cooperative defendant."

I threw my napkin down atop my congealing tuna melt. "I don't want to be a cooperative defendant. I'm a plaintiff in my own divorce filing."

"I'm not too excited about your counterclaim, Randle, tell you the truth. What evidence do you have?"

"I have financial records. Every penny of debt was either spent by her or on her. She's like a car thief who sees the keys in a Beamer and can't resist taking a ride."

"Drop them at my office. Do you have any proof that she's been fooling around?"

In March and April, the clues had piled up like flotsam on a deserted beach. "Back in the spring she used gas like she had a pipeline to Saudi Arabia. Wouldn't tell me where she was going. There were long, unexplained absences. Wouldn't tell me where she had been or with whom."

I took a breath, and Tony said, "It's all circumstantial, Randle."

"She got a Brazilian wax job that I wasn't supposed to discover."

He grinned. "I won't ask how you 'discovered it.'"

And what about Mother's Day? I surprised her with a large yellow diamond on a thick platinum chain with matching earrings. We both knew she didn't deserve an extravagant gift. I had hoped it would prompt a confession or an apology and an offer to repair the relationship. Or she could have declined the gift in a dignified admission of her guilt. She did none of the above. She had worn the diamonds the day the process server came to serve me.

I said, "What would you think if your wife was doing this stuff?"

"Cheating on me, but the judge expects to see naked pictures and hotel receipts."

"Can we subpoena her cell phone records, see who she was texting?"

Tony looked at me over a forkful of salad. "I'm not sure."

"Check it out. See if we can subpoena her email records too."

"I'll see."

"The legal system has to let me defend myself, Tony."

Tony hurriedly scooped leaves into his mouth as though he had to eat them all before he could swing a golf club. Chewing, he said, "The good news is that your marriage was short and there were no children. My partners tell me that despite what the law allows, a childless wife doesn't get permanent alimony until she's been married for ten years. However, you established a very high standard of living for your wife that you'll have to maintain for the alimony period."

"So if a man treats his wife badly during the marriage, he can get a better divorce deal than if he treated her well? That makes no sense."

Tony raised his arms in an exaggerated shrug. "Makes perfect sense. The divorce laws are designed to encourage the parties to mediate, settle, and go their merry ways."

"Total crap. The laws are obsolete, designed to protect stay-at-home moms in the 1950s."

"The law allows you to walk away from a lifetime commitment, Randle. If we issue subpoenas and file a Baker Act petition, this is going to be a war."

"We have to file the Baker Act petition."

Tony waved a hand in front of me. "The document you wrote is excellent, but it paints an ugly picture of your marriage, my friend." I just nodded, so he continued. "Melissa will transcribe it onto a deposition form, and you'll have to sign it and swear to it."

I nodded again.

"My partners tell me it's not difficult to get an order to have someone examined. The unknown is the outcome of the examination. They can hold her for up to seventy-two hours to perform the examination. Then the psychiatrists have three choices: They can declare her sane; they can order outpatient care; or they can detain her for in-patient care. If they do order detention, it is for a period of not more than six months during which she may get well."

"People with her issues don't 'get well.'"

"You're convinced she's insane, but it's harder to convince the shrinks, especially state-funded shrinks. The shrinks like to prescribe drugs and let the crazy ones walk around free. If she's institutionalized for three years or more, it becomes grounds for divorce and you can walk away not owing her a cent. Otherwise, your current divorce progresses normally."

"If she's institutionalized, wouldn't alimony be forgiven? She wouldn't need support if she were a ward of the State."

Tony shrugged. "I suppose."

"Do it, Tony. I'll stop at your office on the way home and sign the deposition."

"Your divorce will take a lot longer if we take steps like this."

"Now you're the one who's being naïve. They're not going to let anything happen fast."

"You're probably right." Tony considered me like any professional would consider an amateur. "Don't send me anything more from your known email account. I should have told you before to delete your old email account and its history and open two new ones: one for our privileged communications, and one for any friends you'll have left after the divorce. Delete all your social media accounts too—they're poison. Do it today."

"You're making me nervous. I don't have any social media accounts, and all my emails are innocent."

"Trust me on this one. You want to be invisible. No leaks to the other side."

A cold shiver of fear bounced up and down my spine. For the past couple of months, I had locked my office door when I was away, but the lock was the simple doorknob type, easy enough to pick with a large hairpin. About a year ago, we agreed to be open with one another and shared our passwords. I nodded, dazed.

Tony leaned back in his chair, sated and exhausted by the effort. "This is going to be expensive. I can't give you any breaks on fees and expenses, Randle."

"Don't worry about the money, Tony. There'll be plenty after the settlement."

My lawyer pushed his chair away from the table. "Want to take care of lunch, or you want me to put it on my monthly invoice?"

"I'll take care of the check."

"Wonderful, less work for me. I won't charge for my time; I'd have stopped for lunch anyway."

"You're all heart, Tony," I said to his back as he rushed off to meet his golfing partners.

Sally appeared with the check. "Thanks for taking good care of us today," I said.

"My pleasure," she said with a hand on her hip. "I work weekdays, so I'm always here if you drop in for lunch." She winked at me.

Disgusted, I hustled out of the club. I pulled the Bronco to the end of the driveway and waited to see if the van would reveal itself. The kid was nowhere in sight, but I took Alternate Route 19 to Dolphin Beach instead of Gulf Boulevard, where he may have been hiding.

Following Tony's instructions, I opened a new email account that I would use only for privileged communications. I decided not to close my old personal email account because it was too much of a hassle to notify friends and credit accounts to use a new email address.

From my secure email account, I wrote Tony a note about Carrie's mental health history. Attached to the note was Carrie's application for employer-sponsored medical insurance in which she listed her counselors and psychiatrist and all the drugs she had been taking when we got married.

Next, I went to work on the property inventory that Tony had to submit on Friday. As I listed possessions that obviously were mine, it depressed me to realize I had been a guest in my own home, sequestered in a few spaces Carrie had ceded to me. I felt as though I were in a TV news scene of survivors picking through the ruins of their homes after a devastating tornado—an attempt to salvage a bit of a life that was gone forever. The approach I took with the division of property seemed fair to me: Each list represented half the value of the contents of our two homes. Of course, I listed for myself the things she had stolen from the beach house. When I was done, I emailed the inventory to Tony.

CHAPTER SEVEN

O n Tuesday, I packed an overnight bag, climbed into the Bronco, and headed for Atlanta. I hated the whole commercial airlines experience: park at the Tampa airport; get mugged by the TSA; wait in the gate area; endure delays and cancellations; squeeze into a seat too narrow for the average human being; suffer through boring airplane conversation; traverse the Atlanta airport; rent a car; return the rented car; reverse the process. As a result, I often made the seven-hour journey to the company's home office in the comfort of my Bronco, making and answering phone calls, being productive.

As I proceeded through Tampa and into the countryside toward Cortes County this morning, I scanned the southbound lanes for a red Jaguar convertible. *Pathetic.* No red Jaguars were out for a spin.

Driving was hazardous, visibility reduced to a few yards, the windshield drenched in the spray from the big rigs. I drove carefully, stayed in the slow lanes, and made it impossible for the white panel van to conceal its presence. The van had picked me up on Gulf Boulevard in Dolphin Beach as I exited my neighborhood by the only route available. Apparently, the kid had camped in the Walgreens parking lot and waited for me to make a move.

Irritated that Carrie was figuratively looking over my shoulder, I called Melissa, and Tony Zambrano agreed to take my call. *No golf in this weather.*

"Carrie's private investigator is violating my protective order again," I said when Tony picked up the phone.

He cleared his throat. "What you have to do is call the cops, get them to come out and identify the PI, check his license and so forth, and measure the distance from your home to his van."

"It's not like that. I'm driving to Atlanta for business meetings, and he's on my tail like a dog in heat. Can you call the cops to get him off me?"

"I believe I-75 is a public thoroughfare," Tony said sarcastically, "but I can check if you want me to."

"The judge can't issue a warning or something?"

"Your word isn't proof of anything, Randle. You seem to have trouble with the legal concept of proof."

"Don't be a prick, Tony." I hung up on him.

The white van peeled off at the first Ocala exit. No doubt the kid wanted to ensure I wasn't heading for the country house to harass my wife. If I really wanted to sneak up on the country house, I could just drive north until he gave up, then turn back south and do whatever I wanted. The kid was either a rookie or an amateur.

After checking into the Hilton Hotel at Technology Park, just a couple of blocks away from the company office, I called Jerry Louks, the company's technical guru, and told him I needed some technical advice.

Jerry and I had collaborated on many projects and spent many an evening together at Atlanta's finer watering holes. We made an incongruous pair, as Jerry was the perfect caricature of a techno-weeny, complete with horn-rimmed glasses and a pocket protector, while I'm tall, dark, and handsome. Well, I'm tall.

"You married guys kill me," Jerry said. "Surfing porn and getting infected with viruses. Do you know how many viruses I remove in an average week?"

"It's not a virus, Jerry. My wife has filed for a divorce, so I want to do a background check on her, see if she's got any skeletons in her closet."

"Sorry to hear that, bro, but you should have done that before the ceremony."

"I know, Jerry. There are online sites that pop up whenever you Google someone's name. Can I use one of those to see who she was before I married her?"

"Sure, easy enough, but most of them are scams." He gave me the URL of a site he trusted.

I keyed in the URL, searched for "Carrie Marks," and got hits in Oregon and Nebraska, but not Florida.

"Try her maiden name. These sites are slow to update files."

"Which one?" I said. "She's been Tomkins, Dickson, Simmons, and Marks. Like a law firm."

"Damn, bro, wasn't that a clue for you?"

I didn't have a smart retort, so I kept my mouth shut and searched for Carrie Simmons. A page popped up with a familiar picture I had taken of Carrie as we were preparing to go out for her birthday. I had rented a stretch limo to take a bunch of her friends on a tour of Ybor City nightclubs. At a club with a live band, we danced together until Carrie turned it into a raunchy performance. Her movements became so suggestive that I abandoned her on the dancefloor, embarrassed to be near her. Other men had then left their dates to join her, three and four of them at a time. When the set ended, she returned to our table overjoyed that she had been the center of attention.

"We're done here," I had said, and jerked her out of her seat.

"I'm having fun!" she had screamed as she tried to twist out of my grasp.

People at nearby tables had gawked at the scene. Her "twentysomething" son, Travis, who had cowered in shame, grabbed her other arm and together we'd dragged Carrie out of the club, kicking and screaming.

The incident was not unusual. When I took her to nightclubs, there was always a risk she would go home with someone other than me.

The site claimed to store everything there was to know about Carrie Simmons, including marriages, divorces, relatives, home addresses, phone numbers, and criminal records. I had to pay to get the report. In seconds, I was prompted to download a twelve-page PDF file.

As I scanned the report, I found familiar information—father: Harlan Tomkins; mother: Annabelle Tomkins; sister: Connie Tomkins; son: Travis Dickson; the address where she had lived when I met her and her phone number at that time. Further down the page it listed ex-husbands as Chance Dickson and Philip Simmons—men I knew about—and a third guy named Richard Puralto with an address in Pinellas Park.

"It lists an address and a guy I never knew about—Puralto," I said, trying the name on my tongue. "Is he another ex-husband?"

"Maybe not a husband, Randle. Maybe they co-owned the home."

Nonetheless, history she had never divulged. I scanned the rest of the report and found nothing very useful. The other phone numbers were old, the criminal records merely traffic tickets, and the court records listed two divorces, but not a third from Richard Puralto.

"There's nothing else in the report, but I also want to be sure she isn't snooping on my email."

He whistled. "Do you have your machine with you?"

"No, just my work computer."

"Next time you're up here, bring me your machine and I'll have a look."

"Can't you just tell me how to do it?"

"Too complex, bro. If you want to smoke her out, send some phony emails and see if she reacts."

Interesting. "Good idea. I'll bring my box next time."

"I drink single malt Scotch."

"I know that, Jerry."

Inspired, I gave Jerry's idea a test drive. Maybe Carrie was still friends with her ex-husband Phil Simmons. She had often praised him for his romantic charm, and I wasn't certain she had gotten over him. He also lived far enough away to explain her gasoline consumption. I wrote Tony a note from my old email account, the one Carrie knew about.

> **Hi Tony,**
> **I've figured it out: She's having an affair with her ex-husband, Phil Simmons. Can you put Fred on his tail, get those naked pictures and hotel receipts you need?**
> **Randle**

I should have felt better, but lethargy and loneliness engulfed me. Too lazy to go out for dinner, I fell asleep in my clothes watching something forgettable on TV.

At three a.m. my cell phone rang and woke me from a disturbing dream. Jamie and I were staying in what seemed to be a barn. Glenda's father and brother were there, and they were armed with shotguns. Outside the barn door, an angry group of hoodlums called for me to come out of the barn, but Glenda's father blocked the door and threatened to shoot them.

Disoriented and frightened, I answered the phone ready to tell a wrong-number caller to go to hell and then saw that it was my security company.

A young man said, "Your alarm is sounding"

"How come?"

The young man probably wanted to say, "Duh!" but instead he said, "It's been tripped. Can you check the doors and see if they're secure?"

"What? Why would I endanger myself? You guys are supposed to protect me."

"All sorts of things can trip the alarm, sir. Just have a look around before we file a false police report."

I shook my head to clear it. "I'm out of town, so I can't do your dirty work for you. Which sensor was tripped?"

"Number three. Know which one that is?"

My voice rising, I said, "No, I don't know which one that is! Don't you?"

"Calm down, sir. Let me pull up your security map."

After forty-five long seconds, the young man said, "The door between the dining room and the screened porch on the back of the house."

"Sure, an intruder would be out of sight back there, so it's not a false alarm."

"It's almost always a false alarm, sir. I've disabled your siren so it won't disturb your neighbors."

"Don't we want to alert the neighbors, get them to investigate?"

"No sir, that wouldn't be safe."

"Then call the cops before the robber gets away."

The young man gave a little huff and said, "Okay, stay by your phone, and I'll call you back after the police check it out."

I put my head down on the desk and considered all the possibilities. Only one seemed likely: Carrie had let herself into the house. But why? To let me know my protective order wouldn't stop her if she wanted to get to me? To steal something she had forgotten to take with her? I nodded off. Over an hour later, my cell phone woke me again.

The young man said, "Your house is secure. No sign of forced entry, all doors locked."

"So it was a false alarm?" *Carrie has a key.*

"Yes sir, like I told you. Now you're unprotected until you can reset the alarm."

With all the sarcasm I could muster, I said, "Golly gee whiz, I feel so exposed without your protection."

CHAPTER EIGHT

I had convinced my partners that it wasn't productive for me to work from the company office in Norcross—too many interruptions, too many meetings to attend. My job required deep thought, mathematical modeling experiments, and analysis of model run results—tasks better performed in the solitude of my homes in Florida. On the other hand, I missed the social aspects of working in an office. I enjoyed seeing my partners and the other employees when I came to Atlanta, and this Wednesday morning was no exception. I walked the halls, shaking hands, trading barbs, catching up on events in personal lives. I did not mention my divorce to anyone. My colleagues were acquaintances, but other than Jerry Louks, they were not close friends.

My focus today was the status of the IPO, so I met with Bob Platt, the CEO, and Richard Barker, the CFO. They assured me that the IPO would happen according to plan. The seven partners would all be rich—on paper—within a month. The good news was that the

IPO was on track; the bad news was that it would happen before my divorce was final. I challenged the timing—gently, not wanting to raise any suspicions—but my partners were firm in their drive to get the IPO done.

In the afternoon, I endured a two-hour demonstration by my team. They wanted me to see how the end product was now taking shape. My mathematical models were embedded in an application stored in the "cloud" and used by medical staff to predict the future health of their patients. The latest delay in the IPO had occurred when the bankers insisted the application be demonstrable to investors before taking the company public. The team could now demonstrate the end product. It was too late to change the IPO date.

The money I would earn from the IPO was important only as a means to an end. Unbeknownst to my partners, I had no intentions of working for a commercial business for the rest of my life. After the IPO was completed and my patents were approved, I would cash out and resign so that I could travel the country lecturing on the use of predictive modeling and analytics to solve medical issues. Maybe write a book. Maybe become an adjunct professor at a university with an affiliated medical center. My company, AMA, held a free perpetual license to my patents and would continue to commercialize the models while I proselytized. After a respectable period of time, I would issue free licenses to research universities so that the technology would become accessible to everyone and not just to those who could afford to be healthy. Carrie had objected to this plan, saying, "I'm not ready for retirement." What she had meant was that *I* was too young to stop funding *her* exorbitant lifestyle. She wanted me to work for AMA until I reached retirement age so we could reap the commercial value of my inventions. I argued that we could live nicely on two million dollars plus honorariums, but she would have none of that.

The chief information officer and the chief marketing officer, my closest working associates, treated me to a long lunch and then I headed back to Florida.

———✺———

Hours later, Tony called as I passed Gainesville and the University of Florida campus.

"I was in court filing motions for you today. We went two for three with a sacrifice." He sounded excited.

"Pretty good if we were playing baseball. Which one was the strikeout?"

"The subpoenas. Her Honor Phyllis Matthews-Bryant said, and I quote, 'You're not going to turn this civil proceeding into a criminal case,' unquote. De Castro argued that since you are legally separated, Mrs. Marks's records are her personal property and not community property. The judge agreed. Of course, it is reciprocal so they can't ask for any of your records either."

"They can have all of *my* records, Tony. *Her* records would prove she's been unfaithful. How are we supposed to get justice if we can't use the facts?"

"Whoa, buddy. Are you okay?"

"No, I'm not okay. This is business as usual for you, but it's once in a lifetime for me. When you lose a fight in court it has dire consequences for my future."

"This is the way it works, Randle. Cases are assigned sequentially to a roster of judges, and de Castro got lucky when Matthews-Bryant was assigned to us."

"So luck will determine my fate, not your good work?"

"We won more than our share today. The judge ordered mediation as soon as possible and gave us the privilege of choosing the mediator. De Castro was upset because she knows I'll choose Ross Smallwood, a guy I've dealt with who has a reputation for being sympathetic toward male defendants. I'll get us on his calendar tomorrow."

"Alright. And the other hit was . . ."

"The judge ordered your wife to allow you access to the house so you can move your things. De Castro objected on the grounds that you have a home of your own and you're under a restraining order, but I informed the judge that Mrs. Marks had the foresight to remove property from the beach house before she filed her complaint. Then she blindsided you with the filing and you left Cortes County with just a suitcase of clothes. Your wife's behavior annoyed the judge so she approved our motion. The judge also noted that if Mrs. Marks wanted to protect the privacy of her records, she had to allow you to move your records to protect their privacy."

"Well done, Tony, but of course my records and everything else I own are in Carrie's care until I move the stuff. When do I get into the house?"

"That was the sacrifice. Mrs. Marks is to give us three dates that are convenient for her, but not later than thirty days from today."

"Thirty days! Tony, it'll be like a sale at Filene's Basement— everything will be picked over. So much for protecting my privacy."

"Calm down, Randle. The *quid pro quo* is that we'll have agreed property inventories before the moving date."

"The way the court supervises divorce cases is ludicrous."

"Bloated as the government is," Tony said, "there aren't enough bureaucrats to closely monitor every litigant. We have to assume you and your wife will follow the rules, behave yourselves."

"Uh-huh," I said, and filed that information away for future reference.

"Next thing I have to do," Tony said, "is get a ruling on the stock options—are they in or out—so we know what we're dividing at mediation. Any word on the IPO?"

"Still on schedule, unfortunately."

"Okay, I'll get us back in front of Her Honor next week and schedule mediation as soon as possible."

Despite the ponderous pace of activity, Tony seemed pretty pleased with himself. Lawyers have different standards of performance than businessmen.

When I reached the beach house, I checked all the doors and windows and found them secure. Inside the house, nothing seemed to be missing—my iPod lay on the bedside table, my pistol was in its drawer, my lonely TV posed invitingly on its stand—so my intruder had not been a common thief. Carrie may have been surprised that I had changed the alarm code and may have escaped before irate neighbors discovered her. However, the screaming alarm siren had not prompted any of the neighbors to alert the police. With my car sitting in the front drive, I doubted Carrie would make another attempt, but I loaded a clip into my pistol and laid it on the bedside table. Just in case.

CHAPTER NINE

O n Saturday, I put on my happy face and decided to enjoy living alone. I wasn't comfortable in bucolic Cortes County and wasn't adept at sharing space and time with another person. Since I had no schedule to negotiate with Carrie, I ate when hungry, napped when tired, and floated on a raft in the pool until I was pruned from head to toe.

The alternating rain and sunshine in Florida produces weeds as fat as your wrist and as tall as a fourth grader. Chop them down this week, and they're back next week. I was chopping them down on Sunday, in the row of hibiscus bushes between my yard and the neighbor to the left of me, when a little girl's voice said, "Hey you, with the plumber's crack. Can you spare me the nasty visual?"

As I turned toward the voice, I saw that a tall, slender, attractive woman, just turned fifty, had slipped through the side gate. I said, "Are you Jehovah's Witnesses? Got a bunch of brochures under that blouse?"

"I'm the welcome wagon, dummy. Got cookies and milk under this blouse."

I chuckled, and she walked around the pool to meet me in the lower yard. Glenda was smoking, so I guessed she was more nervous than she looked. She wore Bermuda shorts and sandals and a slipover top with a lot of sparkly stuff on the front. Her hair was pinned up haphazardly with strands pointing in every direction, like those signs that say Dubai is ten thousand miles one way and Hong Kong is twelve thousand miles the other way.

I stood to meet her, bareback and sweating. She wasn't deterred. She walked into my arms, put a hand behind my head to hold me in place, and kissed me like she meant it.

"Welcome to the neighborhood," she said.

"I hate to destroy the mood, but were you followed? White panel van?"

"He's still on duty?"

"We can't let him catch you here. I'm going to take a look out on the street, and I'll open the garage door so you can pull your car in."

I started to walk away, and Glenda said, "Randle, this is crazy. You can do anything you please. Screw 'em."

I grunted and nodded but walked through the gate and around the side of the house to get a look at the street. No white panel van. *Screw 'em.* In the backyard, I found Glenda sitting on a chaise lounge chair. She said, "Get me a drink?"

"White wine okay?"

"If it's cold as a witch's titty."

When I returned, I also carried a frosty beer for myself. Glenda was smoking again so I got an ashtray off the screened porch, took a seat on the chaise lounge chair next to her, and lit a cigar. Saluting her with my bottle, I said, "Of all the gin joints in all the towns in all the world, she walks into mine."

She cocked her head and gave me a rueful smile. "*Casablanca*—our movie, like most couples have a song that's just for them."

I smiled back. As Glenda took a sip of her wine, I admired her. Bright green eyes, fire-engine-red lips, fingernails, and toenails, hair as bright as a stoplight, and skin as white as new snow on a ski slope. She was well kept and tastefully polished, but less artificial than Carrie—sort of the difference between a cold glass of water and a syrupy soda.

"How did you know where to find me?"

"Jamie gave me your address and phone number long ago—in case of an emergency."

"Do we have an emergency?"

She looked directly at me so she could see my reaction. "Minor emergency. I've left Wesley and moved in with my mom."

"Oh no, Glenda. I'm sorry to hear that. I know Jamie really liked him."

"Jamie didn't have to live with him. It takes unbelievable courage to help an alcoholic through each day, and I'm not Mother Teresa."

I wanted to avoid all the funeral parlor sympathy clichés, so I said, "I wish you didn't have to go through the pain of a divorce. Do you need a lawyer?"

"Our divorce won't be contentious like yours. I don't want anything from Wesley. He can keep his momma's house and his rental properties. All I want is my store and my freedom, so I hired Sam, the guy who did our divorce."

"Well, then I'm envious. Where will you live after the divorce?"

She gave me a mischievous grin. "I don't know, but this is certainly nice."

Please don't go there, Glenda. "We're a lot better at fooling around than we are at cohabitation, sweetie. And I have this private dick watching me."

She lit another cigarette. Exhaling, she said, "That makes it all the more interesting."

"Still a danger junkie?"

"Actually I've changed a lot in the seven years we've been divorced. You must have changed too."

I grimaced and slowly shook my head. "Not sure I've changed much, but I have learned a few things. I know to stay away from country girls with big tatas."

She howled. "They're not real, are they?"

"No, no—store bought, but high quality."

"Did you buy them for her?"

"No, her second husband made that investment."

"Mine are just average, but they'll still look good when I'm sixty-five. In ten years, she'll have to tuck hers into her panties."

We shared a laugh, but she turned reproachful. "Was that the attraction? Her body?"

Why do women always pry into places they shouldn't go? "Sure, I fell for the honeytrap."

Glenda pointed an accusatory finger at me. "She was a little piggy, and you liked it."

I shrugged. "She thinks it's okay to catch a man by being a little piggy and then not keep him happy after the ceremony. And she has mental health challenges I can't cope with. I'm not Mother Teresa either."

Glenda stared at me a long time before handing me her glass. "Can you get me another one?"

I took the glass into the house and poured a refill. When I returned, I found Glenda standing at the edge of the pool with her back to me. She stepped out of red thong panties and flipped them with her foot onto her tiny pile of clothes. Naked, she grinned at me over her shoulder and said, "I'm tired of talking about Wesley and Carrie, aren't you?" Then she dove into the pool.

Damn! I set her glass on the Cool-Crete and picked up my own. Standing at the edge of the pool, I waited for her to surface. She turned toward me and dug chlorine out of her eyes.

"Come on in. But drop those shorts first. You can't have a free show."

"Come on out, Glenda."

"You ever do it with her in the pool?"

"No, she said it was uncomfortable."

"Poor thing. What about the hot tub?"

"Nope."

She batted her eyelashes at me. "I can be your little piggy, Randle. It's one way I'm different now."

"We can't do this, Glenda. Get your divorce and I'll get my divorce, and then we'll date like normal people. How's that sound?"

"Sounds old-fashioned," she said in a disappointed voice, but she was already wading toward the side of the pool.

I went into the house, grabbed a beach towel, and got back to poolside as she started up the steps. That's when I spotted the kid.

"Get back in the water! Duck down!" I shouted.

She obeyed without question, half-squatting in water up to her chin. Her eyes sparkled as she said, "Are the neighbors watching?"

She'd have liked that! "It's the kid with the camera," I said.

He stood in a center console fishing boat floating slowly down the inlet just beyond my dock. He had the camera to his face, presumably snapping pictures every few milliseconds.

"Stay where you are."

I picked up my cell phone and jogged around the pool, down the yard, and onto my dock. Feet spread for stability on the floating dock, I snapped pictures of the PI snapping pictures of me. Having gotten enough, he waved, took the helm, and slowly cruised back up the inlet toward the Intracoastal. Looking back at the house, all I could see was a fuzzy red splotch on the surface of the pool. *There's an outside chance he didn't get any full-frontal nudes of the only white woman in Pinellas County with a red Afro.*

I walked back up the yard and waved Glenda out of the pool. I spread the towel like Superman's cape and held it for her. She walked into my embrace and said, "I'm sorry, Randle. Are you upset with me?"

"He must have seen your car turn onto my street. We've got to get you out of here before he comes around the front taking pictures of your license plate."

"Can I use your bathroom?"

"Sure."

Glenda picked up her clothes and padded into the house. I relit my cigar and paced alongside the pool. I wondered how much damage this indiscretion would do to my claims that Carrie had been unfaithful. After Glenda had been gone a long time, I went inside to investigate. In the bathroom, I found the blow-dryer in the sink. On the counter, my hairbrush was clogged with red curly hairs. The wet towel was lying on the floor. *Just like being married.* The medicine cabinet was standing open. *Checking to see if I've got a stock of Viagra?* When I closed the cabinet door, I saw that Glenda had written a note, in lipstick, on the mirror.

If you want me, call me.

⸺◦◦◦◦◦⸺

Labor Day passed slowly. I walked the three blocks to the Walgreens for some milk and snacks and discovered the white panel van keeping vigil. I had a jailer; all I needed were bars on my windows.

Back home I logged onto my computer. Since the Simmons note hadn't smoked out any spies, and with a taste for revenge after being spied

on again this weekend, I wrote Tony Zambrano another exploratory
note from my public account:

> Tony,
> Carrie is hiding a third ex-husband, a guy named
> Richard Puralto, in Pinellas Park. She may have committed
> bigamy when she married me. Have Fred track him down.
> Randle

From my secure account, I wrote Tony a real note:

> Tony,
> This PI kid is really getting under my skin. Attached are
> pictures of him violating my restraining order and taking
> pictures of me. Do something!
> Randle

CHAPTER TEN

E arly Tuesday morning, I drove to the Cortes County seat to meet
with the judge. If the kid in the white van had followed me, he
did a good job of hiding.

The iconic county courthouse is a broad, substantial building
constructed of bricks, standing three or four stories tall with a dome
on top. In most county seats, the courthouse sits on a square in the
heart of town, emblematic of justice in America, the centerpiece
of civilized society. The courtrooms in these courthouses resemble
scenes from a John Grisham novel. Judges' chambers are luxury
suites, paneled in wood, equipped with bars. Some courthouses
are so impressive in stature they are pictured on postcards. Such
is not the case with the Cortes County courthouse. It is not an
attraction for spring breakers. It is not pictured on any postcard. The
courthouse is a nondescript glass-and-steel office building spirited
out of some Eastern European country in the 1950s and plunked

down on an unremarkable street to hide anonymously among other unimpressive buildings.

Her Honor Phyllis Matthews-Bryant had agreed to hear motions in her "chambers," so Ms. de Castro, Carrie, Tony, and I gathered in an office that would have been suitable for a middle manager of an insurance company. The judge was a slender woman in her fifties with a patrician face and long gray hair she didn't bother to conceal. Aging hippie is the phrase that came to mind, except that she wore a business suit just like a middle manager of an insurance company.

It had only been a couple of weeks since I had moved out of the country house, but in this official setting my wife seemed a stranger I was meeting for the first time. She seemed smaller, vulnerable. The spiky gelled hair she favored when she wanted to attract attention was gone—her hair was brushed like a little boy's—and she had applied no makeup. She wore no rings, no jewelry of any kind, was dressed in slacks, a conservative sky-blue blouse, and low-heeled sandals. She did not make eye contact with me and stuck close to her attorney's side. Poor little Carrie was now a supplicant in front of the judge.

Roberta de Castro turned out to be an attractive woman in her early forties, dressed in a navy suit and wearing fire-engine-red heels. I liked the bold statement made by the heels—"I'm a flamboyant attorney, and I don't mind you knowing it."

The judge's assistant wheeled in two swiveling desk chairs borrowed from other offices, and everyone took a seat.

The judge said, "Let's get started. We have three motions to consider: stock option disposition, mediation, and personal property division. Let's take the stock options first. Ms. de Castro, we'll start with the plaintiff's argument."

In an accented voice that sounded like a dull razorblade scraping a three-day-old beard, de Castro said, "Thank you, Your Honor. Our position is that the option award itself is tangible property, and therefore all options became community property when the couple wed. The IPO has been scheduled to occur twice during the marriage, so Mrs. Marks had a right to believe she would share equally in their value. When the marriage was irretrievably broken by Mr. Marks, my client was forced to file her complaint for divorce, but the timing of the divorce shouldn't influence the Court's view of their community property. All two hundred thousand options should be divided equally, as will be the case with all other community property."

No reaction from the judge; she didn't even take a note. Carrie wore a brave smile.

The judge said, "Mr. Zambrano?"

Dressed in his trademark chalk-striped suit and bowtie, Tony shifted in his chair and then leaned forward to deliver his argument. "Your Honor, the stock options are not tangible property as they have no value until or unless the company goes public and shares are sold on the market for a value as yet to be determined. In order to gain ownership of the options, Mr. Marks must be employed by the company on the date the options vest, and therefore the thirty thousand shares that vest on the company anniversary and the fifty thousand shares that vest on the IPO date have no legal standing whatsoever. He's under no obligation to remain employed by AMA, and we can't limit his freedom by compelling him to be employed there. It is also our opinion that the thirty thousand shares that vested prior to the marriage are a premarital asset, so a ruling is only required for the ninety thousand shares that vested during the marriage. We would argue as well that those shares will not become real property unless the IPO occurs prior to the final divorce decree."

Tony leaned back, pensive. A frown rose from Carrie's neck and crept across her face. De Castro wore a confident smile. The judge hadn't taken any notes during Tony's monologue either. She wore a little smirk.

Judge Matthews-Bryant said, not unkindly, "I'll decide what rulings need to be made, Mr. Zambrano." She folded her hands on her clean desktop. The arguments made by the attorneys had been anticipated. The ruling to come had been decided before anyone entered her chambers.

"So, we have opposite ends of the spectrum: all . . ."—Matthews-Bryant motioned toward de Castro—". . . or nothing at all." She motioned toward Tony. "That was to be expected, so I'll be Solomon and divide the baby. I agree with Mr. Zambrano that the options had no value when awarded, but my opinion is that they do have a value once vested. Before the IPO, the value of the vested shares happens to be zero because the shares can't be sold. After the IPO, the value will be set by the market. Thus, the hard currency value of the shares fluctuates, but once vested there is always a value between zero and something to be determined. The IPO date is a trigger for market valuation of vested shares, but the vesting date is the trigger that turns potential into real property."

Nodding to de Castro, she continued, "I will agree with Ms. de Castro that Mrs. Marks had a right to believe all options would vest during the marriage and would be community property with a monetary value to be established by the market. Since she filed for divorce before the last eighty thousand options have vested, she has left those options up for debate. Any questions so far?"

Tony spoke up. "Yes, Your Honor. I'm confused by your ruling. Since the options become property on their vesting date, and since the first thirty thousand shares vested before Mr. Marks had the misfortune of meeting the future Mrs. Marks, it would follow that those shares belong to Mr. Marks as premarital property."

The judge frowned at Tony. "Watch your tongue, Mr. Zambrano."

Matthews-Bryant donned a pair of reading glasses and paged through a file on her desk. She found what she wanted before looking up. To Tony Zambrano she said, "Let me try to explain it to you. The

IPO was originally scheduled for the summer of last year and then it was rescheduled for March of this year. Mrs. Marks filed her complaint just last month, in August, after the couple had been married nearly four years. Clearly all one hundred and twenty thousand shares should by now have been shared by both parties. Although there is no guarantee that AMA will ever go public, and there is no guarantee that more options will vest in the future, the options that are vested will be shared equally by the parties. Is that clear?"

Abashed, Tony said, "Thank you for the explanation, Your Honor."

Matthews-Bryant waved a questioning hand toward de Castro.

De Castro said, "I'll hold my questions, Your Honor."

Matthews-Bryant resumed her pose as the oracle dispensing judicial wisdom and continued. "It is not appropriate for Mrs. Marks to remain in a broken marriage in order to obtain her fair share of community property. On the other hand, I will not allow the plaintiff to drag her feet on this proceeding simply to acquire a bigger slice of the pie."

The judge paused to look at Carrie and de Castro. Carrie smiled and de Castro nodded. Tony and I were quaking in our boots.

"The shares that will vest with the IPO and on the next company anniversary will also fall under this ruling if the divorce isn't final before those triggering events. However, this is a simple divorce and we want this process to proceed with speed; therefore, I order the parties to reach an agreement during mediation on the split of the eighty thousand options and to keep those two timings in mind as you negotiate."

I could feel the air being sucked out of the room.

As we all stared at the judge, she said, "Questions or rebuttal?"

De Castro raised her hand as if she were in a classroom. "Your Honor, what happens if the parties cannot reach an agreement on the unvested options?"

Matthews-Bryant was quick to respond. "Then I'll divide those shares. Don't make me do it, Ms. de Castro. Anything else?"

No one said a word, so the judge continued. "To make my point about dragging feet, I order that mediation occur on the earliest availability of the mediator." She consulted the file on her desktop. "The last Monday of the month, in the offices of Ross Smallwood. Ms. de Castro?"

De Castro immediately realized that the divorce could go final before the IPO and the vesting of fifty thousand options. She considered an objection but swallowed her words and simply said, "We'll be there, Your Honor."

"Good. Mr. Zambrano, you may choose a date for the division of personal property."

Tony said, "We'll take the earliest offered moving date, Your Honor, the Friday before mediation."

"Then we're done."

The judge began to rise, but de Castro interjected, "Excuse me, Your Honor, but we haven't reached agreement on the property division. Each side filed different versions."

Matthews-Bryant sank back into her chair. "Ladies and gentlemen, you are starting to annoy me. You will have a property division agreement in my hands by this Friday, or you will be held in contempt. You follow?"

The attorneys nodded.

"That means Mr. Marks can move his belongings the following day, Saturday. We aren't at the mercy of a mediator's calendar here, right? So let's just get this done." She looked over the top of her reading glasses at the women, who were frozen in shock, then added, "Unless you have a nail appointment on Saturday, Mrs. Marks."

Carrie flushed. She and de Castro huddled and whispered hisses like two snakes in a mating ritual. De Castro broke the huddle and said, "Your Honor, the plaintiff would like more time to prepare for the move."

"What's to prepare? He's doing all the heavy lifting." She snickered.

Carrie surprised us by saying, "Your Honor, I'd like to separate my things from his so they are out of harm's way and his are easier to access."

The judge gave her a look of amused respect. "Fine. I'll give you all weekend to prepare. Can you move on Monday, Mr. Marks?"

"I can, Your Honor. Thank you."

The judge didn't give Carrie another chance to object. She rose and said, "Mr. Zambrano, if you would please, wait here a few minutes until the ladies have left the building."

"Of course, Your Honor."

The women were seated closest to the door so they could leave without passing by us, but at the doorway Carrie paused, popped out a seductive hip, and, looking back over her shoulder, stuck her tongue out at me. The judge noted the insult before she picked the file folder off her desk and followed de Castro out of the office.

Tony put a hand on my shoulder. "I can see why you were attracted to her, Randle. That's quite a body."

Mimicking the judge, I said, "Watch your tongue, Mr. Zambrano. She's still my wife."

He tried to put an arm around me, but I pulled away and put some space between us. "I just lost somewhere between six hundred and eight hundred thousand dollars."

"We held our own."

"They're kicking our butt. All you said was, 'Thank you, Your Honor.' Like some kid in prep school saying, 'Thank you, sir, may I have another?'"

"It was just a ruling. You win some and you lose some."

Tony tried to wander away, but I grabbed his arm and turned him around. "You said the thirty thousand startup shares were mine. You don't seem to know what you're talking about."

That insult hurt him. "My offer still stands: If you want a new lawyer, now is the time to get one."

"I don't want a new lawyer; I want a fair settlement. You know they'll want a fifty/fifty split of the remaining options."

Tony clapped me on the shoulder. "You don't get it. If the judge wanted her to get half of those shares, she would have given them to her. The judge is expecting your wife to accept something less than half."

"She could have said so."

"Judges don't want to dictate settlements, Randle. They want to approve settlements and rule on points of law." Tony started for the door. As we walked through the maze of clerks to the hallway, he said, "I don't think you have to give her more than twenty thousand shares."

I grunted my disgust. When we rounded the corner into the elevator well, we saw Carrie and de Castro conversing animatedly. De Castro wagged a scolding finger in Carrie's face. Tony grabbed my arm and pulled me back into the hallway.

"What's that all about?" I said.

"I'll bet the judge warned them about that look your wife gave you as she left the room."

"A warning won't make Carrie behave. Judges seem to think they have power, but I see no proof of that."

Tony peeked around the corner and said, "Still there." Then he gave me a stern look. "Maybe I should warn you too. Don't fool around with the property inventory. When de Castro sends the next version, just accept it so we can get the list to the judge by Friday."

"I get it now," I said. "The people the judge has the power to control are the lawyers. You're afraid of her, but Carrie's not and neither am I."

"Then you're dumber than I thought."

I let that pass. My point had been made. Tony peeked around the corner again. Waving his arm like an infantry sergeant leading troops into battle, he said, "Come on, they've disappeared."

As we rode down in the elevator, I said, "Where do we stand on the Baker Act petition?"

"Putting it together."

I spun my hand like a clothes dryer, signaling "hurry up." "When will you file?"

"Next week, Randle. You're not my only client."

"How will Matthews-Bryant react to this happening in the middle of the divorce?"

"It doesn't go to circuit court," he said. "It goes to state court, to a judge name of George Smithson. Matthews-Bryant won't know about it unless someone tells her."

"What are our chances?"

"According to my colleagues, Judge Smithson never rejects a petition, likes to get them on his docket, keep himself busy. He'll schedule a show cause hearing and let both sides submit briefs and make oral arguments. Then he'll decide whether to have your wife examined."

"Okay."

We exited the elevator, walked through a revolving door, and were soon on the street. "What about that PI? Can you get him off my tail?"

Tony gave me a serious glance. "What did he get pictures of?"

I debated whether to tell the truth. I settled on a half-truth. "My ex-wife was in the pool."

Tony set his briefcase down so he could use both hands to massage his temples. He decided against a tongue-lashing. "In that case we'll wait for them to bring it up in court, and then we'll object to the stalking. You'll just have to avoid giving him anything to use against you."

I was about to object, but Tony shook his head. "One more thing. I thought I told you not to write me notes from your old email account."

"That was intentional, Tony. I want to see if they're reading my mail. See if we get a reaction."

"What do you want me to do with them?"

I explained Carrie's relationships to Philip Simmons and Richard Puralto and asked him to track the guys down. Tony didn't see the relevance of the Puralto investigation, but I rather rudely insisted, reminding him that I was the client and I was footing the bill.

CHAPTER ELEVEN

I t was no accident that Connie phoned me first thing Wednesday morning. The day after I filed the countersuit, she had invited me to lunch to lobby for a retraction of the countersuit, and now she was on the line the day after we met with the judge. Carrie had asked the "fixer" to help her again.

"Hey, brother," Connie said. "Carrie says you have dates for moving and mediation, so you should be happy."

Fishing for a reaction to the option split? "Happy enough. The judge just followed state law. The subjective pieces remain to be decided—the unallocated options, alimony, property."

Cautiously, she said, "All to be decided at mediation. Carrie is nervous about it. Are you?"

De Castro knows the mediator doesn't coddle wives. "Not at all. We've chosen a mediator who will help me get a fair deal."

"Just be reasonable, Randle. Carrie wants to put this behind her."

Feeling cocky, I said, "Sure, with all the other stuff she has behind her."

Connie took a breath that sounded like the return vent on your home air conditioner. "Carrie hid some things from you because she didn't want you to judge her for her past."

Pretty close to an admission that Carrie had read my email. "Shame on me for not digging into her past before I married her."

"Well." Connie stretched the word into three syllables. "Why don't I treat you to dinner tonight? I can fill you in on some history."

Is she defending her sister or hitting on me? "Can I have a raincheck? I have to go to Atlanta for business."

"We need to talk, Randle. About things." She sounded perturbed, but then she softened. "You can drop by anytime for dinner, you know?"

Hitting on me. "That's . . . kind of you. I'll take you up on it."

"Okay. Open invitation." I thought we were about to hang up, but she was just mustering her courage. "There's one thing I should tell you before we hang up, if you have another minute."

"Yeah, of course."

She cleared her throat before continuing. "When Carrie and Chance divorced they were poor, and Carrie had to start with nothing and build a life as a single mother. That was hard on her."

She waited for me to commiserate, so I did. "She was lucky to have a supportive family."

"Yes, she was. Then she divorced her second husband, Phil, and she got nothing out of that either. Phil walked away with everything, even though he was the one who cheated."

"Maybe I should hire Phil's attorney."

"Don't make light of it, Randle. After Carrie divorced Phil, she got lucky and fell in love again. It was a storybook romance except that the man was married."

"Not a storybook romance for the guy's wife."

"Let me tell it, Randle. He separated from his wife, bought a condo, and moved in with Carrie. They were madly in love, lived together for more than a year. Then one day he up and went back to his wife. Did it for his kids."

More likely, he decided his wife was the lesser of two evils. That's what I should have done: lived with her long enough to know the real Carrie Tomkins Dickson Simmons before adding Marks to her name.

"Happens every time, Connie. The guy always goes back to his wife."

"Broke her heart and made a real mess of things for the man."

I filled in the blanks. The "man" must have been Richard Puralto, Carrie's putative third husband. He was the guy she used for revenge on Simmons, and Carrie got nothing out of her divorce from Simmons because Phil caught her cheating with Puralto. To me, she had represented her revenge as a one-night stand, but it had actually been a yearlong affair. *Liar.*

"What's his name?"

"His name isn't important, Randle. He still lives with the same wife in the same neighborhood and doesn't deserve any negative attention."

"Lucky guy—disposed of Carrie, got his life back, and you're still protecting him."

"Let me make my point, Randle. You don't have to be sarcastic all the time."

As she so often did to me, I ignored her admonition and plowed ahead. "This man must have had some money to keep a wife and kids in one house while he kept his mistress in a condo for months."

"Yes he did. He was a doctor. But the breakup was messy because Carrie's name was on the deed . . . to hide it from the wife, while the mortgage was in the doctor's name. Of course, Carrie couldn't afford it after they split up, and the doctor wanted to sell it, but Carrie wanted to live in it. They got into a scuffle about the condo, and Carrie filed an injunction to block the sale."

"I can see the complication."

"Yeah, the judge denied the injunction, and Carrie was homeless again."

Filling in some more blanks, I guessed the doctor and Carrie worked at the same clinic and that her desire to quit work when we married was to put distance between her and the doctor. No problem for Carrie; she found a new sugar daddy—me.

"That's why the country house is so important to her," I said.

Connie sighed. "*You* were important to her. You could heal her wounds and give her a fresh start. Now she's heartbroken again."

Now I was infuriated by this whole set of lies and excuses for bad behavior. "Heartbroken? Let me reimagine *The Life and Times of Carrie Tomkins*. She messed up her marriage to Chance Dickson and got nothing material out of the divorce, so she traded up for Phil Simmons."

"Randle—"

"To get revenge on Simmons for his cheating, she seduced the simple-minded doctor, but Simmons caught her and she got nothing out of that divorce either." I was like an avalanche, gathering power as I careened downhill. "She conned the doctor into setting her up in a condo, but the relationship soured as soon as he got to know the real Carrie Simmons, and he ran back to his family."

"Unh!" She sounded like she had cut herself while dicing onions.

"So Carrie tries to steal the condo out from under him, but the judge knew a scam when he heard one and he ruled for the doctor."

"My sister is just trying to build a good life, Randle."

"By sucking the life out of her husbands. She plays the same game every time, but she picked the wrong sucker when she picked me. She won't get a windfall out of this divorce, but don't worry about her, she'll just find a new sugar daddy."

"Stop it!" she exclaimed. "You're going to get hurt if you don't cooperate."

"Was Carrie coming to hurt me when she broke into my house last week—three a.m. Thursday morning, to be precise?"

"Carrie didn't break into your house. She stayed with me Wednesday night, and we went shopping together on Thursday."

"Amazing that's so easy for you to recall. If it wasn't Carrie, which person with a key was it? The alarm was tripped, but the door was locked when I got home."

"Well, it wasn't her, Randle. She slept at my house."

I snapped my fingers like you do when you have an epiphany. "You were her alibi, Connie. She had someone do it for her. She gave him a key, but I had already changed the passcode, so he tripped the alarm."

"Maybe it was a false alarm, Randle."

"If they're trying to scare me, it's not working."

"You've become a problem, Randle, and they've discussed solutions."

"They, who? What kind of solutions?"

Connie composed herself, took a deep breath. "We were all at Momma's—Carrie, Momma and Daddy, Travis, Carrie's friend Jerilynn, and me. Carrie was nervous about meeting the judge on Monday, worried she'd get screwed again. She got very emotional and said, 'Randle needs to roll over and play dead. I'm not walking away with nothing again.' So Daddy spoke up and told her, 'I'll take care of that son of a bitch. You want me to?'"

I said, "He was showing off for the women."

"He'd do anything to help Carrie. They all would. You had to be there to feel the vibe, see the dynamic. Momma and Jerilynn egged her on, encouraged her to invent ways to hurt you. I think Jerilynn was having fun with it, but Carrie was serious. Momma was too."

"Your momma's demented. So Carrie would what? Snip my balls and roast them over a fire like chestnuts?"

Connie was serious. "Carrie said she could show up on your doorstep unannounced and dressed to kill. Sorry, bad choice of words." She tittered. "You'd let her in because she looks like she wants sex."

She paused again for a reaction, but I didn't know whether to laugh or get angry. When she didn't continue, I barked at her, "Then what?"

"Well, she's not going to have sex with you," Connie said as though I was thickheaded. "She shoots you, and then there's no divorce."

"That's laughable, Connie. When I answer the door, I'll be holding my Glock, not my—"

"Randle!" I could hear heavy breathing as she composed herself. "Momma warned her not to knock on your door. Said you're too volatile, and she doesn't want Carrie to get hurt."

I shook my head as though I needed to dislodge something foreign in my brain so it could exit through an ear.

"They're discussing ways to kill me, but I'm the one who's volatile?"

Connie ignored the absurdity. "You can be volatile, Randle."

"That's the plan? Carrie seduces me like she seduced the doctor? Then she shoots me in cold blood?" I laughed out loud—a fake laugh. "They were blowing off steam."

The phone line was as quiet as a church between Masses. Connie was barely audible as she said, "I don't think so, Randle. They came up with several ways to . . . do it. Daddy could bring her by boat and drop her off in your backyard. She'll strip and float on a raft until you find her. You always wanted to skinny-dip, so you'll join her in the water, where you'll be less mobile and unarmed. Then she'll . . . you know."

My outburst was spontaneous. "Ha ha! Tell them to do it that way. I want to see which orifice she uses to hide the gun."

Connie grunted. "You need to take this seriously."

The kid PI came out on a boat. Harlan's? But I can't let her think they're scaring me. "Okay, how is Carrie going to get away with murder?"

"She'll tell the police you tried to rape her."

"Um-hum, and who's her witness?"

"Huh?"

"She can't shoot her lawfully wedded husband and claim it was attempted rape without a witness and forensic evidence."

"Oh," Connie said. It wasn't quite a question, and it wasn't quite an exclamation.

"They'd have to find my DNA in her, and she'd have to be bruised. Down there."

"Well, she's not going to have sex with you just to make it look good."

"Then her plan won't work. What was your daddy doing while Carrie was plotting?"

"Listening. He doesn't interfere with the women."

Sure, passive-aggressive old coot. "Connie, your sister had the best deal on the planet, and she dropped it in the dirt and kicked it around. All she ever had to be was a halfway decent wife, and she couldn't do it. Now she'll be held accountable for her failure."

"She just wants to be free, Randle. Don't make this difficult."

"Tell your sister to give in at mediation, because if that doesn't work there'll be a trial and we'll expose every ugly thing she ever did."

A pained, strangled cry came though the phone, as though the executioner had opened the trapdoor and the noose had tightened around Connie's neck. Her mission had failed once again.

"See, Randle, you're caught in a vicious cycle. You do something and they retaliate and then you respond and so on, until it becomes a nuclear chain reaction."

Neither of us spoke for a minute. I didn't know what Connie was thinking, but I figured I should maintain a connection with my "Deep Throat."

"Listen," I said. "I've got to run, but let me take you to a nice dinner when I get back from Atlanta."

"Oh, I can't do it this weekend. We're all helping Carrie pack."

Pack? "Okay, then the following week?"

"I'd like that, Randle. Call me when you get back."

After I hung up, a locksmith came and changed all the locks. I didn't expect Carrie to show up dressed to kill and she never did. *Bunch of crazy crackers.*

CHAPTER TWELVE

A t five a.m. the following morning, I left the house for Atlanta. The white panel van sat alone in the Walgreens parking lot at the corner of my street and Gulf Boulevard. It did not follow me as I turned toward the Pinellas Bayway and I-275. I had slipped the kid's notice while he was napping.

When Tony called I was already north of Gainesville. He asked if the PI was on my tail, and I told him I had lost the kid in Dolphin Beach. He said he had complained to de Castro, and she claimed Carrie knew nothing about a PI. De Castro said I must have problems with many women. *Yeah, right.*

"One more thing," Tony said, "and I'll let you go. I can't be a part of your schemes, Randle. Don't send me any more mail from your old account."

Wimp. "Treat them like spam. Don't open them. Just delete them."

I could hear him breathing down the line, considering. Eventually, he said, "Drive safe."

⸻ ∞ ⸻

When Bob Platt, the CEO of Atlanta Medical Analytics, had asked me to come to Atlanta for a partners meeting, I was perplexed. It had been only a week since my last office visit, and everything had been copacetic. When I spoke to my closest associates, Terry Johnstone and Harry Higbee, they speculated that there were new problems with the IPO. That could work in my favor so long as only the schedule was in question.

AMA's seven partners gathered in the main conference room. Other than them, the only persons allowed in the room were the CEO's secretary, Mary Jane Abbott, who would record the minutes of the meeting, and Patricia Masters, our Wall Street banker. AMA consisted of only eighty employees, but our little startup had all the CxOs found in a major corporation—a chief executive officer (CEO); chief operating officer (COO); chief financial officer (CFO); chief marketing officer (CMO); chief people officer (CPO); chief information officer (CIO); and a chief science officer (CSO).

The seven partners were all chiefs of something. I was the CSO. Unlike the fabled startups that begin with friends in a garage, a venture capital firm with a novel idea and a bit of scientific intellectual property had fabricated AMA. None of us had more than a passing awareness of the other partners before we had all been recruited. Now the Silicon Valley-based venture capitalists wanted to take the company public and walk off with a gargantuan return on their investment. Everyone was nervous except me. If we were going to reconsider the IPO date, I knew how I would vote.

Platt called the meeting to order and thanked those who had traveled to it for making the effort to be present. Like me, the CMO,

Terry Johnstone, and the CIO, Harry Higbee, lived in different states. The banker had flown in from New York.

Platt said, "We have to decide whether we need internal closed case trials before going public and, if so, how that would impact our IPO date. With that said, I'll turn it over to Patricia."

Patricia Masters was an ugly woman with severe features and severe attire. There is no kinder way for me to describe her. She was, however, highly respected in business circles. If Masters was your banker, your IPO would be a success. She stood and moved to-and-fro around the head of the table, making eye contact with all the partners as she spoke.

Facing me and Peter Hayes, the COO, she said, "Thanks to Peter and Randle, we've passed our lab tests and we've been certified by our internal medical board. That was a big hurdle. And thanks to Harry," she said, gesturing toward the CIO, "we've built the technology for a demonstrable prototype. Another big hurdle and enough to take us public."

Masters paused and looked at the floor as she paced back to my side of the table.

She looked up and said, "However, our research shows that your initial offering price will be lower than we anticipated—perhaps as low as five dollars a share—if we go public without conducting clinical trials."

A shocked murmur filled the room.

"Naturally your share price would increase down the line as you passed clinical trials, but that would delay the exit for your VC firm. It would delay your rewards for sweat equity as well."

Terry Johnstone, the CMO, said, "You don't mean live clinical trials with patients, do you?"

Masters said, "That would be the best case, Terry, but that takes too long."

"And costs too much money," Richard Barker, the CFO, chimed in.

"Right," Masters said. "But we can push the initial offering price north of fifteen dollars if we conduct closed clinical trials before going public, using medical case histories for patients no longer under treatment. Of course, we would have to get the results certified by an external board of doctors, as our internal board wouldn't be considered objective by investors."

No one reacted, so I filled the void. "This is a typical approach for science-based startups, right, Patricia?" I waited for her to nod yes. "If we were a pharmaceutical manufacturer, we would take exactly this approach: lab tests, internal trials, IPO, and then live clinical trials. First you announce the drug, get the investors excited, hook them with the IPO because they don't want to be left out, then you prove the efficacy of the drug and get FDA approval. It's too capital-intensive to place the burden of live trials on the angel investors. You need public money to make it happen."

"Bravo," Masters said. "You could work on Wall Street, Randle. You have it right."

Barker, the CFO, said, "We have live clinical trials scheduled for first quarter of next year. Isn't it enough for investors to see that we have them scheduled?"

"Unfortunately, no," Masters said. "Investors are nervous about bleeding-edge ideas like this one."

I interjected, "We may have difficulty recruiting live patients and their practitioners if we haven't passed internal trials."

CEO Platt said, "The obvious question is why didn't we think of this sooner. And the answer is this: The market was willing to give us twelve dollars a share back six months ago, but now the climate isn't as favorable. We can still get the number we want, but only with more effort."

Barker said, "So it's a foregone conclusion, and we don't need a vote?"

"We need a formal vote, Rich," Platt said.

Barker replied, "Then I vote no. We're going to run out of cash if we keep delaying . . . unless Patricia can get us some cash."

Masters said, "You'll get your cash with the IPO, but till then you have to get funding from the VC."

"That well is dry," Platt said. "We're two years behind schedule now. Let's take a vote."

Platt cast the first vote to delay the trials and then went clockwise around the table asking each partner for his vote. It was three to three when it reached me. Hayes and Barker had voted "nay," as had Archie Eckhart, the CPO. I looked around the table at the men who had joined with me in this risky venture, men who were counting on payback for their efforts. I felt a pang of remorse about what I had to do, but I couldn't settle my divorce for half of five dollars a share.

Platt grew impatient. "What's your vote, Randle?"

I feigned resignation as I said, "I vote to delay, Bob."

Platt nodded. He knew it would go this way. Turning to the chief people officer, Platt asked, "What's your objection, Archie?"

"I'm worried about keeping the people, Bob," Eckhart said. "Every time we delay, a few folks lose confidence and leave."

Platt said, "Let's address the question of how long this takes and see if you feel better about it then."

Masters took her seat, her job done, and Platt stood to take the floor. He said, "Peter, you'll have to manage the trials. How long will it take to collect the case histories and recruit an external board of respected physicians?"

Hayes tapped his pen on his notepad as he thought about the question. He wanted to minimize the delay. He squirmed in his chair a bit as he answered, "If we put all other work aside, maybe a month?"

Platt turned to the CIO. "Harry? You have to load all the data, make all the test runs."

Without thinking, Higbee said, "I can load and run them in two weeks."

"Okay, Randle," Platt said, "you're the end of the chain. How long will it take you to produce and publish results?"

Here we go. I said, "With all due respect, we're being unreasonably optimistic. The board of doctors we've lined up expects to engage sometime next spring for clinical trials, not internal trials. You're asking them to radically change their schedules and do different work, so we may have to recruit different doctors. We have live patients identified for clinical trials, but we haven't yet collected any closed cases. That will take time. Even if Harry's team worked 24/7 to load and run cases, it will take longer than two weeks because the runs always require interim reviews and adjustments."

My partners glared at me.

Hayes said, "I'll work my ass off, Randle, and I expect the same from you."

Higbee, my friend, said, "We're building a tool to automate case loading, so I'm confident I can do it in two weeks."

Platt said, "Let's not question one another, Randle. Just give me an estimate."

If Hayes and Higbee kept their promises, I could probably complete my work in three weeks, meaning a one-month delay in the IPO, but I didn't want to give them that option. I wanted to move the IPO date well out of range of my divorce action.

"Not only do we have to analyze the results ourselves, but we have to walk each doctor through the results, document their opinions, get them to certify the overall findings, and make sure they turn out the way we need them to turn out," I said. "Then we'll prepare final results that are as flattering as possible for publication to investors. The doctors will want to take time off for Thanksgiving and Christmas, so the best case would be January 15th of next year." That would give me two and a half additional months to settle my divorce.

Everyone spoke at once, most of it vile and aimed at me. Platt stuck two fingers in his mouth and whistled, like coaches do on the practice field. "Settle down, everybody."

Masters jumped in with, "Anything later than Thanksgiving gets us into the holidays, and then it's January before we can do the IPO."

Thank you, Patricia. That makes it easy. "Well, there's no hope of getting done before Thanksgiving," I lied.

Around the room partners inhaled sharply from shock, as though they'd been stabbed in the back. Of course, they had been. Each partner looked at every other partner to see if anyone had a way around me. The room was silent for some time. Platt planted his hands deep in his trouser pockets and looked at me with anger in his eyes.

After several minutes, he said to no one in particular, "Where does that leave us?"

No one offered an opinion, so it was left to me to shatter their dreams. "Let's change the IPO date just one last time," I said. "If we miss November, we'll scare investors and employees with another delay. Give Peter an extra month to collect cases and recruit a board. Give Harry three weeks to load and run the cases. My team will work through the holidays, but the bulk of the work will happen in January. The IPO date should be February 15th." And that would give me exactly the average amount of time to settle a divorce in Florida.

The room filled with angry murmurs and the harsh scraping of chairs. Masters interceded. "I agree with Randle," she said. "You'd lose all credibility if you announced another slip in November."

Platt nodded like a man resigned to bad news. He said, "Richard, you'll have to stretch our cash, maybe find a sympathetic lender to supply bridge funding. I don't see any other way to stay afloat."

Barker flipped his pencil in the air and let it hit the table and bounce disrespectfully. "No hiring, no business travel, no capital expenditures until further notice." He stared each of us down, and no one objected, so he added, "Bring your own shit paper if you intend to use the restrooms."

A few titters escaped, and the mood lightened a bit. I said, "We'll work our butts off to make February 15th, but let's remember that the panel of doctors will have to work to our schedule to certify the results. Make sure they are aware when you recruit them."

Platt sat back down. He said, "Okay, let's formalize the plan with another vote."

Barker, Eckhart, and Hayes all voted "nay," but this time Platt cast the deciding vote in favor of a February 15th IPO, and fifty thousand options slid off the negotiating table. Although Barker was adept at managing AMA's money, rumor had it that his personal finances were a mess. He wanted to go public as soon as possible to keep himself afloat, and Eckhart was legitimately concerned about staff defections.

Platt said, "I presumed Rich and Archie were voting for November 1st, but why did you vote against February 15th, Peter?"

"I'd have voted for anything before Christmas." Looking at me, he added, "But if Randle can't go faster, we can't go faster."

For the first time in my life, I had allowed my personal needs to influence my professional judgment, but it had been necessary. There wasn't enough money on the table, after taxes and debts, for both Carrie and me to have a future. The judge had screwed me out of fifteen thousand shares that had vested before I met Carrie, and now I would get them back by moving the IPO to a date beyond the end of my marriage. The question was how to hide the news from de Castro and Carrie.

Platt directed Eckhart to draft an announcement to the staff, and the meeting was adjourned. I didn't want to explain my position to my partners, so I hustled out of the building and hightailed it back to the hotel.

———⟨⟩———

Jerry was waiting for me in the lobby. When we entered my room, he couldn't fail to see a sealed bottle of Glenlivet on the desk.

"Okay," he said, "get online and follow my instructions."

I did as I was told. At the halfway mark of scrolling through the apps installed on my machine, Jerry stopped me. "That's a redirector. Someone is snooping on your account."

"What's a redirector?"

"An app that makes a copy of every mail you send and every mail you receive and sends the copies to another email account. Businesses use it to create audit trails of incoming and outgoing mail, but it can also be used for nefarious purposes."

I'll be damned. "How can I find out who's snooping?"

Jerry gave me another set of instructions, and a few minutes later said, "There it is! Your mail is going to shadylady44@spiritnet.com. Know who that is?"

Carrie's public email account was catmarks38@flaweb.net. The letters c-a-t were the initials of her maiden name, Carrie Ann Tomkins, and her family and childhood friends still referred to her as "Cat." She'd added the number "38," her bust size, pretending she had to distinguish herself from the dozens of other "catmarks" in the world. She was smart enough not to use her public email address to steal my mail.

"My wife is forty-four years old, and she thinks she has the right to snoop on me."

"Easy to remove—just highlight the app and click 'uninstall.'"

I had nothing to be ashamed about in my emails, but I felt violated— the sensation you get when you find that a tick has burrowed into your body. The urge to pull it out was powerful, but I had an epiphany. "I don't want to remove it, Jerry. She'd know I found it. I can send her misinformation through this link."

"You read too many spy novels."

Indignant, I said, "How did she get this onto my machine?"

"Easiest way is to log onto your machine and install it, but the sneaky way is to embed it in an attachment to an email and hope you open the attachment. That's how most viruses are spread—through spam mail."

I couldn't remember receiving any email from Carrie with an attachment, and she wouldn't know how to install an app so she'd had help. *Does Phil Simmons have the technical skill to install a redirector?*

"Listen, Jerry, are there ways to get something like this onto her machine without having physical access to her computer and without leaving any evidence behind?" I held my breath.

"Yes, there are." After a long silence, in which I wasn't about to incriminate myself, he said, "You want me to help you with that?"

"I do. I want to see everything she's doing on her computer." It would be ironic to catch my wife sending sweet nothings to boyfriends using the same devious trick she played on me.

Jerry pointed to the bottle of Glenlivet. "Mind if I crack that before we move into the high-tech stuff?"

"No, it's yours." I went to the bathroom to get Jerry a water glass. He offered me a drink but I declined, so he poured one finger and chugged it. Then he poured two fingers and set the glass down.

Motioning to the chair, he said, "May I?" I watched as Jerry paged through a search engine list of websites. When he chose one, a garish red-and-black page popped up showing cartoonish characters in various spying poses. Jerry grabbed his glass and took a sip of Scotch, then leaned back to let me have a better view of the screen.

"You can embed a redirector in an attachment to an email. Hope she opens it. Hope she's sending the mail you want to find from the account you choose to monitor. Having spied on you, she may be wary of attachments in emails from you." Jerry pointed at a picture on the screen of a box of software. "This would be a good product to buy, but you could get caught."

"Or . . ." My word dangled in the air.

Jerry savored a sip of the whiskey. "You could buy a keystroke recorder that can be installed remotely." He leaned toward the screen and paged down to another product picture. "This is the one I recommend," he said. He turned the screen so I could read it.

The software wasn't as expensive as I had feared. "Okay. How do I use it?"

"Do you know her machine account name?"

"Her computer says 'Hello, Carrie' when you boot it. Then you enter a password."

Jerry got up and told me to take the desk chair. "We don't need her password; we just need the directory name to load the software into. Buy this product and download it to your computer. Then we'll transfer it to your smartphone. Next time you're within range of the wireless router in your house, put your smartphone in Wi-Fi mode so you're connected to the same router. Open the app and follow the instructions to load the software onto the computer named 'Carrie.' It's that easy. The software will record all her keystrokes and put them in a file on the cloud. When you want to see what she's doing, you log into your account on the cloud and read the file."

"Is this what the NSA does to snoop on us?" I said, referring to the National Security Agency.

Jerry laughed. "No," he said. "It wouldn't be efficient to gather data from millions of individual computers, so the NSA breaks into the service provider databases where everyone's emails are stored. To do that, the NSA twists the arms of the email services to get their encryption keys or else breaks the codes."

"Well, I only want to spy on one computer, so the challenge is to get my cell phone within Wi-Fi range."

I could see myself sneaking through the woods behind the house, creeping into the swimming pool area in the middle of the night, and doing the dirty deed like the CIA would do it. When I was in college, I was attracted to that lifestyle.

Jerry showed me how to buy the software, download it, and then transfer it to my smartphone. It felt like I carried a concealed weapon.

"You didn't get any of this instruction from me," Jerry said. "You never saw me today."

I said I understood.

Before he left with the bottle of Scotch, Jerry made me change my account name so my computer was less vulnerable to hacking. I called it "Sneaky Pete."

Hours later, I approached Cortes County Highway 98, running east to west across the interstate. Before I could consciously resist, the Bronco took the exit and headed west toward the country house. I doubted there was any sort of surveillance on the house or that Carrie would be rocking on the front porch, yet my heart was pounding as I turned onto my own road.

I drove past my house at full speed, just a random vehicle on the road, so I only noted that there was no visible activity around the three-story faux plantation manor. Two miles down the road, after ensuring there were no cars following me or coming at me, I made a U-turn. On the second pass, I slowed down and took in the details. Two yard lights had burned out. The water pump for the homemade rock waterfall in the center of the yard wasn't running. Carrie's car was not in its usual position under the carriage porch. The garage door was closed.

Down the road, I pulled over and put my smartphone in Wi-Fi mode, then made another U-turn and crept up to the house. I let the smartphone search for a Wi-Fi signal, but after more than a minute it was obvious my phone could not connect to the Wi-Fi from the street. I wasn't brave enough to pull into the driveway because Carrie could catch me violating my restraining order. Since she lived alone now, she may have adopted the safety measure of parking her car in the garage. Carrie could see me if she glanced out a front window.

So I did yet another U-turn, accelerated away from the house and through the turn onto Highway 98. When I rejoined the southbound traffic on I-75, I felt like a kid who had disobeyed his mother and gotten away with it.

A little voice in my head said, *Why do you care where Carrie is or what she's doing? You aren't a couple anymore.* I answered the voice with, *I don't care about Carrie. I wanted to prove that I could violate the restraining order too.* And the little voice said, *Uh-huh.*

I took the back way to Dolphin Beach and snuck up on the Walgreens parking lot. The white panel van was waiting for me. I parked and went into the store, waving to the driver as I did so. Inside I bought myself a bottle of chocolate milk and a candy bar for the kid. When I came out, I shocked him by placing his chocolate on the hood of the van, and then I went home.

In a chaise lounge chair next to the pool, drinking my chocolate milk, I wondered if I should be worried about myself. The cat and mouse game with Carrie had become an interesting, almost exciting, contest of wits, and I was enjoying it. *That's pretty alarming, isn't it?*

CHAPTER THIRTEEN

had called Glenda on my way back from Atlanta and asked her to dinner on Saturday night, but I was far from deciding that I *wanted* her. The last thing I needed to do was jump back into a relationship that had failed once before.

We agreed to meet at Bern's Steak House in Tampa so she didn't have to cross the causeway to St. Petersburg. My task was to lose my tail. When I exited my neighborhood, I turned left onto Gulf Boulevard, toward Pass-a-Grille, and the white panel van pulled out of the Walgreens parking lot and fell in line one car back. I timed the lights so I could stop for a red light at the head of the straight-ahead lane, waited for a few cars to use the left-turn arrow, then pulled the New York taxi trick of turning along with and outside of the cars in the turn lane. While I headed in the opposite direction for the Corey Causeway, the kid was forced to wait for oncoming traffic to stop for the next light change. Around the corner on Corey Avenue, I pulled into the Ace Hardware parking lot and waited for him to pass. When he flew by, I doubled back down Gulf Boulevard and took the Pinellas Bayway to I-275 North and across the Bay to Tampa.

I arrived early at the restaurant, sans the tail. When Glenda pulled up to the valet parking stand, I opened her door for her and gave her a quick kiss. The restaurant's Howard Avenue location was an easy jaunt from her shop in Oldsmar, so I expected her to be in work clothes, but she wore a little black cocktail dress with a modest neckline, three-inch open-toed heels, dark hose with a seam up the back of her legs, and evening makeup.

"You are stunning," I said. *And provocative.*

She smiled. "So you do have taste."

Walking into the restaurant, I placed a proprietary hand on the small of her bare back and enjoyed the rocking of her hips, accentuated by her high heels. A mixture of cigarette smoke and *Obsession* perfume, the most effective aphrodisiac ever concocted, wafted from her and triggered an automatic response in my loins. Inside, the lobby décor reminded me of a Roman palace—marble floor, statuettes on pedestals, heavy red draperies on the walls—and belied the quality of the wine and steaks. I strode up to the hostess station and announced myself. Soon we were led to a semiprivate back room where the light was low and the conversation muted. Walking behind her, I noted that Glenda had no visible pantyline.

At the table she was ebullient as we progressed through the rituals of ordering drinks—white wine for Glenda, Crown and Seven for me—appetizers—beefsteak tomato and buffalo mozzarella salad for me, warm spinach salad for Glenda—and entrées—filet for me, petite filet for Glenda, and sweet potato casserole to share. I did all the ordering, specifying how steaks were to be cooked, selecting Glenda's pinot grigio, telling the waiter to please space the courses to allow us time with one another.

She lifted her glass and said, "Here's looking at you, kid."

The salads arrived, and I asked how her store was doing. She owned a shop that attracted "earth muffins" and New Age spiritualists to whom she sold an eclectic combination of candles, scents, books, figurines, and even clothing. It was sort of the Florida version of a New Orleans voodoo shop. While we were married, she had devoted all her energy to it and I had gotten little attention. She knew that was the point of my question.

"I have a good team now and a lot of regular customers, so I have time for a personal life."

The conversation turned to updates on families from which we had been separated for over seven years. While we were married, Glenda had lost a brother to suicide, and since our divorce she had lost her father to cancer, but her mother was well and still lived on her own in Lakeland. "You'll have to come visit her, Randle. She always liked you." I promised I would.

When she asked for an update on my family, I had little to say. I considered myself an only child because I was older than my siblings and had no real relationship with them. My sister was six years younger than me and my brother was two years younger than her. It was as though my parents had decided to build a new family after discovering I would never be a fulfilling child for them.

I recounted my father's passing and told Glenda that my mother still lived alone in our childhood home in Augusta. Although she was mentally sharp, her physical health was in decline. I had not seen her since my marriage to Carrie had fallen apart and would have been embarrassed to admit another failure.

Talking about my father's funeral, I said, "I couldn't recognize him, lying in his casket. He reminded me of a banker or a television personality. I touched his arm but it wasn't an arm, it was a board. Why would they do that? I didn't touch anything else."

Glenda reached across the table and placed a hand on my arm.

I added, "I had to do an impromptu eulogy because the priest had no idea who my father was or what to say about him." She squeezed my arm.

"To make matters worse, my sister and I agreed that my brother should take control of Mom's finances and Carrie had a hissy fit. She said, 'You're too soft. As the oldest child, you should take control or you'll never see a penny of inheritance. Your brother will steal it all.'"

Glenda looked shocked. "Was she right or just being a bitch?"

"She's a greedy control freak."

"Doesn't say much for your taste in women."

The entrées arrived, and there was a break in the conversation as we served ourselves, sampled our steaks, and smiled at each other as we chewed.

"I didn't go to work today," Glenda said. "Wesley was served with papers, and I didn't want him coming around and causing a scene."

"I'm happy for you, Glenda, and I hope it works out."

She gave me a sly smile. "I think it will. How about your situation? Going okay?"

"It's become a dogfight, but we're holding our own. We're filing a petition to have Carrie examined by State psychiatrists, see if she belongs in an asylum. And my company's IPO has been delayed, so a lot of my stock options are off the table."

She nodded and smiled appreciatively. Nibbling on the sweet potato casserole, she said, "So tell me again what you do now."

"Predictive modeling."

"Huh? I've heard of nude modeling and runway modeling, but not whatever you said. Did you mean to say perverted modeling?" Coy, having fun with it.

"Ha ha, the guys at the office will like that one. We've built a tool to help doctors plan their patients' treatment programs and preventative care. Basically, we can predict whether the patient will be diagnosed with cancer or hepatitis or heart disease sometime in the future. The bigger potential is then to predict the therapies most likely to cure their disease."

"Really? How do you do that?"

"We build mathematical models that use patient histories—not just yours but millions of histories—combined with DNA, again from millions of people, to forecast medical outcomes."

"I'm very impressed." She looked at me with interest. "Is this going to make you rich?"

"You know I don't care about that, but I will have the luxury to quit my day job so I can write and lecture." While Glenda's store had robbed me of her participation in our marriage, my career had robbed her of my time. I fashioned a sincere look and added, "I'll have time for a personal life too."

I loved the way Glenda looked when she was thinking. Her brow furrowed, and her nose twitched like a bunny rabbit's.

"You're treating this like a real date," she said.

"Of course, isn't that what it is?"

"I thought you'd just want to start where we left off last weekend—me naked, running around your backyard. Which would be okay with me, by the way."

"Glenda, we should have a normal dating experience and fall in love like we did years ago. This is our first date. The second date should be something fun, see if we enjoy each other's company. On the third date, you can let me get in your pants. That's the American average, sex on the third date."

She laughed, loudly enough for nearby diners to stare at us. I thought of a line from the movie *As Good as It Gets*: ". . . if you make her laugh, you got a life."

Glenda tilted her head. "Who taught you how to play this game? Your mother?"

"It may sound old-fashioned, but we owe it to ourselves to be certain we aren't making a mistake by getting back together."

Shrugging off my dull but good sense, she said, "You know they have private rooms upstairs for dessert and coffee. I didn't wear panties so you can have a quickie if you want one."

Smiling, I said, "You are an incorrigible little wench and an irresistible temptation, but . . ."

She gave me one of her patented stares. "If you think you can resist me until our third date, I'll play it your way, but the mistake we made was getting divorced, Randle. Now we can correct that. Let me take care of you as you grow old, and you can take care of me."

"That's the nicest thing anyone has ever said to me." Mutual commitment had been a foreign concept to Carrie.

Glenda nodded to confirm her sincerity. "Don't take me to the beach for our next date. I don't like sand in my crack, and I burn in the sun."

I couldn't agree more, and it had been a point of contention with Carrie, whose only real hobby was baking in the sun, soaked in grease, like a turkey on Thanksgiving. While Carrie's deep tan obscured and blurred her features, Glenda's pale skin made her look more naked without clothing. Carrie was sexier clothed; Glenda was sexier nude. *I prefer classy clothed, sexy nude.*

"We can take a ride on my boat, find a secluded spot to swim and relax."

"Saturday is busy at the store, but I could do Sunday."

That worked for me as I planned to spend Saturday on the boat with my male friends. "It's a date."

We didn't wait for our check. I threw two hundred dollars on the table like a drug dealer flush with cash, and we left the restaurant.

Outside, the parking attendant took our tickets and sprinted away to find the Bronco and Glenda's sedan. I turned to her and said, "You haven't had a cigarette all evening. Want to have a quick smoke?"

Her smile was part gratitude, part disappointment. "I don't need one. I'm not nervous, and I didn't get laid."

I took her in my arms with attendants and other waiting diners watching, and she slipped her hand behind my head and pulled me down to her. This kiss was hard, passionate. She broke away and said, "Something to remember me by."

We both smiled broadly. I opened her car door for her, and when she got settled behind the wheel, I said, "Text me to let me know you got home safely."

She gave me that long look of hers and nodded. "Okay."

I watched her drive away before I got into my Bronco and headed for the marina. Half an hour later, I received Glenda's text: *Home*, signed with a heart emoticon.

CHAPTER FOURTEEN

M oving day: It would be either a parade or a funeral procession, I wasn't sure which yet. I drove north on I-275, through Tampa and toward the country house in Cortes County, leading a moving van with three laborers aboard, and a PODS rig carrying a large portable storage container. After three days of wrangling over the property inventory, Tony cut off the debate in order to meet the judge's deadline. As a matter of principle, I wasn't happy with the result—Carrie would acquire most everything we had accumulated during our marriage—but in truth I cared little about the possessions Carrie coveted.

What bothered me was that the property division wasn't a fifty/fifty split of possessions acquired with my earnings. Why should a woman who hadn't worked a day during the marriage walk away with a windfall of extravagant furnishings just because she had declared the marriage over? Neither the judge nor the lawyers seemed to have any interest in fairness—they just wanted to facilitate the dissolution of the marriage

107

and declare a legal victory. I knew I should approach the moving exercise as I would a business transaction; instead, I felt combative. Tony had of course coached me to be civil and avoid confrontation; I hoped de Castro had given Carrie the same instruction.

When the caravan pulled into the circular driveway, I saw that a ragged pickup truck was parked by the carriage porch. Carrie's red Jaguar, top down, sat in front of the main entrance. I stopped short and got out of the Bronco as Carrie emerged from the front door. She wore sandals, shorts that were indeed short, and a low-cut top with a bare midriff. Her hair was done in the prickly style that matched her personality. I guessed she wanted to remind me of what I was losing. When she got closer, I saw that she wore the Mother's Day present again, rubbing my nose in it. She was made up for going out and had fresh paint on all her nails.

"You're late," she said flatly.

Trying to sound civil, I said, "Hey, can you move your car so we can set the PODS container at the front door? Easier to bring things out through the double doors."

"No, you'll be loading from the garage. I've packed your stuff and it's all in the garage except for big items in the attic and your office."

"What?"

Carrie walked toward the garage and used a remote to open the double-wide door. In the garage were boxes and totes with "Randle" inscribed in magic marker.

She said, "Give me your remote and keys and get started."

I was annoyed that Carrie had once again jumped the gun, planned further ahead than I had planned. I moved toward the front door and said, "I'll just walk through the house, check things off the list, make sure you didn't forget anything."

"Stop, Randle! You can't go in the house."

Two men stepped out of the interior shadows onto the front porch. One was the redneck named Larry and the other was a carbon copy.

I turned back to my wife. "You buy them at a two-for-one sale?"

Carrie's face turned the color of her Jaguar, but she held her breath and swallowed her anger. "Keep your nose out of my business."

I figured that was a reference to Puralto. "Likewise. Next time your private investigator trespasses, I'll shoot him."

Carrie looked befuddled, eyes wide, eyebrows raised. *Nice acting job.*

"I have no idea what you're talking about."

I changed the subject. "You can't stop me from entering my own home. I pay for this place."

"It's my home now, and I have a restraining order."

"All you have is permission to stay here while we're separated. The house will be negotiated in mediation."

She scoffed at me. "Here's how it's going to work, Randle: Your movers will go up and get your stuff out of your office and the attic. Larry and Danny will escort them to make sure they don't take anything they shouldn't. You'll sit in your car and stay out of trouble." Carrie sounded like a mother lecturing a young child.

I could feel the PODS driver and the movers loitering behind me, wondering how good a show this might become. I pulled my cell phone from my pocket and dialed 9-1-1.

Not knowing whom I had called, she said, "Stop wasting time, Randle."

I put the phone on speaker, held it toward her.

The operator answered, "Cortes County Sherriff's Office, what's your emergency?"

I answered, "We have a domestic disturbance. Do you have my location?"

Carrie clenched her fists and gritted her teeth. She made a sound like a wounded lioness. "Put that phone down, Randle!"

The operator said, "Is that the other party I hear?"

"Yes, it is," I said. "You need to hurry."

"Has there been a physical altercation?"

Carrie screamed, "Give me that phone!"

She grabbed for the phone, but I pirouetted out of the way. The movers snickered in the background. Larry and Danny headed down the driveway toward me.

I said to the operator, "No violence as yet, but she has two men with her and I fear for my safety."

Larry and Danny stopped, looked at each other, and turned back toward the house.

The operator said, "Is it your residence, sir?"

"Yes, ma'am, it is."

"One of you should go inside and the other should stay outside. Got it?"

"I get it, ma'am, but my wife doesn't get much of anything."

Carrie lunged at me, but a little Mexican guy with broad shoulders and a Pancho Villa mustache stepped between us.

The operator said, "I have a car on the way to your location. Please stay on the line with me until it arrives."

"Yes, ma'am. And thanks very much."

"No problem, sir. Just speak up if you need me."

Carrie threw up her hands in disgust and started back to the house. Larry and Danny inched toward their pickup truck. I put the phone on mute and told the PODS driver to drop the container outside the garage.

To the movers I said, "Cut open all the boxes in the garage. Let's see what's in them."

The movers were all smiles as they walked to the garage. Pancho Villa said, "El jefe in charge here."

Carrie glared at me from the porch as I followed the workers into the garage. They cut the boxes open so I could mark items off the property list. Each box contained a random assortment of items from various rooms of the house: a toaster, a golfing trophy, a dictionary, and a small couch pillow in one; a broken DVD player, a lampshade, and a pack of shop rags in another. Fragile items were combined with heavy items; nothing was wrapped or cushioned. Some items weren't on my inventory but had been packed because Carrie wanted to dispose of them. The packing had followed no logical pattern, so I had no idea how I could verify that I had gotten everything that belonged to me. It reminded me of movie scenes in which the wife throws the husband's possessions out on the front lawn.

I stacked unwanted items in a corner of the garage, repacked boxes to contain like items, and carried some of the fragile items to the Bronco. After about fifteen minutes, I heard a siren, so I told the movers to load the boxes into the container and I retrieved my file of legal documents from the Bronco. The sheriff's car, lights flashing, pulled into the far leg of the driveway, the side that wasn't blocked by trucks. I told the 9-1-1 operator goodbye and hung up. The deputy, young and fresh-faced, left the lights on when he emerged from the cruiser. As I approached the officer, Carrie materialized, waving a handful of paper and yelling, "I've got a restraining order!"

The officer—his nametag read "Dobbins"—looked from Carrie, hurrying toward us, to me with a question on his face. "What's going on, sir?"

I explained that it was a divorce situation, and I had a court order that allowed me to move my possessions out of the marital home today. However, my estranged wife wouldn't allow me to enter the house and wanted the two guys standing next to the pickup on the carport to guard the movers while inside the house. The cop, pretending to be in control of the situation, nodded his understanding and asked to see the court order. I handed it to him as Carrie reached us, out of breath.

Dobbins and Carrie exchanged surprised looks of recognition and anxiety. A hint of fear danced across Carrie's face.

Pushing her document at the deputy, she said, "I have a restraining order. He doesn't need to go into the house to get his stuff. It's all packed."

Deputy Dobbins said, "Take it easy, ma'am. Let me have a look at this document." He indicated my court order and started reading.

When he was done, Dobbins said to Carrie, "The court order says your husband can enter the home for the specific purpose of moving the possessions listed on a property inventory. It says right here . . ."—Dobbins ran a finger under the passage for Carrie—"'enter the marital home.'"

"He doesn't need to," Carrie repeated. "The movers can get his stuff."

Dobbins stared at her for a moment, thinking. Having reached a conclusion, he said, "I'll accompany your husband while in the home. I'll make sure he only takes things on the property inventory." He glanced at me and said, "You have a list, right?"

I produced the list from my file.

Dobbins said to Carrie, "Let's keep this simple. Pretty much the only people allowed in the house will be the movers, your husband, and me. Those guys"—he waved toward Larry and Danny—"have to stay outside. Move your car away from the front doors. You can come in, but please don't get in the way."

Carrie grunted something unintelligible. She held her clenched fists down at her sides, spun on her heels, and walked toward her car.

Dobbins looked at me. "Don't turn this into World War III. Don't make me call for backup."

I waved the mover over, and we all entered the house. Immediately a large dog began snarling and growling. It was somewhere in the back of the house, in the sunroom or out on the deck. *Carrie has a dog?* Our mantra had been: no pets, no kids, no problems. We all climbed the stairs to the second floor as Carrie came back into the house.

Dobbins waited for her and said, "Your dog sounds vicious. Is it secure, ma'am?"

"He's a trained German shepherd attack dog, responds to my voice commands."

The movers and I walked across the balcony overlooking the ground floor toward the third-floor staircase. I motioned for the workers to climb the narrow stairs but I waited, out of Carrie's sight, so I could hear the rest of the conversation.

Dobbins said, "I believe you, but lock him up. We don't need an incident."

Carrie said, "He's locked in the sunroom. I bought him in case my husband tries to get into the house."

Dismissively, the cop said, "I don't see your husband as a cat burglar. He's more a white-collar crime kind of guy."

"Don't patronize me, officer. The dog isn't a burglar alarm; he's trained to attack intruders. I know what Randle's capable of, you don't."

"I'm only concerned about today, while we're all here," Dobbins said. Then he ascended the stairs to join me and the movers.

On the third floor, I instructed the men to leave the office furniture for last so that it could be offloaded first at the beach house. My empty family room at the beach house would now become my home office. While they boxed books and knickknacks and carried bookshelves and tables down three flights of stairs, I sat in my desk chair and pulled out my smartphone. Dobbins took a seat on the couch, my former bed.

"You get everything on this floor, right?" he said.

"Yeah, this was all mine before we got married. The contentious stuff is on the lower floors."

The deputy relaxed, nothing to worry about yet. I motioned at him with my smartphone and said, "Work mail. Just never stops."

He grunted. Pretending to scan my mail, I put the phone into Wi-Fi mode and connected with the router that was located in my office. While the deputy lounged and the movers packed and carried, I opened the snooper application and followed instructions, downloading the application and directing its installation on the networked computer named "Carrie."

Waiting for the app to install, I moved to the dormer windows that looked out into the backyard and saw that Carrie had fenced a portion of it for the dog, enclosing an area that included the deck off the master bedroom but excluded the pool, which was on a hill at the back of the property. Several pieces of outdoor furniture from the beach house were now positioned around the pool. Carrie hadn't expected me to have this view.

Turning back to the deputy, I said, "Do you and my wife know each other? You seemed to recognize one another."

The deputy looked pensive, decided to be candid. "I stopped her once, about a year ago. We got into a bit of a hassle."

"Oh, you're that cop. She said you wanted to trade sex for letting her go."

The deputy, assuming I was accusing him of wrongdoing, stood and straightened his uniform. "I didn't assault your wife, sir. She went berserk because I stopped her."

"Started yelling rape?"

As though he still found the incident incredulous, Dobbins said, "No, but she put her hands on me and told me very matter-of-factly that she'd tell everyone I came on to her."

"And you gave her a ticket anyway."

"Damn right." Proud of himself.

"That's how I knew you hadn't assaulted her. If you had let her go, I'd have been suspicious. She was angry with me for not filing a complaint against you, but I know my wife lies to get out of trouble. I figured she was lucky not to be in jail."

"I should have arrested her. I gave her a ticket, but I should have done more."

"Maybe you can. I've filed a Baker Act petition to have her examined by a State psychiatrist. She needs help. Would you be willing to testify?"

The deputy was relieved. "I would. I'd like to help." He handed me his business card.

On my smartphone a message appeared: **Installation Successful.** I found it ironic that I had discussed Carrie's transgression with a cop while committing my own transgression.

The movers returned to the office and asked us to move out of our seats. Two movers grabbed the couch, and the third took my desk chair downstairs. I walked into the attic, where the rest of my pre-Carrie possessions were stored, and the deputy followed. It looked like a staged home invasion. Carrie hadn't bothered to disguise the intrusion because she hadn't expected me to see this room. She had left boxes open, lids off the totes, and paintings and framed pictures strewn around the floor. Totes that should have been full of documents and records were half-empty.

As I restored order to the photo albums, pictures, and paintings, I noted a pattern—there were no pictures of Carrie. All pictures in which she had appeared with my parents, pictures of vacations, pictures of our dating days, pictures of our wedding, were gone. Early in our marriage, she had made me dispose of all photos of my life with Glenda. An acute form of insecurity, I supposed; something I thought I could cure with love. I had pretended to comply with her demand but had gotten many of those pictures into Jamie's hands. I regretted not having taken the same precaution with the photos of life with Carrie. Despite the impending divorce, our marriage had included events I wanted to remember when I sat in a rocking chair on the veranda at some old folks' home.

Furious, I leapt to my feet and hustled out of the attic and down the stairs. Startled by the sudden action, the deputy trailed behind. I found Carrie sitting at the dining table, looking innocent.

"Where's my stuff?" I shouted at her.

Carrie shrugged. "I don't keep track of your things."

"What did you do with all the pictures?"

"Calm down, Randle. I don't have anything of yours."

Pointing my finger at her, I said, "You won't get away with this."

Carrie moved around the far side of the table, putting space between us. To the deputy she said, "Get him out of here. He's dangerous."

Dobbins came up beside me and grabbed my right bicep. "Be cool, sir. We can take a quick look around the house, then we have to get you out of here."

Carrie gasped. "You can't go in my bedroom."

Dobbins dragged me along with him as he said over his shoulder, "We won't disturb anything."

I told one of the movers to get a packing box and join us. Then the deputy and I began our tour of the ground floor. In the master bedroom, a room I hadn't entered for six months, I examined the furnishings as though I were touring a museum. On the nightstand stood a framed photo of Carrie and her family that was at least twenty years old. In the photo, her son, Travis, was a toddler, and her first husband, Chance Dickson, was a grinning father. On her dresser, a large wedding photo was now displayed. Carrie's second husband, Philip Simmons, looked ready for happily-ever-after in a smart tuxedo. Carrie had secretly preserved her past while she demanded that I erase mine.

Disgusted, I opened the top drawer of her nightstand revealing reading glasses and a trashy romantic paperback. In the next drawer, I found a vibrator and lubricant. As I pulled the bottom drawer open, the deputy said, "You shouldn't do that, sir."

Carrie's chrome-plated .22-caliber pistol lay on top of several file folders. I said, "Just trying to see if she's hidden anything of mine in here."

I lifted the edge of the top folder to see what was inside but was careful not to touch the gun. The folder contained her mental health records.

"Please, sir," the deputy said as he started toward me.

I pushed the drawer shut and straightened. Walking away from the nightstand, I said, "How can I see whether she's hidden my stuff if I don't look in her drawers?"

"If you want to look in any concealed space, you'll need a search warrant. You have probable cause, based on the items missing upstairs."

I gave Dobbins a look of resignation. I walked a circuit of the master suite and found one of my favorite paintings hung in an alcove that served as a dressing area, separating the bedroom proper from the walk-in closets. I pulled it off the wall, and Dobbins made a questioning sound.

"It's on my list."

The deputy nodded, understanding that Carrie hadn't intended to surrender it. "More probable cause."

I carried the painting down the hallway to the foyer. Carrie, sitting at the dining table, said, "Oh, forgot that one."

I said, "Yeah, mistake anyone could have made. Ha ha." I handed the painting to one of the movers and told him to put it in the Bronco.

Dobbins and I resumed our search of the premises, trailed by Pancho Villa with empty boxes. We went from room to room and found items Carrie had taken from the beach house and things that should have been on my list. Dobbins watched the proceedings but made no comment. All the while, the dog howled and made a racket.

In the sunroom, the blinds were cranked open, and through the slats I saw the German shepherd. Over and over, it jumped against the door, threatening to break through the glass. It was huge, perhaps seventy-five or eighty pounds of unbridled violence. On the floor were the tattered remains of two stuffed rabbits, their innards scattered around the room like driftwood on a beach. I took a picture of the dog in midleap.

Two movers now held full boxes waiting for instructions. I told them to carry the boxes straight out the door without stopping, without even looking at Mrs. Marks. I went first, followed by the movers, and then Dobbins, who had become a part of the boys' team.

When Carrie saw the boxes, she jumped to her feet. "What's all that?"

The movers kept walking toward the front doors. I said, "Stuff that you forgot to pack for me."

To Dobbins I said, "Let's go through the second-floor rooms. Then we can get out of here."

I started up the main staircase as Carrie took off after the movers. She yelled, "Wait! Let me see what's in the boxes."

The movers didn't stop. They walked right out the front doors. The deputy was now confused about what to do next: stop Carrie or join me upstairs? He decided to stop Carrie. He stepped in front of her and said, "Your husband only took what's his. Don't cause a scene."

Carrie stared at the deputy with hatred, astonishment, and bewilderment all competing to be her primary emotion. She backed down and walked through the dining room and the kitchen to have a look at the garage. Dobbins went to the front doors and surveyed the scene outside. The movers were loading boxes from the attic and packing the furniture from the office into the container. Dobbins walked off the porch and toward the garage apron so he could referee if Carrie objected to what the movers were doing.

Upstairs, I looked through spare bedrooms and bathrooms, opened closets, and knelt to peer under beds, but I found nothing that had been taken from the attic. In the room that Carrie called her office, she had a three-drawer filing cabinet. I tried the drawers, but they were locked. In the media room, I noticed that the door to the second-story balcony had been fitted with a doggy-door so the beast could go in and out as it needed. The door seemed more appropriate for a dog the size of a collie, but once through the door and onto the balcony, it could go down a set of stairs to the deck and into the fenced portion of the backyard. Ingenious, I had to admit, eliminating the need to defile any of the formal rooms on the main floor.

In the second master, the suite I had used after I had been kicked out of the downstairs master, I found a few scraps of clothing hanging in the closet and a few more in a corner of the room, but the drawers had been emptied, the bathroom cleaned out. I had been eradicated from the country house.

I guessed it was time to get out of Dodge. Bouncing down the main staircase, I saw the deputy out on the driveway with his back to the house. Carrie was no longer sitting at the dining table. Did she go to her bedroom or the other way, to the garage? *It's now or never.* I wasn't sure if it was terror or excitement I felt as I darted down the hallway to the master bedroom and scampered around the bed to the nightstand. The whole day had been a microcosm of life with Carrie: Carrie would do something childish and I would respond in kind. We were a bad match—not like oil and water, substances that don't mix; more like two harmless chemicals that when combined create an explosive compound.

I lifted three file folders from the bottom drawer and wrapped them in the jumble of clothes under my arm. Considering the pistol, I hesitated. Was it better to take it or leave it? *Take it so she can't use it to shoot you.* I stuck it in my belt in the small of my back, under my T-shirt, like some gang hoodlum. It was a small weapon—a girl's gun that could be hidden in any of Carrie's designer handbags—but it dug into my flesh and threatened to pop out or slide down my pants as I walked. *Hollywood makes this look easy.*

With the folders under my arm, buried in the clothes gathered from my bedroom, I eased down the hallway to the staircase. If I got caught,

I'd say I had taken one last look around the ground floor. I reached the staircase without being noticed, shuffled up several steps, and waited for someone to see me descending.

The deputy came through the front doors and was relieved to see me come down the stairs. He said, "If you're done, let's bring this to a close."

"All done here." I walked into the dining room, pulled a garage door opener and a set of keys from my pocket, and plunked it all down on the table.

Carrie heard it, walked in from the kitchen, saw the keys and opener on the table, and said, "Are you finally getting out of my home?"

I said, "You have a restraining order, a guard dog, an alarm system, and a gun." I turned to the deputy and said, "She has a pistol here somewhere, officer." Facing Carrie again, I finished with, "What's next, a moat and a drawbridge?"

Speaking more to Dobbins than to me, she said, "I'll do whatever I have to do to protect myself against this man. And I don't have a gun, but I should probably buy one."

I stifled a grin. She was right: She no longer had a gun.

I said, "Give me the garage door opener and keys to the beach house. Please."

Carrie went back to the kitchen and returned with my keys and opener in a yellow mailing envelope.

With a smile for Carrie, I said, "Thanks. See you at mediation. I'm sure that will go as well for you as today did."

As Carrie lunged at me, claws bared, Dobbins slipped between us and pushed me toward the doors. We were on the front porch before we heard Carrie shout, "I have proof, Randle. You don't."

Huh? The deputy and I sauntered toward the movers and the PODS truck, all poised for action.

"Button it up," I said. "We're outta here."

I dropped the clothes and the files onto the backseat floorboard of the SUV. Pancho Villa closed the door to the container, and the PODS driver winched it onto his flatbed.

As we watched the operation, Dobbins said, "You headed for I-75?"

"Yes, Dolphin Beach. I have a little bungalow down there."

Dobbins nodded. "I'll follow you out and make sure she doesn't."

We shook hands, and he slapped me on my shoulder while Carrie scowled at us from the front porch.

CHAPTER FIFTEEN

As the sun rose over the Intracoastal Waterway, lighting and warming my backyard, I sat beside the pool drinking a cup of coffee, thinking how odd it was that with the simple move of a few possessions, I had erased four years of my personal history and reverted to my former status as a bum in a beach bungalow. Sitting there in my new chaise lounge chair, I couldn't stop thinking about all the outdoor furniture now at the country house. It drove me crazy that I hadn't taken the pieces, so I retreated to the air-conditioned interior. By the time I got home the previous evening and the movers had offloaded the office furniture, I had been too exhausted to do anything but affix a padlock to the PODS container and collapse on my bed. Now I turned my attention to my prizes—the three files I had taken from the bottom drawer of Carrie's nightstand.

The medical file was innocuous. No maladies had been diagnosed or treated while we were married. Mrs. Marks was healthy and could expect to live for several more decades. Too bad—alimony ends with the death of either litigant.

The mental health file was a goldmine. It contained receipts for Carrie's irregular visits to the counselor I had met. There were periods when Carrie saw the counselor once a month; occasions when she saw the counselor twice in a single week; stretches when she didn't see the counselor at all. If the visits were plotted on a graph, they would depict the peaks and valleys of our relationship. We had been happy in inverse relation to Carrie's counseling visits.

The file also contained receipts for prescriptions written by a psychiatrist on a quarterly basis over the entire length of our relationship. Over time, the drugs and dosages had changed. When I met her, she was taking two drugs, one for depression and one for anxiety. I looked them up on the Internet and found that among the side effects of the antidepressant was a loss of interest in sex. No kidding.

Instead of the antidepressant, Carrie now took a drug prescribed for "major" depressive disorders, and instead of the "mother's-little-helper" drug, she now took a powerful concoction for "anxiety disorder." Among the side effects of that drug, *Wikipedia* listed aggressive, angry agitation. No kidding.

Recently, Carrie had been prescribed two oft-advertised antipsychotics. It wasn't my imagination: The drugs she had listed on the employee benefits questionnaire had been replaced by more powerful medications as her mental health deteriorated. Diagnoses once described as generalized depression and anxiety were now major depressive disorder and anxiety disorder. More shocking still, Carrie wasn't just an irascible golddigger; she was one of the millions of people who swam in the open sea of humanity while hiding serious mental health problems that were suppressed—just barely—by powerful drugs. *You don't take antipsychotics unless you're psychotic, right?*

The third file contained statements and cancelled checks written against the home equity line of credit. The checks, totaling to the account's maximum limit of one hundred fifty thousand dollars, were made out to Carrie Marks and endorsed by Carrie Marks. There was no way to trace the expropriated funds—there were no payees identified and no records of deposits to other accounts. My body shook with anger until embarrassment settled over me like a shroud. *How could I have allowed my own wife to extort me?* I placed the three stolen files in a black plastic garbage bag, wrapped them into a neat waterproof package, and taped it closed.

The fourth item I had stolen was Carrie's little peashooter. I wiped the gun of fingerprints and placed it in a shoebox. Then I carried my loot down to the dilapidated wooden dock. Under the dock, a shelf formed by the junction of the pilings with the support beams created a perfect hiding place.

Next, I unlocked the PODS container and sorted through my belongings. Some of the valuables—a vase, a painting, decorative platters—I brought into the beach house and displayed in the living room. I opened totes and selected pictures to place on side tables and paintings to hang on walls. Buried in one tote I was surprised to find several old pictures of Glenda and a couple of candid shots of Susanne. I was amazed and confused that the tote had survived Carrie's purges. As a balance to Carrie's pictures of Simmons and Dickson in her bedroom—*our bedroom*—I set the pictures of Glenda and Susanne in prominent locations around my house.

Boxes containing work files were the next items to unload. The files that were current I carried into the house and stacked on my desk. The rest I taped closed and carried into the garage, where some of my most important files had been stored in totes under a workbench. As I entered the garage, my mouth fell open and I had an Oh-my-God moment. The totes were gone! I hadn't spent any time in the garage and hadn't noticed the empty space under the workbench. The conclusion was obvious: Carrie had broken into the house to steal the totes.

One missing tote contained old tax records, medical records, house closings, and long-closed bank accounts—records that had been saved in case of an IRS audit. The other tote contained my proof of Carrie's spending habits, and she had stolen the records to keep them out of the hands of attorneys and judges and mediators. That's why she didn't throw away the pictures of Glenda and Susanne when she rummaged through the attic—she had looked for incriminating evidence and couldn't have cared less about the pictures. Although it would be tedious, I could reproduce some of the records online, but the receipts were likely lost forever and other records would have to be requested from retailers and creditors. That could take weeks or even months.

Connecting more dots, I realized that, full of paper, the stolen totes weighed forty pounds apiece, more than Carrie could haul around in a panic with the alarm siren blaring in the night. She would have needed a man to do it for her. Connie had told the truth: Carrie was at her house and the shopping trip was an alibi. Therefore, the intruder was Harlan! Or Harlan *and* Travis. Then again, it could have been Larry the Yardman, playing prince to the damsel in distress. Maybe his carbon copy helped him.

I locked the PODS container and grabbed a cold beer. It was childish, I know, but the urge to strike back at Carrie for stealing the financial records was irresistible. I called Tony's office and Melissa answered his phone. She said he was in a meeting, which I took to be a euphemism for playing golf. He surprised me by calling five minutes later.

"Have you filed the Baker Act petition?"

"Tomorrow."

"Great! I've been going through the files I moved out of the country house yesterday, and I found my copy of Carrie's mental health records. There's a record of all her appointments with a psychologist and all her prescription receipts. She gets antipsychotic drugs from a psychiatrist every quarter like clockwork."

"Holy crap! No, wait. Why do you have her medical records?"

"I kept a copy for insurance claims, and she didn't know that."

Tony hesitated, then said, "Bring them over here."

"I also caught up with a sheriff's deputy she falsely accused of sexual assault. He's willing to testify to her behavior."

"Given Judge Smithson's tendency to approve requests for hearings, I'm going to save witnesses for the hearing."

"Will I have to testify?"

"I don't even want you in the room; don't want you available for cross. When we get a date, schedule a business trip out of town."

"When will Carrie hear about this?"

"When Smithson sets a hearing date. Maybe next week."

"We're rocking and rolling now, Tony. Thanks."

I called Connie. When she answered, she called me a crook for stealing things from Carrie. I thought she meant the files and the pistol, but it turned out she meant vases and statuettes and paintings. Carrie hadn't yet opened the bottom drawer of her nightstand to discover that she had lost more than material goods. Relieved, I reiterated my dinner invitation. She demurred, hemmed and hawed, castigated me for my behavior toward her sister, questioned my character, and then accepted. We would have dinner on Friday.

Like a kid who had saved the best piece of candy for last, I had saved electronic snooping for last. I logged onto my personal computer and followed Jerry Louks's handwritten instructions to access the account in the cloud, where Carrie's keystrokes were stored. I was pleased to find the file contained a massive amount of data, but as I marked each keystroke on a notepad, like a code-breaker, I realized it was just a couple of website visits. Each visit was short but required numerous keystrokes to make access. Late this afternoon she had logged into her public account, deleted a couple of spam mails, but hadn't written de Castro any notes about moving problems.

The other website she had accessed was Facebook, password: lonely38s. She wasn't referring to gun calibers. Hoping to find pictures of her cavorting with a boyfriend, I opened Carrie's Facebook account and was disappointed to find only photos of her family. She had not logged into *shadylady44*. I signed off before she could catch me rummaging around in her online life.

Disappointed, I showered but didn't bother to shave. Dressed in a grubby T-shirt, cargo shorts, and flip-flops, I drove to Tony's office and dropped off the incriminating mental health evidence. Then I drove all the way back to the Hurricane restaurant in Pass-a-Grille. At the restaurant, I sat alone at a table among happy couples and families at the beach on a Saturday night. After three Coronas and a fried shrimp dinner, I returned to my house to protect my property.

It was after dark when I wheeled my trashbin out to the curb for Wednesday morning pickup. Four doors down I spotted a white panel van parked across the street, but I gave the kid no indication that I had noticed. I returned to the house as though nothing were wrong and reenacted a scene from some Mafia movie I had seen. In the movie, the wise guy's wife delivers sandwiches and soft drinks to the FBI agents watching their house from a van. I prepared a ham and cheese sandwich and grabbed a plastic bottle of water. Using a Sharpie I wrote on a piece of notepaper: **Tell Carrie you're an idiot**. I carried the stuff out the back door, through the screened porch, down the side of the house where you could park a small boat on a trailer, and under a line of palm trees to the sidewalk. Staying in the shadows on my side of the street, I walked up the street as though I were taking a snack to a neighbor's house.

When I was abreast of the van, I darted across the road, set the sandwich and water on the hood, and stuck the note under the windshield wiper, writing facing into the cab. Then I rapped on the blacked-out side window and yelled, "Relax. I'm in for the night."

Feeling cocky, I strolled down the center of the street, back to my house. If it wasn't the PI wannabe in the van, the neighborhood cats would have a feast and the van owner would wonder, *Who the heck is Carrie?*

Before I turned out the lights, I stepped outside and looked up the street. The panel van was gone.

CHAPTER SIXTEEN

C onnie and I arranged to meet at the municipal marina on Friday night and walk to our dinner "date" from there. The marina was convenient for Connie, who lived in a middle-class neighborhood in St. Petersburg, midway between her job in Manatee County and the Tomkins family enclave in Cortes County. It was also convenient for me as I planned to spend the day on my boat.

Given the turmoil in my marriage, I hadn't been aboard in months, but when I unlocked the padlock that secured the hatch to the interior spaces, I had the sensation that someone had been aboard the boat. It was nothing alarming, just things not quite as I would normally leave them—glasses in the dishwasher, trash in the receptacle under the sink. I peeked in the master stateroom and found that the bed was not quite made to my usual precision. Goosebumps formed on my arms.

I had named the forty-two-foot Carver aft cabin cruiser *Wahine II*, in honor of Glenda's brother who had committed suicide after losing his battle with drug addiction. His boat had been named the *Wahine*—Hawaiian/Polynesian for "girlfriend." Fifteen years old, the interior furnishings, appliances, and TVs were dated, but the engines and mechanics were in fine operating condition. The boat stood three levels tall, like a floating condominium. Belowdecks were a master stateroom in the stern, a guest stateroom in the bow, and a galley in between; on the main level was a sitting/dining room above which perched the bridge. There were two heads: one in the bow, and one in the master stateroom. On the bridge were two captain's chairs and a built-in lounge seat for passengers. Behind the bridge, half a level lower and sitting atop the master stateroom, was the aft cabin—essentially an enclosed patio equipped with a wet bar and furnished with a wicker couch and two side chairs. Powered by two massive Caterpillar diesels that were geared for torque rather than speed, the boat could start, stop, turn, spin, and maneuver like a sports car.

Carrie hated the *Wahine II*—hated the name; hated the fact that I had entertained on it before we were married; hated the fact that it wasn't sleek and sexy and fast. She wanted me to buy a speedboat, but I had wisely resisted.

During the rest of the morning I straightened the spaces, and in the middle of the afternoon I took her out for a sea trial. The rumble of the big diesels, the vibration of the deck, the salt air, and the whooshing of the massive wake she created as she plowed through the Bay thrilled me. Many of my dock neighbors were uncomfortable on the water by themselves, but I enjoyed the solitude, not to mention the freedom from landlubbers who might fall overboard or throw the wrong switch or foul a line. The Bay was busy with boats of all kinds, but I wound my way past fishermen and around sailboats to a stretch of open water. Moving at cruising speed so I didn't attract any attention, I casually leaned over the gunwale and dropped Carrie's pistol into the Bay. On the bottom I imagined it coming to rest alongside murder weapons discarded during Tampa's Mafia heydays.

After burning fuel for two hours, I returned to the dock, showered, and dressed in date clothes. With a beer in my hand, I waited for Connie in the aft cabin. From my boat, I had a clear view of the locked gate at the land end of the dock and the parking spaces beyond. When Connie's blue sedan pulled into a space, I climbed down onto the dock and walked to the gate to meet her. She was all smiles in a floral-print sundress and a pair of real high heels. Her face showed a hint of blush, and her lips revealed a faint coating of lipstick.

We kissed—on the lips as always—then walked down Beach Drive toward Cassis, the trendy restaurant at the edge of the Central Yacht Basin. I calculated that a trendy restaurant was a safer rendezvous than a romantic one. It was an awkward stroll because I didn't want to hold her hand or clutch her arm in mine. To cover my uneasiness, I chatted up a storm and used both hands to accentuate my words. The expanse from my boat to the restaurant, with the park on our right and the harbor to our left, was one of my favorite places on earth and I wanted to share it with Glenda, not Connie Tomkins.

At the restaurant, the hostess led us to a table at the window overlooking the harbor. I held Connie's chair for her, and we both took a few moments to admire the yachts. Comfortable, we disposed of the pragmatic tasks of ordering drinks and discussing the menu. We clinked glasses—sauvignon blanc in anticipation of seafood entrées—and Connie made a toast.

"To a fresh start."

"Just remember that we both need a fresh start, not just your sister."

"Don't play hardball, Randle. This isn't business, it's personal."

"Nice turn of phrase. Mario Puzo would like that. If she wants mediation to work, she has to call off her private investigator."

"If mediation is going to work, you have to give her back the files and pistol you stole when you moved out."

I didn't bother to deny the thefts. I folded my hands, rested my forearms on the table, leaned toward her, and adopted a serious, sober look—the pose a doctor uses to tell a patient he has terminal cancer and only six months to live.

"Carrie's private investigator hasn't gotten a shred of evidence against me."

Connie shrugged. "They know you're having an affair with your ex-wife."

"There is no 'affair.'" I used my little fingers to make air quotes around the euphemism "affair." "I took pictures of him when he floated down the inlet like Huck Finn on a raft, and I'm going to report him to the judge for violating my protective order."

Connie gasped. "Don't do that! He's just a kid—Phil's son, Scott Simmons."

"Why would she use her former stepson?"

"He has a crush on her, does her favors. He's a computer science student at the university, and he helps Carrie with computer problems."

Like installing an email snooper. "If I see him again, I'll report him for stalking me without an investigator's license."

"She already called him off."

"Good, then I won't have to use the evidence I have on her."

"She swears she never cheated on you."

"I have the evidence, Connie. For example, when I moved into the beach house I found two wineglasses in the hot tub and only one had her lipstick on it."

"The other one was mine, Randle. I stayed with her and helped her move. She made me get in the hot tub with her. Not really my thing, but she was distressed."

"I have a pile of evidence, Connie, but the rest is more . . . intimate."
I wish.

Connie composed herself, pulled her dress down under her thighs, and adjusted herself in the chair. "Maybe my sister isn't a saint. So what? Just reach a settlement and put it behind you so you can start a new life."

With the evil twin sister? "I don't think you understand how much money is at stake. It's millions, Connie."

Her eyes popped open, and then her face dissolved. "Millions?" she whispered.

I nodded.

Connie sagged back in her chair. In a tiny voice, she said, "She won't share. She's selfish."

"The beggars will follow the money, believe me. That's how human nature works."

The waiter appeared, and while Connie sat frozen like an ice sculpture, I ordered for both of us: grouper tacos—the house specialty— as an appetizer and scallops as entrées. While Connie was distracted, I switched my smartphone into voice record mode and laid it in the middle of the table, next to my wineglass. When the waiter left, now on the record, so to speak, I said, "If mediation doesn't work, will Carrie and her father kill me to get the money?"

Connie shushed me, didn't want people at neighboring tables to hear the word "kill." She leaned across the table and stage-whispered directly into my microphone: "They talk about the murder plot all the time. She asked Daddy to be a witness for her. You know how vengeful Daddy would get if he thought you raped Carrie."

And who told her she needs a witness? "Your daddy is old school, thinks husbands own wives like they own dogs. He wouldn't understand how you could use the terms 'marriage' and 'rape' in the same sentence."

We were interrupted by the waiter delivering our appetizers. As he positioned our plates and utensils, I remembered a conversation I had with Harlan on his front porch following a family dinner, out of earshot of the womenfolk. During dinner, Carrie had made a nasty remark about me and I had shot her down and shut her up.

Harlan had congratulated me and said, "Those other guys couldn't handle her."

At the time, I assumed Harlan was referring to Carrie's ex-husbands. Now I wondered if the remark included Richard Puralto.

"She can be hard to handle," I had said.

"Needs a firm hand, like her momma." Harlan had slapped his left hand with his right. Smack!

I had laughed along with my father-in-law, to show I could be one of the boys, but I found it ironic that a Bible-toting Christian thought physical force a useful tool in a marriage.

The waiter departed, and Connie and I began to eat. After I swallowed a mouthful of grouper, I said, "Is she still planning to float naked in my pool until she magically produces a gun?" I wanted to get that plot "on the record."

Chewing, Connie said, "What if she was willing to meet you on the boat to make a deal and avoid mediation?"

Is she afraid the mediator will favor the husband—me? "Why the boat?"

"She said you guys always 'did it' on the boat, so you'd be willing to let her aboard if she was dressed for sex. Then maybe you could make a deal."

Connie pretended to organize the grouper in one of her tacos, waiting to see how I'd react. A meeting on the boat was appealing to me. I wanted them to stop messing with my beach house, and the boat was a more controllable environment. Remembering that I would be recorded, I answered carefully, "I can't afford the house *and* the boat *and* alimony. When the beach house sells, I'll have no choice but to live aboard the boat full time until I can cash my stock options."

I paused, and she stopped playing with her food to concentrate on my words. Remembering again to be careful, I said, "She'd have to come alone, and she'd have to warn me she was coming."

"She wouldn't let you in the country house again."

"We can't have an emotional discussion in a public place."

"This is the best way." Still playing the role of family fixer, she said it as though it were an agreed arrangement.

I thought for a moment, a forkful of fish suspended in front of me. "What if it doesn't work? Is it mediation or murder?"

"Oh, Randle, this has to work. They talk about hurting you like it was a parlor game, something to get just right."

"She'd claim I tried to rape her?"

Connie dabbed her lips with her napkin and sat up primly like a 1950s secretary being interviewed. "Yes. She'll bring along a change of conservative clothes so she can look innocent when she meets the cops."

"Your sister would look like a tramp if she wore a nun's habit."

"Now you're being mean just to be mean. From what I hear, you like the tramp look."

Touché. I pursed my lips and spun my wineglass in my fingers. "She'd have to change clothes *before* she shot me so she'd get blood on the conservative clothes. If she shot me at close range, it would produce high-speed blood spatter, not a smear. Anyone who watches *CSI New Orleans* knows that."

Connie made a face like she had bitten into something sour. She finished one taco, then picked up another.

I said, "She'll need help too. She can't overpower me by herself."

Chewing, she said, "Daddy and Travis will help her."

The hairs on my neck stood up like the quills on a threatened porcupine. Did the crazy old cracker break into my beach house?

"They can't kill me on the boat dock. Too many witnesses. Unless it's a sneak attack."

Connie seemed caught off guard. "Ah, no. She'll ask you to take her out into the Gulf so Daddy can get to your boat in a hurry from his marina. You guys always floated off Clearwater, right?"

In the good ol' days, we'd drift off the coast, tie our floats to the boat, and drink in the sunshine. When the lights came on along the coast, we'd watch the shoreline glitter, grill a steak, and sometimes we'd make love. It would be an obvious temptation for me and a safe murder location for Carrie.

"Yes, in the good ol' days," I said.

"If she wants you to go out into the Gulf, up to Clearwater, you'll know she didn't come to give you hugs and kisses."

Connie smirked and I seethed. Had we been in a private place, I'd have flipped her on her head and shook her until the whole story fell out like coins from a piggybank. I leaned toward her, and she shrank away from me. Under control, I said, "Makes sense. Go on."

Connie squirmed. "Well, if you can't make a deal, Carrie could shoot you, rip her clothes, get bruised, you know. Travis and Daddy would rescue her. They would call the Marine Police, and Carrie would tell her story: She wanted to discuss a settlement; you made her go with you to the Gulf, where no one could see what you were doing; you came on to her; she resisted." She paused to look at me, see if I believed her story. Maybe I didn't look all that convinced because she added, "She feared for her life." Other than the change in venue, it was the same old plan they had for the beach house.

I sat back to think about the plan. With the physical pressure relieved, she sat upright. I said, "If your daddy and Travis arrived after I was dead, they'd have to testify to an assault they hadn't witnessed. Would they perjure themselves?"

"Daddy is willing to help his favorite little girl any way he has to." An undercurrent of bitterness inflected her voice.

"How would she get bruised?"

Connie flushed with embarrassment. "Carrie saw a movie where a woman fakes her rape by using a bottle to bruise herself. Down there."

Gone Girl. "Yep, I saw that one." In a voice full of skepticism, I said, "But, Connie, they must see that this isn't a very good plan. She said her gun was stolen, but now she's going to shoot her unarmed husband in cold blood."

Connie's chin dropped onto her chest. She didn't look up. "Instead of shooting you, they could force you at gunpoint to jump overboard. You'd drown, and they'd go back to shore in Daddy's boat. Your boat would be found adrift, but you'd just be a sailor lost at sea." She spread her hands as though I should see how obvious that variation would be.

"The problem with that idea is someone might see Carrie getting on my boat, and then she wouldn't be on the boat when it was found. If she came to the dock dressed for sex, people would remember her."

"She would say you fell overboard and she called Daddy to pick her up."

"I'm not going to commit suicide by drowning, Connie."

She nodded. "Another way is to shoot you when Daddy gets there and throw your body overboard. There'd be blood in the water so the sharks would, ah, dispose of your body. Carrie could still say you fell overboard, but you wouldn't be found."

I could imagine the scene at the Tomkins hacienda—one person would point out a weakness in the plan and another person would suggest a way around it. I had the twisted thought that I should change my boat's name to *Haole*, the Polynesian pejorative for Caucasians, meaning "shark bait."

"What about all the blood? Carrie knows you can never clean it all up."

She had a ready answer: "They could sink your boat so the DNA deteriorates."

"Good God! How much time do they spend on this? Do they ever go grocery shopping? Feed the dog?" It pissed me off that these people were spending their time thinking up ways to make these amateurish plots workable. "Is your insane sister coming up with all these ideas, or are your momma and Jerilynn helping her?"

Connie shrank away from me. "I don't know. I haven't always been there."

While I rearranged my silverware and glasses, I slid my phone off the table and put it in my pocket, turning it off as I did so. I took a sip of wine and said, "Okay, I get it. I have to make a deal, but your sister has to be reasonable."

Connie thought about it. "This is Carrie's last chance to get a stake for the future. She's already struck out three times, and she won't look sexy forever."

"In a couple of years she'll look like her mother, a wrinkled old prune. That's the problem when beauty is your only asset—it fades."

Connie wore a dreamy look, as though she were imagining Carrie as plain as herself. Maybe the passage of time would supply Connie the final advantage in her sibling rivalry. She carried less weight, hadn't abused herself with prescription drugs and UV rays the way Carrie had. The scallops arrived, and we took a few moments to get acquainted with our meals.

"Let's talk about something less depressing than my divorce."

Dipping a scallop into the mustard sauce, Connie said, "Okay, I'll go first. I'm taking the whole family to the beach to celebrate on the weekend after your mediation. The kids will be back in school so it won't be crowded. I'm going to miss having you along, Randle. You were always fun."

I thought I'd rather have a root canal and a proctology exam in the same day than go on a Tomkins family trip, but I said, "Yeah, the sad part of a divorce is that you lose the whole family. Going to make a long weekend of it?"

"We'll drive over to Clearwater on Friday afternoon, spend the night Friday and Saturday, and then people can leave for home whenever they want on Sunday. Travis will need to get to work, but Carrie will want to be in the sun all day."

Showing off her assets. "That's a fact," I said.

"Aren't you lonely, Randle, living all by yourself?"

"I've had to work hard to get the company ready for the IPO. And then there's all the moving out and moving in I've had to do, so I haven't had a chance to be lonely. But this is nice. Tonight."

It was nice. As the sun set into the Gulf on the other side of the peninsula, darkness fell over the yacht basin like a shade drawn slowly down on an enormous window. Boat lights, dock lights, and buoy lights were suspended in the night, hinting at the unseen objects they marked. We both gazed out the window, enjoying the peaceful setting.

Connie said, "Yes, I'm enjoying it. Carrie is high-strung, excitable. You and I are calm, more compatible."

"Carrie is a thoroughbred, and I'm just a plow horse. It wasn't a good match."

"I'm a plow horse too, Randle. You have to break a thoroughbred or it's hard to handle. Plow horses are easier to manage."

I twirled my wineglass, shifted in my chair, and gave Connie a sympathetic look. "You mentioned that other men had made the same poor choice I made and had gotten involved with Carrie when they should have, ah, gone in a different direction."

"I knew you'd ask. I should never have mentioned it." She dipped another scallop to delay a direct answer.

"Come on, you promised to tell me the story."

Connie cocked her head, swallowed, and decided to trust me. "It was just one man."

I nodded.

"In high school I dated the star quarterback. Surprised?" Her eyebrows rose in anticipation.

"No, not at all," I lied.

"Well, you'll be surprised by who it was. It was Chance Dickson."

Shocked was a better word. "You dated Chance before Carrie did?"

"Carrie never dated Chance, I did. He was always around our house, and he couldn't help but notice Carrie."

"Oh no, I see it coming." And I could: Carrie prancing around, showing her butt, to see if she could attract his attention.

Connie nodded in resignation. "When Chance came on to her, Carrie didn't resist. Couldn't resist. He got her pregnant, and Daddy went crazy. Made them get married."

"Shotgun wedding. I am so sorry, Connie." I meant it. Must have been mortifying to be betrayed by her sister. How could they pretend to be friends now?

"Changed my plans, for sure." A weak smile played across her lips as she remembered the shattered dreams.

"I'd have strangled the little bitch."

"Wasn't her fault, Randle. Chance took advantage of her." She used her napkin to stop the moisture forming in the corners of her eyes from becoming tears. She took a breath. "I was away at college, so I didn't attend the wedding."

That stopped me in my tracks. "Whoa, wait a minute. You were already out of high school when this happened?"

"Sure, I was at Stetson. Probably why it happened."

I pressed on, hammering a wedge between the sisters. "That's a nice rationalization, but Chance wouldn't have hung around your family unless he was sleeping with your sister."

"Chance worked for Daddy in the yard," she insisted. Then Connie's face dissolved like a box of chocolates in the hot sun. "Carrie said they slipped up once at the end of my freshman year."

I shook my head. "Carrie let herself get pregnant so she could get back at you."

"Get back at me for what?" She said it loud enough for nearby tables to hear, and diners stopped their conversations to look at us.

"For being Miss Perfect, the good student, the college girl, the daughter who took care of her parents. She didn't want you to have a fairytale marriage as well."

The tears ran freely. Her lower lip trembled, turning words into wails. "It was Chance. He made her do it and got her in trouble."

"And the baby was Travis. He's the baby you should have had, and the baby Carrie never wanted."

"Chance made her do it." She slammed the table, anger overcoming sadness.

"Carrie trapped him, Connie."

"No." She shook her head. "No."

"They were only married a couple of years. Did you try to get him back when they divorced? He was the love of your life."

"I can't do this, Randle. I've got to go." She stood up.

Looking up at her from my seat, I said, "You should have taken him back, adopted Travis."

She shouted at me, "I couldn't! Chance enlisted in the Army to get away from it all. Then he brought home a wife from Germany." She moved into the aisle.

"And you were left alone. My God, what devastation! Carrie destroyed all of you."

Connie barreled away, knocking over her glass of wine, drenching my lap. Nearby diners stared at me in horror. What terrible thing had I done or said? A waiter hurried to the table with a bundle of napkins. I took one and said, "I can do this. Why don't you meet me at the door with the check?"

"Of course, sir," the waiter said and hurried away. He wanted to get the wild man out of his restaurant.

Making no eye contact with the other diners, I signed the check, left the restaurant, and walked back toward the marina. Connie waited beside her car, daubing her eyes with her table napkin. I put my arms around her, and she rested her head on my chest.

"I'm sorry, Connie, but I think you've known the truth for a long time. You suppressed it, but you knew. Your sister has been manipulating you since you were little girls."

She pushed back enough to look up at my eyes, as if straining to see the top of a skyscraper, then switched her gaze to my boat. "I think I should calm down before I drive."

I knew what she wanted but I couldn't do it to Glenda, not even to save my life. "Let's go over and sit on a park bench for a bit until you're calm."

Instantly, her demeanor changed. She stiffened and her eyes burned with evil intensity. She extricated herself from my embrace and moved to the driver's door.

Feeling a measure of remorse, I said, "You shouldn't drive until you calm down."

She forced a smile. "I'm calm, Randle. I'm a plow horse."

Embarrassed that she had been rebuffed, she didn't wait for me to change my mind. As she drove away, I felt genuine sorrow for her. We all harbor unreasonable aspirations that are dashed by reality, don't we? My expectations had been modest: get Connie on tape describing an amateurish murder plot so the tape could be played for a jury if mediation failed. *If mediation failed.* I had no intention of walking into Carrie's trap on the *Wahine II*. If Connie hated her sister enough to be my "Deep Throat," so much the better.

CHAPTER SEVENTEEN

W alking back to the boat I decided not to stay where Connie and Carrie expected me to be and to return to the beach house for the night. I locked up the interior, secured the lines, and drove back across the peninsula. When I reached the beach house I went straight to the refrigerator, grabbed a beer, and took it out to the pool. Then I contemplated my options for dealing with my ex-wife and her crazy family.

There were only two or three ways to play it, and I was trying to imagine the end state for each option. When I rose from the chair to get another beer, I faced the house and saw the broken window. The guest bath window on the back of the house, an old-fashioned pebbled-glass window that allowed a certain amount of sunlight while maintaining privacy, had been smashed. Because of its unusual construction, the security company could not affix a pressure sensor to detect the breaking of the window. It was the one unprotected porthole to the home, and only Carrie would have known that. More alarming was the supposition that Carrie knew I wouldn't be at the beach house. Either the kid "private investigator" had located me at the marina or Connie had told Carrie I would be with her.

I rushed inside and checked for the TV, the iPod, the computer, and artwork. All were in their places. Moving from room to room, pausing to scan walls and tabletops, I couldn't detect anything missing. The last place I checked, at the far end of the house, was the master bedroom. I knew before I opened the drawer to the nightstand what I was going to find. Not find. My pistol and its twelve-shot clip were missing. I turned on my heel and ran down to the dock. Kneeling in shallow water, I verified that my horde of Carrie's files was still on the concealed ledge wrapped in a black plastic garbage bag. Having dumped Carrie's peashooter in the Bay, I was unarmed and vulnerable.

The pistols were the obvious objects of the break-in, but had she found the stolen files, it would have been a bonus for her. My stolen weapon, the .40-caliber Glock, had been Jamie's service weapon in Atlanta. She had given it to me when she was issued a new service weapon in Florida, so it had sentimental value as well as defensive value. I knew I should call the cops and report the theft, but there were downsides to doing that. If I pointed a finger at Carrie for this break-in, she would point a finger at me for the theft of her gun. A crime scene investigation wasn't likely to produce any evidence—Carrie's fingerprints were all over the house and fingerprints aren't time-stamped. If I lost everything in the divorce and was forced to sell the house, a reported crime would stain its safety record and make it more difficult to unload.

I turned on all the lights, set the alarm, and locked the doors. With nowhere safe to go, I took a room at a sleazy beach motel. Lying on the bed, fully clothed to deter bedbugs, I arrived at several conclusions: 1) Carrie and Connie were collaborating as Carrie knew I wouldn't be at the beach house; 2) Connie wanted to sleep on the boat to keep me away from the beach house; and 3) they were definitely plotting to kill me.

—◦◦◦—

On the way back to the beach house in the morning, I contacted a window repairman and the security company. Waiting for them, I swept up the glass on the bathroom floor and dumped the jagged shards into an old plastic paint pail. Then I loaded everything of sentimental value into my Bronco. I had no intentions of returning to the beach house while crazy people were attacking me.

The window repairman was the first to arrive. I showed him to the bathroom and he pulled on a pair of rubber gloves and began picking the remaining shards out of the frame. As he worked I wandered away, paced from room to room, said my sad goodbyes to my safe haven. A few minutes later the repairman called out to me from the bathroom, "Hey, boss, look at this."

Now what? Is he going to tell me it's a non-standard window that can't be replaced? Reluctantly, I joined him in the tiny bathroom and found him holding a glass shard up to the light like a sommelier holding up a goblet of fine wine. "What do you see?"

Now it's a contest? I squeezed next to him and gazed up his arm to the piece of broken glass. The bright light of day illuminated its red edges. Grabbing the repairman's wrist, I pulled the glass close and squinted. The red stain was blood. Had to be.

"The burglar cut himself. There's more in the frame," he said.

Three adjacent pieces in the lower right-hand corner of the frame were spotted and smeared, and on two of them dark hairs were stuck to the dried red stains. *Carrie has blonde hair so this DNA belongs to her accomplice.* He couldn't exit by a door or he would have tripped the alarm, so he climbed out the bathroom and snagged an arm on the broken glass. I told the repairman to leave the evidence on the windowsill and take a cigarette break. Then I called the Dolphin Beach Police for help.

"Help" arrived forty-five minutes later in the form of one squad car and one female officer. By then the security company had arrived and the installer wasn't happy about the delay in the process. I told him to grab a couple of beers and make friends with the window repairman.

The officer reminded me of my daughter—serious, enthusiastic, naïve, determined to protect the public from itself. Her name was Brittany Williams. She filled out a form, dutifully noting the date and time of the break-in, the manner of intrusion, my weapon's serial number, and my contact information. I insisted that my estranged wife did it, but Officer Williams was having none of that. She said break-ins were epidemic up and down the beaches—kids looking for weapons, drugs, and cash. When I showed her the bloodstained shards, she grimaced. Taking the evidence meant tagging it, filling out another form, logging it into the evidence room, and hounding someone to run DNA tests. She grappled with whether one more missing gun was worth the effort. After some hesitation, she promised to file the report and get a detective to contact me. She told me to leave the bloody shards in the paint pail for the detective. Then she gave me her card, which made her the second cop in my rolodex.

By lunchtime, the bathroom window had been replaced with flat frosted glass. The security system installer, two beers happier, had added a pressure sensor and connected it to the alarm system.

My Glock had rested in my nightstand for years, had never been fired even for practice, yet now I felt naked without it, so I climbed into my Bronco and went looking for a new gun. It turned out to be a piece of cake. Shockingly, I was able to walk into a gun shop and purchase a 9-millimeter Beretta and a box of ammo with no questions asked, no waiting period, and no license required. Only three counties in Florida required background checks, and they were clustered around drug-infested Miami. The clerk helpfully informed me that it was illegal for any government agency in Florida to keep a registry of firearms. The only restriction was that I couldn't conceal the weapon and carry it in public. I could, however, keep it in my home.

"What if I'm living on my boat?" I inquired.

"Then that's your home, bro."

Afraid to sleep in the house, I packed up some casual clothes, my computer, and some files and headed back to the boat. On the way, I called Jamie and invited her to breakfast on Sunday morning as I had a favor to ask of her. She declined, saying she wasn't going to let me off the hook with an easy meal in a restaurant. She asked me to come to her apartment on Wednesday, her day off, so she could cook for me. We could have an entire evening together, she said. That scared the hell out of me, but I accepted.

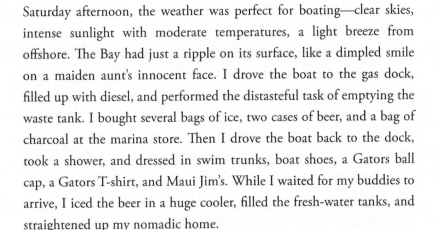

Saturday afternoon, the weather was perfect for boating—clear skies, intense sunlight with moderate temperatures, a light breeze from offshore. The Bay had just a ripple on its surface, like a dimpled smile on a maiden aunt's innocent face. I drove the boat to the gas dock, filled up with diesel, and performed the distasteful task of emptying the waste tank. I bought several bags of ice, two cases of beer, and a bag of charcoal at the marina store. Then I drove the boat back to the dock, took a shower, and dressed in swim trunks, boat shoes, a Gators ball cap, a Gators T-shirt, and Maui Jim's. While I waited for my buddies to arrive, I iced the beer in a huge cooler, filled the fresh-water tanks, and straightened up my nomadic home.

Marty Weinstein was the first buddy to show up—short, skinny, graying, bespectacled, and with a goatee to prove he was a psychiatrist.

Marty came to the boat for a cruise dressed for golf although tennis was his game. Next Fred Tanner shuffled down the dock. The private investigator, who worked for Tony's law firm, was taller and heavier than I and also more athletic. Consistently disheveled, he rocked worn-out boat shoes, cargo shorts, and a button-up, short-sleeved shirt that looked like it was made of bandage gauze. Tony completed our foursome. The swarthy Italian was of average height but thick in the torso with a full head of wavy black hair. He wore dress shorts and a Hawaiian-print shirt and flip-flops. As a group, we defined the term "middle-aged men."

I started the engines, and as we waited for the big diesels to warm up we mingled on the bridge and exchanged small talk. Marty complained that he didn't have enough patients. People flocked to marriage counselors, psychologists, and sociologists because they were less expensive than psychiatrists and few people wanted to invest in deep psychoanalysis. That trend had reduced his practice to writing prescriptions for the patients of counselors who weren't medically qualified to prescribe the drugs that were now a substitute for formal treatment.

"I may have to work for an institution," Marty whined. "Maybe work for the VA, treat soldiers with PTSD."

Fred said, "It's important to stay out of the free-cheese line. I run all kinds of crappy little errands for Tony's firm just to make ends meet."

Addressing me, Marty said, "Weren't you going to recommend me to your wife?"

"I did. She said she isn't going to tell her secrets to a friend of mine. She'd rather cry on the shoulder of a sympathetic counselor than get serious help. She dragged me to one of those sessions so I could hear her complain about me. The counselor told me I should validate Carrie's emotions, respect her feelings. I said, 'In order to be valid, don't her feelings have to be based on facts?' They both got mad at me, and Carrie never took me to see the counselor after that."

Marty said, "Does the counselor use a psychiatrist to prescribe drugs for your wife?"

"Oh yeah," I said, "a boatload of drugs. She uses some woman in Safety Harbor."

"Does Carrie ever see the psychiatrist?"

"Nope. They talk over the phone once a month. If Carrie likes the way the drugs make her feel, she gets a new prescription."

"Modern medicine," Marty said in a depressed voice.

Tony Zambrano weighed in. "We've filed a Baker Act petition so we can get a formal evaluation of her mental state."

"Can you include me in the evaluation somehow?" Marty said.

Everyone turned to me, and I felt trapped. I was saved by the sound of a female voice calling my name from the dock. I stepped down to the aft cabin where the Plexiglas "windows" had been rolled up, and through the openings saw my wife standing on the dock. She was dressed to kill—deeply tanned in a yellow bikini top, cutoff jean shorts, and stack-heeled espadrilles. A soft fabric bag hung from her shoulder. She was smiling.

"What are you doing here?" I sounded more brusque than intended.

"Calm down, the restraining order doesn't apply to our boat. We need to talk about our situation. We could take the boat out and make it pleasant."

My buddies crowded around me, staring through aft cabin windows at the woman below. They reminded me of dogs with their tongues hanging out of their mouths. I gave them a disgusted look and walked out of the aft cabin and down the stairs on the side of the boat to the swim platform at the stern. I was on the same level as Carrie, but with a gap between the boat and the dock. The water between us was a metaphor for the emotional gap in our lives.

I jerked a thumb at the men in the aft cabin and said, "We've got plans."

Carrie looked up at the men and gave them a smile, but through gritted teeth she whispered, "If you want to avoid mediation, let's discuss a deal. I'm not going to keep coming back."

A cold chill ran up my spine. Was it an accident that she turned up unannounced the day after my gun had been stolen? She probably thought I couldn't have replaced it this quickly.

"If I had known you were coming I'd have told these guys to stay home, but I can't change our plans now."

Marty said, "We can leave if you want to talk to your wife, Randle."

I gave Marty a fierce look. "I promised you guys a fishing trip, and that's what you're going to get."

"Fishing?" Marty blurted.

Fred roughly shoved Marty aside, out of view from the dock.

I turned back to Carrie. "We'll have to do this another time."

Carrie turned red. "You just blew your chance for a good deal. And a nice afternoon, if you know what I mean."

She was about to stomp off, so I said, "Now I have proof, Carrie. So we're even."

She looked at me with a mixture of hatred and confusion. I could see her mind working, wondering how much I knew and what exactly I meant. Not able to figure it out, she pivoted and hurried down the dock, tail wagging and head bobbing as she spewed a stream of invective.

Fred whistled. I climbed back up the stairs to the aft cabin and said to Marty, "Make yourself useful. Cast off the lines and we'll get underway."

I headed for the bridge, but Tony stopped me with a hand on my arm. "You should have talked to her. She may have made you an offer."

I lied to the lawyer. "We're going to stick to our plan. No sidebars without attorneys present."

I pulled away and took the captain's chair. Fred, the practical guy in the group, went down on deck and began untying the lines. Tony sank into the other captain's chair, and Marty perched on the lounge seat. When Fred climbed back onto the bridge, he stood behind me with feet spread for balance as I advanced the throttles and maneuvered out of the slip and into the channel leading to the Bay.

Fred said, "You're making a mistake, divorcing her. Bodies like that don't grow on trees."

"She's hot," Marty concurred. "Oh my God, is she hot." He shook his hands like he had touched a hot stove.

Marty was married to a mousy little university professor, and Fred had been separated from his wife for over a year. Tony was divorced. My friends were a bunch of envious losers.

"Cut it out, guys," I said. "She's still my wife, so give me a little respect, okay?"

Fred and Tony looked sheepish, but Marty was irrepressible.

"Just for my professional interest, what sort of troubles did you guys have?" Marty asked.

I looked at him with a question mark on my face. Why was the little weirdo asking personal questions? This wasn't a group of women; it was a group of grown men.

To shut him up, I said, "All the usual." I drove the boat through the narrow opening leading to the Bay and pushed the throttles forward. Wanting to get away from the crowd on the near shore, I headed toward MacDill Air Force Base.

"Sex, money, and religion are the usual," Marty said, as though he were imparting rare wisdom.

Annoyed, I glared at him. "Why are you asking these intimate questions?"

Marty held his hands out defensively. "Men look at a woman like your wife and think they'd do anything to keep her. But you're letting her get away, so I'm curious what went wrong."

The other guys perked up their ears like deer in the woods.

I sighed. "The problem we had with sex is that she doesn't like it."

The three men issued a collective groan. "She looks like sex on a stick," Fred said. "She's advertising."

"She's compensating, Fred. The fake boobs, fake nails, false eyelashes, the polish and jewelry are all compensations for not being sexy in the bedroom. It's like men who compensate for their lack of masculinity with guns and uniforms and Corvettes."

"Hogwash," Fred muttered.

"Tattoos and piercings," Marty said.

We all turned to the weird little psychiatrist. He blinked. "Women use tattoos and piercings now as a signal that they're hot. I'll bet Carrie has a tattoo."

I looked at the little pervert and decided to tantalize him. "She has a tattoo of a butterfly on her butt. Monarch. When I do her from behind, her butt jiggles and the butterfly looks like it's flying."

Fred and Tony laughed appreciatively. Marty licked his lips.

Picking up on the list of our problems, I said, "Money was an issue. We both want more of it, but we use it differently. I like to pile it in a corner and admire it like a work of art."

"You're just keeping score," Fred offered.

"Something like that," I said. "But Carrie sees money for what it can buy: cars, houses, clothes, jewelry. She wants to convert money into possessions, so it was a problem for us."

Marty jumped back in. "And religion. Was that a problem too?"

"No," I said, "but we're different. She's a fundamentalist Christian, and I'm a 'none.'"

"A nun? Like a sister?"

"N-o-n-e. What you put on a form in the space next to religious preference."

"You believe in God, don't you?" The psychiatrist sounded alarmed, as though it would be risky to ride in a boat driven by an atheist.

I pulled back on the throttles and let the big boat settle in its wake. We were standing off the end of the runways at the air force base. I grabbed a pair of binoculars from under the dashboard and handed them to Tony. "See if there's a quiet spot along the Tampa shore," I said.

To Marty, I said, "I don't argue about religion, because there are no facts to argue. You either believe or you don't. I choose to believe. Some people call it faith; it's really more like hope."

"The benefit we get from religion is morality training," Marty said. "A civilization requires a population that is moral."

Tony, the hardened lawyer, sneered. "Morality is the position you hold on abortion *before* your teenaged daughter gets pregnant. After that we all behave in our own self-interest."

"No," Marty said. "Morality is real. We've isolated the chemical in the brain that controls morality. It's called oxytocin."

"Only chemical my wife is missing," I said. "She took two helpings of silicone instead."

They laughed.

"Karma," Fred said, as though he had uttered an entire sentence, and everyone turned to wait for more. "Karma controls the universe, not some moral code. The Hindus believe that every good act and every bad deed is returned to you in kind during your lifetime."

Marty was ready to argue the point, but Tony announced, "There's a clear area up toward Davis Island."

I altered course and crept around the base toward the islands at the mouth of the Hillsborough River.

Marty wore a thoughtful look as he said, "Your marriage can be saved. Given a little counseling, you could hold on to your wife."

"I don't want to hold on to her, Marty. She cheated."

Fred said, "Did you see the news about the two websites that got hacked? The one where you find a married woman for an affair? Thirty million members. Thirty million! And the one where you can find someone for one-night stands? Sixty million members. Twenty percent of our population is cheating. So it's not that big a deal anymore."

I hated Fred for that dose of repugnant reality. "Call me old-fashioned, but it's a big deal to me."

The three men looked at me with pity. Right or wrong, the male opinion of the cuckold is that he's a guy who wasn't good enough in bed to keep his wife from straying. Rather than argue the point, I said, "There is another problem that is more up Marty's alley—her mental health."

Staring at the Bay to avoid looking at me, Fred said, "Too many boats."

"Head farther south," Tony said.

I turned south, cruising slowly. Fred and Tony left the bridge and walked out on the foredeck. Marty slid into the copilot's seat.

To Marty, I said, "She suffers from anxiety and depression and takes antipsychotic drugs."

"Antipsychotics? Prescribed by the psychiatrist she never sees in person?"

"Yep."

"That's unethical. You can't prescribe antipsychotics outside a formal treatment program. Give me the psychiatrist's name and I'll report her."

"I'll have to look it up in Carrie's medical records."

Tony overheard my remark and gave me a warning look.

Marty plowed ahead. "Is there an official diagnosis of antisocial personality disorder?"

Tony, jumping in, said, "We'll find out when the State shrinks get a look at her."

"It's beer o'clock," Fred shouted. "Who wants one?"

Tony and I raised our hands, and Fred played bartender, digging the beers out of the ice chest and delivering them. Marty asked for a Coke.

"What would it mean to be diagnosed with antisocial personality disorder?" I said.

"It would mean she has to take antipsychotics to control her behavior. Or she could get institutionalized, but nowadays you have to commit a crime to get institutionalized."

"She'd have to be a psychopath?"

"Or a sociopath," Marty said. "The clinical diagnosis of antisocial personality disorder is symptomatic of both psychopaths and sociopaths."

"Aren't they the same thing?"

Fred interrupted us. "Look back there to the north. That boat's been following us."

I swiveled in my chair and looked across the Bay at an array of boats. "Which one? There are a million boats."

"The one that's moving along with us, going slow," Fred said. "About a mile back."

All I could tell was that it was a small fishing boat. "Is it a Boston Whaler, Fred?"

Looking through the binoculars, Fred said, "Could be. Definitely a center console boat."

"Who owns a Boston Whaler?" Tony said.

"Carrie's daddy." To Fred I said, "Can you see who's on board?"

"Two men and a woman."

"Yellow bikini?"

"No. White top." Carrie must have covered herself in deference to her daddy.

"Hold on." I advanced the throttles and steered to the south, toward the Sunshine Skyway Bridge, careful to stay out of the shipping lanes.

"Are they coming?" I yelled to Fred.

"Yeah, they've picked up speed. Tracking us but not getting any closer."

"This is creepy," Marty said.

"Hold on again, everybody." I turned the *Wahine II* back to the north in as tight a circle as the big boat could handle and then opened the throttles as far as they would go. I was making twenty-two knots, heading straight for the fishing boat.

"Ha ha!" Fred said. "They've turned around, and they're moving fast. Away from us, heading toward the Gandy causeway."

I cut the throttles. No way we could catch a Boston Whaler.

"What was that all about?" Marty said.

"Carrie and her daddy, keeping a watch on me," I said.

"Why?"

"Because she's crazy," Tony said.

What did they think they could do? Board us like pirates and kill us all?

"I'm hungry," Fred said. "Anyone else hungry?"

The men shouted a chorus of affirmatives, so I headed toward Apollo Beach and Tony climbed down to the galley. He was the grill master.

As I cruised slowly toward the beach, I again picked up the conversation with Marty. "You were saying that psychopaths and sociopaths are not the same thing."

"Two sides of the same coin," Marty said, glad to be back on familiar conversational turf. "They are both antisocial, but their behavior is different."

"How so?"

Marty crossed his legs and spread his arms across the back of the loveseat. He enjoyed the opportunity to pontificate. "The hallmark of the antisocial personality is a lack of empathy, an inability to see things from other people's perspective. It's all about them."

"Sounds like Carrie."

"Sure. They act in their own self-interest without any pangs of conscience. What's good for them is always justifiable. But how they achieve their goals is different."

The little psychiatrist waited to see if I was following. On the foredeck, Fred scanned the horizon, but he was listening as well.

I said, "Yeah, go on."

"The psychopath is impulsive, quick to anger, doesn't plan well, isn't able to weigh consequences. They are usually extroverts."

"That's Carrie."

"You need a formal diagnosis by a psychiatrist to be sure," Marty said.

"Yeah, of course," I said, not wanting to offend my friend.

"The sociopath is in control of his emotions, plans his behavior meticulously, weighs possible outcomes. They are often introverts, loners. The psychopath is dangerous; the sociopath is extremely dangerous."

"Well, thank God for small favors. Carrie is only a psychopath."

Fred guffawed on the foredeck. Tony emerged from the galley with a tray of steaks swimming in marinade and corn on the cob wrapped in tin foil and headed down the stairs to the swim platform where my grill was mounted. Fred came up to the aft cabin, went to the ice chest, and distributed another round of beers. I coasted to within five hundred yards of the beach and cut the engines. In the still air, the smell of burning charcoal and roasting meat now rose from the stern to the bridge. Fred climbed down to the swim platform to keep Tony company.

I turned toward Marty and leaned forward with my elbows on my knees, poised for an intimate conversation. "I've tried to convince her to get better help, but she says I'm the one who's crazy, not her."

Marty smiled, pleased to be of value in this masculine social setting. "That's not surprising. Personality disorders are ego-syntonic."

"What does that mean?"

"It means she doesn't have the self-awareness or objectivity to know there's anything wrong with her. In fact, she thinks her behavior is perfectly reasonable and logical as a response to *your* behavior. *You're* the problem, not her."

"You've nailed her."

"I'm just parroting the textbooks. What you need to understand is that she isn't faking it when she blames you for something that was her fault. She's describing the circumstances as she honestly perceives them. She would be shocked to find that you have an opinion that's different from hers."

"What does society do about these people? If the disorders are ego-syntonic, the sickos don't know to get help for themselves so they slip through the cracks."

"Societywide, it's insoluble, but relative to your wife, the Baker Act petition is the best way to go. Let the professionals decide what should be done with her."

"Will she end up in an institution?"

"There aren't enough beds to lock all the sickos away, Randle. If she's borderline but not psychotic, she'll be treated as an outpatient."

"That's another gap in the mental health system: Until they commit a mass murder, the sickos are free to ruin our lives. And when they do commit a murder, we lock them in a penitentiary instead of an insane asylum. If the Baker Act examination doesn't work, maybe I can get Carrie to do something criminal. That would solve the problem."

The three men smiled indulgently, sure I was being facetious. The steaks were ready, so Tony handed them to me through the window and we all sat in the aft cabin to eat.

After he sampled his steak, Tony said, "At mediation we'll try for a deal that minimizes your ongoing involvement with Carrie, so you can avoid contact with the sicko."

"Why would I be involved with her? What happened to 'settle and go your merry way'?"

He smiled at me. "That just applies to the legal proceedings." Leaning forward into the circular group of men, he said, "You're lucky you don't have kids. You won't have to worry about custody, but you'll still be attached by property rights and alimony, credit histories, and debts and investments. The law doesn't cut those ties." Leaning back again, he delivered the punch line: "The only good news is that when you wake up in the morning, the head on the pillow next to yours won't be hers."

I lost my appetite. I set my plate on the coffee table, walked to the ice chest, and grabbed another beer. Leaning on the wet bar, I said, "I need a trial to prove I'm innocent and she's guilty."

Fred perked up. "Let me dig up some dirt on her so you can nail her in court."

Before I could discourage Fred, Tony climbed on his soapbox.

"Innocence and guilt are just concepts they teach in civics class. All the Constitution guarantees is due process. It makes no promise that every innocent person will be acquitted or that every guilty person will be convicted. Juries acquit people they like and convict people they dislike. It's that simple."

"The O.J. trial proved that," Fred said.

I snorted. "That makes it a game. Each side hires a proxy to climb in the ring and duke it out, and the winner is declared innocent and the loser is declared guilty. The proxies and the referee are motivated to determine a winner, but they aren't motivated to find the truth."

"Why are you getting hostile?" Tony said. "This is the way it works."

I couldn't allow *it* to work that way for me. After we ate, we dumped our scraps, paper plates, and beer bottles in the trash, then I started the engines and we cruised slowly westward, toward St. Petersburg. Fred and Tony stood at the bow with the binoculars, like lookouts on a warship, but only fishermen were out in the Bay. Harlan had disappeared.

After ensuring the boat was tied off and secure, I walked with my buddies to the parking lot and said my goodbyes. For a long time, I leaned against the fence that separated the walkway from the marina and watched the normal people in the park go about their normal lives, oblivious to the possibility that my wife had planned to kill me today. In the eighty-degree heat, I shivered. Mediation had to work or this situation was going to get out of hand.

CHAPTER EIGHTEEN

M y cell phone woke me from a disturbing dream as it vibrated off the bulkhead ledge and dropped into the bedclothes. I had trouble finding it, and, not sure if the call was business or personal—my eyes weren't focused enough to see the caller ID—I answered by saying, "Hello, this is Randle Marks."

"You lied to me again!" Connie shouted.

I pushed myself into a sitting position, my head touching the ceiling of the cramped stateroom. Weak daylight seeped through the Plexiglas hatch above my head. I had slept in the forward guest cabin so I would have a sight line to the entrance to the interior of the boat and would not be where an intruder would expect me to be. If anyone had entered the boat during the night, I could have watched as they came down three steps from the aft cabin and turned to port, toward the master stateroom in the stern, where the intruder would expect me to be sleeping. I could then have gotten the "drop" on the intruder from behind. Theoretically, under prevailing piracy laws, I could have shot the intruder with impunity.

Shaking my brain into working order, I said, "About what?"

"You said you would talk to Carrie, but then you didn't let her on the boat."

"I had people aboard, Connie." I rubbed my eyes, yawned, and tried to become alert enough to deal with her anger.

She huffed down the phone line. "Do you know how hard it was to convince her to go all the way down there and humble herself? She can't stand to appear submissive."

"She should have called first. She just turned up out of the blue at a bad time."

"Make up your mind, Randle. Are you willing to talk to her or not?"

I took a shot in the dark, pun intended. "If she came to talk, why was your daddy following me around on the Bay?"

Silence. Five long seconds of it. "He was there to rescue Carrie if anything went wrong with the negotiations."

Was Harlan her safety net, or were they stalking me to set up the kill? "Why follow me when Carrie wasn't on board?"

"To see if you met up with your ex-wife or some other girlfriend."

"I thought she had all the pictures she needed."

"They're not all that, ah, conclusive."

Scott-the-screw-up-PI didn't catch Glenda naked! "Was Travis with them?"

"Yes, he helped Daddy with the boat."

"Were they armed?"

Another hesitation from Connie. "Daddy always has a shotgun on the boat. He doesn't own a pistol."

Someone had my pistol, and it crossed my mind that it could be used to stage a suicide scene. On the other hand, a shotgun left no traceable ballistic evidence.

"Tell Carrie if she wants to meet she's got to give me advance notice."

Connie was silent for a long time. "I don't think she will now. Her lawyer is going to ambush you at mediation."

"I'm ready for her. Tell your sister I have more surprises as well."

<hr />

After coming fully awake, I dialed Jane Whitehead, the Realtor who had helped me buy the beach house and was now nominally the listing agent for it. Selling the beach house was now a priority. The neighborhood was nearly deserted since the snowbirds had migrated to Canada or New Jersey to escape the heat of the Florida summer. When my home had been broken into the first time, no one reported my alarm sounding in the middle of the night. Friday night, the break-in had aroused no suspicions, and yesterday no one came to investigate even though a squad car was parked in my driveway with its lights flashing. I needed to be in a place that was harder to attack without detection, a place that was easier to defend. I needed to be on my boat, not in the beach house.

Whitehead answered after just two rings, working on a Sunday to match naïve buyers with desperate sellers. "Randle! What a surprise. Why are you calling me?"

"I'm fine. Thank you for asking. And you? Are you well?"

Whitehead didn't answer immediately. I waited, and eventually she said, "Yes, I'm fine. You caught me off guard. Are you going to tell me to delist the house, come get my sign?"

"Exactly the opposite. I need to sell my house fast."

"That will make my broker happy. He keeps saying, 'Move it or lose it.' Did you lose your job or something?" After a pause, as though she'd had a flash of insight, she said, "No wait, it's a divorce, right?"

Is my life that pathetic? "It is a divorce, Jane. Good guess. Can you help me?"

With just a touch of sympathy, she said, "Oh, Randle, it's not a seller's market. What's your payoff balance?"

I told her.

"You're not going to make any money on it. You know that, right?"

"I know, but in the short term I can't afford it and in the long term I'll want to do something different. Give you some more business."

"I always appreciate the business. We can sell it, but to break even will take six to nine months."

That won't work. "Can't we do it any faster?"

"I could dump it on a speculator. They're everywhere now, gobbling up cheap property. When the market turns, they'll bulldoze your place and build a multistory mansion for a profit."

"How long would that take? To dump it?"

"Do you have fifty thousand dollars to put into the deal?"

"I do, actually," I said, thinking of the CD in my name.

"Two or three weeks. Maybe sooner."

I quickly calculated the timing relative to the scheduled mediation. It seemed the only solution and it could just work, so I said, "Okay, dump it."

———— ◦∞◦ ————

Intending to soften Carrie up before mediation, I wrote Tony another email that would get forwarded to Carrie's *shadylady44* account.

> **Tony,**
> **I've canvassed the boat owners on my dock and several confirmed they had seen Carrie at the boat with a man. I've created a list of the people we can depose. The list is attached.**
> **Randle**

There was no such list of witnesses, so the mail was sent "naked." I imagined Carrie checking my account hourly to find the next email that would transmit the missing list of witnesses. I imagined her phoning our boat dock neighbors to find the traitors who were willing to testify against her. The ruse cheered me up.

—∞∞—

Sunday afternoon, instead of taking Glenda out on the boat, I drove all the way to Lakeland, to Glenda's mother's house, for an afternoon of chitchat and an early dinner. I didn't want to expose Glenda to any highjinks on the water.

Glenda's mother, Ruth, made me feel like the prodigal son returning home. Together with my accomplice, enjoying the company of family, it felt like we were Bonnie and Clyde, on the lamb, and excitedly in love. Glenda was in a good mood because Wesley had agreed to settlement terms. She'd be single within thirty days. The best part of the day, however, was dinner. Ruth served fried oysters, fried okra, fried corn, black-eyed peas, and jalapeño cornbread. That's the way I wanted to eat, right up until a fat-induced heart attack ended my blissful life.

CHAPTER NINETEEN

I slid out of bed, padded into the galley, and used the Keurig to make a cup of coffee. With the coffee in hand, I climbed up to the aft cabin and watched the gulls and the kingfishers hunt their breakfast. After three days in the small spaces of the boat, claustrophobia had burrowed into my skull like a rat gnawing through a tenement wall. Loneliness intensified the sensation. Although our time together at the country house had been spent evading each other or spying on each other or claiming defensive positions in case of an attack, we were not lonely. Our mutual antipathy fueled our lives and filled them with purpose. Disgust and revulsion honed my senses and sharpened my concentration. Now, I couldn't work. For hours on end I gazed at the Bay, stared at the boats, replayed the events that led to a disastrous marriage and a traumatic divorce.

Finally, in the middle of the afternoon, Tony called. "Judge Smithson approved our Baker Act petition and ordered a show cause hearing on the 25th of September."

Three days before mediation. "Fantastic, Tony. Will the examination happen before mediation?"

"No way, Randle, but if an examination is ordered, your wife will come to the negotiating table with her arm in a hammerlock. That ought to please you. Just wanted to let you know that de Castro has been informed of the hearing and your wife will know soon enough."

I did my happy dance all around the confined spaces of the aft cabin and realized that in addition to enjoying the sparring match, I was elated over the prospect of the divorce. I had wanted a divorce all along, but I had lacked the courage to admit defeat and take action.

That evening, with a cigar and glass of port in hand, I checked my cloud account to see if there was any chatter about the Baker Act exam or if Carrie had found my last email about dock witnesses. Negative. She had spent considerable time on Facebook, posting messages on other people's walls and uploading photos of her dog, but there was no communication with her lawyer or with any boyfriends. *Odd.*

CHAPTER TWENTY

As the young parent of a precocious and headstrong girl, I had asked my father how I should judge my parenting skills. Parenthood, he told me, is a job with modest goals. If Jamie reached the age of eighteen without going to jail, getting pregnant, or becoming a drug addict, he said I could congratulate myself for a job well done. The truth is that her mother and I had had little to do with how Jamie turned out. We fed her, loved her, protected her from the worst dangers of childhood, but we did little to shape her character. The highly moral, disciplined, college-educated Tampa cop she became was all her own doing.

I had to hunt for Jamie's address, written on a scrap of paper two years ago, because I had never been to her apartment and hadn't updated her contact information in my phone. Luckily, I found the note, plugged her address into Google Maps, and headed for Tampa. The GPS took me north on Dale Mabry, toward Raymond James Stadium, and then east to a spot between Himes and MacDill Avenues, not far from Macfarlane Park. It was a quiet neighborhood with trees and shrubs and kids on bikes and skateboards. The apartment complex was a bit long in the tooth but seemed well kept. Jamie's home was on the second floor, overlooking the parking lot.

When she answered the door, we kissed cheeks and I handed her a bottle of Jordan Chardonnay.

"Thanks," she said. "We're having meatloaf, but I'll save this for next time."

She told me I should help myself to a glass of Kendall Jackson Cabernet or a beer from the refrigerator. I opted for the beer and followed her out the other side of her apartment to a small balcony facing a greenbelt. On the way, I passed through rooms that were neat and furnished in a style that could be called "I'm all grown up now." Gone were the posters and makeshift furnishings of the college apartments I had last visited.

When we were seated on plastic outdoor furniture, she said, "I'm glad you came."

"Me too. I hope we can do this often now."

Jamie and Carrie didn't like each other. After one year of marriage, Jamie had stopped attending Tomkins family events, always courteously declining invitations with work or illness excuses. "It might ruin the occasion if I ripped her face off in front of her family," Jamie had told me. As a result, the frequency of our meetings had diminished to an occasional lunch. I was never more than twenty miles north in Cortes County or twenty miles to the south in Pinellas County, but I may as well have been on another continent.

"How's the divorce going?" she said.

An icebreaker if I'd ever heard one. "It's become nasty. Last spring she installed snooping software on my laptop so she can read my email. But I discovered it, and the day I moved out of the country house I installed a snooper on her machine so I can see everything she does."

"That's illegal."

"I guess, but it's very helpful. I send fake emails to my lawyer and watch her reaction. She's quite sensitive to charges of infidelity, but I don't have any proof. The courts won't let me subpoena her phone records."

"Sounds like you're both making it nasty. It's just about money, isn't it?"

It strikes me that people who have no money—like Jamie—can be very casual about it, can pretend money is unimportant.

"For her, yes. For me it's more about fairness."

Jamie looked at me the way most rational people look at people who believe in astrology. "Blah, blah, blah. Just pay her off and move on."

"I'm not going to let her rip me off. They broke into my house and stole my financial records, records that prove Carrie's spending habits."

Jamie rose to refill her wineglass. "Can I bring you another beer?"

"Sure." Talking to her back as she walked into the kitchen, I said, "Last Friday they broke in and stole my pistol so I'd be unarmed."

That stopped her. She whirled around. "Did you report it to the police?"

"Of course." That made her feel better, too much better, so I said, "Connie says the whole family is conspiring to murder me if the divorce doesn't go their way."

Jamie handed me my beer and sat back down.

"Bunch of crazy crackers," she said dismissively. "Have you reported the threats to the police?"

"What good would it do?"

Jamie gave me the half-smile mothers give their children instead of saying "Duh!" "There would be a report on file. For the detectives, if anything did happen."

"So the cops can solve my murder? That doesn't do me much good. I need help defending myself, thought maybe I could count on you."

"You didn't want me to be a cop, now you want me to help you unofficially? Go to the authorities, Dad." Anger rode just below the waves.

"It scares me that you're a cop, but that has nothing to do with my situation. The murder plot is just hearsay, nothing useful to the police."

"You shouldn't be talking to Connie."

"She's my only source of information, to keep me safe. Reminds me to tell you I'm selling the beach house. It's too dangerous to stay there."

She bounced to her feet. "Here it comes. You're running away again."

"No, it's a safety issue." Jamie wore a skeptical frown. "And a money issue. I'm moving onto the boat until my company goes public. If the IPO goes well and the divorce doesn't destroy me, I'll buy something better. If things go wrong, I can't afford two houses and alimony and all the other debts."

"I'd like to believe you, Dad, but you've established a pattern of behavior, as they say."

She led me into the kitchen, where we made our plates of meatloaf, garlic mashed potatoes, and mixed peas and carrots. Then we sat at her round glass-topped dining table. The meatloaf was excellent, and I told her so.

"Mom's recipe. You always liked it."

"She taught you to make it?"

"Yes. I learned a lot of things when you weren't around." She didn't say it in a mean or provocative way. It was just a fact.

"Okay," I said, and stopped eating. "Let's admit that there's a big pink elephant in the room, and we can't ignore it any longer. I looked forward to coming over tonight because it gives me a chance to apologize for not being around enough as you were growing up. I'm sorry, Jamie."

After judging my sincerity, she said, "Apology accepted. I know you had to travel, Dad, but it was extreme. We weren't a family. We were just people you mailed checks to until you divorced Mom."

"I did what I had to do to support you guys."

"We always had enough money, but we never had enough 'Dad.' I know it's selfish, but I wanted two parents who lived together and cared about me."

"We waited until you were old enough to deal with it." I tried not to sound argumentative.

"A child is never old enough to deal with it. You made matters worse by toying with Mom's affections. She kept her life on hold waiting for you."

"I see that now." She had me on the run.

"As soon as you divorced Mom, you shipped me off to college and you left for Texas."

"Only for a while. I was back by the time you graduated."

"Back to Atlanta. By then Mom had moved to Florida, and I didn't know where I belonged. As soon as I moved to Atlanta, you moved down here. Then you met Carrie, and I never saw you again."

Now I was in full-retreat mode. "I hope I can make it up to you now."

"There's always hope. We're all in the same state, and you'll be rid of Carrie soon. So if you hang around, maybe we can get to know each other."

"I'd like that."

"I won't move again, Dad."

"I know that."

"And Mom is strictly off-limits."

"We have to talk about that."

"No we don't!" she screamed.

That stopped me. If we were going to be honest with each other, it had to start now. "She's left Wesley, and she's staying with your grandmother. Did you know that?"

"No, no, no. You guys are killing me, Dad!"

"I didn't have anything to do with it. Apparently there's been trouble in that paradise too."

She gave me a hard look, shaking her head and causing her auburn hair to sway from one side to the other like a grass skirt on a Hawaiian dancer. "I know she wants you, but do you want her?"

"I shouldn't have divorced her. That's what started this ugly sequence of events."

"That's not the same as wanting a permanent relationship. Permanent, Dad."

"We're not that far along. I just wanted to be honest with you."

"So you're fooling around again but haven't talked about the future?"

Anger enveloped me, and I couldn't completely shake it off. Everyone seemed to feel that my personal life was fair game for criticism. "Whether we're fooling around or not is none of your business. We are talking and we'll reach a mature decision and it will be our decision."

Now her face twisted into a wry smile. "Sure. I guess I should be happy you bothered to tell me."

It was awkward for a while as we cleared the dishes and started the dishwasher.

Then Jamie said, "Why did you dump Susanne? She was strange, but she was nice and smart. If you had stayed with her, you'd have avoided these problems with Carrie."

I shrugged. "Susanne was like medicine I took to get well after your mom and I divorced. When I was well, I didn't need the medicine."

"That's a pretty crappy way to look at relationships, Dad."

She had used the evening to give me a whipping behind the woodshed. "Wrong choice of words. Susanne was a nice part of my life, but I didn't think she was the woman I should be with forever."

Jamie gave me a pass with a shrug. Neither of us was quite sure how to end the evening, and it was obvious we were both uneasy. To fill time, I went to the refrigerator for another beer.

"Two's the limit, Dad. You have to drive."

She was serious; cop on duty.

"Good advice. Listen, I had a terrific evening and—"

"Are you interested at all in what's happening in my life?"

"I wasn't going to pry."

"It's not prying, Dad. It's showing an interest."

I felt like I'd been slapped. "Yes, I'm interested. Do you need anything?"

"You mean money? No, Dad, I can afford myself. You and Carrie can fight over the money."

I needed more practice at this. "So what else is happening?"

"Nothing, but thanks for asking. I have friends, but none with benefits. Ha ha!" I chuckled along with her. "I recently broke up with a guy I was seeing. A cop. Cops—male cops—are all alike. Their badge and their gun are substitutes for masculinity and a healthy ego."

"Compensating."

"Huh?"

"It's called compensating. Firearms, Corvettes, badges, and uniforms. They're compensations for other shortcomings."

"And would collecting younger women be how you compensate, Dad?"

I suppose. Glenda was eight years my junior, Carrie fourteen. Susanne was two full decades younger. Following that pattern, I'd soon be dating a teenager.

We hugged and promised to see each other again soon. We were well intentioned. As I shuffled across the parking lot, I thought I now knew how Catholic penitents felt after confessing their sins to a priest—relief, mixed with the vain hope that the little ceremony actually worked. My soul didn't feel cleansed after confessing my sins to Jamie; it felt soiled and pitted by its encounter with the unvarnished truth.

Not wanting to be lulled into a false sense of security, however, that night I slept in the guest stateroom again, kept the Beretta loaded and cocked on the ledge beside me, and quaked when the boat rocked in its slip.

CHAPTER TWENTY-ONE

At first light on Thursday, I rolled out of the sack, performed my bathroom ritual, and brewed a cup of coffee. Today I would meet Glenda to hide out for the weekend, à la Bonnie and Clyde style, so I had to pack a bag.

Glenda had suggested we go to Asheville, North Carolina, in the mountains, for a romantic dalliance, and that had unleashed a waterfall of unpleasant memories. The Tomkins family had taken a group vacation to Asheville in the spring, and it had been a disaster. While the rest of the family stayed in one large house, Carrie and I had rented a cabin for ourselves so we could hide our marital problems. One night, after dinner with the family, we had returned to our cabin and changed into bedclothes. Carrie found *True Blood* on TV and settled in for a dose of mommy porn. I sat beside her and tried to get her interested in real-life sex. Although Carrie forbade me to surf for porn, she had watched the *Twilight* movies, the *True Blood* series, and read *Fifty Shades of Grey* and both sequels.

It annoyed me that she'd rather indulge in fantasies than have a real sex life with me, so I tried to melt her icy exterior, but Carrie rebuffed me and became infuriated at my advances. Frustrated, I had stood up to leave the room and said, "If you ever get the urge to be a real wife, let me know."

"Alright! If it means that much to you, go ahead and do what you want!" She had pulled up her white cotton nightgown, pulled down her white cotton panties, and spread her legs. That's how I discovered the Brazilian wax job. And for whom had she done that bit of landscaping?

If I could avoid it, I would never go to Asheville again. Disappointed, Glenda invited me to spend the weekend with her at her mother's house instead. As I packed, Tony called my cell phone. I put it on speaker and set it on the dresser so my hands were free.

"I just got an update from de Castro," Tony said.

Carrying clothes from the dresser to the bed, I said, "More bad news?" I went to the closet and grabbed jeans and shorts.

"She's going to file a motion to dismiss your countersuit. De Castro also said we'd be sorry if the case goes to trial."

Piling the last of my clothes onto the bed, I said, "Best thing I've heard all day. Means we've struck a nerve."

"The judge will dismiss your countersuit if you don't come up with some evidence of Carrie's infidelity."

Double-checking the clothes I had gathered, I decided against socks. I hated socks. "I'm working on it."

"Naked pictures and hotel receipts, Randle. Nothing less."

I stuffed the last clothes into my suitcase. "I get it. What about Puralto?"

"Got Fred doing a background check."

It appeared I had everything I needed for the weekend. "When's the Baker Act hearing?"

"Tomorrow at nine a.m. Are you out of town?"

"On my way. Call me with the results."

Tony promised he would call.

After I zipped up my bag I called Officer Brittany Williams at the Dolphin Beach police department. She said the little department was overworked with serious crimes but that a detective should call within "a couple of days" if no higher priority cases were booked in the interim. *Right.*

Before I could get out the door and on the way to Lakeland, Jane Whitehead called and said she had a buyer for me.

"How much will it cost me?"

"You'll have to put forty-five thousand dollars into the deal."

"Does that include your commission?"

"Yeah, that's everything."

"When can we close?"

"Friday the 9th of October work for you?"

"I'll be there."

To fund the deal, I would cash the CD I had managed to keep out of Carrie's hands. The arithmetic worked nicely—the remaining five thousand dollars would go to Tony to cover my legal expenses.

Before World War II, Ruth's home, on the eastern edge of Lakeland, had been a rooming house for travelers making the then arduous trek from the Central Florida orange groves to the big city of Tampa. The white wood-frame structure stood two stories tall, with eight small bedrooms and one shared bathroom on the second floor and large communal rooms on the ground floor. Built long before fiberglass insulation and central heat and air were common, the house could be stifling in the summer and surprisingly cold in the winter. One year a cold wave had penetrated the South, and as we packed the car in Atlanta with Christmas presents, the thermometer hovered near zero. We—Glenda, Jamie, and I—were thrilled to be heading farther south to what we imagined would be a warm, if nontraditional, Florida holiday, but we did not outrun the cold wave. On Christmas Day, it was nineteen degrees in Lakeland. Shivering, we wrapped ourselves in blankets to open presents before we climbed into our car and dashed back to our properly heated Atlanta home.

As I wound through the grove of pecan trees that guarded the driveway, I saw Glenda in the swing on the front porch—she's hard to miss with all that red hair. As I parked, she came down the steps to meet me. She was smoking.

"Are you nervous?" I said.

"A little."

I gave her a bear hug. "It'll be okay. I don't leave my socks on the floor, and I put the toilet seat down."

"It's three days together in the same room, Randle."

"I lived with you for eighteen years, so I know what I'm getting into."

"Don't you ever get nervous?"

"Not around you."

"And do you always say the right things?"

"It helps to be with the right woman."

"See?" She heaved a sigh. "Alright, let's go have lunch with Momma."

I followed her into the house and admired my roommate. Today her hair was pinned up, and she wore a sleeveless blouse and modest shorts that exposed her long, shapely limbs. Around her neck was a fragile necklace with a small pendant holding a semiprecious stone that might have been aquamarine or topaz. Sandals finished Glenda's ensemble and revealed pretty feet with blue toenails. To me, blue said, I'm unique and have unusual tastes.

Once again, Ruth extended a warm Southern hospitality I didn't really deserve after dumping her daughter seven years ago. After a lunch of cold cucumber salad, cold macaroni salad, and cold potato salad, washed down by iced tea so sweet my teeth ached, we repaired to the massive sitting room and talked about the good ol' days, carefully avoiding anything controversial or embarrassing. Soon Ruth nodded off in her recliner, and Glenda joined me on a fifty-year-old burgundy velour couch.

After a bit, she said, "We'll be better this time, won't we?"

"A lot of things have changed. Jamie is grown and on her own; I'm not chasing success anymore. After AMA goes public, I'll be more like a volunteer helper to the medical industry, so I'll have a lot more time to devote to us."

"And I have a team I trust at the shop," she said. "It's not my entire universe anymore."

"If we make it all about us, it will work."

She smiled and leaned into me. "I love you."

It wasn't difficult to tell her that I loved her too.

Southern families revolve around food and gatherings for meals. Ruth prepared fried chicken for dinner, and then we laughed along with her as she enjoyed her favorite TV programs. As the evening dragged on, ennui and angst attacked my being like parasites crawling through my veins. Soon I'd be sleeping with my ex-wife for the first time in many years. Tomorrow morning a judge would decide whether my current wife should be examined by State psychiatrists.

Finally, Glenda said, "Let's call it a night."

In our room, Glenda used the bathroom first. When she emerged, she wore a plain cotton gown that touched her knees. I must have betrayed my disappointment, because she wagged a finger at me and said, "No, not in my mother's house."

She got into bed and propped herself on a pair of pillows. Pointing to the bathroom, she said, "Your turn. I want to see if you've got Sponge Bob Square Pants pajamas."

I unbuckled my belt and dropped my shorts on the floor, pulled my Polo over my head, and did a pirouette. "I forgot to pack the PJs, but we can buy some in town."

Glenda squealed with delight. "Don't take all night in there. I want you next to me."

I found Glenda's toiletries stacked on the far end of the double-sink vanity, leaving the rest of the countertop clear—a welcome distinction from Carrie, who was a walking bomb, exploding and spreading Carrie-shrapnel everywhere she went. It was a power play, a land grab. I brushed my teeth and peed. When I returned to the bedroom, Glenda was still awake, still propped up. She patted the side of the bed next to her.

I crawled under the covers and she rolled into me and laid her head on my shoulder. We adjusted positions a couple of times and settled on spooning. She felt good. Out of the blue, she said, "You feel good."

When Glenda emerged from the bathroom Friday morning, I sat at the dresser with my back to her, appearing to be engrossed in the text messages I was trading with colleagues as there was no Wi-Fi in Ruth's house. The bath towel wasn't large enough to wrap around her and tuck, so she had to hold it together with one hand as she groped in the chest of drawers for underwear with her other hand. She glanced at me and, satisfied that I was occupied, dropped the towel to put on her bra. I watched her the entire time in the mirror above the dresser. As she fastened her bra, she caught me spying on her.

"You can peek, but it's not polite to stare."

"I'm fascinated by the process—women hurry to cover their breasts while they leave their, ah, lower half, exposed."

One eyebrow arched, but she didn't hurry when she reached for her panties. "I'm sure you have much more experience with how women dress than I do."

Abashed, I said, "You're the only woman I want to watch."

I turned back to my text messages and didn't look up, so in a conciliatory voice she said, "Hit the shower, big boy. You have the rest of your life to watch me."

I took a quick shower, and after declining Ruth's offer to cook yet another meal, we drove into town to have breakfast at a diner. Before we got back to Ruth's house, my cell phone rang. It was Tony.

"I beat her, buddy."

"Way to go, Tony. When is the examination?"

"September 30th, next Wednesday. De Castro complained that the Baker Act was just a way to disrupt the divorce and should be deferred until the divorce is final, but I told the judge you've been trying to get her help for years, but your wife wouldn't maintain a treatment program. That's one of the criteria for an exam—that the patient won't participate voluntarily. It worked!"

"Super, Tony. Where will she be examined?"

"Wherever they find a bed." Then Tony switched back to talking about today's events in court. "Then de Castro puts your wife's psychologist on the stand, and she testifies that Mrs. Marks isn't mentally ill, she's just depressed about her failing marriage and has anxiety attacks because she worries you'll cheat her out of the money. So I walk her through your deposition and you know what? Carrie hadn't revealed any of those incidents to the counselor. So your wife had never been treated for any of her real symptoms of mental illness."

"I told you that was the case. How do they know Carrie will show up for the exam?"

"She'll be picked up Tuesday evening at six p.m. by a sheriff's deputy." That didn't answer my question—will she allow herself to be picked up—but Tony was on a roll. "The judge was particularly upset about the incident where she cut herself with the hedge trimmer and didn't want you to stop the bleeding, because that implies she might hurt herself. And then the incidents in which she attacked you were important because they imply she might hurt others. Another criterion for an involuntary examination."

"Cool. Did you give him the prescription records?"

"Oh yeah. The prescription records were the icing on the cake. The judge wanted to put the psychiatrist on the stand, but de Castro didn't have the psychiatrist in court, so the judge says, 'Obviously, the psychiatrist feels Mrs. Marks requires antipsychotics, so we'll accept that as her testimony.' Then he orders the examination, and de Castro is shocked that it will happen so soon. Isn't that great?"

"It's terrific, Tony. Buy yourself a drink and have a nice weekend."

Tony wanted to bask in more glory, but I cut him off so I could internalize this major victory. People told me I should be sad and depressed about the divorce, and for a while I had been, and maybe when it was over I would be again, but at that moment I was elated. Often were the times I became so infuriated with Carrie's behavior that I wanted to punch her lights out, break her long Irish nose, bash in the pearly-white smile I had paid to perfect. Now I had done it figuratively. Pow! Take that!

My elation was no match for the cloying ambience at Ruth's house. She wanted to play cards, so we passed the day playing gin rummy. Ruth won consistently. In a good mood, she cooked catfish for dinner, breaded and deep-fried, of course. If I married into this family again, I'd be signing my death warrant.

Once again, the television anesthetized us through the evening and then we retired to our bedroom to sleep chastely, albeit with arms and legs entangled like snakes in a den. It felt good to both of us.

———✄———

Saturday it rained. Hard. Glenda suggested we drive to Tampa and find something to do indoors. An hour later, she parked in front of the Tampa Bay Grand Prix, an indoor go-kart track. "You game?" she said.

"Is that a challenge?"

"Take it any way you want, Bubba."

She was out of the car and running to the entrance before I could manufacture a smart retort, so I followed her onto the track.

From our first ride, it was clear that Glenda wanted to compete. I was placed in a kart several positions ahead of her, but she jumped the starter's signal and flew past me on the outside. I got trapped in kiddie traffic and never caught up. When it was over, we went to the back of the line to wait for another turn.

"You cheated."

She grinned. "If you're not cheating, you're not trying." I had no idea she knew that old sports bromide.

She won the second race too. No matter what I tried, I just could not keep pace. I slid through turns NASCAR-style, stayed inside to shorten the track, and tried the police maneuver of tapping her inside back tire to make her spin out. Nothing worked. Glenda knew the correct line to take around the course and stood on the accelerator. There was no stopping her.

When I finally won a race, she said, "I had a bad car." I believed her.

Several races later, I won again and she said, "I let you win. I don't want to destroy your self-confidence."

Overall, Glenda won three of every four races. She was exhilarated, as happy as a kid who got everything she wanted on Christmas.

After hours of racing, we called it a day. There was no one home at the house, but Ruth had left us a note on the dining room table. Her church group had picked her up for an afternoon of Bingo. We had reached the go/no-go point in our rekindled relationship. Glenda gave me a naughty smile, took my hand, and led me up the stairs. We locked the bedroom door and simultaneously undressed each other.

When she was naked, I said, "You're gorgeous."

She gave me a tentative smile. Then she tumbled on top of me and the trouble began. Suddenly we were all knees and elbows and hipbones; movements started and abandoned; arrhythmic thrusts; missed cues; awkward tugging and pulling and pushing. Although we had done this hundreds of times, we were now strangers starting anew. Sadly, we were more accustomed to the patterns of other people, and it hurt to realize that Glenda had learned new moves from other men.

When it was over, we did not lie in bed whispering sweet nothings to one another. Naked, we padded to the back balcony overlooking five acres of pecan trees.

She sat in a rocker, legs crossed, feet dangling, smoking a cigarette. "I'm not nervous," she said.

"I can see that." I lit a cigar and we rocked in unison, gazing at the orchard. It was pleasant with a hint of sexual tension. If she insisted upon walking around naked, I would insist on an encore.

Sounding philosophical, she said, "It takes practice."

"We'll get better at it."

"We'd better, or someone will get hurt." We laughed.

"I have bruises everywhere." We laughed harder, calling attention to ourselves if anyone was listening.

"Something poked me in the eye, but I have no idea what it was." Louder laughter.

"I can guess, but it would sound like bragging."

She choked on her cigarette smoke, coughed, and slapped her chest. When she recovered, she said, "Your ego is the biggest thing you've got."

Waving my cigar like a conductor's baton, I said, "You are a fine musical instrument, my dear, in the hands of the maestro."

"Ha! Too much of the woodwinds and not enough brass and percussion, maestro."

Good-naturedly, I said, "Whatever you wish, my dear."

It was left at that for a while, and I had time to marvel at how comfortable it was to be sitting beside my ex-wife, trading quips, relaxing, enjoying her proximity.

Then she blurted a surprising admission. "It was my fault. I was out of sync with you."

My immediate reaction was to let her off the hook. "I didn't give you a chance to settle into a rhythm."

"No, I tried to control everything. I wanted to show you that I could be as sexy as the women you've been with since me. That was silly. Next time you lead, Randle, and I'll follow. Like we're dancing."

"All I want to do is dance with you."

She looked at me as though she could read my mind by staring at my forehead, where my thoughts might scroll by like the electronic newsfeed in Times Square. I guess she saw what she wanted to read because she said, "I love you, Randle."

"I love you too."

We never heard the car coming up the driveway, but we heard the car doors slamming shut. In a panic, as Ruth called our names from downstairs, we scrambled from the balcony back to the bedroom and into our clothes. When we walked down the stairs, blushing and out of breath, Ruth gave us an indulgent smile. She knew what we had done . . . had perhaps planned her afternoon away.

In the morning, I packed my bag in silence.

"You okay?" Glenda said.

I assured her I was fine, but I don't think she believed it.

Before she could challenge my assertion, Connie called my cell. "Where are you?"

"Away for the weekend."

"With your ex, no doubt. Carrie went to the boat, but you weren't there."

"How many times do I have to say that she needs to let me know when she's coming?"

"She doesn't want you to set a trap for her, Randle."

I didn't bother to remind her that it was Carrie who had concocted a murder plot. Frustrated, I said, "Well, she blew it. Now we'll just have to see how mediation turns out." I rang off.

Glenda said, "Let the lawyers handle it. Don't talk to that bitch."

Probably good advice. Glenda went quiet again. She gave me the by now well-known stare. Not a glaring look and not a mean look, just a look of concentration, wanting to read the answer from my expression.

She cleared her throat. "Was this weekend just another one of our flings?"

"No." I shook my head. "No."

Her head bobbed slowly, like a teacher guiding a student through some convoluted logic and making progress. "Was it a test?"

"Every day is a test for a relationship. We know we love each other, but a relationship requires more than love."

"How did I do?"

"I'm still upset about the go-kart track, but otherwise you were better than average."

"Dammit, Randle. You don't have to be flippant all the time."

"Sorry. It was a test for both of us, and I think we did well. What do you think?"

She leaned into my chest and nuzzled. "We're good together. I love you, Randle. Don't leave me on an island."

"Or at the altar." Trying to be funny.

A big smile lit up her face. "You've thought about it?"

"Of course," I lied. "When this is all over—"

"Can I move in with you? My mother is driving me crazy."

That opened Pandora's Box and the discussion lasted for twenty minutes. I told her almost everything—the PI, the email snooper, the inability to obtain subpoenas, the unfair option split, the break-ins and the theft of my pistol, the sale of the beach house, the Baker Act petition, my threat of a trial—and Glenda's sense of foreboding increased with each point.

"My God, Randle! You've started World War III. Let the mediator deal with her."

"I'm not going to settle for a bad deal."

"We need to get on with our lives, Randle. I don't care about money and neither do you. At least you didn't while we were married."

I inhaled and held it. "I can't work forever, Glenda, and I refuse to work merely to fund Carrie's future. I need enough money to quit AMA so I can write and lecture and spread the word about my work. If mediation works, great. Otherwise, we go to trial."

She took a minute to think about her next comment. "A trial is a backup for a failed mediation?"

"Yes, but I have no concrete evidence. Her affair happened long ago, and there are no naked pictures or hotel receipts."

"Then make mediation work, Randle. I'm ready to get married."

"We have to tell Jamie. About us."

"Leave her to me. She trusts me."

CHAPTER TWENTY-TWO

t was a nice weather day, so I walked with Tony from his office tower on the north side of downtown St. Petersburg to the mediator's office on the seedier south side. As we walked, I considered how many things in my life were undecided: Jamie wanted me to morph into a good father; Glenda wanted to remarry; Connie wanted me to cooperate today or be murdered; AMA might or might not survive to go public. And who was responsible for this state of affairs? Me. Now we were on our way to the financial execution of J. Randle Marks.

I pulled an oversized rolling briefcase behind me, stuffed to overflowing with records, files, and photos that documented my unhappy marriage. Tony found my preparations amusing and said, "Drag it with you wherever we go. Scare the hell out of the ladies."

The mediator's office was a windowed storefront formerly occupied by a failed retailer, and Ross Smallwood turned out to be a gray-bearded black man who was well beyond full retirement age. I sincerely hoped he harbored old-fashioned ideas about marriage and fidelity. The old guy showed us to a small conference room with a window looking out to the side alley. Noting my dismissive glance, he said, "You got the luxury accommodation. Their room has no windows at all. Seems to make people more reasonable 'cause they wanna get out of that place."

I chuckled, but I was nervous. Smallwood told us that Ms. de Castro and Mrs. Marks were waiting in the main conference room. The session would start there, with a briefing about the procedure to be followed, after which the two sides would retreat to their private spaces. Then Smallwood would shuttle back and forth with proposals and counterproposals until we reached agreement.

Referring to my rolling filing cabinet, Smallwood said, "You can leave your things here. The briefing only takes a minute."

Ignoring him, I dragged the briefcase with me as I trailed him and Tony to the main conference room. De Castro rose as we entered and shook hands with Tony.

She said, "I hope this is the last time we'll see each other."

Smallwood butted in with, "That's the idea."

Carrie didn't rise, and I didn't offer my hand. Instead I avoided eye contact, pretended she wasn't present, pretended I didn't notice that she was deeply tanned and had brushed her hair like a boy's again. She wore the yellow-diamond pendant and earrings too.

I paused at the head of the table as Tony and Smallwood took their seats. Without being too conspicuous, I waited until I was sure de Castro noticed the briefcase. When she frowned, I knew that my first objective had been achieved—they knew I was prepared. I took the seat directly across from Carrie, who had her hands in her lap like a demure little girl.

Smallwood reiterated the procedure and concluded with, "When we're done I'll have the terms typed up and both parties will sign. Then one of the attorneys"—he looked from de Castro to Tony—"can prepare the marital dissolution agreement. Are we ready?"

Everyone nodded. He said, "I'll start with the defendant, see what we've got to divide."

Wanting to show us how tough she could be, de Castro objected. "The property is community property, not the defendant's property."

Smallwood said, "Spare me the semantics lesson, Bobbie. This ain't my first rodeo. I'll get the lay of the land then come to you for the first proposal. How's that sound?"

Chagrined smiles popped up all around, then the teams split up and went to their respective rooms. Smallwood joined Tony and me and sat at the head of the table. He had a document in his hands that he referred to as he said, "Okay, Tony was good enough to give me a financial summary. Let's work our way through that." Without acquiescence, he read from the paper: "You have an IRA worth seventy-five thousand dollars, a CD for fifty thousand dollars, and a 401K with forty-five thousand dollars in it. State law says it all gets split fifty/fifty."

I was about to speak, but Tony beat me to it. "The IRA is premarital, Ross. Matthews-Bryant has already ruled on it."

Smallwood made a note and said, "Alright. That's done. Easy peasy." Going down the list, he further said, "You have two homes, both furnished. She's in one, you're in the other. You each get the home you occupy."

Again, Tony spoke before I could assemble my thoughts. "The home Mr. Marks occupies is premarital property. The home in Cortes County, where Mrs. Marks is temporarily lodged, is community property to be divided."

Smallwood said, "That ain't gonna fly, Tony. You know that."

I decided not to mention that the beach house was sold. This was moving too fast, and I didn't want to make a mistake.

Tony said, "We're willing to give up the house, but we need consideration in return."

Smallwood nodded in understanding. "You boys wanna act tough to start, that's okay by me, but we know where we're gonna end up, don't we?"

Tony said, "When we get to the debt part, you'll see our point."

Smallwood said, "In just a minute. Let's talk about the cars first. You got two, and you each drive one. We okay with that?"

I had learned to wait for Tony, who said, "No, Ross. The Jaguar is on lease to Mr. Marks. Mrs. Marks can buy her own vehicle."

Smallwood sighed. "Thought this might be an easy one, but I guess not." He used a pencil to scribble on the financial statement.

Tony and Smallwood were discussing my future as though I weren't even in the room. It felt as though I were in a hospital bed and doctors in the hallway were deciding whether to save me or let me die.

Smallwood, motioning with his head at me, said, "All the debt is in his name, and they'll want him to service the debt—that's forty-five thousand dollars in credit cards, his car loan, his house, her house."

Tony said, "We're okay with the credit cards, his house, his car. The house she temporarily occupies is a different story. There are two liens: the construction loan and a home equity line of credit."

Tony motioned to me, and I extracted the file I had stolen from Carrie's nightstand. He opened the file, pulled out a statement, and slid it in front of Smallwood. As the old guy looked it over, Tony narrated.

"The home is valued at five hundred fifty to six hundred thousand dollars. The original construction loan has a payoff of four hundred thousand dollars. On top of that, they have a home equity account. Mrs. Marks managed the account, wrote all the checks."

Tony slid two handfuls of checks toward Smallwood. "Mrs. Marks has spent the entire account limit of a hundred fifty thousand dollars and wrote the checks to herself, so there's no way to trace the funds."

Smallwood's eyebrows shot up, nearly touching his hairline. "So what's your ask on the house?"

Tony said, "If Mrs. Marks wants to live in it, she has to pay for it."

"All of it?" Smallwood asked. "Construction and home equity?" *Already thinking of a compromise.*

"All of it," Tony said. "We'll deduct the outstanding amounts from her settlement and cure the debts to get Mr. Marks off the loans."

As though struggling to break out of a trance, Smallwood shuffled his papers and consulted a different sheet. He said, "Um-hum. And what's your position on stock options? Judge ordered sixty thousand options apiece with eighty thousand still to be divided. What you gonna give her outta that?"

Tony gave him an exaggerated shrug, both palms up and lips pursed. "Maybe ten thousand? She already got fifteen thousand more than she should have."

Smallwood said, "Yeah, Phyllis may have gone overboard on the shares that vested before the marriage. But if you don't give her any more, Phyllis will do it for you."

I was impressed that Smallwood felt comfortable calling the judge by her first name. Maybe there's an age at which decorum and courtesy can be abandoned, like a reward for growing old. Neither Tony nor Smallwood knew that the IPO date had slipped into next year, and I wasn't ready to tell them.

I said, "I'm not going to give her any more options. Her share is already worth nearly a million dollars, and she didn't earn it as a wife, believe me."

"Lotta money," Smallwood said, nodding his head and scribbling on his yellow pad. He looked up. "But this is just the division of assets, so there's alimony to consider as well."

Tony said, "We don't believe Mrs. Marks requires any alimony since she'll get a boatload of stock. She'll be wealthy, won't require monthly maintenance."

Hoping the old guy was a churchgoer with a traditional sense of propriety, I added, "She violated the marriage contract by committing adultery."

The room went dead as a scowl formed on Smallwood's jawline and crept slowly upward, clouding his eyes. Morality had been injected into a cut-and-dried division of wealth, and he didn't like it. He said, "You established a very high standard of living for the young lady, and she has a lot of years to live. Judge is goin' ta give her something, young man."

Tony shot me an "I told you so" look, which I ignored. *How does it make sense that the better you treat a woman during a marriage, the more you have to pay her when divorced? That just encourages golddiggers, doesn't it?*

I said, "Our lifestyle wasn't established by me and was never supported by my income. The lifestyle was funded by debt, and my wife created all the debt." I lifted a thick file folder out of my briefcase and dropped it on the table with a thud. Recreating that file had cost me an entire night's sleep, and it only contained monthly statements from credit cards and joint bank accounts. I riffled the documents like a Vegas card dealer and said, "If I have to fund the past by paying the debt, I shouldn't have to enable the future as well. Shouldn't she get what she deserves now as opposed to what she didn't deserve in the past?"

Smallwood considered me with a measure of respect. "Good point, young man. Let me go see what they're thinking. They'll be nervous about how much time I spent with you."

I hoped they were as nervous as I was. My strategy before entering this room had been to hold the moral high ground and take a hard line on all issues. But now that we were engaged, every organ from my intestines to my heart trembled with fear.

After Smallwood left the room, Tony went to work on his BlackBerry. Just a routine day of billing for the lawyer. I paced the small room, regarded the litter in the alley through the window. In sympathy with my mood, the weather had turned overcast and was threatening rain.

I couldn't stand the silence. "Well? What do you think?"

Tony looked up, annoyed at the interruption. It took him a minute to rewind and playback what I had said.

"I wouldn't worry about their first proposal. They know we'll counter, and we know they'll counter and then we'll accept. That's the way it works."

Tony resumed typing with his thumbs, a guy caught in the digital past. I leaned against the wall, tried not to count the seconds. After an eternity, Smallwood burst back into the room without knocking. He dropped into the chair, but I remained standing. You should stand in front of a firing squad.

Smallwood said, "We're pretty far apart, but I'm going to give you boys a chance to make a good faith counter." He gave me a look as though I were being discourteous, but I didn't think I could control the shaking of my legs or the bouncing of my knees if I took a seat.

Smallwood gave up and said, "We're okay on the investment accounts, but they say the debt is all in Mr. Marks's name, so it's all his. I told 'em you've got the records, and Bobbie goes, 'He let her spend the money.'"

Tony gave me the same "I told you so" look.

I said, "I'm a scientist, not an accountant. I trusted my wife to handle the money, and now I'm saddled with her malfeasance?"

Smallwood said, "You gonna get the debt, son."

I sank into my chair.

"Your wife wants the house and everything in it," Smallwood continued. "Wants you to sign a quit claim on the deed, put it in her name." *Getting revenge for the incident with Puralto.* "I got her to accept the home equity debt on condition the alimony and stock are

196 | MIKE NEMETH

right." Smallwood gazed at me. "It's a good compromise. Is that three points solved?"

Tony had nothing to say, but I did. "No. My wife stole the money from the home equity account. We need to count the hundred fifty thousand dollars as a joint asset to be divided. That means our assets are two hundred forty-five thousand dollars to be divided equally. I'll settle for the ninety-five thousand dollars we know about, and she can keep the money we're not supposed to know about. The equity account shouldn't be a part of a deal for the house."

"You're pretty slick, young man. You keep the money and punish her for her sins."

"Eye for an eye, Mr. Smallwood."

"Do you read the Bible, Mr. Marks?"

"Not very often," I admitted.

Smallwood nodded. He seemed to be trying to decide which party should have his sympathy. Then he found his place and said, "I got her to give on the car. She'll pay for it and buy the insurance, but she needs the right to use it—she doesn't have credit to buy one of her own."

"Sorry, Mr. Smallwood, that's not a solution. I am not going to stay connected with that woman through her car. We're cutting all the ties today. Her credit rating is her problem."

Smallwood gave a disgusted grunt and a loud deprecating sigh. "Okay, let's talk about the really hard parts. They want permanent alimony at eighty thousand dollars a year, assuming you'll pay the construction loan on the house in perpetuity. State law gives them the right to ask for it."

"They're just negotiating, pounding a stake in the ground," Tony said. "Matthews-Bryant won't grant permanent alimony on a short marriage."

I said, "Alimony is like a jail sentence for me, Mr. Smallwood. I can't quit work until the alimony expires."

"She's gonna get some alimony, son. You plannin' to retire on your stock shares? You pretty young to retire, lay around."

I guessed I looked young to a seventy-five-year-old guy who still worked for a living. "No," I said. "I plan to write a book about my work, maybe lecture. But within a couple of years the concepts will be stale or in the public domain."

Smallwood rubbed his beard thoughtfully. "Your wife claims you wouldn't let her work, so her career has been interrupted. She says it would take her time to find work."

Feeling the stress now, I shot back, "That's a joke. She was a clerk in a medical clinic, filed insurance claims, paid the electric bill. Is that a career?" Before Smallwood could respond, I continued. "When I met her she was being treated by a psychiatrist for anxiety and depression."

I pulled Carrie's medical file from my briefcase and plopped it on the table. "I have all the medical records right here." Tony and Smallwood traded looks. "I took pity on her, told her she didn't need to work. Now she wants to claim I did something bad to her?"

Tony said, "We could get a court order to have her tested for occupational skills."

"You boys just spoiling for a fight, aren't ya? Mrs. Marks has files too. One with all the receipts for her expenses, the standard of living you established for her. So what do you propose?"

I said, "Three years at sixty thousand dollars. I'll pay the construction loan, but the house goes up for sale and we split the upside when it sells. How's that?"

Smallwood shook his head in disgust as he wrote it all down. "You can expect they'll come back in the middle. That what you're looking for? If so, we could save time by offering that now."

I said, "Too many open items to give anything yet, Mr. Smallwood. For example, she can have the furnishings in the house, but only if she returns what belongs to me. She stole property from the beach house, and she stole personal things from the country house before I moved."

Tony said, "I'm sorry, Randle. We got into the house as soon as we could."

Smallwood took a deep breath and blew it out slowly. He continued down his list and said, "They want to split the remaining options fifty/fifty."

They think I'm up against a November 1st IPO date, but I'm not. I said, "As part of a satisfactory overall agreement, you can offer the ten thousand Tony suggested earlier. Added to the fifteen thousand she shouldn't have gotten, that's twenty-five thousand, equal to half of the IPO shares. The last thirty thousand won't vest until March."

Smallwood said, "I already mentioned that number. They won't take it."

"That's my best offer," I said.

Tony shook his head. "We're going to be here longer than I thought."

"Look, I understand you're angry about the divorce, but if you were married you'd be splitting everything every day," Smallwood said. "That's how you should look at it. She's just a sweet little thing from the country, and you're a big-time businessman, so you should feel some obligation here."

"With all due respect, Mr. Smallwood, you have no idea who she is under that innocent façade."

Smallwood considered that and then said, "There's one last thing I wasn't aware of: They want you to split your royalties with her."

"Hell no!" I screamed. "That's my reward for inventing a tool that will benefit mankind. She had nothing to do with it." I swept all the papers off the table in one swift, unexpected motion, and Smallwood had to roll his chair out of the way to avoid being buried in the avalanche. "I'm done with this prejudicial process." I got up and headed for the door.

Tony shouted, "Stop, Randle!"

Smallwood leapt to his feet and grabbed me by the arm. He peered into my eyes. "Lemme go back and give it my best try."

After a dramatic pause, I returned to my seat and the mediator left the room. As though nothing had happened, Tony immediately went back to his BlackBerry, unaffected by my outburst.

I jotted down some numbers. In the worst-case scenario, my share of the options would be worth one point two million dollars—in other words, six hundred fifty to seven hundred thousand dollars after taxes. Paying off the house, Carrie's car, credit card debts, and her lawyer would leave me with about one hundred thousand dollars. An alimony obligation meant I'd have to work for AMA into my mid-sixties. After truing-up the money for the beach house sale, my IRA would be drained. Not only would the pursuit of my dream be impossible, I would have nothing to fund retirement.

I walked around to Tony's side of the table, rested one haunch on it, and looked down at my lawyer. "We need to go to trial, Tony. She stole my possessions, she spent all my money, and she committed adultery. Why should she walk away with a soft life funded by my hard work?"

Tony was too nice to say "Duh!" so he said, "Because you put a ring on her finger. When you do that, you either make it last or you end up here, in mediation, giving half your life away. That's the way it works. When we hear their counter, we're going to accept it. Then we'll get drunk. You can put your mistake behind you, but not until you pay for it."

"Why am I the only one who has to pay for the failure?" I knew the answer, of course: I was the husband and I had the money. I moved back to my side of the table, paced back and forth, head down, thinking about how to get out of my mess. If mediation failed, the obvious next move would be to ask for a trial, but I had no naked pictures and hotel receipts to sway the judge.

Smallwood wasn't gone long. He entered the room, sat at the table, and said, "They've compromised. Let's get this done."

Convinced by his confident tone, I took a seat and waited for him to continue. Using his notes as a checklist, Smallwood said, "She says she doesn't have anything that belongs to you, but that you stole her medical records and her pistol." He pointedly looked at Carrie's medical file, lying on the floor. "Says you took those things the day you moved out of the house, and she wants them back."

"Carrie is lying. A Cortes County Sherriff's deputy was with me the whole time I was in the house. His name is Dobbins. Ask him if I stole anything. Carrie told him she didn't have a gun, now she says I stole the gun."

Smallwood said, "Whatever. She doesn't have your stuff, and you don't have her stuff, so you're even. You both keep what you've got." He made a check mark on his list.

"Swift justice," I said, "like in the Old West."

He ignored me. "They want the judge to divide the remaining options. They know they won't get half, but they're hoping for twenty-five thousand." He put a check mark next to options.

Continuing down the list, he said, "They asked for half the royalties for five years. I told 'em that wouldn't fly, so I'm just going to cross them off the list." Smallwood made a big show of striking a line through that item on his sheet. I watched impassively.

"That leaves the house and the alimony." He looked at me for a long moment before continuing. "She's not going to let you sell the house out from under her. She wants it in her name, wants you to pay for the construction loan, and she'll pay for the home equity loan. It's a deal breaker."

Tony, fearing he'd be tied up the rest of the day, jumped on the mediator's bandwagon. "Do you want that house way out there?"

"Of course not," I said. "There's no *there*, there."

"Then let her have it and fight over the alimony."

An alternative to a trial, one that had been forming in my subconscious for the past thirty minutes, suddenly crystallized and danced in front of my eyes like sugarplum fairies on Christmas. *Maybe Carrie should try to murder me.*

I made them wait a few minutes before I said, "I've sold the beach house. I close on Friday the 9th of October, so you can't give one home to each of us and think you've done a great job. If she wants the house, she has to pay for it."

Tony came out of his chair. "You're in contempt of court, Randle. You're creating a mess and causing me trouble with the judge."

"You're wrong, Tony! I can do anything I wish with premarital property."

Smallwood lost his patience. "You messin' with the law, young man. I have to disclose this to your wife, and she's not goin' ta be happy."

I said, "You ever been divorced, Mr. Smallwood?"

He jerked back in his chair like he'd been slapped in the face. "Been married to the same woman for fifty-three years. Proud of it."

I nodded. "That explains why you don't know what this negotiation is about. The lawyers see it as a game, and you see it as a job, but for the husband and wife it's about guilt and shame. The settlement is the apportionment of blame. Until you get that right, you don't have a deal."

Smallwood slammed his pencil on the table. "You're gonna end up with a raw deal, and you're not gonna like it, boy."

I banged the flat of my palm on the table, making a loud splat sound that shocked the old guy. "If she wants the house for herself, she has to buy me out."

Smallwood shrank back in his seat.

Tony said, "Settle down, Randle. We're trying to help you out of the mess."

"You're no help, Tony. The only way for me to get a fair settlement is to have a trial."

Smallwood said, "I haven't heard anything today that would get you a better deal at trial than I can get you right now. It pisses Phyllis off when she has to hear a trial."

Tony said, "Just get it over with, Randle."

I delayed for a moment and replayed the events of the last two weeks and the conversations with Connie. I made up my mind. As though I were still negotiating, I said, "What did they offer on alimony?"

"They'll accept eighty thousand dollars for five years if she can have half your bonuses during the alimony period. They split the difference between the two proposals just like I told you, negotiating in good faith, and you should do the same."

Obviously, Smallwood had suggested the compromise, but he didn't understand the economics. The bonuses were worth as much as the alimony. I turned nasty and said, "You had no authority to mention royalties or bonuses."

Smallwood was offended by my insolence, but he tried a softer approach as a last-ditch effort. "Your wife seems like a very nice person, a gentle soul who wants a fair outcome. She expected to be married forever, put all her trust in you, and now you're splitting up. She needs some help down the road."

I was exasperated by the "system's" bias toward my wife. "The judge won't order more years of alimony than we had years of marriage."

Tony pulled a face and said, "Who knows what a judge might do. Five years is better than permanent."

Incompetent jerk. Just wants to get this case done. Turning back to Smallwood, I said, "Anything else up their sleeves?"

"Yeah, two more things any smart lawyer gonna ask for: They want you to pay for a million-dollar life insurance policy, in case you kick the bucket before paying all the alimony. And they want you to pay her legal fees."

"No way," I said. "Neither one."

I was genuinely offended by the suggestion, but Tony said, "It's routine, Randle. The plaintiff always gets to protect alimony payments, and the plaintiff always gets legal fees."

"I'm a plaintiff too!" I shouted.

"Alright, young man," Smallwood said, still trying to be conciliatory, "let me give her the house and the furnishings, the insurance policy, twenty-five thousand options, and five years of alimony, and I can set you free."

I spent a few minutes mentally totaling it all up. Initially Carrie had asked for more than three million dollars. Her second proposal totaled around two point two million dollars. Smallwood's compromise was approximately one point seven million dollars. I could have looked at that proposal as a savings of one point three million dollars—like a woman bragging about a sale on something she didn't actually need—but compromise was no longer my goal.

"Here's my best and final offer: We sell the house, and she can have all the upside. I'll pay the construction loan until it sells, but she pays the home equity loan. She can have the furniture and another ten thousand options. I'll throw in one hundred eighty thousand dollars upfront, which is the equivalent of three years of alimony at sixty thousand per year. There will be no ongoing relationship of any kind—no insurance, no legal fees, no bonuses, and no royalties. Otherwise we go to court."

That would be a haul of a million dollars, give or take, but Smallwood said, "You a fool!" Looking disgusted, he got up and left.

Tony said, "You're going to end up right where Ross has you now, but the trial will cost you a bundle of money to get there. How is that smart, Mr. Negotiator?"

"Let her stew over this for a while, Tony. In the meantime, see if you can subpoena her bank records and prepare a motion for a trial."

Tony sighed. He had no enthusiasm for doing more work on the case.

Smallwood returned, his shoulders slumped in defeat. He said, "They didn't accept my proposal but want you to know their offer is on the table any time you want to accept it. And your wife gave me this note for you." He handed me a folded piece of Carrie's personalized stationery.

I opened the note and read: **I have the sex tape. I'll make you a YouTube star if you don't cancel the psychiatrist and give me the house.** ☺

Expressionless, I folded the note and slipped it into my breast pocket. Smallwood and Tony waited for me to react or disclose what the note said, but I remained placid as I said, "Let's get out of here."

The old guy blocked the door. "What you gonna tell Phyllis?"

Another member of the legal fraternity afraid of the judge. "Tony will tell her that they rejected both my offer and your compromise." As I eased toward the door, I said, "Sorry to have wasted your time, Mr. Smallwood."

"You ain't wasted my time. I get paid to watch people act stupid."

I brushed past him and left the room.

In the parking lot, Tony said, "The judge is going to be all over me about you selling that house."

"It's premarital property."

"Did you put money into the deal?"

"Yeah, premarital money."

"Oh my God!"

"As long as we're having a nice chat about strategy, I'll let you in on another secret: The IPO has been delayed until February 15th."

He stopped walking and pivoted, as though he might run back and tell everyone the secret. "We should have told them, Randle."

"We're not going to be the only saps who follow the rules, Tony. This is a negotiation. We want them to agree to a settlement assuming they're going to get a bunch of the outstanding options, then we'll whisk those options away like a magician pulling a tablecloth out from under a four-place setting."

"No, Randle." He shook his head. His lips quivered with anger. "I have to tell the judge."

"No, Tony, you will keep this communication privileged until we go to trial."

His lips were still moving as I cranked my car and drove away. I didn't mean to be rude, but I had bigger fish to fry.

On my way back to the beach house, I stopped at the home goods store and found the aisle where desks, chairs, and filing cabinets were displayed. There were two three-drawer steel cabinets identical to the one I had bought Carrie for her office. A pair of silver keys dangled from each lock. I took the keys from the locks and mixed them up in my hand. Then I tried all four keys on each lock. They all worked—all the locks on the cheap filing cabinets were the same. I slipped a pair of the silver keys into my pocket and left the store.

CHAPTER TWENTY-THREE

The courtroom resembled a community college classroom but with the ambience of a waiting room at a police station. On an elevated platform, the judge's bench was a simple clerk's desk and the witness stand was a lonely chair beside it. A lectern for lawyers to hide behind stood in the center of the room facing the judge's desk, and opposing counsel sat at cafeteria tables on either side of the lectern. A low railing separated a small spectator gallery from the business end of the room. The people in the gallery looked as though they wanted to be somewhere else.

As I entered the courtroom, business was being conducted in a low hum of chaotic activity. Cases started and ended without fanfare. At intervals triggered by some unheard signal, lawyers, witnesses, plaintiffs, and defendants switched prescribed positions like football offenses and defenses taking and leaving the field. I took a seat in the front row between a Hispanic family and an elderly black woman. Carrie was nowhere in sight, probably packing a bag for her psychiatric vacation.

Tony leaned against the far wall, apparently on the defendant's side of the courtroom, waiting his turn to occupy the counsel table. I didn't see de Castro enter the courtroom or approach Tony, but the next time I glanced in my lawyer's direction, she was in Tony's face, hissing and spitting like a King Cobra ready to strike. Tony appeared placid, as though he wasn't hearing anything alarming, was just riding out the storm of viperous emotion, until de Castro jerked a thumb over her shoulder in my direction. Tony automatically looked my way and found me in the crowd. He wore a frown with a question mark over it.

De Castro made her way to the near side of the room, behind the plaintiff's counsel table, and gave me a look that could kill. I smiled and nodded a "hello" in return, as though I had no idea why she would be angry with me.

Several more team changes took place before *Marks v. Marks* was called. Zambrano and de Castro stood side by side behind the lectern as Judge Matthews-Bryant opened a file on her desk. With all the background noise, it was like a conversation in a crowded restaurant— each conversation private because all conversations were shielded by the general noise level of the room.

Tony was about to speak when Matthews-Bryant cut him off. "What do you think you're doing, counselor?"

"Ma'am?"

"The Baker Act, Mr. Zambrano. That's a pretty low blow, don't you think?"

Tony uttered the first unrecognizable syllable of a response but halted as soon as the judge gave him the "stop" sign. "You will not initiate any other legal proceedings without my consent so long as we are adjudicating this divorce. Is that perfectly . . . crystal clear, counselor?"

That made me laugh. I'm sure the judge opted for "crystal" over an f-bomb to avoid offending all the sensitive souls in the gallery.

Tony didn't back down. "Your Honor," he said, "the Baker Act examination has nothing to do with the divorce action. It grows out of Mr. Marks's longstanding efforts to get his wife proper mental health care. I admit the timing is bad, and I apologize for that."

The judge pointed a finger at Tony and said, "Never again, Mr. Zambrano." *I was right—judges have no power, and she let us get away with it.*

Tony said, "Understood, Your Honor."

"Okay, give me an update."

Tony cleared his throat. "Mediation was conducted yesterday, as ordered by the court, but the parties failed to reach a settlement, Your Honor."

Matthews-Bryant peered over her reading glasses at the two lawyers before her. "Why not, Mr. Zambrano?"

"Your Honor, defendant made an offer and the mediator proposed a compromise, and plaintiff rejected all attempts to settle."

The judge removed her glasses. Turning to de Castro, she said, "Any reason you couldn't accept a compromise?"

Shifting from one trademark red high heel to the other, de Castro said, "Our offer was justifiable, Your Honor."

Matthews-Bryant took a moment to digest the information and then wrote a note in her file. When she looked up, she addressed de Castro. "Justifiable isn't the goal in mediation. You know that, Ms. de Castro. The idea is to reach a compromise, right?" The judge wore a questioning look but de Castro treated the question as rhetorical, so the judge continued. "I order that a repeat mediation session be scheduled within two weeks. I'll leave that to you, Mr. Zambrano."

Matthews-Bryant closed the file on her desk, believing the appearance to be concluded, but Tony said, "One more thing, Your Honor. The

IPO for Atlanta Medical Analytics has been delayed again—until 15 February of next year."

Tony!

De Castro threw her hands into the air and dropped her files on the floor. The judge ignored the dramatic response and folded her hands on top of the file. She said, "Then there is something to negotiate in mediation. Where did you stand on that issue in the first mediation session?"

De Castro hoped Tony would respond, but he waved a hand in her direction and forced her to say it aloud. De Castro said, "We asked for half of the unallocated shares."

The judge said, "I can see why Mr. Zambrano felt you were being unreasonable. Don't get greedy, Ms. de Castro, and don't leave this in my hands. Now let me get on to more important cases, please."

Tony stopped her again. "I'm sorry, Your Honor, but I also want to apprise the Court that the defendant will petition the Court for a trial and a directed settlement. We have no confidence that another mediation session will produce an agreement."

De Castro's jaw dropped and her mouth hung open. The judge exhaled a puff of surprised breath and slowly removed her glasses as she considered this turn of events. Defendants rarely asked for a trial, as they had been accused of wrongdoing and usually were guilty. She said, "You can file any motion you like, counselor, but I won't be ruling on anything until you put some effort into another mediation session. My advice: Reach a settlement."

The judge tried to shoo the attorneys away with a flip of her hand, but de Castro begged for a chance to make a point as well. Irritated, the judge said, "What is it, counselor?"

"Your Honor, defendant has disposed of a major asset—the home in Dolphin Beach."

With a questioning look, knowing there must be more to the point, the judge said, "That's his privilege. It's premarital."

Hoping she finally held a trump card, de Castro said, "He used marital funds to complete the transaction—forty-five thousand dollars."

The judge turned to Tony and motioned for him to speak. He said, "It's semantics, Your Honor. Defendant has sufficient premarital funds to cover the payoff, but they aren't liquid, so he used liquid funds to complete the sale and he'll true-up when a settlement is reached. Of course, the settlement now must include an agreeable disposition for the Cortes County home as it is the only remaining home the couple owns."

The judge said, "Don't make me engage an accountant to find all the money, Mr. Zambrano." Turning to de Castro, she said, "That should explain it to you, counselor."

The judge didn't allow a retort. She banged her gavel and called for a recess. De Castro walked away looking as though she'd been stampeded by a herd of normally docile milk cows.

Tony caught my eye and motioned for me to meet outside the courtroom. When I joined him in the hallway, he grabbed me roughly by the arm and dragged me away from eavesdroppers. Shoving me against a wall, he said, "Are you a sadist?"

"You didn't have permission to disclose the IPO delay."

"De Castro gave me an ultimatum: 'If you go to trial, Mrs. Marks will disclose evidence that your client sexually abused her.'"

"Tony, you ruined our negotiation."

"Are you going to answer my question?"

I yanked my arm out of his grip. "It's a bluff, Tony. While we were dating we made a tape of ourselves playacting various scenes. She scripted the scenes."

He rolled his eyes. "I went to bat for you, Randle, and I hope that was the right thing to do. I told de Castro that we won't cave in to her threats and we want a trial. Am I right?"

That made me smile. My lawyer was finally invested in my case. "Yes, but you shouldn't have mentioned the IPO delay."

"I had to tell the judge, Randle. You could see how upset she was."

"You got a gentle slap on the wrist."

His mouth opened, but he wimped out. Seeing that de Castro was headed for the elevators, we turned in the opposite direction and took two flights of stairs down to street level. It was a short walk to a Starbucks crowded with people who had found Lady Justice or been defiled by her. We sat in easy chairs and sipped lattes.

Tony rubbed his chin, thinking. "What was in that note from your wife?"

"The same threat that de Castro made to you." *In more colorful language.* Carrie had taken the tote of old files because the sex tape was buried in that tote.

"They seem desperate."

"We're desperate too. I want a trial. File the motion, Tony." In truth, I merely wanted to put pressure on my erstwhile bride. I had no evidence to turn a trial verdict in my favor.

Tony sighed loudly. "Okay. I'll need a real list of witnesses."

"Deputy Dobbins from the Cortes County Sherriff's Office, Simmons, Dickson, my daughter, my ex-wife, Glenda, and my former girlfriend, Susanne."

"Now you're playing hardball." The lawyer scribbled the names on his notepad.

"What about Puralto? Did you find him?"

"Yes, that was easy. He's a doctor, works at a clinic in Brandon. Married twenty-five years to the same woman, two kids. Upstanding citizen."

"Ever own a condo in Seminole?"

"Briefly. Awarded to him by the court in a case against one Carrie Simmons. The doctor sold the place less than six months later."

"Did she own the condo while she was married to Simmons?"

"Technically. The condo was purchased after the divorce was filed but before it went final."

"She had Puralto lined up before Simmons filed. Add Puralto's name to the witness list."

Tony grimaced. "Why bother the poor guy, after all this time?"

"Why is everyone more concerned about his well-being than mine? Puralto establishes a pattern of behavior. I've seen lawyers do that on TV."

It was Tony's turn to grunt in disgust.

With my lawyer out of the way, I dialed Jamie's cell phone number and was surprised that she answered.

"What's up, Dad?"

It took a minute to organize my thoughts and find the right way to tell the story.

"Carrie has come to the boat twice without warning. I think she's coming to kill me."

"You don't believe that murder plot stuff, do you?"

"Hard to say. That's why I need a safety net—to protect myself if she comes back."

Jamie gave me an exasperated huff. "Make her meet you in a public place, Dad. Not on your damn boat."

"Sure. I'm talking about if she turns up uninvited."

"If you're worried about it, report it to the police. Why are you asking me for advice?"

"I could take her to the cove, down by Fort De Soto Park. Do you remember it?"

"Stop it, Dad. This is crazy."

"Just to be sure, I thought you could meet me there, with your gun and your badge. Give me a hand."

"No, no, no! I'm not risking my badge on your mess. Forget this ridiculous idea and report her to the police."

"What if she snuck aboard? If I called you, would you help me?"

"No! Go stay in a hotel." Jamie hung up on me.

Despite my daughter's reluctance to get entangled in her father's imbroglio, I was in a jovial mood. As I pulled into the marina parking lot, distracted by the joyful snippets of courtroom repartee ricocheting around my cranium, I didn't see her until it was too late.

The red Jaguar sat nose-out, top-down, in the space immediately in front of the walking gate to my dock. A man lounged beside her in the front seat. Unsure of my next move, I stopped dead in the second rank. That was a mistake. My wife and I traded evil stares for a moment before I impulsively stepped on the gas to escape, but the Bronco was not designed to drag race a sports car. The agile Jaguar leapt out of its space and raced up the first rank of cars, parallel to my path, and it outpaced me. In a brazen display of recklessness, Carrie screeched through the corner and slid to a stop at the end of my rank, blocking my flight.

My reactions were barely adequate. The big Bronco skidded sideways and halted with its right bumper inches from the Jaguar's passenger door. As I caught my breath, and Larry caught his, Carrie popped out of her car and ran around the backend, shaking her fist at me. Larry pushed himself out of his seat and onto the rear deck of the convertible. He looked ready to join the fun, but Carrie waved him back.

She hustled up to my door, and I rolled the window down in time to hear her say, "Get out of the damn truck!"

"Get out of my damn way!"

"You can't run away like a little sissy. I'll make you a deal, but you have to cancel the psychiatrist."

"I don't have to do squat. Admit it, Carrie, your tits are in a wringer."

She kicked my car door. "I'm not going to the nuthouse."

"Fine. Then it's jail. You've always looked good in pinstripes."

She kicked my door again, harder. I heard, rather than felt, the metal crumple as she screamed, "I'm not crazy!"

"Sure. Anyone can see that." I waved my arm to encompass the whole scene.

With her left hand, she grabbed my outside mirror and levered herself onto the running board so she could pummel my arm and shoulder with her right fist. On cue, Larry stood in his seat, ready to lend a hand. I wasn't about to brawl with an ex-con, so I threw the Bronco into reverse and jerked backward a few feet, cranking the wheel to the right to get a better angle on the space between the Jaguar and a parked car. The sudden movement flung Carrie off the truck. Like an ice skater doing a leaping spin, Carrie turned three hundred sixty degrees in the air, but she failed to stick the landing. Her right foot struck the ground and acted like a pogo stick, bouncing her up in the air, arms and legs akimbo, before gravity smashed her into the pavement, tailbone first. She shrieked in agony.

Larry was about to run to his boss or mistress or whatever she was to him, but I cut him off by rolling forward until my bumper leaned on the Jaguar's right rear wheel well.

Larry waved a bandaged arm in horror. Carrie yelled, "Stop it!"

Slowly, I increased power until the Jaguar's rear end began to lurch sideways. As the Jag crab-walked, Larry lost his balance and grabbed the windshield to steady himself. Carrie struggled to her feet and shouted at me, but I couldn't hear her over the roar of my engine.

Howling deliriously, I applied full power. Smoke and acrid fumes enveloped the scene as the Bronco burned rubber and bulldozed the Jaguar out of the way. Carrie limped toward my door, shouting profanities, but I did not stop pushing the Jaguar until there was room to pass around it. I backed away from the crumpled Jag, cranked the wheel to the left, and stepped on the accelerator. Accidentally, I snagged her rear bumper, and as the Bronco circled the Jag I ripped Carrie's bumper from its anchors like I was peeling a banana. Her bumper scraped the asphalt as I dragged it through the parking lot to the cheers of a growing crowd of spectators. Larry tried to chase me down, but he was no track star.

When I bounced out into the street, Carrie's bumper wrenched free to lie in the middle of the street, forlorn evidence of the violent confrontation. The onlookers shouted encouragement as I made my getaway like a hit-and-run driver. Three blocks later, I hid the Bronco in the downtown mall-parking garage and inspected the damage. Two streaks of Jaguar red paint on the bumper and the imprint of one size-seven shoe on the driver's door were the only signs that my truck had been in an altercation. The Bronco had won another bar fight.

Curious to see how the other guy looked, I pulled a ball cap low over my eyes, walked back to Beach Boulevard, and blended in with the onlookers. Carrie neither called the cops nor summoned a wrecker. As Larry used a tire iron to pry the quarter panel off her right rear tire, she paced gingerly, stopping every few feet to place both hands on her lower back and push her pelvis forward to relieve the pain. Once the tire was free, the two of them jumped into the Jag and found that it was drivable, at least in the loosest sense of that word. Barely making ten miles an hour, teeter-tottering from side to side like a broken old man, the Jag hobbled through the parking lot as the crowd pointed and jeered and snapped photos with their smartphones.

In the street, Carrie paused to allow Larry to pick up the bumper and prop it over his shoulder in the passenger seat. Then she gave the crowd a one-fingered salute and eased down the street. As the tortured clang, clang, clang of her ruined gearbox receded, the crowd dispersed.

I waited for her to turn out of sight before I retrieved the trusty Bronco and parked it in the space Carrie had vacated. Although Carrie had five hours to reach Cortes County for her rendezvous with a sheriff's deputy, I doubted the Jaguar could be her chariot. I also doubted that Carrie would "go gentle into that good night." Like a wounded bear, she would look for ways to gain revenge. All afternoon and well into the evening, I sat in the aft cabin, watching the parking lot and the walking gate with my Berretta in my lap, but neither Carrie nor Larry returned to the marina.

CHAPTER TWENTY-FOUR

O n Wednesday, the marina was deserted. The tourists had returned to their mundane lives, and the weekend boaters were at their offices and businesses. As soon as Tony's office opened, I called my lawyer seeking confirmation that Carrie was being examined. Melissa answered and told me Tony was conducting a deposition and couldn't be interrupted.

Melissa said, "Your wife made quite a scene. Refused to go with the deputy, so they called her lawyer and the lawyer drove her to the hospital."

"Which one?"

"I assume West Florida Psychiatric Center in Tampa," Melissa said, "but she's way up there in Cortes County, so it could be Orlando or Gainesville or anywhere there's a bed."

"What happens now?"

"She will be interviewed by a psychiatrist today, and then a second psychiatrist will review the findings and decide whether he needs to interview the patient to confirm a diagnosis. Then they'll prepare a report of their findings."

"Tony told me they'll take seventy-two hours to decide what to do with her."

"They can't hold her for more than seventy-two hours to examine her, but they can release her at any time."

"Unless she needs to be kept in the asylum, right?"

"Oh no. Since she hasn't been charged with a crime they won't keep her no matter what their findings." Before I could react, she amended her pronouncement. "Let me take that back. If they advise in-patient care, your wife could take their advice and voluntarily commit herself."

Fat chance. "So if they decide she's crazy, they're just going to let her go?"

"If they conclude she should be detained involuntarily, they have five days following the examination to get a court order for a commitment. That's the way it works. The judge reviews the report and decides whether or not to detain her."

Unbelievable. Why would a judge get to second-guess the experts? "Will we know when she's released?" *Or will I have to walk around with a loaded gun?*

"Since you're the petitioning party, they'll notify us and we'll pass it along to you."

"Terrific."

I checked the cloud account and found that Carrie had not been online since mediation. *Weird.* Sure she was reading my mail somehow, I left her a present to find when, and if, she was released from the hospital.

Tony,

We know about Puralto, but keep Fred looking for other people she cheated with.

Randle

———◦⊗∞◦———

Driving into my old neighborhood in Dolphin Beach on Thursday morning felt strange. I had only been gone a few days, but it already felt as though I were returning to a childhood home after years away. Carrie and I kept our deeds, car titles, and wills in a safe-deposit box at the Community Bank on Gulf Boulevard. If something untoward happened to me, I wanted to be sure Jamie inherited my worldly goods and that Carrie didn't.

Carrie had beaten me to the punch once again. An amendment to her will had been sworn on September 23rd, the day after the Baker Act show cause hearing date had been set. Originally, we were cross beneficiaries in the event one of us passed away. That is common practice in marriages. In the event we both passed away, our estate would be divided equally between our children, Travis and Jamie. Again, a common practice. The new amendment, however, named Carrie's sister, Connie Mae Tomkins, as her sole beneficiary. So Connie had found a way to restore her status as family bank. Why would Carrie agree to that? Loyalty to the Tomkins clan?

I stopped that scam in its tracks by amending my will to name Jamie as my sole beneficiary, cutting Carrie, and therefore Connie, out of my will.

While the bank's notary public prepared my amendment, I received a text message from Tony: *Trial motion filed. Crawl in a foxhole and keep your head down.*

On the way back to the boat, I called Connie's cell phone but received no answer. Presumably, she was at work, as though this were a normal day in the life of a bean counter.

When I reached the boat, I established an alibi for the weekend. I arranged to meet with the IT guys and my team in Atlanta on Friday afternoon to review their design of the new automated loader for closed medical cases. To cover Monday, I set a meeting of all senior executives to walk through the design and approve the implementation plan.

The arrangements with Glenda were far more complex, but she excitedly took notes and reveled in the prospect of assisting me.

That afternoon, Tony called. It sounded like he was in a bar—probably the 19th hole at the Belleview Biltmore. "Melissa texted when I was on eighteen. Your wife was released an hour ago. Kept her less than forty-eight hours, so it's probably not a good sign."

"When will we hear something?"

"They have five days to write a report."

"Yeah, yeah, yeah. Everyone has all the time in the world except me."

<hr/>

I called Connie again and reached her voice mail once more. I wanted to hear the inside story of Carrie's examination, so I left a message to call me back.

<hr/>

Friday, I felt like Henry Hill in the movie *Goodfellas*, running desperate errands with police helicopters following my every move. I packed my bags for a week's stay and waited for thunderstorms to pass. As I waited, smoking a cigar in the aft cabin, I called my friend Jerry Louks and arranged to meet him for happy hour. I needed a favor.

At long last, the rain turned to steam rising from the pavement, and I carried my bags to my car. I dropped the Bronco at the dealer for a routine service and accepted a loaner vehicle, which I drove to the beach house to retrieve my stolen goods from under the dock. Then I self-parked the loaner at the Don CeSar Hotel, the "pink palace" on Gulf Boulevard, and walked four blocks to a strip mall. Enterprise Rent-A-Car met me there with a nondescript rental in Glenda's name, and I took possession. Back in the Don CeSar parking lot, I transferred my luggage and stolen goods to the rental car and took off for Atlanta.

That afternoon I reviewed our product demo with my team. At seven p.m., I checked into the Technology Park Hilton, had a couple of drinks with Jerry, ate dinner, and watched a college football game as though my life were normal. *What do terrorists do the night before they plant a bomb?*

CHAPTER TWENTY-FIVE

On Saturday morning, I waited in the hotel room until the maid arrived. She could confirm I had spent the night. Downstairs in the hotel restaurant I generated a dated credit card receipt by having breakfast. Before I left for Florida at two p.m., I messed the bed to make it look slept in.

Connie had arranged to take the Tomkins family to Clearwater Beach this weekend, and Carrie had been released from the mental hospital in time to make the trip, so the country house should have been unoccupied. Nonetheless, I cruised slowly past the house at ten p.m., checking for signs of life. The place was buttoned up and dark, but I could see that the backyard spotlights were lit. I made a U-turn, cruised back to the house, and pulled into the garage side of the driveway.

Wanting to spend as little time as possible outside, I immediately pushed the "open" button on a garage door remote that I had not surrendered to Carrie. The door opener I had handed over when I moved was an old one that had stopped working long ago. As the door rose, a nondescript beige sedan appeared, nose pointed toward me. I slammed on the brakes. My heart tried to punch a hole in my chest, but I forced myself to wait. No one came out onto the porch, no one walked out of the garage, no one emerged from the shadows. Maybe she was just inside the back door with my pistol cocked. As time drifted by, I realized she probably had hitched a ride with Connie.

If this were a movie, everyone in the theater would be yelling, "No, don't go in there," but I rolled up the driveway, did a three-point turn, and backed into the garage. As a precaution, I left the door open in case I had to fight my way out of the situation. Nothing happened.

Before I got out of the car, I donned surgical gloves and grabbed my MagLite flashlight. Wondering if I could go to jail for breaking into my own home, I pulled on a cord attached to a door in the ceiling and a folding ladder dropped in front of me. I unfolded the ladder and climbed into the storage space above the garage. When the alarm system had been installed, Carrie had objected to mounting it in a closet or any other interior space. It would have been an eyesore or something in the way of her wardrobe, so the technicians had mounted the equipment in the storage space above the garage. It had required running both electricity and a phone line into the space and had cost hundreds of dollars more than a conventional installation. Now I was happy I had made the investment. I pulled the electrical plug on the alarm system and disconnected the RS-11 cable for the phone line. Sure I wouldn't trip the alarm and alert Carrie, I descended into the garage.

I stood quietly in the garage for a moment and listened for the dog, but I couldn't hear him. For a weekend away, Carrie either would have taken the dog or hired someone to feed and water him for her. Since the whole family was at the beach, I couldn't imagine who would have performed that favor, but I couldn't risk getting eaten alive by that beast, so I had to go looking for him. From the car I took a cloth satchel containing the files I had stolen on the day I moved out of the house. I looped the satchel over my head so I wouldn't lose it in the chaos that was sure to follow. Then I reached for my bait, a stuffed bunny rabbit I had purchased at a pet store. It was a toy designed to be torn to shreds by predator dogs, and that's exactly what I hoped would happen.

I walked into the backyard to the near fence line and yelled inanities to flush out the dog. Nothing happened. I shook the chain-link fence, hoping to alert the dog if it was napping inside, but it did not appear. Maybe the dog was enjoying a weekend at the beach. To be sure, I shook the chain-link fence violently, causing it to rattle, and the dog did appear, just its head and shoulders squeezing through the second-story doggy door. There it stayed, glaring at me. I pretended to climb the fence and the dog just watched, assessing the threat as minimal. Dropping to the ground, I showed him the bunny rabbit and shook that at him. Like an alligator emerging from its den to stalk its prey, the dog slowly emerged in its menacing totality and stood on the balcony, snarling at me.

I continued to shake and wave the bunny, but the dog wouldn't budge from its perch. It had been trained to guard the house and not chase outdoor varmints, but I had another inducement for "Fido." I extended the rabbit over the fence and pulled its cord, prompting it to wriggle and squirm and squeak. That got a reaction. The dog sauntered down the steps and then stopped on the deck, growling at me. I pulled the bunny's cord again and again, but the shepherd wouldn't charge. In desperation, I pulled the cord one last time and threw the toy as far as I could across the yard. That provoked him. Instinct caused Fido to leap off the deck and chase the fleeing prey. I turned in the opposite direction and ran for all I was worth.

It was now a race—man against animal—to reach the doggy door. I ran around the house, through the garage, and into the kitchen. Despite my repeated advice to the contrary, Carrie never locked the door that led from the garage to the kitchen. Like most people, she was convinced the garage door was all that was needed to keep intruders from her home. Panting, I ran through the kitchen and took the front stairs two and three steps at a time. The dog would have to sense the ruse, abandon the bait, run back across the yard, across the deck, up the stairs, and across the balcony to its doggy door. I felt I had the advantage, but the shepherd beat me to it. As I reached the gallery, he was already shimmying through the doggy door that was two sizes too small for him. At that point, I had only one option. I leapt across the hallway, grabbed the media room door handle, and threw myself back into the hallway, slamming the door shut as the massive animal exploded into it from the other side. I leaned on the door with all my weight, shaking with fear, but the dog did not jump against it. He raised a racket, barking and crashing into things, but he did not attempt to break down the door. *That is one well-trained animal.* I wasn't concerned about the barking— the nearest neighbor was a squatter's shack half a mile away.

Assuming the door would hold, I ran down the hallway to Carrie's office and knelt in front of her filing cabinet. I used the little silver keys I had lifted from the home goods store to unlock it and pulled the top drawer open. It contained correspondence with retailers, credit card companies—applications denied—and home warranty companies and, in the middle of that junk, a folder marked "legal." It wasn't what I was looking for, but I pulled the file from the drawer and replaced it with Carrie's medical, mental health, and home equity files I had taken from her bedside table on moving day.

The middle drawer was stuffed with files holding bank statements, receipts, and cancelled checks. Hopeful I might find evidence of the secret account where she had hidden the stolen equity account money, I pulled all the manila folders out of the drawer only to find that all of the records pertained to our joint checking account, our savings account (balance of zero), and the investment account I had liquidated and deposited into my CD. The secret account was most likely a joint account with her momma. I wondered if we could get a search warrant for her momma's house.

In the bottom drawer, folders standing in file separators buckled over the top of an obstruction lying beneath them in the drawer. I pushed the standing files to the back of the drawer and uncovered a bonus—the infamous "rape tape."

After we had dated for a couple of months, Carrie said she wanted to test her sexual boundaries but wanted me to "force" her to do it. In particular, she liked fake rape scenes. The tape was a record of one long afternoon of scenes you wouldn't want your mother to see, all staged so it appeared Carrie was the victim of a dominant husband. Years ago, I had tossed the tape in the tote of old financial records under the workbench in the beach house garage and hadn't thought about it since. Carrie had remembered. Her murder plot hinged on a claim of rape, and the tape would be evidence that I had done it before.

I stuffed the tape into the satchel along with the legal file and flipped through the other files. At the very back, I found an unlabeled manila folder, and a glance confirmed it was Carrie's cell phone records. I took them, closed the drawer, and relocked the cabinet. I didn't feel bad about the burglary; Carrie should have moved her precious possessions to a bank safe-deposit box. Phil Simmons probably had one she could have used.

Back on my feet, I rushed down the hallway and took the stairs three at a time. As I hurried toward the ground-floor master bedroom, the flashlight beam illuminated the hallway enough for me to see that Carrie had hung pictures of her past lives with Dickson and Simmons. Another picture I had never seen caught my attention. A tall, fit man with short dark hair and a heavy beard draped a proprietary arm around my wife. I didn't have the time to do it, but I moved closer, angled the beam of the flashlight to eliminate the glare, and examined my doppelgänger. His face was long, while mine was angular, and his complexion was darker—Mediterranean—but the resemblance was uncanny. Puralto.

In the master suite, I walked around the bed and checked the bedside table for my pistol. It had to be in the house somewhere. The sleazy paperback lay in the top drawer along with Carrie's reading glasses, but the middle and bottom drawers were empty, the vibrator hidden somewhere else.

I moved to the dresser, opened the miniature chest of drawers that served as Carrie's jewelry box, and was surprised to find it nearly empty. She had moved her collection to a safer place. All that remained were a few pieces of everyday costume jewelry and the yellow-diamond pendant and earrings that she often wore to taunt me. She wouldn't taunt me any longer. I took them.

Wondering if my pistol might be hidden in the dresser, I opened several drawers and pushed underwear and sleepwear around. In the middle drawer, under pantyhose, bras, and camisoles, lay her diary, a leatherbound notebook the size of a family Bible with a strap to hold it closed. Carrie wrote compulsively in the diary, but she never let me read it. I hefted it in my hand, wondering how I could get it into the hands of the authorities without incriminating myself. I decided to figure that out later. I stuffed it into my overflowing satchel.

In a hurry, I went to her closet and grabbed her furs, encased in storage bags, and three designer purses in their protective boxes. Then I staggered up the staircase and dumped the valuables in the closet in the guest bedroom. If she reported them stolen, the cops would find them and realize she's wacko.

My heart pounding, I raced toward the staircase, glancing into my former bedroom as I passed by. From there I could hear the angry animal clawing at the media room door, but that's not why I pulled up short. I crept into the room and marveled at what I saw in the beam of my flashlight, the way tourists creep into caves and marvel at the prehistoric drawings on the walls. Carrie had used a magic marker to draw a crude stickman on one wall and had then bashed in its head with a hammer, leaving huge holes in the sheetrock. On the opposing wall, she had hung my official AMA portrait. It had been defaced with an angry red "X."

I knew it was unconscionable to be thrilled, but I couldn't help it. *More evidence of her madness.* On my smartphone I turned off the feature that tags photos with a date and time stamp and took half a dozen pictures of the walls. Then I hurried out of there, back down the hallway, and back down the stairs. On my way out of the house, I checked hiding places in the family room and kitchen but could not locate my pistol.

I put the diary, the files, and the sex tape in the car. Then I climbed back into the attic, reconnected the phone line, and plugged in the security system. I refolded the ladder and let it close into the ceiling. Back in the car, I pushed the "open" button and waited for the garage door to rise. It had taken less than twenty minutes to neutralize the dog and move and steal items, but I had the crazy sensation that a hundred cops were waiting on the driveway, in riot gear, guns raised and ready to annihilate me with a hail of bullets like the scene at the end of *Butch Cassidy and the Sundance Kid.*

If any cops were waiting for me, they were hiding. I pulled out of the garage and immediately hit the "close" button. When I was certain that the door was down, I zoomed out of the driveway and turned to the right, away from I-75 and the obvious escape route. There were no other cars on the rural road. Miles from the house, I threw the garage door opener and the little silver keys out the window. I took a circuitous route to the rental agency, avoiding high traffic streets and expressways, speed traps and patrolling cops. After two hours, I arrived at the rental lot, wiped down the car, removed my cargo, and locked the keys inside. Then I set out on foot, walking up Thirty-Fourth Street North in St. Petersburg. It didn't take long for the files to feel as heavy as boat anchors.

At a Publix grocery store, I borrowed a shopping cart and put the files in it. Then I pushed my belongings along the street like a homeless person.

Glenda's car was waiting for me in the parking lot of a twenty-four-hour diner. It took another fifteen minutes to drive to the Don CeSar Hotel on the beach and take the elevator to Room 410, rented in Glenda's name.

At four a.m., I flopped into bed, exhausted. I wondered how thieves withstood the stress and the exertion. Working for a living was far easier.

Glenda had constructed a burrow of blankets, but when I rolled next to her she made sweet little murmurs, as though she were humming an old Southern spiritual.

Sunday morning we took the diary with us to breakfast and paged through it together. Carrie had recorded her suspicions about my behavior when I wasn't at home, descriptions of unpleasant encounters with sales clerks, imagined slights, and run-ins with her family. Page after page was filled with dated and coded entries that made cryptic references to drinks and dinners at secret places with "friends." Most of the entries were easy enough to decode—girlfriends, family members, favorite restaurants, and watering holes. One frequent location was coded "WW," but I knew of no restaurant or hotel with those initials. One person she often met had the code name "MD." I knew no one with those initials. The latest entries, made in tiny, cramped writing with a pen pressed hard into the paper, railed against me, the judge, and her lawyer. In several places she had written, "I'll kill him." "Him" referred to me, I'm pretty sure.

Glenda pushed the diary over to me and gave me an angry look. "Were you so drunk with lust that you didn't notice she was nuts?"

I hadn't expected that reaction. "You're right; I made a huge mistake. But she wasn't this crazy while we dated. Her mental health has deteriorated over the past two years."

She exhaled loudly through her nose. "I have to get over the fact that you dumped me so you could chase trash like her. It might take a little while, so be patient with me."

"Sure." I doubted she'd have complimented me on any selection of a successor but got her point; in retrospect it was glaringly obvious that Carrie was a poor choice.

After breakfast, Glenda went to the front desk to check out and I went back to our room to read the other files. Most of the documents in the legal folder were bills and account statements. De Castro charged Carrie nearly twice as much per hour as Tony charged me and had billed 50 percent more hours. A few pieces of correspondence documented the fact that they had no real evidence of impropriety against me—no naked pictures nor hotel receipts. In her latest communication, de Castro asked if Carrie wanted to name Glenda and Susanne as witnesses if the case went to trial. There was no response from Carrie in the file.

Her cell phone file was even less useful. It contained the call history for her current number, the one she obtained to hide from me when she filed for the divorce, but not for the one she had when she was seeing men in the winter and spring. Now most calls were to or from her momma, and all the text messages were between her and her son, Travis. There were no calls to or from Connie.

There were two calls to numbers I didn't recognize. I was hopeful as I looked up the unfamiliar phone numbers using the *Whitepages* reverse phone lookup feature, but a number in Largo belonged to Roberta de Castro and a number in Plant City was for a wholesale food company. That call was a mystery, but it didn't seem to be relevant.

I wrapped all the stolen property—the diary, copies of Carrie's medical files, a copy of the home loan file, her legal file, her cell phone bills, and the sex tape—in plain brown paper and sealed it with packing tape. It looked like something the Unabomber would mail.

When Glenda returned from paying the bill, I took the bundle off the desk and handed it to her. "This is all the evidence I have on her. Can you store it in a safe place?"

"I'll hide it at my mother's."

"Good. If anything happens to me, give it to the Pinellas County DA."

She held the package away from her as though it were indeed a bomb. "I'm nervous now, Randle. Stay with me at my mother's house."

As attractive as that arrangement sounded, I couldn't entangle her in the rest of the plan. "I can't yet," I said. "I have some more business to take care of. In the meantime, I'd like you to have these." I held out the yellow-diamond pendant and matching earrings.

Glenda's eyes widened. I hadn't earned enough money while we were married to give her expensive gifts. "Did you steal these from Carrie?"

"She didn't deserve them, but you do."

She put the jewelry in her purse and said, "I'll hold them until this is over and you can give them to me legally."

"Alright."

I retrieved the loaner car from the self-park and made the long trek back to Atlanta. I drove carefully. Although I carried no contraband, a speeding ticket along the route would be damning evidence against me.

That evening I was sitting in the hotel bar watching a pro-football game when Connie called. I walked out of the bar so I could hear what she was saying. From the sound of it, she was hopping mad again.

Out in the lobby I could finally hear well enough to understand her. "You stole Carrie's furs and purses and jewelry!" *They're home from the beach.*

"What are you talking about? I'm in Atlanta."

"Where were you yesterday?"

"I've been in Atlanta since Friday. Company meetings."

"Someone broke in while we were at the beach and stole all her jewelry."

That's a lie. "Did they get the Rolex watch, the wedding rings, the chocolate diamonds?"

"Everything, Randle. They took it all."

Carrie probably stored her jewelry at her momma's house. She's lying to make it a big enough deal for the cops to investigate. "How did the thieves get in?"

"She doesn't know. The doors were locked, the alarm was set, and the dog was on guard."

"Did they harm the dog?"

"No, they tricked it with a stuffed toy."

I broke out laughing. "Your sister is quite a comedienne. No, she's the joke."

"She says it was you. How is stealing from her going to convince her to come see you? She's going to call the cops and tell them you did it."

"I hadn't heard from you or Carrie, so I stayed in Atlanta over the weekend instead of driving back and forth."

"Tell the cops when they knock on your door."

"Tell Carrie I'm ready to negotiate now. See if she can do it next weekend."

Connie grunted something like "Awrrhaw" and hung up on me, so I went back to the bar and resumed my deliberations. Every time I reviewed my plan, it worked.

CHAPTER TWENTY-SIX

In the morning, we explained our time-saving designs to Bob Platt and the executive team. We were ready for an independent board of doctors to use the technology to review closed medical cases and give our little startup the blessing it needed to convince investors to buy into our IPO offering. While we were presenting the design, my phone vibrated in my pocket. I looked and saw that it was my attorney. I didn't answer; this wasn't the time or place for a chat about the divorce.

The executives were pleased with our progress, and several wondered if we couldn't reestablish a November or December IPO date. I couldn't allow that to happen, so I deftly shot the idea down like a bird hunter bagging a pheasant. On the other hand, I was quite confident we would have a successful February launch and I'd reap the monetary benefits.

I found Jerry Louks in the communications room with his arm buried up to his elbow in a wall of electronics. Without being asked, he pulled a small square ticket stub out of his shirt pocket and handed it to me. It felt like another CIA spy operation, the two of us hiding in an equipment closet to exchange secret material.

"Enjoy the game?" I said.

"My niece went with her boyfriend. Braves lost."

Waving the Braves ticket stub at Jerry—a stub for the game Saturday night—I said, "I owe you one, buddy."

As I walked to my car, I peeked at my phone, which had continued to vibrate in my pocket. Tony had left me a text message: *call ASAP, cops looking for you.* I slipped the phone into my pocket and drove to the hotel. Back at the Hilton, I changed clothes, packed my bags, and checked out. When I was on the road to Florida, I called Tony.

Without preamble, he said, "There was a break-in at your wife's house on Saturday."

"I'm really tired of people referring to it as my wife's house. That's yet to be decided."

"Did you do it?"

"I have dozens of witnesses in Atlanta, so stop stressing."

"They suspect it was you because files that went missing when you moved out are back now and the legal file is missing. A thief wouldn't steal her legal file."

"She misplaced some files, but now she's found them. She'll find the legal file when she remembers where she put it—and her gun, if there ever was one. Of course, she could be faking it for the insurance money."

"Maybe. She claimed her furs and purses were stolen, but the cops found them in a second-floor bedroom. The problem is that a Lieutenant

Callahan told me the alarm was tripped by someone who had a key to get in and locked up on the way out, so that would be you."

What? I almost said I didn't hear an alarm. In a daze, I said, "I don't have a key."

"There's no way to prove you don't have a key, Randle. You didn't give her the keys the day you were served. You waited until you moved your stuff out of the house, so you had plenty of time to make a copy."

"She's lying to get back at me for the psychiatric examination."

"It happened, Randle. Don't you want to know what's missing?"

"Not really."

"Jewelry worth a hundred thousand dollars. Did you buy her that much?"

"I bought it, but I didn't steal it. Never earned me any gratitude either."

I received no commiseration from my lawyer. "The cops want to know when you'll be back in Florida."

"Tomorrow. I need to print some pictures of the house so you can get them to the shrinks. Forgot to give them to you before."

"Too late, the examination is over."

"They haven't published their findings. These pictures are conclusive proof of insanity."

Silence crept down the phone line like a high tide sweeping over the shoreline as he calculated the probability that I had taken the "forgotten" pictures when I broke into the house this past weekend. "They have a date and time stamp for the day you moved?"

Uh-oh. "Nah, I don't use that feature."

To mollify me, he said, "Send them to me electronically, and I'll decide if they're relevant enough to break the rules. If they are, I'll print them for you."

And charge me for it. "Thanks, pal."

"Don't have any jewelry with you, Randle. The cops will be waiting for you."

This call had become a nuisance. "I don't have her jewelry, Tony."

"Drive safe, buddy."

Fewer than a dozen cars were scattered around the Municipal Marina parking lot when I arrived on Monday evening. I drove slowly up and down the aisles verifying that no one was sitting in any of the cars—no cops, no Carrie. Pulling to the curb at the walking gate entrance to the docks, I scanned the dock but the only suspicious person in the marina was me. I dumped the luggage on the sidewalk and drove down the street to The Vinoy hotel, where I left my car with the valet. Mumbling to the attendant that I was going to get a bite to eat, I walked back up the street, collected my bags, and punched the security code into the dock gate. My dock was the left-most arm of a "Y" and my boat was third from last in the row, near the channel that exited the harbor. Backed into the slip, the boat faced the hotel anchorage and, across the street, The Vinoy. It was a lovely, peaceful setting, and on this night, a quiet one.

I climbed onto the *Wahine II* and found nothing amiss on the decks or in the aft cabin until I approached the sliding hatch to the interior spaces. Someone—it had to be Carrie because cops hand you search warrants—had used a bolt cutter on the padlock. Through the hatch, I walked into the aftermath of a small tornado.

A trashcan had been dumped onto the galley floor, and the garbage had been trampled as the intruder walked around the spaces. The bow stateroom had been used as a collection point for possessions moved out of other spaces. Bedclothes had been torn off the bow bed and bedclothes from the master stateroom had been piled on top of them. The under-bed storage had also been emptied onto the bed, and all closet contents had been stuffed into the small stateroom. In the galley cabinets stood open, their contents dumped into the sink and onto the counters.

As I moved through the salon, I saw that one edge of the salon carpet was curled under the lounge settee as though it had been pulled up and not replaced correctly. The hatch to the engine room was under the carpet. *Did they sabotage my boat, plant a firebomb that would ignite when I cranked the engines?* I pulled the hatch and dropped into the tight space between the two big diesels. Like a greenhorn, I tugged on hoses and checked caps and bolts to ensure they were tight. No expert at engines, I saw no obvious signs of tampering and nothing that looked like a bomb. Promising myself to test the engines tomorrow, I climbed out of the pit and resumed my tour.

In the master stateroom, the mattress had been moved off the bedframe. The master closet had been emptied; the master bath had been trashed. The contents of the medicine cabinet lay in the sink; the contents of the trashcan lay on the shower stall floor. Begrudgingly, I gave them credit for being thorough. It crossed my mind to call the police, but nothing had been stolen and Carrie obviously had broken in to find *her* missing things. Add the fact that no detective had contacted me about the beach house break-in and reporting this intrusion seemed a waste of time. Too tired to clean the place, I grabbed a pillow and blanket from the bow stateroom and lay on the couch that encircled the dining table in the salon. I cocked the Beretta and laid it on the dining table. I considered a barricade. I considered sleeping on the foredeck. I considered hiding at The Vinoy. Before I could decide what to do, I was asleep, too fatigued to be scared.

CHAPTER TWENTY-SEVEN

I n a funk over the fact that I had no private space immune to Carrie's tampering, I spent the next morning cleaning and organizing the interior of the boat. As promised, I started the engines and let them idle long enough to become convinced they were in good working order. After shutting them down, I found a small padlock in a kitchen drawer and affixed it to the engine room hatch.

I didn't feel obligated to work, so I sat in the aft cabin, drinking port and smoking cigars as I watched the walking gate. No one came to visit. I did not hear from Connie. The cops did not come to interview me. That evening I walked through the park, up to Beach Drive, and ate dinner at a Cajun restaurant. Afterward I sat for a long while on a park bench watching the parking lot for suspicious activity. It did not appear that I was under surveillance. Neither was I being watched, nor protected.

On Wednesday, I felt like a sitting duck on the boat, so I camped out in the park with my tablet computer. I monitored my email as I monitored the marina. There was no sign of Carrie or any co-conspirators. Connie never called. Nonetheless, I felt safer in the park. If Carrie came alone, "dressed to kill," I would execute my plan. If she arrived with reinforcements or snuck up on the boat, I would exit stage left to The Vinoy, retrieve my car, and escape via Fourth Avenue North.

I was about to walk down the street to grab some lunch when a black four-door sedan pulled into the front of the parking lot. A middle-aged, heavyset guy exited the driver's door and two younger men with Marine Corps haircuts also emerged from the sedan. All three wore cheap sports jackets and polyester slacks. They had to be cops. At the gate they were met by the marina store clerk, who let them onto the dock.

It was easy enough to guess they were looking for me, so I followed as they strolled down the dock, checking names on the backs of boats, looking for the *Wahine II*. When they reached my boat, they immediately climbed aboard, which told me they weren't experienced mariners who would have respected the privacy of a boat. I boarded my boat and found the senior cop and one of his minions in the aft cabin. The third cop had gone belowdecks.

To the senior cop, I said, "Since you've already invaded private spaces, I hope you have a search warrant."

He gave me a surprised look and said, "We do."

He handed me a stapled sheaf of paper, and I took a look. The warrant authorized them to search my boat and my car for jewelry, a pistol, and "personal items," i.e., a diary. Attached to the boilerplate was a detailed list of all Carrie's jewelry, including the yellow pendant and matching earrings. Photos of the jewelry were appended to the list.

I handed the warrant back to the senior cop and said, "My wife's jewelry collection. Very comprehensive. Kind of amazing she'd have all that information at her fingertips."

A thoughtful look crossed his face as he folded the document and stuffed it into his jacket pocket. "I'm Detective Lieutenant Michael Callahan of the St. Petersburg Police Department. Are you John R. Marks?"

"I am. People call me Randle."

"Do we have permission to execute the warrant?"

"You already are."

He motioned to the younger cop, who immediately opened the cupboard under the wet bar and began pushing things around to see if there was a hoard of jewelry hiding behind the liquor bottles. Callahan waved me to the couch, and he took a seat in a side chair. He pulled out a notebook and a pen and said, "You mind if I ask you a coupla questions?"

The younger cop moved onto the bridge and peered under the dashboard.

I said, "Not a bit."

"Where were you last Saturday?"

"In Atlanta. I had business on Friday and Monday, so I stayed the weekend instead of driving back and forth."

"Where did you stay?"

"The Technology Park Hilton."

Callahan wrote that down. "Where were you at ten p.m. on Saturday?"

I took a second to reply. "On my way back to the hotel after a Braves game. I think I have the ticket stub in my wallet."

One of his eyebrows twitched just enough for me to notice. I reached for my wallet, but he waved a hand to let me know it wasn't necessary.

"We're going to run a check on your credit cards, see where you filled up with gas over the weekend."

I shrugged. "Okay." *Dry hole, my friend. I paid with cash at every stop.*

"We're going to pull your cell phone records too. See which towers you were pinging on Saturday."

I shrugged again. "Okay." *Another dry hole. I left my cell phone in Atlanta and carried a disposable with me on the trip. I never had to use it.*

The younger cop went belowdecks, and soon we heard pots and pans clanging and glasses clinking as he searched the galley.

Callahan said, "Do you have a key to your wife's house?"

"No I don't, officer." *Honest answer.* "I'm sure she changed the locks the second I moved out."

Lieutenant Callahan's fleshy face formed a self-satisfied smile. "Your wife says she never got around to changing the locks."

I shot him an incredulous sneer. "Have you checked with Jimmy's Lock and Key in New Port Richey? That's who we use."

He blinked a couple of times, wrote a note.

I went on, "My lawyer told me she reported a break-in, but I don't know the security access codes."

Callahan recovered quickly. "Neither did the thief. The alarm was tripped, but Mrs. Marks had it on silent so the thief wouldn't know it was sounding. She wanted to give the police time to react and catch the thief in the house."

It took me a few moments to figure it out. *Battery backup.* I had forgotten the system has a battery backup, and I hadn't disconnected it before I entered the house. I heard no alarm because it was on silent alert. *Sloppy!* "I guess they didn't catch the thief or you wouldn't be here."

Callahan looked resigned to that failure. "No call was ever made to the monitoring station. We haven't figured that out yet."

"Maybe the call was made, but the monitoring station screwed it up."

"Maybe." He sucked on his pencil a minute, then said, "Tell me somethin' else: You friends with that dog of hers?"

"Hell no! She bought it after she kicked me out. I saw it the day I moved my furniture. Had to keep the monster locked in the sunroom."

"The burglar trapped it upstairs. Tore the hell out of the media room. She's pretty upset about that."

"Maybe there was no burglar. My lawyer tells me you found the things she thought were missing. Maybe my wife is lying about the whole incident."

"Why would she do that?"

I laughed. "To frame me."

Callahan looked thoughtful again. Just then, the two cops who had been searching belowdecks popped through the hatch. They shook their heads at Callahan—they hadn't found anything incriminating.

Callahan asked me, "Can we have the keys to your car please?"

I reached over to the side table, grabbed the keys, and tossed them toward the younger cops in one motion. It took them by surprise and they got in one another's way and fumbled the catch. One cop stooped to pick them up while the other glared at me. Then they left for the parking lot.

Callahan turned back to me. "If your wife was going to frame you, who would help her?"

Without hesitating, I said, "Larry Pardeaux—P-a-r-d-e-a-u-x—her handyman. Uses him as a bodyguard. They assaulted me in this parking lot a few days ago. I didn't want to hire him, but Carrie liked watching him work bareback in the yard. He was a bodybuilder when he did time, and he's covered in prison tattoos."

Callahan jerked in his seat. Cops like nothing better than a suspect with a criminal history. "Did he have a key to the house?"

"Yes." *And a garage door opener and the access codes.* "So does the maid and Carrie's momma. We used to hide a key in the yard too."

"Not anymore. We asked."

"And you believed her?"

Callahan sighed. "Walk with me to the parking lot, see what my boys found in your car."

As we walked down the deserted dock, Callahan questioned me about the boats in the marina: how much to buy one, what did they cost to maintain? He was shocked by my answers. Clearly, he was disappointed at how far out of his price range even the smaller boats were. In the parking lot, the two younger cops were leaning against the unmarked cruiser. They shook their heads in unison. I wasn't sure either of them had vocal chords. One of them threw my keys at me, and I made a leaping catch. I gave them my sports hero smile, and they glared back.

Callahan thanked me for my cooperation, and they drove away. As I walked back to the boat to see how badly they had trashed my private spaces, I wondered if they'd get another warrant for the beach house.

After cleaning up the boat yet again, I logged into the cloud account to see what Carrie had been doing on her computer. As had been the case since installing the keystroke recording software, Carrie had logged onto Facebook and her public email account once per day, but she had not checked her secret account, *shadylady44*. Was she doing that from a computer I didn't know about?

Irritated that Carrie received more attention from the police than I did, I called Officer Williams again. The young cop was apologetic and promised once again to follow up with detectives. *Right.*

Later that afternoon, Tony called me to his office. When Melissa ushered me through the door, I could see it wasn't going to be good news.

Tony's mouth drooped, and his heavy Italian face sagged. "I got the psychiatrists' report on your wife's little holiday at the funny farm."

"Are they going to put her away?"

"No," he said in a dejected voice. He handed me a packet of documents.

As I scanned the ten pages, Tony said, "They presented their findings to Judge Smithson this morning. She doesn't qualify for an involuntary commitment."

I tried to interrupt, but he held up a hand and continued. "She *is* sick, but not in the right way. You'll see in there that she has several personality disorders—narcissistic, paranoid, avoidant, and histrionic. Probably antisocial disorder, but they'd need more time to decide."

"They could have kept her another day. The woman is a psychopath!"

"She's a nasty piece of work, but that's not enough for a commitment. Even if they had diagnosed her as antisocial, it wouldn't have mattered. The statute explicitly exempts antisocial personality disorder as a reason for involuntary commitment because we have drugs to treat the problem. You have to hallucinate and hear voices to get a room at the asylum."

"Psychopaths commit mass murders. They should be committed."

"The legal definition of insanity is knowing the difference between right and wrong. Psychopaths know the difference; they just don't care about the distinction. So we convict them and send them to jail."

"So you'll wait for her to hurt someone—probably me—and then you'll throw her in jail for a while. *That's* what's insane!"

Tony was tiring of the debate. "If we sent every sicko to the funny farm, we'd need more asylums than prisons." He said it as though the absurdity were evident.

"Exactly! We don't have a criminal behavior problem; we have a mental health problem."

Tony waved the argument away with both hands. "Bottom line: Smithson ordered mandatory outpatient care from the hospital, not from her shrink in Safety Harbor."

"Did you get the pictures to the shrinks before they wrote this report?"

"Those pictures were very disturbing. I showed them to Smithson, and he agreed. He had them hand-carried to the shrinks, but it was too late to question your wife. She had been released."

"File another Baker Act petition and include them as new evidence. Keep doing it until they finally realize they should hold her."

"You're not going to get a second bite of the apple, Randle. It's on to the next phase. Mediation has been rescheduled for a week from Friday with Ross again. He cleared his calendar just for us so we can comply with the judge's order."

"I'm not doing another mediation, Tony. My offer is on the table. Mediation is a waste of time, so cancel it."

There was a pause as he struggled to form sentences that wouldn't completely enrage me. "You won't get a trial without mediation, Randle."

As fiercely as I could, I said, "You can tell the judge she won't get a settlement unless I get a trial."

Tony gave me a look as though he no longer recognized his client. He exhaled. "Have the police interviewed you yet?"

"You could call it that. They had a warrant and tore the boat up but didn't find anything."

"I'm glad the police didn't find anything, Randle. Would hurt to fire a client."

But wouldn't hurt to fire a friend? "Relax, Tony, I'm clean as a whistle."

———∞———

I couldn't relax. The powers that be had thwarted my quest for justice once again. In a pique, I wrote another fake email although I was no longer sure they were being read by anyone.

> **Tony,**
> **Let's not wait for the trial to be approved. We know who MD is, so depose him ASAP.**
> **Randle**

CHAPTER TWENTY-EIGHT

T he closing on the beach house sale took place at the West Florida Title Company in South Pasadena first thing Friday morning. While I attended to the closing, Glenda met the movers at the beach house where all of my earthly possessions were loaded into a PODS container and driven to a public storage lot.

At the closing there was no happy young couple acquiring their dream home, just the speculator's agent and attorney. I signed a pile of documents, handed the closing attorney a check for forty-five thousand dollars, and gave Jane Whitehead a hug. She didn't offer to take me to breakfast or to Starbucks. She climbed into her black GMC Denali with her commission check and drove away with a perfunctory wave. I consoled myself with the thought that after the IPO, I'd be back in the market for something bigger and better than the little bungalow.

I tried Connie's cell phone multiple times without success. Instead of answering my calls, she sent a text: *lose my number.*

My only home was the *Wahine II*, so I went there and waited for fate to find me.

It took no time at all for fate to locate me. The boat rocked to starboard, toward the staircase that led from the swim platform to the aft cabin, interrupting the rhythmic rise and fall caused by swells off the Bay. Someone had come aboard. I slid out from behind the dining table in the salon, where I had been working, and grabbed the Beretta. I crouched at the bottom of the short staircase to the aft cabin with the cocked gun aimed at the hatch.

The hatch slid open, and I squeezed the trigger to the safety point. Tony recoiled, but he wasn't nimble enough to jump out of my view. "Damn, Randle! What are you doing with that gun?"

"Never, ever come aboard a boat without permission. You'll get yourself shot."

"Well, can I come in?"

He looked like he had had a bad day. He was in shirtsleeves with the cuffs rolled up and his tie loosened. Sweat ringed his collar and soiled his underarms. "We need to talk," he said.

I laid the pistol on the dining table and slid into the circular seat. He took the opposing couch. I said, "Shoot."

Tony flinched, puffed his cheeks, and blew his stale breath into the chilled air of the salon. "Can you put that thing away?" He meant my pistol.

I took it off the table and slipped it into my waistband. He gave me the look parents reserve for recalcitrant children. "Cancelling mediation was a bad idea, Randle. When I informed Her Honor, she said, 'This won't get you a trial, buster. Ms. de Castro will reschedule mediation with a mediator of her choice. Your motion will be held in abeyance until you make a deal at mediation, at which time the motion will be moot.'"

"Tell her again that I will not submit to mediation. If she won't give us a trial, ask for one in my countersuit."

Tony showed no emotion. "The judge upheld de Castro's motion to dismiss your countersuit. Called it 'frivolous and superfluous.'"

The judge was herding me into her legal paddock like a steer going to slaughter. "All your legal system is good for is running up legal fees."

"I won't be billing you anymore, Randle. What comes next is painful for me, but my partners insisted. I have to ask you to find another attorney."

"What? Why?"

"Number one: The judge thinks I'm toying with her, and that will hurt your chances. Number two: The cops have gotten a search warrant for your storage unit. We're not a criminal defense firm. Number three: I'm very nervous about the provenance of the pictures I gave to the judge. And number four: Some woman mysteriously turned up at the hospital with your wife's diary. I don't know who she was and I don't want to know, so don't say a word."

"Must have been her sister."

"Her sister isn't a redhead. Your wife had already been discharged, so the hospital turned the diary over to the cops. It's one of the items missing after the break-in at your wife's house."

Glenda! "I had nothing to do with it."

"Knock it off, Randle. When you get caught for the break-in, I don't want to be within a hundred miles of you."

"When you're back to sitting second chair, wining and dining fat cats, remember that I gave you a chance to be more than that."

It took a long time for Tony to compose himself and respond. During all that time, I wished I could stuff the words back down my throat and turn them back into air in my lungs.

Appearing thoughtful, Tony said, "I used to wish I was more than a schmoozer, but after representing you, I realize I'm not a shark. I'm a panfish, and I'm okay with that."

"Fine. I can take care of myself."

He looked at me with pity emanating from those wet, brown Italian eyes. "You'll need a lawyer, Randle. I can send you a list we recommend."

"Seriously, Tony, don't worry about me."

Tony didn't seem to know what to do—he just sat there like an overripe Roma tomato—so I motioned toward the hatch and he took the hint. He ascended the three steps, then bent down through the hatchway to say, "Don't send me any more email. You can't claim attorney-client privilege anymore."

And my best friend walked out of my life.

CHAPTER TWENTY-NINE

aturday morning dawned routinely bright and sunny, Mother
Nature oblivious to my plight. In a foul mood, I drank my
wake-up coffee and marveled at how often my life seemed a
neutralized combination of good news and bad news. The good news:
Carrie had no motive to kill me. The bad news: If Carrie didn't come to
kill me, I had no way to win the divorce game.

I dialed Connie's cell phone one more time. As my phone beeped
and beeped in my ear, I imagined Connie staring at her caller ID,
waiting for the ringing to stop, waiting for me to leave another message.
Tired of playing that game, I hung up and climbed into the Bronco
and headed straight out to Central Avenue. At Thirty-Fourth Street, I
made a right turn and drove north, past the Walmart Supercenter, past
a row of no-tell motels, and into a nicer residential area. I had only
been to Connie's house once, but I was fairly sure I could find it. When
I turned onto Twenty-First Avenue North, a neighborhood of retirees

living on Social Security, I realized it might not be easy—all the houses were white, single-story, wood-frame bungalows with royal palm trees in the yards. I cruised slowly down the street and circled the block on Twenty-Second Avenue North.

As I approached Thirty-Fourth Street again, nearly drained of confidence, I spotted Connie's blue sedan in the driveway of a house that was somewhat distinctive. When I saw it, I remembered it. A miniature portico, supported by two skinny poles that couldn't honestly be called columns, extended from the roof to the sidewalk that led to the driveway and provided shelter for guests as they approached her front door. I pulled in and parked behind her car, blocking it in. If she wanted to run, she would have to do it on foot.

She may have seen me arrive because the moment I rang her doorbell, the front door swung open to reveal a tousled Connie Tomkins, barefoot and wrapped in a faded blue terrycloth bathrobe. She didn't seem enthusiastic to see me.

"You okay, sis?"

"Sure," she said, like a patient fresh from surgery. "Why wouldn't I be?"

"You didn't answer the phone. I thought there was something wrong."

She leaned out the door and glanced up and down the street before walking into her living room, giving me a view of white, sturdy legs over ankles as sharp as knife blades. I followed and closed the door behind me.

As she walked, Connie said, "I'll be okay. You're the one with problems. Momma told me your trial has been denied, your countersuit has been dismissed, and Carrie can choose a new mediator." Over her shoulder, she gave me the cat-who-ate-the-canary look. "She knows your lawyer quit. He notified the court that he is no longer representing you."

Tony wasted no time distancing himself. Wimp. I returned her look and said, "Carrie is smart enough to realize that none of that matters. I won't do mediation. I'll force the judge to grant a trial, and now I can hire a shark to swallow that little panfish she hired."

Connie stopped and gave me a doubtful look. "Your plans always fall apart. Carrie has won as usual, and you've lost. She even fooled the shrinks at the asylum. You should be used to this. I am."

"You're forgetting there are things she wants."

A look of genuine surprise erupted on her plain face like the sun peeking through the clouds to signal the end of a storm. Walking again, in a tentative voice she said, "You do have her diary and jewelry?"

I found it interesting that Connie thought her sister had been lying. "She knows exactly what I have. So what's her next move? Will she come to the boat to talk, or will she come to murder me?"

Connie spun on her heel, her face flushed with emotion. "How would I know? I've been ostracized. In front of everybody she said, 'What the hell do you think you're doing? He's still my husband.'"

I spread my hands in the there-you-go gesture. "That's what you get for trying to help her."

"They used me, Randle. My entire life they used me, and now they don't need me."

I knew, of course, that Connie wanted to be used. She wanted the family to be dependent upon her because that was her only source of self-esteem. "Carrie still needs you. Reach out to her."

Pointing an angry finger at my face, she said, "You used me too. You had no interest in me as a person."

I stopped, and heat rose through my neck and into my cheeks. "I'm sorry about how our dinner ended. I shouldn't have pressed you about Dickson."

She shook her head. "Was it too much to ask that you comfort me for one lousy night? Who were you being loyal to? Surely not my sister."

Easing toward her, I gently said, "I didn't want you to think I was taking advantage of you."

Her nostrils flared and heat flashed in her eyes like summer lightning. "So, you were saving me from myself? I wouldn't have been sorry in the morning, Randle. You wouldn't have had a crybaby on your hands."

That pissed me off. "You aren't interested in me either, Connie Mae. You just wanted to sleep with me to get revenge on your sister."

Connie collapsed and knelt in front of me like a Catholic at Mass. "I did hope you'd like me, but not anymore. I'm done with you and my sister."

"And she's done with you. She played you for a fool. When she gets her settlement, she'll become the family bank and you'll become irrelevant."

She began to weep, silent grief flowing down her ruined face. I moved to her, and she let me help her to her feet and steer her toward the couch. After I wiped her tears with my handkerchief, I chose an easy chair across from her. A low wooden coffee table separated us. As I remembered, the furnishings were humble. She folded her hands in her lap, waiting for hope.

I cleared my throat. "On Monday, someone broke into my boat and trashed it. Had you heard about that?"

She didn't make eye contact as she said, "No."

"On Tuesday the cops searched my boat. They were looking for her diary, her pistol, and her jewelry. Did you know about that?"

She jumped to her feet and wandered toward the dining room. She didn't turn around, so I couldn't see her face as she said, "No."

"The night we went to dinner, someone broke into the beach house and stole my pistol. Did you tell her we'd be at dinner?"

She spun toward me, like a revolving door set on slow speed, her face blank and her chalky skin the color of a bleached hospital bedsheet.

She sounded like a mechanical announcement on an airport tram as she said, "No."

"The cops know who did it. They have a warrant for his arrest."

Connie nearly collapsed again, but she caught herself with one hand on the dining room table.

"You should let her know, Connie. And let me know what she wants to bring this to an end."

Stunned, she said, "Carrie doesn't tell me everything."

"Only enough to use you. Did they talk about a settlement when you were at the beach?"

Her face drew a blank again. She was behaving as though she had taken drugs that had dulled her senses and slowed her thought processes. "Just a minute," she said as she headed for the kitchen. I heard her run tap water into a glass. When she returned, she sat on the far end of the couch, putting some distance between us. Holding the glass, she looked at me and said, "She wants the house, a car, alimony, and enough stock to be set for life."

"If I'm dead, there's no alimony."

She grunted and took a sip of water. She ran her hands through her hair, pulling the stray strands away from her face, holding the hair back as though it interfered with her thoughts. Squeezing her head to force the next thought into the conversation, she said, "If you're dead, she gets all the options, life insurance, and the house."

Not anymore. My share goes to Jamie, but you're next in line for Carrie's jackpot. I stared at her, and she matched my gaze. "So she wins either way. She won't wait for another mediation?"

Talking more to herself than to me, she said, "She knows you won't cooperate. Her lawyer is useless. The judge doesn't like her."

"Okay, Connie, tell her you've negotiated a deal with me. You convinced me to give her the house and a new Bentley to replace the Jag. She wants a Bentley."

Connie went somewhere far away, lost in her own world of conflicting emotions. I stood and started pacing. It was dark in the house, the blinds closed, the shades drawn. There were no sounds from the street.

I waited a lifetime for her to say, "I can try." She watched me pace.

Over my shoulder, I said, "There'll be alimony, of course, and I'll split the options with her. I just want this to be over."

"Sure. If she'll talk to me."

"I'll want a few things in return, but I won't prosecute her accomplice who broke into the house. Wouldn't want Travis or your daddy going to jail for Carrie."

She choked back a scream just as her cell phone rang. She looked at the caller ID screen and said, "I have to take this." She turned away and walked to the kitchen before answering the call. I couldn't hear what she said, but she was back in less than a minute.

I moved toward her so we were standing close together in the foyer. For an awkward moment, we jerked back and forth, hinting at an embrace and mutually deciding against it.

She looked at me with faded blue eyes. "I have to meet someone."

"Sure. Let me know if she's coming."

"She's dangerous, Randle."

"I know."

Before I passed through the door, she said, "You have a new gun, don't you?"

Over my shoulder, I said, "Of course."

***

As soon as I got back to the boat, I checked the cloud account. Once again, Carrie had failed to check *shadylady44*. *There's something wrong with this picture.* Remembering how stunned Connie was by the news that the cops knew the identity of the beach house robber, I decided to launch one last rocket at my target.

> **Tony,**
> **The cops know who broke into my house and stole my gun. Probably the same guy who broke in a couple of weeks ago. They've asked for a warrant, and we should have an arrest any day now.**
> **Randle**

It was of no importance to me whether that note was attorney-client privileged. By late afternoon I was certain Carrie would not come to the boat today, but, not wanting to deal with her in diminishing light and not wanting to be in blue water after dark, I walked to The Vinoy and took a room. I slept like a well-fed baby for the very last time.

CHAPTER THIRTY

I n the movie *Straw Dogs*, the Dustin Hoffman character rigs his house to defend himself against the roughneck laborers who've been tantalized by Hoffman's recklessly teasing wife. The Susan George character had taunted Hoffman's character by arousing the laborers without any awareness she was creating a deadly situation. Carrie Marks could have played the Susan George role without having to act at all. I hoped I was clever enough to play the Hoffman part.

In the hope that my visit to Connie would produce results, I spent Sunday morning rigging my boat for a potential encounter with Carrie. I rolled up the Plexiglas windows in the aft cabin so I would have a clear view of any intruders and a clear shot at them, if it came to that. The Plexiglas was old, stiff, and cloudy and might deflect a bullet fired through it. I climbed down on the dock and released all the mooring lines except the port bowline and the compensating starboard stern line. I wanted to be able to get underway as soon as Carrie arrived so I could get a head start on her daddy. If Carrie wanted me to go to the Gulf, I assumed her daddy would exit his marina via John's Pass and intercept us off Clearwater Beach. He wouldn't come through the Bay and risk being detected again as he followed us all the way up there.

I went belowdecks to get my Beretta. I checked the clip but did not chamber a round. Carrie wasn't strong enough to operate the slide to cock the gun, so if she grabbed it she wouldn't be able to use it on me. I carried the gun back to the bridge and hid it in a pile of grease rags on the shelf under the instrument panel. Lastly, I pulled out the western Florida sea charts and determined the exact latitude and longitude of Mullet Key Bayou and the sheltered cove where we often anchored overnight. When I issued my Mayday, I wanted to have the coordinates handy.

Ready for her, I sat on the bridge from which I could see the front rank of cars in the parking lot. Santana's "Put Your Lights On," an eerie song that drips with suspenseful and portentous rhythms, blasted through the speaker system. Sweat dripped from my brow. The coffee turned cold and bitter. Dock noises annoyed me. The salt air smelled putrid. Minutes became hours. If Carrie didn't come to the boat today, the game was lost; I had no more aces to play. By noon, I had lost my edge and the heat had sapped my energy. Rather than waste the day, I decided to cruise to the cove and anchor there for the night. Perhaps Glenda could drive to Fort De Soto Park and join me for some afternoon delight. The big diesels were warming up when my phone dinged. Connie's text message read: *Carrie is on the way to the boat.* On cue, my adrenal glands pumped energy into my flagging system.

I hustled down the dock to the parking lot and found a spot on a park bench that gave me a good view of arriving cars. If Carrie came alone, I'd meet her at the boat. If she was escorted, I'd walk away from the boat, up to Beach Road, and sit in a bar until they gave up on me.

Fifteen minutes later, Connie's blue sedan pulled into the lot and stopped near the street where I wouldn't have seen it had I been on the boat. Carrie emerged and walked across the lot as Connie drove away. Carrie didn't plan to disembark my boat at the marina. The good news was that her only help would arrive by water.

Carrie was "dressed to kill" in high-heeled sandals and a beach cover-up that flapped open as she strutted, revealing a red bikini. It was an outfit designed to titillate, à la the Susan George character, so that I would be distracted and welcome her onboard.

As she wound her way between cars, I loped down the dock and up the staircase to the aft cabin. I leaned out the side window, puffing on a cigar as she walked down the dock.

When she reached our slip, she constructed a disarming smile and said, "Can I join you?"

"Have we put the little problem with the Jag behind us?"

"Connie said you'll buy me a Bentley. Convertible, right?" She sounded like a little kid asking Santa for presents.

I shrugged. "You're not upset about the psychiatric exam?"

She shrugged. "They didn't find anything wrong with me."

That wasn't entirely true. Pointing to the soft fabric bag slung over her shoulder, I said, "Planning to spend the night?"

She gave me a coquettish smile. "I brought something comfortable to wear later."

A cold tremor, like an arctic earthquake, shook my body. I would have bet the Ferrari that the cloth bag contained conservative clothes so she wouldn't look like a temptress when the cops came.

"So you came to make a deal?"

Carrie didn't hide her frustration. Her charms were usually more than enough reason for men to let her have her way. In the exasperated voice all wives know how to use, she said, "My lawyer won't do a damn thing for me, and she makes me ask for things I don't care about so she can brag about the great job she's doing. We can do better without the lawyers."

"I agree, but I have one condition: I want to know the truth about what went on in our marriage. Call it closure." It depressed me to say that.

"Then we need to have an adult conversation right now, to clear the air. You can ask me anything you want and I'll tell you the truth, if you think you can handle it."

I didn't want to hear a confession calculated to blame me for her indiscretions. I didn't want to hear the grisly details of her affairs. I didn't want to stare at her half-clothed body as she described what other men had done to her. I didn't even want to hear the truth. I wanted her to lie, to deny her infidelity, so I could catch her in the lie and punish her for it.

Pretending to be convinced by her argument, I acquiesced. "Come on up."

Relieved, she stepped onto the stern platform and headed up the built-in staircase to the aft cabin entryway. She walked straight to a deck chair, placed the cloth bag gently on the wicker couch, and flopped into the seat. "The engines are running. Were you expecting someone else?"

"I was on my way to the cove down by Fort De Soto. Going to spend the night."

A faraway look came into Carrie's eyes as her mental wheels spun. "You could get me a drink before we shove off."

I went down to the galley and mixed her a rum and Coke. When I returned to the aft cabin, she looked tense, her legs tightly crossed.

I said, "If you're ready to go, we can shove off."

"Aren't you going to have a drink with me?"

"I'll get a beer when we're ready to talk."

I went down to the dock and released the mooring lines. As I reentered the aft cabin, Carrie emerged from belowdecks with consternation on her face.

"What's wrong?"

"Nothing. I used the head."

Looking for her stuff. I climbed onto the bridge. She followed and took a seat in the co-captain's chair. As we eased out of the berth, into the channel, and through the mouth of the harbor, she said, "I miss this. Let's go out in the Gulf and ride up along the beaches like we used to do. Then we can go to our spot offshore and wait for the lights to come on in Clearwater."

I remembered what Connie had said: *If she wants you to go out into the Gulf, up to Clearwater, you'll know she didn't come to give you hugs and kisses.* I neither agreed nor disagreed. We sat in silence, the breeze in our faces, as I sailed southward through the Bay toward the Sunshine Skyway Bridge. Carrie sat motionless, sipping her drink, appearing to enjoy the wind in her face. It was like a pet rattlesnake was coiled on my living room floor. It seemed passive but could strike at any moment. As we approached the massive bridge, I carefully maneuvered away from the shipping channels crowded with container ships and tankers, all in a line like airplanes landing at a busy airport. I swiveled in my chair to scan the water behind us. There were no Boston Whalers following us.

When I turned back around, she made a toasting gesture with her glass. We drank, and more at ease, she said, "Can I have my diary back? You can keep the yellow diamonds. I'd have preferred sapphires to match my eyes, but you were never good at selecting presents for me."

You ungrateful slut! You don't even know why I gave you the present. I said, "The cops searched the boat and didn't find anything of yours."

Her sneer became a snarl. "The cops couldn't find their ass with two hands and a flashlight. Before I leave the boat, I want all my stuff back."

"And I want my gun."

She smirked. "I don't have your gun."

"You broke in once to steal the financial records and the sex tape, and you broke in a second time to steal my gun, so don't act like you're innocent."

A faraway look came into her eyes. If she had been strapped to an MRI machine, her brain activity would have looked like a Google map tracking Manhattan taxi traffic. Hundreds of thoughts were leaping from synapse to synapse.

She said, "I took the financial records with me when I moved out of the beach house. I had forgotten about the tape, only found it because my lawyer made me go through the records. I thought I could use it to twist your arm, but you outmaneuvered me." She made another toasting motion with her glass.

Liar. You tripped the alarm. As we motored westward, under the Pinellas Bayway and toward open water, I said, "I know you've been reading the emails I send to my lawyer. You had Scott Simmons put an email snooper on my computer."

She laughed an unladylike guffaw. "Scott wouldn't pee on me if I was on fire. He hates me for stealing his daddy away from his mommy."

"It's a crime to tap email, *shadylady44*. Did you know that?"

For just an instant, a thundercloud passed behind her eyes but the weather cleared quickly. She said, "You have me confused with someone else. If you want the truth about us, get to it."

I shrugged. "Did you do it for the money?"

"The divorce?"

"The marriage."

"No, not only. My family was broke, so I needed someone to support us, but I was also attracted to you. You were handsome, classy, a professional man with good prospects, as they say. We made an attractive couple. I got what I wanted, and so did you—you got a trophy wife. Now we want other things."

"I would have kept my end of the bargain, but you cheated on me."

She wasn't surprised by the allegation. "It's not cheating if you're in love. Lots of men saw how unhappy I was and wanted to comfort me, but I only let the man I love have me."

I believed her. Carrie judged her self-worth by the reflection she saw in the eyes of others; her entire life was like a selfie posted online, hoping someone would give her a "like." Those other men were used to build her self-esteem but not to sleep in her bed.

"MD?"

She snickered. "So you *have* read my diary. I wasn't smart enough to wait for his divorce the first time, but this time I insisted. When you stopped caring about me, he came back into my life and I needed that."

*Came back into her life. I'll be damned. Dr. Richard Puralto, **MD**, is the other man.*

"So you did cheat."

"You can call it cheating if it makes you feel better, but I don't. I only did what you forced me to do." *Men cheat for sex; women cheat for emotional comfort.*

Carrie sat primly, exuding self-righteousness—a woman as innocent as a golddigging cheater could be because her sins were the natural byproducts of a modern marriage.

"Where is WW?"

She laughed and swept her hand from horizon to horizon. "Right here on your White Whale."

Of course! That was her derogatory nickname for the *Wahine II.* "Are you going to make a life with this guy? Is that why you want to take me to the cleaners?"

"We won't get married anytime soon. For a relationship to work, a woman should be financially independent. That's where you come in."

You insulting bitch! We reached the go/no-go point, and instead of turning northward to run past the beaches, I turned the boat to the south, toward Mullet Key and the private cove. As soon as I made the turn, she knew what I had done.

"Where are you going? I want to go up to Clearwater."

"The cove is a better place to talk. There are big rollers out in the Gulf, so the cove is safer."

Her voice rising with irritation, she said, "I thought this ride was for me."

"I told you I was going to the cove, and you asked if you could come along. Why are you getting testy?"

"Well, shame on me for thinking you might do something I want to do." Carrie gritted her teeth and growled. "I'm going to get another drink." She picked up her cell phone and her bag and went belowdecks, but she neglected to take her half-full drink glass with her.

For several minutes, I cruised slowly southward and wondered if she'd emerge from the cabin with guns blazing. I considered locking her in the cabin, but it was too soon for that.

When Carrie returned, I had my hand under the dashboard, close to my gun. She wasn't carrying a drink and she wasn't holding a gun either, so I relaxed. She seemed calm as she came to the bridge to collect her drink. Then she took a seat in the aft cabin. I guessed she had given her daddy new instructions about our destination.

I said, "Come back up here so we can talk as we're cruising."

"I can talk from down here. I want the Bentley you promised me."

Getting right to it. "Sure. What will you give me in return?"

"Why do I have to give something up?"

"Because it's a negotiation. You have to give in order to get. You always had trouble with that principle."

"Connie said you agreed to the car and the house."

I shrugged. "The house is no problem. You can buy it from me."

Shouting now, she said, "I don't have credit, and you know it!"

Still calm, I said, "You don't need credit, you have stock options. Give me back forty thousand options, and you can have the house and everything in it."

She stood up and stomped her foot. "Forty thousand! You think I'm stupid?" She gesticulated with her glass, and her rum and Coke sloshed over the rim and onto the deck. "The wife always gets the house. My lawyer said so."

"Let's go to trial and see if she's right."

She wore a nasty smirk as she said, "There will never be a trial."

"That's right." I snapped my fingers like I had just thought of something. "You'll be in the looney bin after the shrinks read your diary."

"I'm not crazy!" She whirled around and grabbed a candy-striped cushion off the wicker sofa and threw it across the cabin. It ricocheted off the wet bar, bounced end over end, and dove through the entranceway and into the ocean.

"You've kidnapped me," she said. "I'm going to scream for help if we pass a boat."

"Go stand up in the bow showing your ass. It's what you're good at. I'll stop for the first boat full of horny rednecks so you can have some real fun."

Carrie moved toward the steps to the bridge and gesticulated with her long-nailed hands. "All I've ever been to you is a sex toy."

"That's all you've ever wanted to be, for me and everyone else."

"Must be nice to think you're Mr. Clean, but I know you cheated with Glenda, and Connie told me how you tried to get her into bed. I'm surprised she didn't let you; she's tried to steal every boyfriend since Chance Dickson in high school."

"Look who's rewriting history. I know you stole Chance from Connie. She told me all about it."

That unladylike guffaw erupted again, this time with a touch of hysteria. "My sister is delusional. I made him take her to the prom so she wouldn't be a wallflower, and she tried to get him to do her. He brought her home early and took me to all the after-parties. Travis was conceived that night, in Chance's car."

Later I would take the time to process this conflicting information, but right now all I wanted to do was hurt her. "You always seal the deal with sex. Only way you ever get a man."

"You son of a bitch!" She threw her drink at me, and it bounced off the windscreen, showering the instrument panel with ice and a sticky liquid. As she stepped over to the wet bar to grab a liquor bottle by its neck, I pulled my cell phone from my pocket and put it on video record. I aimed it at her as she cocked her arm to throw the bottle at me.

"I wouldn't do that if I were you," I said. "It won't look good to the shrinks."

She slammed the bottle back into its rack. Smiling for the camera, she said, "I'm going below to change clothes. I'm not comfortable with a rapist leering at me."

"Too late. I've got your costume on tape," I said, but she was gone down the hatch to the cabin. *To change into the modest clothes she wanted to have spattered with my blood.*

I grabbed the Beretta, racked the slide, and placed it within easy reach. Then I cut the engines back to idle and sprinted down the steps to the cabin hatch. I peeked inside but couldn't see Carrie. Guessing this would be my last chance to neutralize her, I swiftly pulled the hatch closed, flipped the hasp across the eyelet, and slipped the padlock into place. With more than a little trepidation, I slammed the padlock shut and officially committed a kidnapping.

Trembling uncontrollably, I moved back to the bridge and inched the throttles forward. That's when I picked up the radio microphone, dialed in the emergency frequency, and broadcast a Mayday: "Being attacked by armed men." I gave as my positional coordinates the latitude and longitude of the private cove. As I cruised, I picked a rag from beneath the instrument panel and wiped down the gauges and controls.

Carrie attempted to open the hatch and come topside but found it locked. She pounded on the cabin hatch repeatedly and shouted profanities. It reminded me of the time she had trapped a scorpion on the kitchen floor by placing a large water glass over it. When I tried to dispose of it, I found the scorpion relentlessly striking the side of the glass in a vain effort to escape. It was an impressive display of blind anger, and that is the display Carrie now made—blind anger at being locked belowdecks. I advanced the throttles as far as I dared given the traffic on the Intracoastal Waterway. At eleven knots, it would take me another ten to fifteen minutes to reach the cove. Traveling at blue water speeds from his marina near Clearwater, Harlan would be close behind, but marine cops patrolling the Fort De Soto area should beat both of us to the cove.

The insistent ringing of a phone broke my concentration. It wasn't my phone in my pocket and it didn't sound muffled, as though it were coming from belowdecks. I looked around the bridge and then walked down into the aft cabin. In her agitated state, Carrie had failed to take her phone with her below. It lay on an end table and was vibrating and jumping around like a tarantula ready to strike. I saw that the caller was Travis, probably wanting to confirm the rendezvous location and time. When I answered the phone, the kid nearly choked.

"Is my mom there?"

"Oh yeah, but she's busy doing what she does best . . . you know what I mean?"

"It's not a joke, Randle. I need to be sure she's alright, so have her call me."

"I'm not joking, Travis. I'll have her call you as soon as she's done."

I punched the "end" button and chuckled. Since Carrie had failed to take her phone with her, she wouldn't be broadcasting any Maydays of her own.

As I neared the cove, I slowed to a snail's pace, eased through the mouth of the cove, and reversed the engines to halt the boat's momentum. I wanted to be certain I wasn't sailing into an ambush. No other boats were in the cove, so I turned to the right, into the cove's open water, and spun the boat around so I could back up to the dock. When I was about ten yards away from it, I threw the throttles into neutral and went down to the bow to lower the anchor. When it touched bottom I gave it ten more yards of chain, then locked the anchor chain so no more slack could play out. Back in the bridge, I put the boat into reverse and gave it some power until the anchor set and the boat was caught up short. The stern platform was less than three feet from the dock. When the police got there, they could just walk out onto the dock and step onto the boat.

There was nothing left to do but wait. When Julius Caesar decided to cross the Rubicon, he reportedly said, "The die is cast." I said those words aloud. If Harlan and Travis never turned up, the cops would arrest me for kidnapping. If Harlan and Travis did show up, I would fight for my life. Belowdecks, Carrie threw dishes against the bulkheads, but her effort to alert passersby was futile; the cove and its banks were deserted.

CHAPTER THIRTY-ONE

I heard them coming long before I could see them. From more than a mile away, the piercing squeals of twin Mercury outboards, operating at maximum RPMs, opened a hollow crevasse from my sternum to my testicles and filled the vacuum with a frozen stream of fear. The speed at which the onrushing boat was closing the distance to the cove was consistent with a police boat answering my Mayday call, but I knew the difference between the soprano duet being sung by these two big motors and the lathe-grinding-metal alto notes produced by the three smaller Evinrude motors mounted on police boats. Harlan's boat would be the first to arrive.

For the tenth time, I scuttled down into the aft cabin and scanned the dock and the sloped land that led up to the roadway. There was no sign of any cops or witnesses. *This is the definition of lonely,* I thought. I climbed back into the bridge and grabbed my gun. The Beretta was ready to fire bullets as fast as I could pull the trigger.

The sound of the oncoming motors dropped an octave as Harlan's boat slowed to make the turn into the mouth of the cove, and the pitch dropped again as the boat maneuvered around the cypress knees choking the entrance to the open cove. Harlan's Boston Whaler whipped through the right-hand turn and headed straight for my Carver, but then it staggered like a late-night drunk, stutter-stepping first to the left then to the right and back to the left again. Harlan was surprised to find himself nose to nose with my boat and not approaching his target from its vulnerable stern. After a few moments of indecision, Harlan gunned the motors and headed down my starboard side, the side that afforded more open water between my boat and the shoreline. As he passed the bridge, I saw that the passenger held a shotgun aimed more or less in the bridge's direction. I also noted the passenger wasn't the fat kid, Travis. It was Chance Dickson, former Green Beret and Harlan's former son-in-law.

I ducked low, slid down the steps to the aft cabin level, and moved through the doorway out onto the starboard wing above the steps from the stern platform. I kept my right arm extended inside the aft cabin so that the pistol was out of sight. Harlan pulled his boat alongside the junction between the dock and the stern platform, and Dickson leapt onto the swim platform in one athletic movement. As he moved, Dickson fired his shotgun once in my general direction like a combat troop assaulting an enemy stronghold. I dropped into a squat, like a baseball catcher, to evade the shotgun blast, but Dickson had fired from his hip to cover his movements, and the shotgun pellets harmlessly sprayed the canopy above the aft cabin. Dickson then disappeared around the stern of my boat before I could react.

In the heat of battle, when I could have been thinking of any number of life-saving tactics, all that came to mind was the sardonic quote from a World War I German general that went something like, "No plan survives contact with the enemy." The actual quote, I knew, was longer and decorated with arcane language, but I had no time to remember trivial history lessons. With Dickson trapped on the stern platform, I focused on my father-in-law.

Harlan struggled with the assault. He tried to grab a cleat on the Carver with one hand and hold his shotgun with the other while he steadied his boat with one foot and raised his other leg to climb onto the swim platform. But Harlan's boat swayed under him, and he was frozen in that precarious position like a bug stuck to a spider's web.

Before he could gain control of his situation, I shot the old man somewhere in the upper chest. Harlan tumbled backward into his Whaler, which promptly drifted away from the dock. *Now the odds are even*, I thought. Dickson was trapped on the stern platform, and I owned the high ground.

I wheeled to my left to reenter the aft cabin and climb into the bridge from which I could command the fields of fire for the entire boat; but before I could get inside, a shotgun blast came from the opposite aft cabin entryway on the port side of the boat. My legs were blown out from under me, and I hit the deck before I could break my fall. I had the odd sensation one gets in dreams that I had made a serious mistake and caused my own demise. There were no stairs on the port side of the boat, so Dickson must have grabbed the aft cabin window ledges and used the handholds on the side of the boat as footholds to inch his way from the stern platform to the walkway on the boat's port side.

I'm battling some comic book character. Travis couldn't have done that. I pointed my gun at the entryway, but Dickson had gone off to some other tactical objective. He had again taken a shot merely to cover his maneuvers, but this one caught me flush in the left leg, shredding flesh and shattering bone from my upper thigh down to my calf. I took a quick look, and what I saw made me retch. My leg looked like a column of freshly ground hamburger meat.

There was no pain—I must have been in shock—but I could not make my left leg work to stand up. The boat rocked gently forward, so I figured Dickson was moving around the bow to come at me from behind. I rolled to the right and used my good leg and right arm to shimmy across the aft cabin like a swimmer doing the sidestroke. Laboriously, I crawled to the portside steps to the bridge, dragging my bad left leg behind me.

After what seemed eons, I traversed the steps, reached the bridge, and crawled toward the captain's chairs and the instrument panel. At any moment, Dickson could burst through the port entrance and shoot me from behind, so I kept checking over my shoulder; but then I heard Carrie down below, banging on the galley windows that faced forward, yelling, "Get me out!"

She sees Dickson. He's still on the bow. In pain now and unable to move fast, I crawled between the captain's chairs and squeezed as far under the overhang of the instrument panel as possible. Looking back between the chairs, I could cover the bridge, the stairs, the starboard entranceway, and some of the aft cabin. Unfortunately, a broad smear of blood dotted with bits of torn flesh led from the bridge steps to the space where I hid. I had left a trail no one could miss. Then the side-to-side rocking of the boat told me a new story. The Green Beret was climbing the bridge's steeply sloped façade. *How can he do that?* It was slippery polycarbonate, and there were no built-in handholds or footholds. *He's using the windshield sills to pull himself up and look over the top of the windscreen.*

Dickson's shotgun banged against the windshield, and I thought of that ominous music from *Jaws* when the shark stalked its unwitting victims. *Ta dum, ta dum, ta dum.* I craned my neck to peek out from under the dashboard and saw Dickson's shotgun and face appear over the windscreen then retreat before I could take a shot. I watched as his hand moved along the windshield, and I realized that he was moving toward the portside to get a good look at me. As he shuffled toward the center of the windscreen, I slid in the same direction to remain out of sight under the overhanging instrument panel and behind the swiveling bridge chairs. It was a raw game of predator stalking prey, and I felt like an antelope cornered by a pride of hungry lions. The terror I felt as I crawled toward cover must be what antelope felt when they were about to be eaten alive.

When Dickson reached the center of the windshield, I heard a woman's voice shouting something unintelligible. For a moment Dickson stopped, and I gained ground on him. Where I lay under the dashboard, behind the two captain's chairs, I was concealed from his view and had a clear shot at the space above the port windshield, where Dickson would have to appear to get a shot at me. I pointed my gun at that patch of blue sky and waited for him to come into view.

The woman yelled again. This time I understood her words.

"Drop your weapon or I'll shoot!"

I recognized Jamie's voice. Where did she come from?

Jamie yelled again. "Stop! Drop it!"

Dickson began moving again, and the barrel of his shotgun came into view and caused me to flinch. I could not see Dickson's head because he had not reached the open space where I was aiming. *Keep moving, damn you!*

Small dogs have a yappy, high-pitched bark, while big dogs howl in deep-bass tones. The same is true of handguns. The small calibers pop like firecrackers, but the heavy calibers boom like little canons. The pistol shot that echoed around the cove came from a high-caliber firearm. Dickson's shotgun clattered to the floor of the bridge just feet from my face, and I heard his body striking the side of the bridge and thudding to the deck.

Two things happened at once: A small-caliber pop came from belowdecks combined with a metallic smack, and Jamie began yelling

"Dad!" over and over. I heard splashes made by someone in the water. *Dickson or Jamie?*

At first I thought Carrie may have tried to shoot me through the bridge decking, but shortly afterward a second shot came from below and the bullet struck something hard and ricocheted off the back wall of the aft cabin. Carrie was trying to shoot the lock off the sliding hatch so she could escape. I couldn't allow her to emerge with a loaded pistol and find me cowering under the instrument panel. Once again I turned on my right side, mustered all my remaining energy, and slithered toward the hatch.

I heard more splashing, and Jamie screamed, "Dad! Oh my God, are you alright?" I didn't have the energy to respond. The high/low wail of a police boat siren suddenly ruptured the air and competed with Jamie's repeated screams.

Carrie kept firing through the fiberglass hatch—one shot, a second shot, then a third, in a paced sequence as though she were aiming carefully. The lock being too difficult to hit with a direct strike, she was trying to blow the old fiberglass to bits. I inched into a position above the hatch and looked down at it. Carrie must have realized she was close to escape because she fired three more shots in rapid succession—*crack/ thwack, crack/thwack, crack/thwack.*

I watched from above as Carrie pushed the ruined fiberglass aside to create a hole to crawl through. From outside the boat came the sounds of Jamie plowing through the water, wading toward the boat, yelling "Dad?" over and over. In the distance, two, or possibly three, sirens blared as cops rushed toward the scene from all directions.

Carrie pushed her gun hand through the ragged opening, followed by her head and her upper body. I raised the Beretta in my right hand as high as I could stretch and brought it down with all my remaining might on the back of Carrie's head.

Carrie screamed and poured out of the hatch and onto the aft cabin deck like a fish slithering out of a net. Her hands went to her head, and her pistol skidded three feet away from her. It was another peashooter, a little Saturday night special. She moaned. I had to smile; she wore gym shoes, Bermuda shorts, and a top that covered all her feminine charms. The top was ripped from the neck to her cleavage. She was dressed to meet the cops, and that's exactly what she was going to do. She would even have blood on the conservative clothes—but it would be hers.

Carrie rolled onto her back to look up at me with unadulterated fury. Then she looked for her gun and calculated her chances of grabbing it and shooting me before I could shoot her. The sirens were growling and winding down; the cops were drawing near. Lazily, Carrie stretched her left arm toward her gun, but it was a full foot beyond her hand.

With my gun arm hanging limp, I said, "Make your best move."

Carrie shriveled up into a fetal position and started wailing. At that moment, Jamie rushed through the port entranceway and instantly read the situation. "Don't do it!" she shouted.

With two long strides, she advanced into the cabin, snatched the gun out of my hand, and tossed it onto the stuffed chair at the back of the aft cabin. Then she hastened over to Carrie and stepped on Carrie's outstretched wrist to pin it to the floor as she retrieved her pistol. Carrie yelped; Jamie tossed the pistol onto the chair and climbed onto the bridge to see about me. Carrie sat up and leaned against the wall of the aft cabin. Kneeling beside me, Jamie pointed her pistol at Carrie and said, "Move a muscle and you're dead."

A center-console police boat, with lights flashing and siren whooping, came skidding to a stop at my stern. One cop, with short red hair, freckles, and muscles, leapt onto the swim platform and took the stairs three at a time. Hunched low, gun drawn, the cop entered the aft cabin. He dropped into a shooter's crouch, aimed his weapon at Jamie with both hands, and yelled, "Police! Drop your weapon!"

Jamie dropped her Sig Sauer and responded, "Law enforcement," as she grabbed the badge pinned to her blouse and shoved it toward Redhead.

Redhead, whose nametag above his breast pocket read "O'Shea," said, "Law enforcement? What agency?"

"Tampa Metro."

O'Shea was confused. "What is Tampa PD doing here?"

"This is my father," Jamie said, indicating me, "and she's your perp." She pointed to Carrie.

"She did all of this?"

"Caused it. Help me with my father. He needs an ambulance."

The second cop, the driver of the police boat, burst into the room. He was very young and tan, with buzz-cut black hair. His nametag said "Riordan." O'Shea gave the orders.

"I've got it in here," he said. "Secure all the weapons, and then see about the guy out on the deck."

Jamie handed her gun to the driver, who then collected the weapons from the chair. Riordan went out on the deck and returned a minute later. He said, "That one's still alive, weak pulse, so we need Life Flight."

O'Shea said, "Get two. This one"—he pointed to me—"needs to fly."

The driver went back out to the deck and made a radio call for two Life Flight helicopters.

A second police boat pulled alongside, and the cops in the boat conversed with Riordan on the deck. I heard them decide the situation was under control and that Harlan could be transported to a hospital by water. The boat left with Harlan lying inert on its deck like a rescued manatee.

On the bridge, O'Shea and Jamie gently flipped me onto my back. I tried to tell them what happened, but they didn't seem to understand me.

"He's bleeding out," O'Shea announced. "His skin is cool. We need to get a tourniquet on that leg STAT."

My vision was blurred, but I saw Redhead pull his thick leather belt off his shorts and dump all the cop paraphernalia onto the bridge. He secured the makeshift tourniquet and yelled at his driver to call again for helicopters.

"They're in the air," Riordan shouted back.

People were talking, but they sounded like they were in a tunnel and growing more distant. At the sound of people clomping up the stairway, Jamie and O'Shea turned toward the entranceway and went on guard. A uniformed cop warily entered the aft cabin, followed by the ubiquitous Lieutenant Callahan, the cop who had searched my boat.

Callahan glanced around and addressed O'Shea. "What's the story here?"

O'Shea summarized for him: "We transported one casualty by boat. We have choppers on the way for this one"—he was indicating me—"and for a guy out on the deck. This officer"— he nodded toward Jamie—"is Tampa PD, and this is her father." He touched my shoulder.

"What's she doing here?" Callahan said, pointing to Carrie. The blood oozing from Carrie's scalp was drying in rivulets that streaked her ashen face and hung suspended in clumps in her stiffly sprayed hair. She looked like a member of a rock band made up for a Halloween concert.

Carrie motioned toward me and answered weakly, "He kidnapped me, and then he shot at everyone who came to rescue me."

Jamie piped up. "All lies. She and her friends attacked my father, and I had to defend him. I made the 9-1-1 call. When I got here, the guy outside had my father down and was going to finish him off, so I shot him."

"He tried to rape me," Carrie insisted.

"Run a rape kit on her," Jamie said to Callahan.

Callahan ran his fingers through his hair and whistled. "Okay, Murphy," he said to his uniformed cop, "secure the crime scene and get forensics out here. The two casualties will go by chopper, and I'll take the wife and the Tampa cop to the station in our cruiser. We'll sort it out after we get statements from everyone."

"I'm going to the hospital with my father," Jamie said.

"You know procedure better than that, officer," Callahan said. "You're a material witness, and you've just described an officer-involved shooting. You're suspended pending a hearing on the shooting, and you aren't going anywhere until I get a statement."

"There won't be room on the choppers," O'Shea said kindly to Jamie.

"Then take my statement here. Now, while we're waiting for the chopper."

The lieutenant shrugged, exasperated. He looked around but couldn't find his sidekick. "Murphy, where the hell are you?"

The uniformed cop came back inside after checking on Dickson on the foredeck. "Right here, lieutenant."

"Alright, Murphy, you keep an eye on the wife. I'll take this officer back to the cruiser to get her statement." Callahan turned to Jamie and said, "Come with me."

O'Shea told Jamie, "Go ahead. I'll take care of your father, and I'll wait for you at the hospital."

Jamie bent over me and gave me a kiss. Then she and Callahan walked out of my vision.

I heard a helicopter. It sounded far away, as though it were on television in another room. I was cold and felt as though I were falling off a cliff backward with nothing to stop me. *Please, God, don't let her win.* At some point, I felt motion. It made me nauseous, but the nausea didn't last long as I drifted toward unconsciousness. To our left the sun dove into the Gulf. Then I was engulfed by darkness.

CHAPTER THIRTY-TWO

T he first time I woke, I was in the ICU. *Thank you, God. She didn't win.* I wasn't confused or surprised to find myself in a small glass-walled room hooked to IVs and monitors. It was to be expected. Through the window wall, I could see a command center of computer terminals and vigilant nurses tracking the recoveries of the patients in the unit. There was no pain. I was like a butterfly in a cocoon morphing into a caterpillar. It didn't occur to me to check my leg to see if it was still there. In a moment, the sweet juice flowing into my veins sent me back to dreamland.

―――∞∞∞―――

The second time I awoke, I was on a gurney and several white-jacketed attendants were pushing me through a hurricane. Then I heard the rotors and realized the hurricane was the downwash from the propellers. They loaded me onto the chopper and locked the gurney in place. One of the attendants asked if I was okay, and I think I nodded. We levitated, swooped and rotated, and darted away. It was a short flight and it was fun, like an amusement park ride. As we descended, I thought to check my ability to make my limbs obey my brain. I couldn't tell if I had moved anything. The sign on the helipad read "Tampa General Hospital." Somewhere between the helicopter and my new hospital room, I lost consciousness.

———⟨⟩———

The third time, I awoke in a surgical recovery room. The nurse told me how lucky I was to be at "TGH." "We're ranked number two in the state of Florida and number nineteen nationally in orthopedics," she said proudly. *They've saved my leg!* Many times I had sailed past the sprawling TGH campus, located on the northern tip of the big Davis Island across a narrow channel from downtown Tampa. I had never thought I might someday be a patient here.

When they moved me to my private room, on the fourth floor of the Bayshore Pavilion, I was pleased to find a huge window that overlooked the channel, a marina, and a row of high-rise condominiums known colloquially as "God's waiting rooms."

My surgeon visited later that day. He was a big burly guy, balding but with a waxed mustache more appropriate for a British swashbuckler. He explained that on the day of the incident, the Life Flight chopper had flown me to the emergency room at St. Petersburg General, where doctors performed emergency blood transfusions and repaired ruptured blood vessels. Their actions not only saved my life but also restored blood flow to the leg before a critical mass of cells had died, and so they were able to save my leg. Two days later, I had been transported across the Bay by helicopter to Tampa General Hospital for continuing orthopedic care.

Here, surgeons reconstructed my shattered tibia, fibula, and femur and inserted rods and plates, which left my damaged left leg three-eighths of an inch shorter than my good leg. The surgeon warned me that this differential would not only cause me to limp, but would also damage the muscles that knit the hip to the sacroiliac, causing intense pain and limiting my mobility. As a result, in my left shoe I would have to wear an insert to level my hips. Philosophically, I said goodbye to flip-flops and hello to the foam-rubber-soled "nurse" shoes popular among the old guys at the club. I hoped they were available in colors other than white and gray.

It may have been the next day or possibly two days later when Jamie walked into the room during visiting hours. She sported civilian clothes and a smile, but her expression changed when she got a look at me. I hadn't shaved or showered; I was bandaged from toe to hip; I was pale and bleary-eyed from all the drugs.

She rushed toward me as though she could change things. "Oh my God, Dad! Are you going to be okay?"

"Sure, they saved my leg." I sounded like a bullhorn. "And you came to my rescue. How did that happen?"

She grabbed my hand, bent toward me, and then thought better of it and gave me an air kiss with plenty of space between us.

"Travis called me, scared out of his wits. Told me to go to the marina, but I knew where you were going. I missed the turn to the park and ended up on top of the hill overlooking the cove. Had to crawl down through the trees to get a shot at Dickson."

So Travis had wanted to defuse a violent situation. He got replaced on the attack team and wanted to protect . . . whom? His mother? Or his father?

"Your timing was perfect," I said. "Nice shot, by the way. Must be fifty yards from the waterline to the boat."

"I braced against a tree."

"I was ready to shoot him when he got into position for a shot at me, but you beat me to the punch."

"He was aiming at you, Dad, over the top of the windshield, so he must have had a shot at something."

My body had been concealed by the dashboard, and my head had been under a chair, but I wasn't about to argue with the woman who had saved my life.

Jamie rocked from one foot to the other, nervous about something. "That brings up an important point, Dad. Did you hear me warn him?"

"Oh yeah. He stopped moving, so I know he heard you too."

"This is pretty important to me, Dad. How many times did you hear me warn him?"

"Three times."

She nodded yes, like a grammar school teacher getting the right answers from the slow kid. "That's right. You have to give three warnings before firing. And did you hear me identify myself?"

"As a police officer?" She nodded. I didn't recall it, but I knew what she wanted to hear. "Yes, sure. Is it a problem?"

"Dickson says it was just some crazy lady running down a hill, so he didn't listen to her. To me."

"He's alive?"

"In this hospital somewhere."

I looked at my daughter with what I hoped was love smeared all over my ragged face. "He's lying," I croaked.

She smiled in apparent relief. "The cops will be here to see you as soon as your doctors give them permission. They'll ask the same question."

"No problem." She squeezed my hand. I think she meant "thank you." "Listen," I continued, "go in the closet and find my cell phone so I can call your mom."

She gave me a wry smile. "I already talked to her. She'll be here to see you as soon as you can have two visitors. She let me have today so we could have our little chat about the incident."

"Thanks, sweetie. Drop by anytime."

She looked at me as she always did when it was time for Dad to get a lecture. "You were such a fool, thinking you could take on those crackers by yourself."

"I did ask for your help. Remember?" Her face turned dark as hurricane clouds, so I added, "If I had told the cops about the threats, they'd have caused Carrie to change her plans. Now I have a resolution."

She spread her arms to encompass the entire hospital scene. "You think?"

CHAPTER THIRTY-THREE

The medical team allowed me to see unlimited visitors beginning Saturday, and Jamie appeared as soon as the afternoon visiting period opened. Again she wore street clothes but she seemed relaxed, gave me a tentative smile as she entered my room. The nurses had cleaned me up a bit—a sponge bath and a shave—so Jamie gave me a proper hug and kiss. Then she related the news from her perspective. The cops would take my statement next week as the last step in the police investigation, then a panel would decide whether Jamie's actions were justified. She didn't seem as concerned about it as the last time she visited, so I suspected she had gotten some encouragement from the investigators. *Cops will protect cops.*

I was interested in a couple of other angles. "Is Carrie in jail?" I asked her.

"I belong to a different agency, so they're not sharing anything with me. The excuse is that I was directly involved and I'm your daughter, but really, if I was St. Petersburg PD, they'd tell me everything."

"So the government learned nothing from 9/11. Has Connie been charged with a crime?"

Jamie gave me a disgusted look. "I bumped into her in the cafeteria. She was here to see Dickson."

"Sure," I said, "getting their story straight before they have to testify. If I had died that would have been easier."

"The nurse said your lawyer has come by a couple of times and peeked in, but you were always asleep."

"My lawyer? You mean Tony?"

"Yeah, the guy with all the hair."

Maybe he feels guilty for abandoning me, wants to remain friends. "Oh good. Did you call your mom?"

"Yes, Dad." An indulgent smile played across her lips. "She was taken completely by surprise. I think she was irritated that you hadn't told her the whole story."

From the doorway, a little girl's voice said, "Yes, I was."

Our heads swiveled in unison, like two ventriloquist's dummies. I was overjoyed to see Glenda, whether she was irritated or not. As Glenda advanced she tried to smile, but I saw that tears dripped from the corners of her eyes. She went to Jamie first and gave her a motherly hug. Then Glenda draped her upper body on mine and gave me a big lover's hug. When she straightened up, my face was wet with her tears.

"You still have your leg and you look like you'll live, so tell me what the hell happened," Glenda said.

I told them both the whole story, trying very hard to convey the uncertainty surrounding Carrie's intentions. Nonetheless, Jamie interrupted several times with, "That's when you should have called the cops," and Glenda interrupted with, "That's when you should have told me." The women quickly sensed an opportunity to go two-on-one against a helpless male. *Women are pack animals.*

To Glenda I said, "I know you were trying to help, but I wish you hadn't taken the diary to the hospital."

"It wasn't doing you any good at my mother's house."

I gave her a soft but troubled look. "The shrinks had already finished the examination, so they turned the diary over to the cops. They can't prove it was at the Cortes house to be stolen, but it makes me nervous."

Glenda shrugged. "We'll tell them she left it at the beach house, and I found it when I moved your furniture. I was returning it to *her.*"

"Not a bad story."

"I also took the broken glass to the Dolphin Beach police so they can test for DNA."

"I don't think the cops care about the break-in, sweetie."

Disappointed that I didn't give her credit for her efforts, she said, "Well, it would have been dumped in the trash if I hadn't saved it."

Troubled by her parents' brewing argument, Jamie changed the subject. "Where are you going when you get out of here, Dad?"

"Back to the boat."

Jamie snorted. "Not anymore. It's impounded, not to mention shot to pieces."

Glenda gasped. For five seconds, we all looked at each other. Finally, Jamie said, "My place is too small, and it isn't wheelchair accessible."

Glenda said to Jamie, "I'm still at Grandma's, living up those rickety stairs." They weren't including me in the conversation.

They both shuffled from foot to foot, and then Jamie brought the talk to a close. "We have some time, Mom. We'll figure it out."

During the rest of the visit, we laughed a lot. It was like old times, from before our divorce. At the end, Jamie walked around the bed so they could each hold a hand and kiss me on opposing cheeks.

Jamie asked her mom, "Do you have time for a cup of coffee?"

The women left together, and I was alone again. I wondered who'd win custody of the damaged goods known as Randle Marks.

———∞∞∞———

Uncertain about my risk of exposure as an email thief, I logged into the cloud account to delete the files containing Carrie's keystrokes. In the process, I found a series of emails that revealed who was tapping my email and explained why Carrie had come to the boat. Five of the fake emails I had sent to Tony—all except the first one about Simmons—had been forwarded from *shadylady44* to *catmarks38*. *Forwarded*. Why would Carrie forward the notes from her secret account to her public account? She wouldn't. In addition to my forwarded notes, there was a note from *cmt1117* to Carrie. The sender had written: **Since you won't talk to me you need to read these. I'll explain later.**

In her response, Carrie wrote: **WHAT HAVE YOU DONE, MAE? NOW I HAVE TO FIX IT.** And that made everything crystal clear. After I had barged into her house, the family fixer had tried once again to help her sister. Connie Mae Tomkins, born on November 17, aka *cmt1117*, had stolen and then forwarded the notes. She couldn't forward the notes from *shadylady44* because Carrie didn't know who that was and might not open the notes. The note accusing Carrie of an affair with Phil Simmons was missing because I had sent that one before the first break-in at the beach house. Someone must have installed the spyware on my personal computer during that break-in. Did Scott Simmons do it for Connie? Obviously, Carrie hadn't come to the boat to negotiate; she came to the boat "to fix it."

———∞∞∞———

At the crack of dawn on Tuesday, the surgeons opened me up again. This time they stitched up the lacerated tendons and ligaments that tie the lower leg to the upper leg, and removed numerous fragments of knee cartilage to produce a kneecap in the shape of an inverted pyramid, a disfigurement the surgeon said would make me unique.

Two more surgeries were planned. The first, which would take place within a week or ten days, would complete the leg repairs by removing damaged muscle tissue and restoring connections to healthy muscles. The second surgery, planned months into the future after the leg healed, would be cosmetic, to make the tower of ruined flesh resemble a human limb.

Although I enjoyed the view of downtown Tampa, trusted my surgeons implicitly, and loved my nursing team, I hoped with all my heart and soul that Carrie's incarceration—and I knew now that she would go to jail—would be at least as painful as my hospitalization.

CHAPTER THIRTY-FOUR

On Thursday morning, I was reading two-week-old company email—just to make sure the IPO was still on track without me—when a loud knock rattled my door. It was Callahan, the cop who seemed to be involved in every aspect of my "case." He wore a faded brown-and-green plaid sports coat that once may have been a horse blanket, a Florida Gators tie in orange and blue, and a beige shirt that wouldn't stay tucked inside his navy trousers. I couldn't stop thinking of him as "Frumpy."

"Can I help you, lieutenant?"

He nodded and shuffled toward me. "I need to take your statement, Mr. Marks, just as I'da done at the scene if you'da been conscious and able to speak." He motioned to my bandaged leg and said, "If you're up to it."

I pushed the food tray and computer out of the way. "Shoot."

He snickered at my play on words and explained that statements had already been collected from Carrie, Jamie, Harlan, Travis, Dickson, and Officer O'Shea, the first responder. The fact that he hadn't been allowed to get a statement from me annoyed him. "Your doctors are like a barbed-wire fence. Case is gonna go cold as a corpse before I get all the statements," he said.

He hadn't taken a statement from Connie—a fact that bothered me. Callahan dug his little notebook out of his breast jacket pocket and cleared his throat.

"Mr. Marks, on the day in question, did you know your wife was going to visit you?"

"Yes, my sister-in-law texted me to say that Carrie was on her way."

"Why would Ms. Tomkins tell you your wife was coming to see you?"

"Carrie didn't want me to have her new cell number, so Connie sent a text for her."

That didn't quite answer his question. "I mean why would your wife come to see you?"

"Connie told me Carrie wanted to negotiate a settlement. She had come to the dock twice before when I wasn't there."

"Were you willing to see her?"

"If she wanted to negotiate. Connie said she would dress provocatively to get on board, but if the negotiations didn't go well Carrie and her family were prepared to be violent."

Callahan didn't hide his confusion. "She was dressed in shorts and a blouse and had a bikini in her bag in case y'all went swimming."

I chuckled. "She's smart. She wore the bikini to get aboard, then changed into street clothes so she could tell you that story after she killed me. Canvass the dock. If anyone saw her they'll remember that bikini."

He sighed and made a note. "Were you expecting your wife to be armed?"

"She may have had a gun in her bag, so I treated her like you would treat a dog that's been known to bite."

Callahan took another note. "She borrowed the one she had with her from that Dickson fella. Belonged to his wife. You knew her pistol had been stolen, didn't you?"

"I didn't know if her pistol had really been stolen or if she was crying wolf."

Callahan considered that for a moment, then said, "Alright, Mr. Marks, go ahead and tell me in your own words what happened that day."

"I was in the park, having a cigar, when I saw her walk through the parking lot and onto the dock. She asked if she could come aboard. I agreed but not because of the bikini."

Callahan gave me half a smile. "Okay, she comes aboard the boat and then what happens?"

"We shoved off and everything seemed to be fine until I turned south toward the cove down by Fort De Soto. Then she got angry because she wanted to go out into the Gulf, up to Clearwater. She became verbally abusive, didn't understand that the cove was a better place to talk—if that's what she wanted to do. She said she needed another drink and went belowdecks, but she didn't take her glass with her. She was gone a long time, so I figured she was making phone calls. I'm sure you guys have pulled her call logs."

"We have," Callahan said, but he did not elaborate. "What did you do while she was belowdecks?"

"Her behavior scared me, and I was sure she was giving people directions to intercept us. So I made a Mayday call."

"So you weren't evading the police, you were asking for help."

"That's right."

He made another note. "Is that when you locked her downstairs?"

"No. She came back topside, and we argued some more. She became very angry and violent. She threw her drink glass at me, tossed a couch cushion overboard, threatened me with a liquor bottle. Then she went below again, said she was going to change clothes. Wanted the blood spatter to be on conservative clothes."

He didn't react to that. "What did you argue about that second time, when she came up top after making the phone call?"

So she did make a call. "She said I had kidnapped her and was going to rape her at the cove. I told her I'd be happy to drop her off somewhere, because I wasn't interested in having sex with her. That's when she became violent."

"So you argued about sex, not about the house?"

Oh! He's heard a different story from someone else. "We talked about the house, but she didn't get angry until I refused to fall for the sex angle. Maybe she wanted a semen sample, to prove rape."

The lieutenant grimaced and took another note. "When she went below the second time, is that when you locked her up?"

"Yes. I assumed she was going for her gun, so I locked her belowdecks. The hatch that leads belowdecks has a padlock so that it can be secured when the boat is vacant in the marina."

He seemed to decide whether my actions constituted kidnapping, scribbled something, and said, "Why didn't you turn around, go back to the marina?"

"I wasn't sure of my legal standing at that point. I was defending myself against her violent behavior, but did trapping her belowdecks constitute kidnapping, or that other charge, false imprisonment?"

"'Unlawful restraint' we call it in Florida."

"Yeah. So I thought I had to see if I was right about her daddy coming to kill me." Frumpy gave me a sad look similar to the one Jamie had given me. With a bit of force, I said, "Naturally I thought you guys would get there first."

He snorted.

I added, "And she wasn't raped."

"We had her checked; there were no signs of rape or sexual abuse."

There were lots of bottles in the galley if she had wanted to bruise herself. "It was all a ruse to kill me, lieutenant."

"Okay, Mr. Marks. She's locked up and then what?"

"I sailed down to the cove and anchored the boat. Harlan was the first to get there. He drove up to my stern, and Dickson hopped onto my boat, firing his shotgun at me."

"Dickson fired the first shot?"

"Yes, while he was boarding my boat."

"Did he say anything before he took a shot at you?"

"No, he just fired as he was jumping aboard, like you see combat troops do in movies."

"What about the old man, Mr. Tomkins? Did he say anything, hail you from his boat?"

"No, no words were exchanged at all."

"So they didn't ask where Carrie was or want to talk to you about kidnapping her?"

"No sir. They did not want to talk. They just wanted to shoot."

This time Callahan wrote several sentences. When he finished, he looked at me and said, "Why did you shoot the old man?"

"Because he was armed and boarding my boat without permission." *That's straight out of the Florida maritime statute on piracy. I looked it up.* "I already had one commando aboard and needed to even the odds. The police hadn't responded as yet."

Frumpy was tired of hearing that. "Mr. Marks, are you familiar with the piracy laws?"

I laughed. "He wasn't after gold bullion, lieutenant. He wanted to kill me."

Unabashed, Frumpy said, "You took the captain's course. I looked it up."

Touché! A thorough cop. "Piracy didn't cross my mind at that moment. I was thinking more along the lines of self-defense."

"Sure. What about 'stand your ground'?"

I feigned a puzzled look. The media had made sure that everyone had heard of the "stand your ground" law in Florida, but I was a bit nervous about the implications of premeditation.

"I've heard of it, but I don't know much about it."

"There's a law in Florida, Mr. Marks, that allows people who are attacked with deadly force to respond with deadly force. I wondered if you were familiar with it."

"Lieutenant, when you're attacked with deadly force the only law you have time to think about is the law of survival."

"Alright. Keep going."

"I turned to go back into the aft cabin, and Dickson was on the opposite side of the boat. He took another shot at me and hit me in the legs, and I went down on the deck."

"Why didn't Dickson finish you off right there?"

"He was exposed in the doorway. I guess he thought I'd shoot back. He moved up around the bow and intended to come at me from behind, but I crawled up onto the bridge and hid under the instrument panel. Next thing I knew, his shotgun came over the top of the windshield, aiming at my midsection, between the two seats in the bridge." *Either Jamie was correct and that's what he was doing, or it was a plausible story to protect my daughter.*

The lieutenant said, "Did you hear anything during this time?"

"I heard a shot, and then I heard his body hit the bridge and then it hit the deck."

Frumpy grimaced at the graphic description. He was looking for a different answer. "What I mean is, did you hear voices?"

"Oh sure. I heard my daughter yell at him."

"What did she say?"

"She told him to drop his weapon."

"Did she identify herself?"

"As a cop? Yes. It was all very official."

"How many times did you hear your daughter challenge him?"

"Three." No hesitation.

Frumpy wrote something in his notebook. "Did he ever respond to her or react?"

"I never heard him say anything and I couldn't see his face, but he stopped moving so I'm sure he heard her." *Up yours, Chance!*

"He says he was just standing there, waiting for you to come out so he could make you open the hatch, release your wife."

"He's lying. He was trying to get another shot at me."

"He says he couldn't hear your daughter clearly."

"He's lying. It was quiet as a graveyard in that cove."

Frumpy gave me the look your buddy would give you if you won the lottery. "Lucky for you your daughter happened to be in the right place at the right time."

"For sure. She told me that Travis, Carrie's son, had called her and asked her to prevent something bad from happening, so everyone knew that Carrie planned to kill me."

Frumpy was faraway in thought for a moment. "Okay, what happened next?"

"Carrie began shooting her way through the hatch. I was afraid she'd get out and then shoot me, so I crawled across the bridge until I was above the hatch, and when she stuck her head out I hit her with my gun. She fell down onto the floor and lost her gun. That's when Jamie entered the aft cabin. I don't remember much after that."

"Just to clarify, did your wife go for her gun after she was on the floor?"

"Yes, she reached for it. Scared me to death because I was so woozy I didn't think I could fight back if she got to it."

Frumpy's brow furrowed with consternation. "Did you say anything to her?"

"I can't remember. I may have passed out from blood loss."

"According to your wife, you said, 'Make your best move.'"

As though I had to trust his rendition because I had no recollection of the situation, I shrugged and said, "I guess I gave her a fair chance, like in a cowboy movie."

Frumpy stared a hole through a spot between my eyebrows. "Maybe you wanted an excuse to kill her. Who did your daughter disarm first when she came aboard?"

Callahan was earning my respect, but I knew where he was heading; he trusted another cop to know which of us posed the greater danger, so I took a calculated risk that Jamie would recognize the ploy as well. "She knew I was no threat, so she picked up Carrie's gun first."

Callahan pursed his lips. I didn't think he believed me. "You're lucky you didn't shoot her, you know?"

"Don't you mean *she's* lucky I didn't shoot her?"

"Her gun was empty. Did you know that?"

"I wasn't counting bullets, lieutenant; I was dodging them. Obviously, she thought it was loaded; she tried to grab it."

He relaxed a bit, leaned back. "Ya know, if you had shot her, this would be a complicated case. The prosecutor might wonder if you lured her aboard so you could kill her, save yourself the trouble of a divorce."

"Are you kidding me? I would have called you guys after I shot her, not before. And I could have shot her before I locked her up. How does a prosecutor see a conspiracy in that?"

Callahan appeared to like the twisted complexity of the various scenarios. He gave a "Who knows?" gesture, then said, "There's no telling how a prosecutor might read the situation."

I thought I knew when I was being conned, but this time I couldn't be sure. "Are you my new best friend, lieutenant, letting me in on the prosecutor's thought process?"

"I hope you have better friends than me, Mr. Marks. You're gonna need 'em."

CHAPTER THIRTY-FIVE

I t took three weeks of relentless official pressure before my panel of doctors caved in and admitted that I was well enough to endure a grilling by Pinellas County prosecutors. The prosecutors needed to depose me so they could use my deposition as testimony at a grand jury inquiry into the incident. My third surgery had been delayed, so the prosecutors wanted to slip the deposition into the window between surgeries before the medical staff had new excuses to exclude them from my visitors' list.

On the morning of the deposition, I had to forego my pain meds to remain lucid for the interrogation. As a result, I shifted uncomfortably in my bed as my orderly, Giuseppe, shaved my three-day-old beard.

"Almost done," he said. "Just have to do the neck without slitting your throat, so sit very still for me. I'll get you a pillow to put under that leg when I'm done making you pretty."

I tilted my head back to give Giuseppe easy access to my throat, but in my peripheral vision I saw my LPN, Sharonda Lucas, sweep into the room as some people loitered in the doorway behind her.

"Good morning, Mr. Marks," Sharonda chirped. "You have visitors."

Giuseppe stopped his work to let me turn my head toward the doorway. There I saw Jamie, in full battle dress, and Glenda, whose mass of copper-red hair was under a measure of control. A wide, red smile broke Glenda's field of freckles. I grinned like a kid at Christmas.

I waved my arm and said, "Come on in. We'll be finished in a minute."

Giuseppe turned my head back toward him and pushed my jaw upward to gain access to my neck. "Stop smiling or you'll lose your Adam's apple," he joked.

Meanwhile, Sharonda readied the room for the interrogation session. She moved my rolling bedside tray, with my laptop computer and mobile phone on it, to the area in front of the sink, and then pushed the overstuffed bedside chair into the near corner at the head of the bed so that there was standing room all around it.

When Giuseppe finished shaving me, he dabbed a hot towel on my face to remove the residue of shaving cream. Afterward, he backed out of the way and went to find an extra pillow. Jamie and Glenda moved bedside and leaned in for hugs and kisses.

I said, "Let me introduce the team. This is Giuseppe. He's a nursing student from the Philippines, and I'm his guinea pig. That lovely creature over there is Sharonda." I emphasized the second syllable and rolled the R's in the middle of the nurse's name, like I was speaking Spanish. Sharonda responded with a curtsy and primped with one hand behind her head, lifting her dark curls.

"Why is everyone so happy?" Glenda said.

"Apparently, if you almost die but then survive," I said, "you are happier than you were before you almost died. It's a well-known phenomenon. Am I right, team?" I looked to Sharonda and Giuseppe for confirmation. Both nodded.

Glenda said "Oh" as though a new spiritual concept had been revealed to her. She turned to Giuseppe and said, "How do you do? Thanks for taking such good care of Randle. And thank you," she said to Sharonda. "Obviously, Randle is quite happy with you too."

"Not as happy as I used to be," I said. "She won't bathe me anymore. Got a little embarrassed once. So Giuseppe does the honors, and it's not half as much fun."

"He's a rascal," Sharonda said as she moved in to brush my freshly shampooed hair into place. When she approved of my appearance, she announced she would return and then departed.

Giuseppe retrieved a pillow from the closet and slid it under my left leg. "There you go, pal. Should help a little." To Glenda he said, "Pleased to meet you, ma'am."

Giuseppe walked away, and we were left in private. While Glenda and I held hands, Jamie shifted nervously from one foot to the other.

"I'd say 'get a room,' but I guess you'd have a room if I left the room," Jamie said.

We gave no indication that we had heard Jamie speak. "Don't give up on this old wreck from Georgia Tech," I said to Glenda.

"I can't stay away," Glenda said.

"Oh God," Jamie groaned. "Dad, when you're well enough, we want to move back to Atlanta."

"What?" I was dumbfounded.

Jamie tried to explain. "You need to get back to business. You won't be able to travel for a very long time, so you need to be where people can come to you. The country house is up for sale, and I think you know the boat's been shot to bits."

We're going back to Atlanta, where we met.

I looked at Jamie and said, "Why are you going back to Atlanta? I thought you had a thing going with that O'Shea kid."

"Cops for boyfriends are a dime a dozen, Dad. My career opportunities are much better up there. It's a good ol' boys' network down here."

Confused, I said to Glenda, "Are you sure about Atlanta? What about your store?"

She winked at me. "It's all settled, Randle."

She lifted a gift bag onto the bed. "I brought you a present. Help you look good for the cameras today."

I pulled the giftwrap paper out of the bag and then lifted a pair of satiny pajamas up for inspection. They were blood red with gold piping.

"Thanks, sweetie. You're too nice to me." I pulled the pale blue-and-white striped hospital gown over my head and slipped my arms into the pajamas. "How do I look?"

Jamie chuckled as she said, "You look like Hugh Hefner ready to lounge around with his Playmates."

Now everyone laughed. "Perfect. I'm sure the prosecutors will be hot chicks, and they'll drape themselves over the bed as they depose me."

Jamie became serious. "Only give them direct answers to their specific questions, Dad, and never change your story once you tell it. Suspects get in trouble when they volunteer information or change their story."

"Understood," I answered.

I was about to ask about Carrie but the daytime duty RN, Julia Russell, entered the room, clapped her hands twice to get everybody's attention, and announced, "The police and the lawyers are here, and they look like a pride of lions in search of red meat. They said your lawyer could have a minute with you first if you wish, Randle."

My lawyer? "Everybody, this is Nurse Ratched, and she runs a tight ship."

Julia said, "Ha! If you think you are Jack Nicholson, you're delusional, and I'll have to report you to the head shrink. I'll ask your lawyer to join us."

Julia didn't have to summon Tony Zambrano, as he had been eavesdropping from the doorway. He entered the room smiling and nodding to Jamie and Glenda and Julia. He wore a gray chalk-striped suit, a blue-striped, straight-collar shirt, and his trademark maroon bowtie with its blue-and-white polka dots. He resembled Indiana Jones's father more than a shark-toothed lawyer.

"Glenda and Julia, I don't believe you've had the pleasure, this is my . . . friend, Tony Zambrano."

"I'm his lawyer," Tony said to the women. Then to me he said, "If this paragon of male pride will allow me to help him today."

I gave him a nod and a look that welcomed him back to the team. To the women I said, "Tony's so terrifying in the courtroom that Carrie chose to kill me instead of divorce me."

Tony wore a modest smile as he graciously shook hands with Glenda and Julia, bowing slightly each time, and gave Jamie a parental pat on the back.

"You're embarrassing me with all this praise," Tony said. Referring to Glenda, he said, "Tell me about this beautiful apparition."

"Glenda is Jamie's mother, and she's immune to your sticky sweet advances."

"Not entirely," Glenda said with a taunting smile. "I'm always pleased to meet a Southern gentleman, and I sympathize with his impossible task to keep you out of trouble."

"I can make no guarantees, ma'am," Tony said in his fake drawl. "But that's a good segue to the business at hand. Today, Randle, the prosecutor will be interested in relationships and motives. Why did it happen, who's at fault, and what were you thinking when you willingly walked into a madwoman's trap? Are you ready for all of that?"

"Sure, I'll just tell it like it was." My police statement had been factual, and nearly truthful, but I had saved my surprises for this session, the legal proceeding that would determine who would be tried for crimes. Since Lieutenant Callahan had tipped me regarding the prosecutor's theory, I was prepared to testify.

Tony studied me for signs of sarcasm but could detect none. He said, "You can be candid within limits. You can't give any answers that will incriminate yourself if you are charged with a crime. You can take the fifth on those questions, so watch me for signals." To Julia, he said, "Could you ask the authorities to join us, please? They're anxious to get started."

Julia left to run the errand as Tony bid his goodbyes to Jamie and Glenda. The women wished me luck and hustled out of the way.

I said to Tony, "What changed your mind about me?"

"I changed my mind about *me*. I don't want to be a panfish."

"Good. Has there been a lot of media coverage?"

"Not a lot, Randle. You're not a black guy shot by white cops, so you're not a lead story. Maybe if you had died . . ." He turned his palms up and made a stupid face.

Into the room came a young guy pushing a hospital cart loaded with electronic gear: a TV monitor, a video camera and tripod, a boom microphone, two large studio lights and their tripods. Behind him came a young chubby woman pushing a small rolling cart on top of which sat a machine that appeared to be the ugly love child of a typewriter and an old-fashioned adding machine. She would be the court recorder, I surmised.

As the kid deftly plugged in cables, connected wires, and positioned equipment, Julia came to my bedside and placed one hand on my shoulder. I patted her hand and whispered, "It will be okay."

The technician worked efficiently, swiftly conducting tests of the lighting, sound, and video quality. As if on some silent cue, the instant the technician was ready, Tony led the pride of lions into the room. Julia edged away from the bed and into the corner formed by the closet and the sink. She would stand guard and halt the proceedings if they had any negative effect on my health.

Tony made the introductions: Donald Eastwick, Esq., the assistant district attorney, and Derrick Sullivan, the DA's lead investigator, followed by my "friend," Lieutenant Callahan. Eastwick came to the near side of my bed, so Callahan had to weave between the lights and camera to station himself on my left, between the bed and the window. That left Sullivan against the wall next to the monitor and Tony farthest away in the crowded room, next to the court recorder, who wasn't introduced at all.

Eastwick took charge and laid down the rules of engagement. He was an odd-looking fellow, late thirties, about the size of the average eighth grader, wearing an IBM-issue blue suit and sporting an FBI-regulation haircut above black plastic-rimmed glasses with Coke-bottle-bottom lenses. The glasses exaggerated the size of his eyes and made me feel like a specimen on a slide under a microscope. When the recording equipment was ready to roll, the court recorder swore me in.

Eastwick said, "If everyone is ready, maybe we can get this done before Halloween." He thought he was being cute, but no one so much as smiled. Forced to continue, Eastwick—I thought of him as "Bug-Eyes"—informed us that he had previously obtained depositions from Carrie Marks, Connie Tomkins, and Travis Dickson and would take a sworn deposition from Chance Dickson when he was well enough.

Tony indicated that we understood the procedure, and Callahan tore his eyes away from the view out the window to join the scene. The court recorder returned to her machine and confirmed she was ready to put it all into the public record.

Like a priest ascending the altar to say High Mass, Eastwick strutted into the picture and made a small speech. "Mr. Marks, the people of the State of Florida thank you for consenting to this deposition. You have been sworn in so that your deposition can be entered in the court record as testimony at a grand jury inquiry if you are not able to appear in person."

He looked at my lawyer, and Tony nodded in agreement. Eastwick asked me to state my name and address for the record, took a deep breath, and began the questioning.

"In your police statement, Mr. Marks, you said that Ms. Connie Tomkins, your sister-in-law, informed you that your estranged wife had agreed to meet you at the boat on the day in question. Is that correct?"

I had appeared on television on several occasions and was comfortable speaking to the camera rather than to my questioner. In a steady, sincere voice, I said to the camera, "No, it isn't, Mr. Eastwick. You must have misread my statement. There was no 'agreement.' Connie *warned* me that Carrie was coming."

I wanted to be sure Eastwick didn't think I was an intimidated pushover, and Eastwick wanted to be sure I didn't dismiss him as a funny-looking little guy without power. He said, "Alright, Mr. Marks, just answer the questions as asked and refrain from editorial comments, if you please."

"Of course, Mr. Eastwick. I just want you to get all the facts . . ." Neither of us blinked so I finished my thought, ". . . for the grand jury." I motioned toward the camera, knowing I was speaking to that panel and not some second-string prosecutor.

We stared at each other with open hostility, two gladiators poised for battle. Eastwick said, "Did Ms. Tomkins act as a go-between, arrange the meeting between you and your wife?"

"I have no idea what Connie may have said to Carrie. Twice my wife had come to the boat unannounced, of her own volition. Since my wife and I weren't communicating, I asked Connie to tell Carrie to give me advanced warning if she intended to come back. Connie sent me a text, presumably on Carrie's behalf."

Eastwick raised his eyebrows and said, "Ms. Tomkins stated that you wanted your wife to come to the boat."

I gave the camera a look that said, *This guy can't get much of anything right.* "Either you misunderstood Connie's testimony, Mr. Eastwick, or she lied to you. Carrie wanted to negotiate directly, and I told Connie that I was willing, if it wasn't a ploy to murder me."

"Mr. Marks, the court doesn't need your inflammatory remarks. Just answer questions directly."

Tony cut in and explained the situation to Bug-Eyes as though he were a professor educating a first-year law student. "Mr. Eastwick, this isn't cross-examination, it is a deposition. So we're all looking for the most complete rendition of the facts as possible, are we not? Please allow my client to acquaint you with those facts as best he can so we don't have to cut this proceeding short."

Eastwick flushed and buried his face in his notepad, aware that cameras were recording his reaction and his associates were watching with interest. He paced in the tight space between the bed and the camera equipment before turning back toward me.

"So your wife may have wanted to negotiate, and yet you think she wanted to harm you. Why is that?"

"You forgot that she may have wanted to get laid. That's how she was dressed."

Everyone laughed; the court recorder nearly choked on her coffee. Eastwick whirled around to Tony, but my lawyer merely shrugged. Eastwick faced me again and took a deep breath. "Just answer my question, Mr. Marks. Why did you fear your wife?"

"Because she had threatened to kill me."

"We'll get to the so-called threats, but why would your wife want to harm you?"

I gave the camera a look that meant *duh!* "If I was dead, she'd get all the money."

The prosecutor gave me an "Oh really" look. "Didn't you amend your will so your daughter was your sole beneficiary?"

The one thing "the authorities" do well is apply manpower to dig into the details. Unperturbed, I said, "Carrie didn't know I had changed my will. Connie told me the day before the assault that Carrie thought she'd inherit everything if she killed me."

The prosecutor's jaw dropped, so I helped him out. "If Connie didn't give you that tidbit, she lied by omission."

Eastwick straightened his shoulders and sucked on the end of his pencil as though my simple statement required deep thought. He said, "Your wife would have gotten a couple million without committing a murder, isn't that right, Mr. Marks?"

"My offer was half that much, which wasn't enough for Carrie."

Eastwick nodded and took a note on his legal pad. "Would the Baker Act evaluation jeopardize her financial settlement?"

"Not according to my lawyer; our assets would be divided equally in any case."

Eastwick smiled as though I had made his point, and I wondered if I had made a mistake.

He said, "Your motion for a trial was denied, wasn't it?"

Hmm. "Deferred. We'd have gotten a trial eventually."

"And your counterclaim was dismissed as well, wasn't it?"

This is not going well. "I could have introduced my evidence in defense of her suit."

Eastwick looked pleased with himself as he did a little two-step and thought about his next question. "Evidence," he said slowly, as though he could taste the word. "You never provided any, did you?"

Okay, I get it now. "We had submitted a list of witnesses, but we hadn't deposed them as yet."

"The truth is, you didn't want to give her a fair settlement, so you kidnapped her."

Well, no finesse to that question. "When Carrie became violent, I locked her up to protect myself and I issued a Mayday for the police. She had a gun with her and later she used it, as I'm sure you know if you've read the police report." I held out a hand and said, "Julia, would you hand me my cell phone, please?"

The nurse gave me a questioning look but gave me my phone. I fiddled with it a minute until I had queued up the video of Carrie about to throw a bottle at me. I held it up for Bug-Eyes.

"Have a look at this, Mr. Prosecutor."

He leaned in and watched the tape with his mouth agape. I wasn't sure if it was the violent intent or the revealing bikini that captivated him. Without warning, he made a grab for my phone but I was too quick for him.

"Let me have that!" he yelled.

"Get me a search warrant," I responded calmly, "and you can use this to prosecute the real criminal."

Eastwick took several moments to calm himself before he said, "Then your story is that you feared your wife, but the prospect of sex overpowered your fear and you allowed your potential murderer onto your boat."

Now I was exasperated by his repeated attempts to put words in my mouth. "Sex had nothing to do with it. I wanted closure, and I had a plan to stay safe."

"A plan, yes." He wanted to appear as though he were deliberating. "So you planned to take your wife to Mullet Key all along?"

"Yes. Carrie wanted me to go into the Gulf because it was a short trip from Harlan's marina up near Clearwater and they could use shotguns without being heard or seen. Connie said, 'If she wants you to go out into the Gulf, up to Clearwater, you'll know she didn't come to give hugs and kisses.' That's a direct quote, and that was the trap I wasn't willing to walk into. If Carrie wanted to negotiate, the cove was far better than bouncing around on ocean swells. More importantly, it had access from shore and was easier for the police to find than some undefined spot out in the middle of the Gulf."

Eastwick blinked twice. "Did Ms. Tomkins know your plan to take your wife to the cove?"

"No, I didn't tell her."

"So you let your wife believe you'd go to the Gulf, but you planned to trap her at the cove and Ms. Tomkins had no knowledge of your plan. Is that right?"

"I couldn't trust Ms. Tomkins because I wasn't sure whose side she was on. Now I know that she wanted me dead too."

Eastwick exploded. "I'd like to strike that answer, Mr. Zambrano, and I'd like you to control your client. Please."

Tony walked over to Eastwick and stood toe-to-toe with him. "Mr. Eastwick, my client is not willing to adjust his answers to make you happy. My client has a limited amount of energy for this deposition, so I suggest you stop slowing the proceedings down with your objections and just get through your list of questions as fast as possible."

Tony ordered the court recorder to record my answer precisely as given. Eastwick looked on in amazement. Then Tony ambled back to his spot between the recorder and Julia and leaned nonchalantly against the wall.

Eastwick took a deep breath. "Didn't you supply Ms. Tomkins with a list of enticements to lure her sister onto the boat?"

Tony shot me a warning look, but I answered the question. "No. Connie told me what Carrie wanted for a settlement, and I told her I'd be willing to give up the house and the car if I received other consideration."

Eastwick made sure the camera caught the doubt on his face. Then he consulted his notepad to find the next question. "Didn't you tell Ms. Tomkins how your wife should plan her rescue so it would look to the police like a murder plot?"

"You think I asked her to recruit a trained killer, wanted him to shoot me to make it look good? That's farfetched even for you, Mr. Eastwick."

Eastwick moved very close to me to deliver his coup de grâce. He was like a little boy who had solved a riddle, and he wanted the grand jury to recognize his brilliance. "You expected Ms. Tomkins to pass the information back to your wife so she'd walk into the trap."

I could see that coming, so it didn't affect me. "Carrie plotted a murder and her sister ratted her out, probably for revenge. Connie passed the plan on to me so I could outwit her."

Eastwick paused for dramatic effect. When everyone was quiet and attentive, he said, "Ms. Tomkins rarely spoke to her sister, because Mrs. Marks was upset with her for associating with you." He pulled a stack of paper from behind his legal pad and waved it at me. "We checked your wife's phone records. There have been no calls between the sisters since July." He turned toward the camera to smile with me in the background of the shot, as though he were taking a selfie with a celebrity.

He had a point; I possessed the same useless phone records. I said, "A murder plot is hatched in person, not over the phone."

"They lived fifty miles apart, Mr. Marks. They would have corresponded somehow."

"Yes, they would have," I agreed. "How else could my 'instructions' make their way back to Carrie?"

That took him by surprise. He wavered in front of me like heatwaves over an asphalt highway. Dumbfounded, he bent over his legal pad and read for a while as though the answer to that riddle might be among his notes.

When he was composed, Eastwick went for the kill. "Here's how it looks to us, Mr. Marks." As he made each point, he unfurled a finger of his right hand. "You lured your wife to the boat with incentives." Pinky. "She had no motive to murder you, so you kidnapped her." Ring finger. "You had a plan to trap her, and you didn't share that with anyone else." Middle finger. "There was no plot to murder you, so you waited for her family to rescue her." Index finger. Voice rising to a crescendo, he threw out his thumb and shouted, "You'd have shot her if Officer Marks hadn't stopped you!"

Oh crap, Jamie told them she disarmed me first. "You're writing a fairy tale, Mr. Eastwick, and wasting taxpayer dollars. Listen to this, please."

I fumbled with my cell phone again until I queued up my surreptitious recording of Connie at our "romantic" dinner. I punched the "play" button, and Connie's voice filled the room with an elaborate description of a murder plot. Eastwick looked around as though his momma might appear and help him out of this mess.

He said, "Stop that tape." Turning to the technician, he said, "Stop recording!"

No one obeyed his orders, and Connie prattled on about the plot in a conspiratorial voice.

Eastwick said, "Did she know she was being taped?"

"No."

"Well then," he said, raising his arms triumphantly, "it's not admissible."

"Maybe not," I said, "but it is exculpatory and now"—I pointed to the camera—"the grand jury has heard it."

Looking into the camera lens, Eastwick said, "I have to work within the bounds of the law, Mr. Marks. If it's not admissible, it never happened."

Looking into the camera, speaking to the grand jury panel, I said, "You may be willing to ignore evidence, Mr. Prosecutor, but our good citizens aren't going to."

Whirling around, looking for support, he yelled, "Strike that!" He swiveled between the technician and the court recorder, barking at them, "Strike that and rewind the tape!" No one moved.

I stuck my finger in his face, and in my best imitation of Jack Nicholson in *A Few Good Men*, I shouted, "You wanted the truth, Mr. Prosecutor! Well, you got the truth."

I thought he might jump on the bed, jump on me, so we could wrestle like grade-school children trading insults about our mothers. There was spittle flying from his mouth as he said, "You concocted the murder plot so you could trap your wife. You used Ms. Tomkins so you could . . . could get rid of your wife."

I shouted back into his face, not a foot from mine. "You dreamed this conspiracy up, to make a name for yourself. My wife concealed a weapon and brought it aboard my boat. Then two armed men attacked the boat and shot me. Other than inventing fairy tales, what are you doing about the crime that actually happened, Mr. Prosecutor?"

As soon as I said that, chaos reigned. Tony shouted, "This deposition is over!" Eastwick screamed at the court recorder to strike my last answer. Tony rushed to the foot of the bed to cup one hand over the camera lens as he told the technician to shut down the equipment. Julia slipped between Eastwick and the bed and herded the prosecutor toward the door. Eastwick shouted over his shoulder, "I'll put him on the stand, and then I'll get the truth!"

Callahan didn't stir from his perch, leaning against the windowsill, but he shook his head in wonderment. The fracas calmed down swiftly as the investigator traipsed behind Eastwick and the court recorder hurriedly wheeled her recording contraption out of the room. The technician packed his gear carefully, not in a hurry.

Tony said, "I haven't had that much fun since I discovered masturbation. He won't show that tape to anyone."

"I hope he shows it to everyone," I said.

Callahan pushed himself up from the windowsill. "Counselor, you mind if I ask your client a couple more questions?"

Tony shook his head. "I think my client has had enough for one day, lieutenant."

"It's okay, Tony," I said. "We're old friends."

My "old friend" Frumpy smiled. "Why didn't you tell me about those tapes when I took your statement? One proves your wife lied about the bikini, and the other implicates her in a conspiracy."

"I didn't mislead you, lieutenant. I gave you factual answers to the questions you asked, but you scared me with talk about the prosecutor's theories, so I thought I should save the tapes for this session."

He cocked his head, considering that. "Can I have them now?"

"Not without a warrant," Tony said.

But I handed the phone to the cop. "I'll get a new phone, and I'll only give my number to people who want me alive. And I have another present for you—those papers on the food tray."

With a question on his face, Frumpy picked up the papers and perused them.

"They're emails," I said. "I sent them to my lawyer and *shadylady44* intercepted them and then *cmt1117* passed them along to my wife. In response, my wife wrote that angry note to 'Mae,' which is what she calls her sister. Connie stole my mail, as *shadylady44,* but sent Carrie a note from her personal account to be sure Carrie read the emails. If you get a warrant for Connie's computer, your techs will prove I'm right. Connie used the emails to entice Carrie to come to the boat. At the same time,

Connie convinced me that Carrie wanted to kill me. Connie hoped I would kill Carrie, because she was the sole heir to her will."

There was more to it: revenge for a lifetime of playing second fiddle to the favorite daughter; revenge for being ostracized; and the compulsive need to be the family's queen bee; but you have to keep things simple for cops.

Frumpy took a long time to digest all of that, paged through the emails, and took a deep breath. "You aren't copied on the emails, so how did you get them?"

"Sorry, lieutenant, I have to plead the fifth and trust that you'll do the right thing."

He shook his head in disgust, folded the papers in half the long way, and stuffed them into his inside jacket pocket. Returning to his list of questions, he said, "When you had your stepson on the phone, you intentionally insulted him. Why did you do that?"

"I don't like my stepson, lieutenant, but I regret being mean to him. At the time I thought he'd be coming with his grandfather and I wanted to scare him."

"That kind of backfired on you. He told Dickson to rescue your wife."

"And he told my daughter to rescue me."

Frumpy wore a look of small respect. The technician finished packing his gear, gave me a thumbs-up, and carried the equipment out the door.

The lieutenant waited for him to leave before saying, "Did you steal your wife's jewelry?"

If he thought he could catch me off guard, he was wrong. "No, lieutenant, I had no way into that fortress. She must have stored the jewelry at her momma's house."

"It's not there. We already checked."

"I was in Atlanta that weekend, lieutenant. I'm sure you've verified that. Maybe the redneck yardman—Pardeaux—stole it. Have you interrogated him?"

Frumpy threw up his hands and said, "We've interrogated everyone, and no one did it."

"Maybe it didn't happen, lieutenant. My wife is a pathological liar."

He nodded, started for the door, and then called over his shoulder, "Good luck with that leg."

When the cop was gone, Tony said, "Would have been nice to know all of that."

"I didn't know I had an attorney."

Tony puffed out his chest and said, "We made a great team, just like you said we would. Beat the pants off 'em."

I meant it when I next said, "Thanks for being a good partner, Tony."

He beamed. "Okay, buddy, get well. When your wife is indicted, I'll submit a motion for a directed divorce decree." He nearly ran Julia over as he walked through the door.

Julia came to my bedside and said, "The redhead is still waiting. Do you want to see her?"

"Yes, Julia, I hoped she'd wait. Do I look okay?"

"You look like a pimp."

CHAPTER THIRTY-SIX

For more than a month, I had wondered when they would come. I wasn't fearful exactly, but I wasn't relaxed either. I was living in limbo. When the guard at the front desk called for permission to let three visitors ride up in the elevator, I knew it was them.

The visitors turned out to be Lieutenant Callahan, a younger, hardboiled cop in a black suit that looked like it had been borrowed from the Blues Brothers' wardrobe locker, and a reincarnation of Ichabod Crane, who introduced himself as an assistant DA for Cortes County.

As I held the door for them, I said, "Where's my buddy, Mr. Eastwick?"

They all looked sheepish. "He's decided to go into private practice," Ichabod said.

Bug-Eyes got himself fired. I did an about-face and hobbled down the Mexican tile foyer, past the French doors leading to my book-lined office and into the living room. The three visitors traipsed along behind, then halted in the middle of the sunken-floored, cathedral-ceilinged living room to stare through the wall-to-wall, floor-to-ceiling windows at the majesty of downtown Atlanta twenty-one floors below.

Callahan—or Frumpy as I liked to think of him—called out to me, "What are we looking at here?"

I turned back around as Frumpy swept one arm from horizon to horizon to punctuate his question. I decided to be nice.

"To your right is the Georgia Tech campus, all the way down to the Georgia Dome. Straight ahead is what we call Midtown. The tall building with the gold filigree and phallic symbol on top was the Southeastern headquarters of a national bank, but they sold the building and moved out during the market crash in 2008. Beyond that are the convention hotels that make Atlanta a great place to work if you're a call girl. Looking down Spring Street, right below us, the beige stucco building is our most famous gentleman's club. And over there to your left is the main drag—Peachtree Street. As you look to the south you can see the Fox Theatre, which is a national landmark."

"Quite a place," Frumpy ventured, referring to the condo. "The carpet is so thick I can't see my shoes."

I limped toward my recliner in the family room. After a long look at the skyline, they followed me. I didn't offer them anything to drink or anywhere to sit, so the three men gathered around my chair like family around a sick relative in a hospital bed.

"This view must cost a fortune," Frumpy said.

"I traded two homes in Florida for this place," I said testily. "And my boat if you ever release it."

"Sure," said Frumpy. He turned away from the windows and pointed to my bandages. "Still healing?"

"One more surgery scheduled here at Emory in two weeks."

"You're lucky, but Dickson wasn't. Your daughter shot him center mass, severed his spinal cord. He'll be in a wheelchair the rest of his life."

"Sorry to hear that."

"I'm sure you are," Frumpy said, and I caught the sarcasm. "His wife is divorcing him too. Apparently, he fooled around on her for years, and she was tired of it. We checked with his employer, a company in Plant City, and that was his reputation—ladies' man. We never had any evidence that he fooled around with your wife, but who knows?" Frumpy cocked his head, hoping to get a reaction.

Carrie made a call to the company in Plant City, but it was just one call. I remained stoic, but the gears in my mind began spinning like a roulette wheel. Dickson had been an automatic addition to the witness list because he was an ex-husband, and that turned out to be a lucky guess. "Obviously he was part of the conspiracy; he shot me."

Frumpy shook his head. "Your wife convinced him to take his son's place on the team. Told him you were going to name him a co-respondent in the divorce trial."

Hoping my eyes weren't bugged out like a cartoon character's, I said, "Was the other ex-husband involved?"

"Simmons? Nah," Frumpy said. "That guy hates your wife as much as you do."

"I was more suspicious of Simmons, but I suppose Dickson was better trained to commit murder. What about Harlan?"

"Well, he's happy you had steel-jacketed slugs in your gun. Bullet went through and through and just broke his clavicle."

"I should have aimed better."

Frumpy gave me a dirty look. "He said he was just trying to stop you from raping his daughter, but your wife's friend"—he consulted his notepad—"Jerilynn Wilson, said that the old goat was the one who wanted to pull the trigger if the women could come up with a plan."

"And Carrie came up with a plan."

"This Jerilynn person said your mother-in-law . . ."

He started flipping pages in his notebook again, so I filled in the blank for him. "Annabelle."

"Right. Annabelle was the one with the ideas the one time she was part of it."

Again, with emphasis, I said, "But in the end, Carrie plotted my murder, right?"

He shrugged. "Ms. Wilson says it was just a bunch of nervous women blowing off steam. It never came up again because your wife got what she wanted from the judge."

I remained still as a stone statue. Black Suit, acting bored, wandered over to the bar that separated the family room from the gourmet kitchen and surveyed the Sub-Zero appliances he'd never be able to afford on a cop's pay.

"Lieutenant, it went down exactly like Connie told me it would. Carrie had a plan, and she carried it out."

"Your wife testified that her sister convinced her to go to the boat, told her what to wear, and had her bring a change of clothes."

My eyebrows shot up like a space shuttle launch and collided with my hairline. *Connie drove Carrie to the boat too.* "Okay, so Carrie and Connie conspired together, but Carrie called Dickson and told him to come murder me."

Callahan shook his head. "She wanted him to get her off the boat 'cause it wasn't going well. When you didn't let her son talk to her, they were sure you had kidnapped her and they would have to use force to board your boat."

Thinking aloud, I said, "You know she called them before I locked her up."

Frumpy nodded. "Sure, we worked out the timing. She got scared."

A disgusted snort forced its way out of my nose. "It's beginning to sound like nothing bad happened at all. I must be imagining the bandages on my leg."

Frumpy shrugged nonchalantly. "We didn't charge the old man, couldn't get anyone to corroborate Ms. Wilson's statement." *Of course you couldn't corroborate her statement; everyone else is a part of the Tomkins clan.* "Harlan never got onto your boat and got himself shot for his trouble. The fat kid backed out before it was too late and then tried to stop the violence. Dickson we downgraded to assault with a deadly weapon and let him go with probation in exchange for his testimony. Green Beret, war hero, and all that. He'll have to live with his disability now."

Lady Justice isn't blind; she wears corrective lenses. Black Suit pushed away from the bar and strolled into the living room. I followed him with my eyes.

Frumpy regained my attention by saying, "We gave your daughter a pass, of course. She acted in her capacity as an officer of the law, and the shooting of Dickson was righteous. You were damned lucky she can handle that gun of hers. As for you, the law was on your side. Whether you knew it or not, you were the poster child for the 'stand your ground' law. Florida is a 'no duty to retreat' state."

My patience had been exhausted. "Is anyone going to be charged with a crime?"

"You familiar with the KISS principle?"

"Keep it simple, stupid."

"That's what we did, nothing fancy. At your deposition, you said we should concentrate on the crime that actually happened, not some farfetched conspiracy theory. That struck a chord with me. Your wife has been charged with carrying a concealed weapon without a permit."

"That's it? She conspired to kill me!"

That got a reaction from Ichabod. "For Christ's sake, Marks, your wife never even pointed her weapon at you!" He flapped his spindly arms in disgust like an ungainly cormorant taking to the air.

"I'll be damned. She got away with it."

Frumpy said, "No, no, it's a serious charge, a third-degree felony, and carries a maximum sentence of five years in prison and a fine. Her trial starts next week."

"She deserves a life sentence."

Frumpy seemed to enjoy the repartee, wanted to see my reactions to his revelations, but Ichabod was exasperated, wanted to get back on a plane to Florida. He said, "You don't get it, Marks. We charged the one person we can convict of the one crime for which we can get a conviction."

A jagged, cold rock sank to the bottom of my stomach. "Sure, conviction statistics are important," I said sarcastically.

Ichabod ignored the sarcasm. "We are closing the investigation and will not file any further charges with regard to the incident on the boat. As the lieutenant said, we have completed the investigation of your ex-wife, and no one else merits an indictment."

Frumpy was happy to have the help. He said, "Yeah, that's the way it works."

Ichabod moved over to the bar separating the kitchen from the family room and took a seat on a barstool.

"I suppose I should be glad you're not charging me with getting in the way of a lawful shotgun blast. What about Connie? If it wasn't my wife's conspiracy, it was Connie's. She wanted me to kill her sister because she was her sister's heir. In Carrie's will."

Frumpy and Ichabod traded looks, deciding who should tell this part of the story. Frumpy got elected. "Now you're the one with the conspiracy theories. We charged Ms. Tomkins with a violation of the Florida Computer Crimes Act, for tapping your email."

"That's all? She describes the plot on that tape I played for you."

"Inadmissible, just like Eastwick said."

"She convinced Carrie to come to the boat. Gave her a ride to the marina. Told her what to wear."

Now Frumpy was exasperated. With some force, he said, "That's not evidence of a conspiracy, Mr. Marks. Ms. Tomkins says she was helping you get a settlement. That one time at dinner, on your tape, she was speculating about what *could* happen, trying to scare you so you wouldn't harm her sister. On the tape, she says, 'They *could* do this" and 'They *could* do that.' You took it the wrong way."

I don't remember it that way. "So I made it up?"

Frumpy pursed his lips. "It was a misunderstanding."

I was lightheaded and close to fainting. "What does she get for computer crime? A vacation in the Caribbean?"

"Her violation is also a third-degree felony and carries a maximum penalty of five years in prison and a fine. Her accomplice, the Simmons kid, will testify against her in exchange for probation."

"He installed the snooper software for Connie?"

"Sure. He's going to testify that he used Ms. Tomkins's key to get into your house and routed your email to one of Ms. Tomkins's accounts, *shadylady44*."

I may have fainted. "So I should pat you on the back for a job well done?"

"We're not done quite yet." Frumpy snapped his fingers, and the cop in black walked back toward us pulling a pistol from under his jacket. He grabbed it by its barrel and handed it to me butt first. I could tell by the weight that it wasn't loaded.

"Your gun," Frumpy said. "It's never been used in a crime. We checked."

"Who had it?"

Frumpy recoiled as though dodging a rattlesnake strike. "No one," he said. "It was under the bed in the master, ah, stateroom. We confiscated it the day of the incident."

I laughed, the way you laugh when you've been a sucker. "Carrie broke into my beach house and stole it so I wouldn't be armed when she came to kill me. She must have stashed it on the boat when she was belowdecks."

Frumpy laughed too, but it was a dismissive laugh. "We found the stolen weapon report, but the Dolphin Beach police closed the case. It was the only item reported missing, but then it isn't, is it?"

I thought he was playing a game, testing me. "Did Officer Williams tell you about the bloody glass from the broken window?"

All too casually, he said, "Sure. They were on the lookout for the gun, but they didn't spend the money on lab tests. Missing weapons always turn up at another crime scene, and there it was." He pointed to the Glock in my hand.

"Did you check it for fingerprints?"

"Sure, they're all yours."

"There was a break-in, lieutenant, and you have the glass to catch the perp. It's your job, dammit, and you owe me for the video and the emails."

"Hey!" Ichabod said.

Frumpy held up a hand for Ichabod, like a school crossing guard.

I said, "It will get you another conviction, raise your average."

Frumpy looked at his companions as though he had just heard a terrific idea. I held the gun out to him, but he wouldn't take it.

He said, "I can't prove the gun was in your house at the time of the break-in."

"The burglar will tell you why he was there and who sent him. Then you can reopen the conspiracy case against Carrie. Or Connie. Or both."

Frumpy shrugged. "I'll see what Dolphin Beach wants to do."

In a desultory tone, I said, "Thanks. Can I go back to recuperating now?"

"You remember that cop show with the guy in the trench coat?" Frumpy looked around at his colleagues for a reaction, and they nodded in unison.

The hard, black-suited cop chimed in with "Columbo," proving he hadn't just been a mule toting my gun.

"Yeah, I feel like Columbo in the trench coat, saying, 'Oh wait, there's one more thing.'" He turned back to face me. "See, the jewelry case is still on the books, but I'm gonna close it today."

"Congratulations. Was she lying, or did you actually find the jewelry?"

In a self-satisfied voice, Callahan said, "Oh, we found the jewelry, Mr. Marks. On your boat."

"What?"

"It's funny 'cause we had your boat impounded for several weeks before we got the idea to have a marine expert do a search insteada the regular detectives. He knew that the hatch to the engine room was under the carpet in the salon." He chuckled. "I've learned all these nautical terms. The padlock on the hatch tipped him off there might be something valuable down there. We figure you padlocked it to keep your wife from finding it when she was on the boat." *Crystal clear.* "Down in the engine room there's a little compartment to store tools. The freezer bag fulla jewelry was in there. Most of it, anyway. We're still missing a yellow-diamond pendant and earrings."

That little slut! "You're not going to fall for that, are you? Carrie hid the jewelry while she was trapped belowdecks. Just like she hid my gun. To frame me. You see that, don't you?"

"The engine room hatch was padlocked while she was down there, Mr. Marks."

He let me think about that, and I realized that she hadn't broken into the boat to look for her things; she had staged the break-in so she could hide her jewelry. *That is one street-smart little brat.* Since the cops didn't find the jewelry during their first search of the boat—the cops couldn't find their ass with two hands and a flashlight—she came to the boat to retrieve the jewelry, but I had padlocked the engine room hatch.

"She broke into my boat and hid the jewelry the day before you searched my boat. She wanted you to find it then."

"You didn't report a boat break-in, Mr. Marks, and you didn't mention it when we searched your boat."

Had Jamie been there, she'd have said, "I told you so, Dad." All I could think to say was, "I don't have a key to her house."

Lieutenant Frumpy waved a hand like he was clearing the air after someone passed gas. "Yeah, you were right about your wife changing the locks. We canvassed the local locksmiths and found the one your wife used after you moved out. That's why we took the security company to your house to check out the alarm system to see if there was something wrong with it. And that's how we learned that it's in the ceiling, above the garage. You can pull the plug on the system up there and disconnect the phone line too. You didn't need a key to get into the house, just a garage door opener."

I shrugged. "I don't have a garage door opener either. I gave mine to Carrie."

"You mean the one that doesn't work? I figure you kept a good one."

I gritted my teeth and said, "I didn't steal the damned jewelry, lieutenant."

"You musta forgot to unscrew the case and disconnect the battery backup, so it recorded the break-in even though it couldn't make the call. It was on silent, so you didn't know you had tripped the alarm."

Think, Randle, think. "Larry Pardeaux had a garage door opener."

Callahan looked at me as though I were a man on the way to the gallows. "We found the pet store where you bought that toy rabbit. The product number was on the tag, you see, so it was just a matter of puttin' in the time to track down every sale of that bunny in the states of Georgia and Florida. You stopped off in Macon on the way to Florida that Saturday and paid cash, but you're on the surveillance video."

"I did not steal her jewelry!" I sounded like a common criminal in denial.

Callahan shook his head. "Your neighbor lady, not the one half a mile down the street, the one directly behind your house through the trees, heard the dog and walked over to see what the commotion was about. She had been feeding it for your wife. She saw you leaving but didn't know you weren't supposed to be there. That's why it took us so long to find her."

I didn't know there was a house back there. I thought it was a farmer's field. How did Carrie know that woman? I felt as though I were in the electric chair with repetitive pulses of current searing my nerve endings. I jerked. I thrashed. I flopped around like a gut-hooked fish.

"Listen, lieutenant, I admit that I violated the protective order, but her jewelry wasn't even there. This is a setup."

"Last thing I'm gonna mention, Mr. Marks: Your friend Mr. Louks admitted that his niece went to the Braves game for you."

"If you're waiting for me to confess to something I didn't do, you'll be here all night."

"No need for that, Mr. Marks. The party's over." Callahan waved Black Suit over and said, "This is Detective Sam Brownell of the Fulton County Sherriff's Office. He's gonna do the honors 'cause I'm pretty far outta my jurisdiction."

As Officer Brownell approached me, he lifted a set of handcuffs out of his jacket pocket and said, "Stand for me, please, and turn around."

Holy crap! They're not going to listen. I struggled to my feet and yelled, "Glenda!"

Then I remembered that she had gone out to the drugstore.

Brownell said, "You're under arrest for grand larceny. You'll be held in the Fulton County Jail until you can be extradited to the State of Florida." He clamped the cuffs roughly on my wrists. Then he read me my rights.

A discreet electronic bell sounded as the security system alerted us to the opening of the front door. We all went silent, waiting, staring at the space where she would appear. When Glenda came around the corner and saw our cops-and-robbers tableau, she stopped dead and dropped her plastic shopping bag. Something broke. Shock and fear contorted the features of her freckled face. Carrie's platinum necklace draped her neck and its huge yellow-diamond pendant rested on her chest. The matching stones dangled from her ears.

Callahan smiled at her and said, "Ah, there they are. Mind if I take those?"

As Glenda removed the jewelry, Detective Brownell said, "Ma'am, if you know where the other things are, please get them for us. It will make this much easier."

Glenda didn't say anything as she scurried away, head down, eyes averted, arms clamped to her sides, like a rat startled by headlights during its nocturnal foraging.

Callahan tapped his breast pocket. "We've got a search warrant, but we don't need to tear your place up again. All we need is the sex tape."

I stood unsteadily, in a daze, unable to form rational thoughts. Glenda soon returned, holding the "Unabomber" package in front of her as though it might explode at any moment. She handed it to Callahan.

Callahan smiled again and thanked her. He tore open one end, leaving the package mostly wrapped, and saw what he wanted. He nodded to Brownell, and we all moved toward the door.

Over my shoulder, I said, "Bail me out, Glenda."

Brownell pulled me roughly along as he said, "There's no bail for extradition cases. You won't be arraigned until you get back to Florida."

Callahan said, "Yeah, that's the way it works." Indicating Ichabod, he added, "Mr. Dunkel will file the extradition order this afternoon, and you'll be outta here in no time."

So they all had their roles to play, and I never saw it coming. I looked back over my shoulder, a clichéd pose from the end of many crime movies, and caught one last glimpse of Glenda, crying and pulling her sweater tightly around her as though she were chilly.

Through her sniffles she paraphrased a line from *Casablanca*: "We'll always have Atlanta."

Epilogue
MID-STATE CORRECTIONAL UNIT

It's not as bad here as you might think. Unlike most "normal" people, I don't find the solitude uncomfortable. While others chafe at the regimentation, I welcome the routine. I'm something of a celebrity— tales of my break-ins and gunfights are whispered from cell to cell and the younger convicts, mostly nonviolent offenders, stare at my wounds in the shower. My leg looks like a neglected country road dotted with angry red potholes and bisected by zipperlike incision scars. Cosmetic surgery has been deferred until I am a free man with medical insurance.

My job now is to teach math in the GED program, and my course is very popular. Teaching leaves me plenty of time to work on my book. My publisher has imposed strict deadlines on drafts and edits, more structure comforting to a scientist. The schedule is tight as we plan the book launch to coincide with my release from prison. In an ungraceful transition from one form of celebrity to another, I will immediately embark upon a book signing tour. That's my life now—teaching and writing—and I'm already adjusted to it.

When I was arraigned in Cortes County, I was charged with second-degree grand theft for stealing property with a value between twenty thousand and a hundred thousand dollars. It's a felony carrying a sentence of up to fifteen years in prison. I didn't have the money to hire a good lawyer, so I was represented at trial by a public defender who was overworked and undermotivated.

We argued that Carrie had framed me, but the freezer bag of jewelry had my fingerprints all over it. Literally. Carrie had reused a bag in which I had stored fish I had caught. Of course, the yellow diamonds and the rape tape were impossible to explain. When Carrie testified, she dressed conservatively and wore no makeup or jewelry. She couldn't color her hair while she was in custody, so it was her dull natural brown, and she brushed it like a boy's.

Her voice never faltered as she swore to the jury that she had not planted the bag of jewelry on the boat. She described her unlawful restraint as a harrowing experience for an innocent country girl. The prosecutor played an edited version of the sex tape, showing only the scenes in which I tied Carrie to the bed and clamped a hand over her mouth as I worked above her. "Juries convict people they don't like. It's that simple," Tony had said.

The jury took less than thirty minutes to find me guilty, and the judge gave me the minimum sentence of twenty-one months, which means I'll serve fourteen or fifteen months, which means I'll be released in about a year. Had I been convicted only of stealing the yellow diamonds—third-degree grand theft—I'd have gotten probation.

Glenda watched the trial from the spectators' gallery. She visits regularly and has petitioned the warden for a conjugal visit. She says we need the practice. Her divorce from Wesley is final, and she spends her time running her odd little store and caring for her clairvoyant mother. She assures me this is our destiny, just as her mother predicted.

Jamie refuses to visit. She says it's embarrassing for an officer of the law to have a convicted felon for a father, but Glenda says Jamie will come around after we've remarried. That would make me very happy. After years of wandering in the desert of failed relationships, it will be gratifying to get our old lives back.

I wrote Tony an apology for deceiving him, but he hasn't responded. According to those who deal with him, he's reverted to being a panfish. The last thing he did for me was get Matthews-Bryant to issue a final divorce decree. The judge didn't waste any judicial wisdom on the settlement; I don't think she liked either of us. She decreed that we each pay our own counsel, that there would be no life insurance policy safety net, and that I would retain all royalties. However, she dumped all the debt on me, including both liens against the house and the outstanding debt on the Jaguar; gave Carrie all our household furnishings, but gave the mortgage collateral—the house—to me. In effect, the judge made our creditors whole, an industrial-judicial conspiracy to be sure. Jane Whitehead dumped the house on speculators, and I broke even.

With all the finesse of Solomon dividing the baby, the judge split the options down the middle, and for a day or so Carrie and I thought we would each get $1.5 million. Quick to react, Bob Platt invoked the morals clause in my employment contract, fired me, and revoked my options, so neither of us got a penny. I didn't care about the money; I granted free, perpetual patent licenses to a pair of major research universities. When Platt heard about that, he offered to reinstate my job and my options if I would curtail the license grants. I declined his offer, as Carrie would have received a windfall of options. Instead, I extended my philanthropy to four more universities and two research institutes, and the commercial marketplace collapsed. Without exclusivity, and without a talented scientist to build new models, it appears AMA will fail.

Five of the six universities have invited me to guest lecture, and both institutes have asked me to consult on their research projects. No one is going to take my book to the beach or read it on an airplane for entertainment, but it should sell a few copies to academics. More importantly, it will add credibility to my lectures. We won't be rich, but lecture and consulting fees will keep food on our table.

Adding a poison pill to the divorce decree, the judge awarded Carrie three years of alimony at eighty thousand per year, contingent upon an acquittal in her criminal case. She wasn't acquitted, but her sentence of three years of probation got her released, along with her fistful of prescriptions, to mingle with the unsuspecting masses. I don't know if the shrinks ever looked at those house pictures, but they declined to reconsider their diagnosis. The cops returned Carrie's diary directly to her, so the shrinks never knew it existed.

When Carrie was released, de Castro petitioned the court to reinstate Carrie's alimony and the court approved the request. Since the State wouldn't provide my wife with three squares and a cot, I was ordered to do it! As a favor, my buddy Fred, the private investigator, tracked her down and found her living in a Treasure Island condo with Richard Puralto, MD. Once his kids left for college, he had divorced his wife to be with my ex-wife.

Believing that the statutes on the books are too punitive, an assistant prosecutor reduced the charges against Carrie's evil twin, Connie Mae, from a third-degree felony to a first-degree misdemeanor. Connie was sentenced to one year in prison, suspended, and was fined five thousand dollars for tapping my email. Fred says she's moved Chance Dickson into her home, and she's caring for him.

Lieutenant Callahan is the big "winner," of course. He milked a simple divorce case for three convictions and two plea deals. Probably get a commendation, maybe a promotion, although Callahan wouldn't have caught anyone if we hadn't screwed up and handed him evidence. As it was, no one was punished for their most egregious transgression, but everyone was punished for something. That's the way it works.

───────※───────

And that's the way I thought the story had ended until Callahan came to see me today, sheepishly apologetic and anxious to deliver good news. Glenda had formed a motherly bond with Officer Brittany Williams, and the two of them hounded Callahan until he agreed to pay for the testing of the four bloody glass shards. The Dolphin Beach PD couldn't justify the testing since the missing property—my gun—had been recovered, but Callahan reopened the investigation into the incident on the boat and ordered the testing in support of that case. No surprise to me, the DNA matched Carrie's yardman, Larry Pardeaux, a paroled felon on the lamb from the State of Louisiana. Faced with ten years in prison, Pardeaux confessed that my wife promised him sexual favors if he would break into the beach house to steal my gun and break into my boat to hide her jewelry. He says she never paid up. Yesterday, Callahan arrested Carrie for home invasion burglary, a second-degree felony punishable by up to fifteen years in prison. Carrie thought she could simply hide my gun on the boat and evade justice, but she didn't know we had the thief's DNA.

Carrie's probation has been revoked, and along with it, her alimony award. She's now eating mystery meat and watery mashed potatoes at the county jail, awaiting trial on the burglary charge. When she gets released, we'll be waiting for her. Glenda has been practicing with the Beretta, and she reports she can hit a moving target at twenty-five paces. In that case, I'll let her do the shooting.

We've sold the Atlanta condo, and we did alright. Florida is where we belong, so we asked Jane Whitehead to contact the speculators who own my beach bungalow. They are willing to sell it back to me, at a profit for them, of course.

My wrongful conviction for the jewelry theft troubles Callahan, but it doesn't bother me. By the time the judicial system grants a new trial, at which I'd be convicted of a lesser charge, I'll have served my sentence. Nonetheless, Callahan is considering perjury charges for Carrie's testimony in my case.

I feel sorry for Dr. Puralto. For a second time, he's abandoned his family for Carrie only to spend the rest of his life visiting his paramour in prison.

On the other hand, I do not feel sorry for myself. It cost one damaged leg, one shot-to-pieces boat, one point five million dollars, and fifteen months behind bars, but the resolution is satisfying—Carrie received no windfall of ill-gotten gains, and she is not free to ruin our lives. Fred would call it Karma. I call it justice. The apportionment of blame is fair.

CPSIA information can be obtained
at www.ICGtesting.com
Printed in the USA
BVOW04s1209220317
479038BV00025B/91/P